THEIR GAMES WILL CHANGE YOU.
THEIR LOVE WILL RUIN YOU.

WILDE FAE

LORDS OF THE HUNT

USA TODAY AND INTERNATIONAL BEST SELLING AUTHOR

KATE KING

ALSO BY KATE KING

WILDE FAE

Lords of the Hunt

Lady of the Nightmares ~ coming in 2023

THE GENTLEMEN

Red Handed

Thieves Honor

Damned Souls

THE BLISSFUL OMEGAVERSE

Pack Origin

Pack Bound

Pack Bliss

OMNIBUS EDITIONS

The Gentlemen

The Blissful Omegaverse

THEIR GAMES WILL CHANGE YOU.
THEIR LOVE WILL RUIN YOU.

WILDE FAE

LORDS OF THE HUNT

USA TODAY AND INTERNATIONAL BEST SELLING AUTHOR

KATE KING

Lords of the Hunt © 2023 by Kate King

ISBN: 979-8-9872003-2-2 (hardback)

ISBN: 979-8-9872003-1-5 (paperback)

ASIN: B0BKG44J66

First cover edition February 2023

Cover design and typography: Story Wrappers

Special Edition Cover and typography: Flowers and Forensics

Copy Editing: Noah Sky Editing

Character Art: Rin Mitchell

Published by Wicked Good Romance

For my husband, John.

I'm fucking obsessed with you.

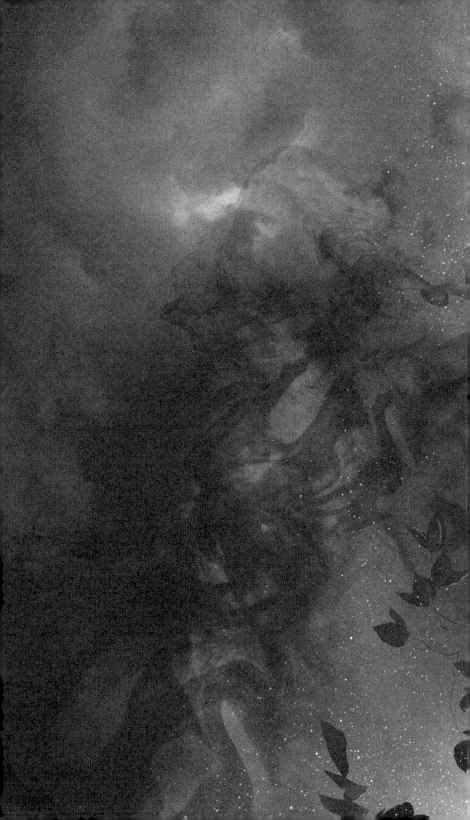

LORDS OF THE HUNT

WILDE FAE
BOOK ONE

KATE KING

AUTHOR'S NOTE

To all my readers who know me from Raegan and Bliss's stories, thank you so much for joining me on this slightly different venture. To all new readers, welcome!

This book, and series as a whole, is intended to be a median point between high fantasy and dark romance.

If you have read my stories before, this might be a little different than what you are used to. The world is quite large, and it will take more than one book to reveal the whole picture.

Up front, **this story will be a why choose romance.**

The characters are morally gray and will stay that way, and the POV narrators are not always reliable. The fae can be quite mean, and this first book has elements of bullying.

It is also a slow burn. There will be spice—a lot of it as the series progresses—but if you are looking for smut without plot, then you will be disappointed.

I promise there will be a happy ending to the series, and all secrets will be revealed…but not immediately.

I hope you will put your faith in me to reveal everything in due course, and enjoy the ride.

Xoxo, Kate

PRONUNCIATION

- "Aine" – An-ya
- "Aisling" – Ash-lin
- "Ambrose" — Am-broz
- "Auberon" – O-ba-ron
- "Baelfry" or "Bael" – Bale-free or Bale
- "Beira" – Bay-ruh
- "Belvedere" – Bell-ve-dear
- "Caliban" – Cala-ban
- "Celia" – See-lee-uh
- "Ciara" – Keer-ah
- "Dullahan" – Doo-luh-han
- "Elfwyn" – Elf-win
- "Elowyn" – El-lo-win
- "Gwydion" – Gwid-ee-in
- "Iola" – Eye-oh-luh
- "Lysander" – Lie-san-der
- "Mairead" – Muh-raid
- "Mordant" – Mor-dnt
- "Penvalle" – Pen-vail
- "Raewyn" – Ray-win
- "Rhiannon" – Ree-ann-in
- "Roisin" – Row-sheen
- "Scion" – Sigh-on
- "Slúagh" — Slew-uh
- "Thalia" – Ta-lee-uh

The Everlast Family Tree

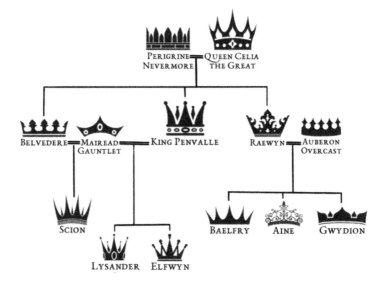

- Perigrine Nevermore — Queen Celia the Great
- Belvedere
- Mairead Gauntlet — King Penvalle
- Raewyn — Auberon Overcast
- Scion
- Lysander
- Elfwyn
- Baelfry
- Aine
- Gwydion

THEIR GAMES WILL CHANGE YOU.
THEIR LOVE WILL RUIN YOU.

WILDE FAE

LORDS OF THE HUNT

USA TODAY AND INTERNATIONAL BEST SELLING AUTHOR

KATE KING

PROLOGUE

LONNIE

*T*he most honest people in the world were liars.

From the time I could talk, every other word out of my mouth was a lie, and I was glad of it. People usually lied for good reasons—to protect loved ones, to lessen bad news, or simply without conscious thought.

The Fae never lied, but they told more falsehoods than any human I knew.

They never downplayed their exhaustion, or told a friend they looked lovely to spare hurt feelings. They twisted their words into knots, taking pleasure in confusion and cruelty, while hiding behind the moral superiority of forced honesty.

Lying well and often was a necessary skill in the high court of Elsewhere. It was our best weapon against the Fae. At least, that's what my mother told me.

Mother had three cardinal rules:

1. Never make a bargain with a fairy.

2. Never enter the Waywoods on a hunting day.

3. Never give the High Fae a reason to notice you.

Lying was one of Mother's unwritten rules. One should always lie, like one should never tell a fairy your true name. One should always lie, like one should never ask questions about the old world.

The rules were part of me. As ingrained in my early memories as breathing. As I grew older, however, I realized that Mother's rules had never done shit for her or for me, so I put less and less stock in them.

Lying, though—that, I could get behind. Especially to guard my secrets. Especially to protect those I loved.

PART I

♔

AS FLIES TO WANTON BOYS ARE WE TO THE GODS; THEY KILL US
FOR THEIR SPORT.

—WILLIAM SHAKESPEARE, "KING LEAR"

1

LONNIE

I bent my head against the warm summer wind as I ran along the thin, winding alley on the cheap side of town. In other provinces, "Cheapside" might be an insult, but not here. "Cheap" meant you were paying your own way, and in the free-human village at the edge of the Fae city of Everlast, they respected self-sufficiency.

Envy and pity churned in my stomach in equal measure as I took in the thatched roofs and peeling paint along the street. Overhead, a string of bedraggled flags hung across the alley. I scowled up at the faded colors whipping in the breeze—a macabre reminder of the upcoming hunt.

Last month, these houses were full of life. Now, half the street stood abandoned and broken, ransacked by rebels during their last raid. Still, colorful decorations covered the broken windows and cold chimneys of every home, as if someone still lived inside.

It was a pretty lie, and a story I was intimately familiar with.

Several paces ahead, under another string of flags, I spotted the faded and cracked sign of the apothecary. I sighed in relief. I was already late to meet Caliban, but I'd promised myself I would make one stop in the village first.

Before I could take another step, the apothecary door flew open. I jumped back, startled.

A short, middle-aged woman with a green scarf tied over her flyaway gray hair looked over at me. I knew her by sight, if not by name. Ciara's shop assistant.

I groaned internally. That woman hated me with every–

"Morning, Rosey!" The shop assistant waved and smiled widely, flashing several broken teeth. "Out early for hunting day?"

I faltered, confused, before bobbing something between a curtsy and a nod. "Hello." I self-consciously flicked my long auburn hair over my ears. "Yes, I'm—"

"Oh." The woman laughed, talking over me. "I suppose you'll be there serving the court?"

"Yes," I repeated, not bothering to correct any of her many misconceptions. If this woman thought I was my sister, all the better for me.

The people of Everlast adored Rosey, while they treated me as something to be feared and avoided at all costs. I could hardly say I blamed them. It had been the same for my mother before she died, and her death had only confirmed their fears.

The woman stared expectantly at me, and I flinched, realizing Rosey would likely ask something polite in return. "Er, are you going?"

Not polite exactly, but not the worst I could have said.

"'Course." The woman reached down and flicked some invisible speck of dust off her stoop, then faced me again. "There's not much else to do around here, is there?"

"Of course," I repeated, nodding vaguely.

Her warm smile was jarring compared to the treatment I usually received in the village. But then, this smile wasn't for me. It was for Rosey, and for all I wished otherwise, I was not my sister.

I took an eager step forward. "Is Ciara here?"

The woman shook her head. "Not yet. Did she leave something for you?"

"No. I wouldn't think so."

Ciara, the local cunning woman, should have no way of knowing I was coming to see her. Though, that was no guarantee that she wouldn't. She always knew, for example, that I was not my sister, no matter how much we looked alike.

"Is everything alright?" the woman asked.

"Oh, yes," I lied. "I just had a question."

The truth was that my sister's persistent cough was growing more worrisome by the day. I'd hoped Ciara would have something to help her, but I would simply have to try back later. *After.*

The shop assistant waved as I hurried away. "I'll tell her you were here. Perhaps we'll see you this evening."

I bit my tongue to keep from doubling back. From shaking her and screaming in her face. *Don't go to the hunts. Don't play their games. You're cheering while they slaughter us.*

Not everyone shared my personal hatred of the hunts. Most feared the Fae. Resented them. But hatred of the Wilde Hunts was most often associated with the northern rebels, and they were feared in the capital almost as much as the royal house of Everlast.

No matter what the High Fae King preached about fairness and tradition, the evidence spoke otherwise. The Fae were the hunters, and we were the prey, and anyone who thought otherwise was only lying to themselves.

2
LONNIE

*T*wo streets away, the pungent scent of pine and moss from the Waywoods dampened the smoke and burnt sugar of the village. I ran as I neared the last row of houses and darted toward the wall that bordered the trees.

Slowing to a walk, I crept along the shadow of the wall, my eyes darting side to side, scanning the tree line ahead. Far in the distance, the Palace of Everlast was tattooed against the misty lilac sky, taller even than the swaying trees.

Without warning, fingers wrapped around my upper arm and tugged me roughly through a break in the stones.

"Took you long enough," Caliban said into my hair, his familiar charred leather scent filling my nose. "I thought I would be standing here like a fool until Samhain."

I smirked at him and matched his slightly annoyed tone. "I'm sorry to keep you waiting. It is a long walk from the palace, you know."

That, and I'd stopped by the apothecary, but he didn't need to know that. It was my own personal rule. One selfless deed canceled out a selfish one. And meeting with Caliban while skipping out on my chores was undoubtedly selfish.

Tall and suntanned, with dark eyes and powerful arms, Caliban was almost too handsome for his own good. Particularly now, in plain clothes rather than his palace guard's uniform. That was why I kept coming back—that, and he wasn't afraid of me. Or rather, of the misfortune that seemed to follow wherever I went.

He smiled sheepishly. "Sorry. Don't worry Lon, it won't be like this forever. We'll figure something out."

I didn't believe that, and neither did he, but it was a nice statement.

Caliban was several years older than me, with four generations of family in Elsewhere, while I was a kitchen maid, with only my sister for family. In short, he would need a wife—soon—and that wife would never be me. No mother would let her son marry a penniless orphan, even if half the city did not consider them dangerous and odd.

Caliban grabbed my small, calloused hand in his large, equally rough one, and pulled me toward the trees on the opposite side of the wall. Dipping his head to run his mouth over the exposed skin of my neck, I felt him smile and flutters erupted in my stomach.

Eyes peeked out from within the trees, some large and fearsome, some small and nervous. Caliban had never noticed the Underfae, and it would only upset him to point them out. Still, I widened my eyes at them until they turned away. *Peeping toms, the lot of them.*

Caliban stepped back a little so I could meet his wide, brown eyes as he ran one long fingered hand up my leg, under my dress, to cup my core. He trailed his fingers over me, and a high-pitched sound escaped my lips. I squirmed, twining my fingers into his soft hair.

"If I had to wait any longer for you, I was going to join the hunting party," he joked.

I froze. "What?"

Caliban shrugged and licked up my neck to my ear. "They haven't started yet, and they're in the forest for this one, you know."

Of course I knew. Everyone knew, what with the way that the palace had been preparing for weeks. "You're not serious."

The hunting season lasted from the first of May, today, to the summer solstice on the twenty-first of June. There were five hunts, each taking place in a different province. The first hunt was always in the capital city. The last, in the province of After-math, where I was born.

There had been talk for weeks in the kitchens from loud-mouthed idiots bragging that they planned to join the hunts for their chance to be king or queen. I hadn't thought Caliban would ever be so foolish.

Caliban pulled back to look me in the eye, and I caught the moment his gaze darted to my right ear. "Maybe I am. I could be a king, you know."

"But it's dangerous."

That was an understatement, but Caliban would not have liked to hear what I really thought, and it would not have made any difference, anyway.

He grinned almost apologetically and moved his mouth to hover over mine again, capturing my bottom lip between his. "I like danger."

You like picking fights with Ezra and Thaddaeus Windom. Not battling the Everlasts. "I don't think they'd allow a human king."

Caliban narrowed his eyes. "There's no rule against it."

I took a deep breath and rearranged my face into something pleasant. Calm. "Alright," I murmured, chasing his mouth. "Then you would be an excellent king."

"Really?"

"Absolutely," I lied, desperately wanting to leave behind both the subject of the hunts and of how long it had taken me to arrive.

Caliban stepped closer, and I pressed my back harder into the tree, my heart pounding wildly against my chest. He pushed my skirt up until it pooled around my hips. "I missed you."

He waited for me to return the sentiment. Instead, I undid the top of my bodice. "It hasn't been that long."

"Too long." He pressed a firm kiss to the exposed top of my breast. "I feel as though it's been forever."

I said nothing, shifting, stretching closer as he reached down to undo his belt. He lifted me, and my legs automatically wrapped around his waist.

"Fuck," he said into my hair, sliding into me in a single stroke.

"Mmmhmm." I ground down onto him, setting my own rhythm, taking the lead as always. I bent my head to suck on his neck and dug my nails into his arms hard enough to leave marks.

A twig snapped, and hooves pounded against the ground somewhere off to our right. "You can't be fucking serious," a high, imperious male voice shouted. "You might not care about wasting your own time, but do not waste mine."

Panic rose the gooseflesh on my arms, and I froze, going cold and stiff in Caliban's arms. There was no mistaking the voices of the High Fae. Musical and enticing to most human ears. Discordant and terrifying to me.

"Go back, then," a second male replied, and I could hear the laughter in his tone. "No one is holding you captive, Sci, least of all me."

"If I didn't know better, I'd call you a fucking liar."

I pushed at Caliban's shoulders, urging him to stop, my heartbeat pounding in my ears as the first Fae laughed. They were growing closer. Too close.

Every tiny creature in the bushes scattered, running for their dens and homes in hollow trees. I longed to follow. We needed to leave now. To run. To hide. "Put me down."

Caliban pulled his mouth back from my ear. "What's wrong?"

"Shhh."

He released me and my feet landed back on the ground far too hard, stumbling in the fallen dust at the base of the moondust tree. Around us, the forest had gone silent, like whoever I'd heard speaking had frozen in their tracks. Shaking, I peered through the branches and pressed a hand to my mouth, stifling a scream.

Somewhere in the back of my mind, I almost wanted to laugh. I should have known better.

Humans who entered the forest on hunting days never came out alive.

3
LONNIE

I hated all High Fae, but none so much as the Everlast family. The royal family had spent centuries killing thousands of innocents: humans, Fae and all manner of other creatures, in the name of holding on to their power.

It had been years since I'd come face to face with one of the Everlasts, but I would recognize their crest anywhere. I'd seen their symbol countless times before. On coins. On the gates of the castle. On the armor of the soldiers that took my mother away from me—the same armor I dreaded seeing on Caliban. And now, on the saddles of the two Fae males riding toward me.

"Bael!" one of the Fae barked. "What the fuck are you doing?"

My stomach sank. It was too much to hope that perhaps there was more than one Fae male named "Bael" who wore the Everlast crest.

Prince Bael was the youngest son of House Everlast. The prince was a favorite among those who worshiped the royal family like gods.

At a distance, Prince Bael was beautiful. Almost angelic. His perfect square jaw, sensual mouth, and bouncing red-golden curls gave him the look of a tragic hero in an oil painting. As he got closer, however, that cherubic facade cracked. There was something unnerving and predatory about his cat-like, yellow eyes. Something cruel in his razor-sharp smile that sent shivers down my spine.

Bael swung down from his enormous black horse and strode forward at double the speed any human could have walked, the pace blowing his curls back from his face. His gaze skimmed over our heads as though he were looking for something in the sky, or perhaps in the village just visible through the trees.

"Patience," he said, his tone full of amusement. "I want to check on something."

His gaze was so intense, it took me a moment to realize he was answering his companion's question of a moment ago, and not speaking to me.

"As I said," the other male complained, dropping from his own horse. "I don't see why you have to waste our time chasing after…what? Shadows?"

My gaze darted to the second male, and I blanched.

I'd hardly interacted with Prince Scion of the Ravens. The Queen's Executioner. Only once, in fact, and it was a scar on my memory.

Sometimes I wondered if our brief meeting seven years ago had made any impression on him, or if the torment was mine alone. It seemed unlikely that he would remember me, and I prayed he did not.

I hadn't seen the heir apparent up close since our last meeting, as he spent most of his time away from the capital enacting punishments on behalf of his house. He was taller than Prince Bael, but only slightly. He wore a black brocade jacket buttoned to the neck and carried an enormous raven—too large to be a normal bird—on his shoulder. His dark hair fell into his face, forming a curtain, but when he turned toward me, it was the eyes that made me jump back.

They were Silver. Not blue, not gray. *Silver.*

Prince Scion set his jaw and came to stand beside his cousin. My heart pounded against my chest, threatening to escape, and goosebumps erupted over my skin. It was rumored he could flatten a village with a single wave of a hand, and looking at him now, I could believe it.

I reached slowly for Caliban's hand, wishing I could tell him it would be alright. But that would be a lie that would benefit no one in the end. It would only kill us faster when the Fae heard my whisper.

Prince Scion looked directly at me through the leaves, piercing me with his gaze. He cocked his head to the side, something like recognition sparking in his eyes. For a moment, I thought he was going to lunge for me, and I went entirely still. But then he glanced away, as if I weren't there at all.

"Fuck this," he said sharply, his tone rougher—harsher—than I was used to. "I thought you saw something interesting. If I've seen one guard fucking some Slúagh whore in these woods, I've seen them all."

Prince Bael laughed, and I relaxed slightly. Perhaps they would simply leave?

Caliban pulled his hand roughly from mine. "What are you staring at?"

His voice was loud as a whip crack, and I looked frantically between him and the approaching Fae princes.

I swallowed hard, caught somewhere between terror and confusion, and then a horrifying idea crossed my mind. He couldn't see them.

"Be quiet—" I breathed, as softly as possible. Though it was pointless. Prince Bael was close enough to hear my heart beating.

"Why?" Caliban scoffed. He reached for my arm, pulling me around to look at him. "What the hell are you doing, Lon?"

I shook my head to clear it, blinking furiously, but when I opened my eyes, the Fae still stood before me. *By the Source.*

My skin, hot a moment ago where Caliban's fingers had run over me, grew cold and clammy. "I—"

Caliban grinned, but there was a slight edge to it. Like he was trying to make light of a terribly uncomfortable situation. His eyes shuttered as he looked back and forth between me and the clearing.

I could feel one more shred of normalcy slipping through my fingers. *He thinks I'm insane.*

Prince Bael laughed, his teeth glinting, and leaned over to his cousin. He kept his gaze firmly fixed on me. "I think you're losing your touch. The pretty Slúagh girl can see us."

Prince Scion had obviously reached the same conclusion. He took a quick, aggressive step forward, raising one arm in a gesture I recognized as the beginning of an enchantment.

I gasped, squeezing my eyes shut, fully expecting to go flying back against the tree behind me. And yet, the pain did not come. I waited an infinitely long moment before cracking my eyes open.

"Did you mean to stop?" Bael asked thoughtfully, speaking to his cousin while watching me. "Fascinating."

At my side, Caliban shifted, annoyed, and stepped back in the direction of the wall. I barely noticed. Prince Scion now stared at me with clear horror on his too-handsome face.

He spun on his heel, nearly dislodging the raven on his shoulder, who flapped its wings, disgruntled. "Let's go."

Prince Bael watched me for half a second longer, and I was frozen, transfixed with mingled terror and panic. Something flared in his gaze that I knew all too well—interest—and dread settled in my chest. I'd learned before what happened when you drew the attention of the Fae. I'd spent years hiding in plain sight, trying to blend in, but no matter what I did, they always seemed to see me.

"Bael!" Scion barked a harsh command.

"I'm coming," the prince called after his cousin, even as he cocked his head to the side, watching me. "I've seen all I needed to see."

4
LONNIE

My feet pounded a violent rhythm, and I heaved heavy breaths as I retraced my steps back through Cheapside. For the first time in a long while, I barely considered the pinching in my too-small shoes.

Later, I would have to face Caliban and whatever he told the other guards—but not now. Now, I was grateful—and surprised —to be alive.

The gates of the palace appeared out of the mist. The pointed iron spires gave the impression of jagged teeth about to clamp down around me, swallowing me whole.

I crossed through the open gates and started up the long cobble-stone road beyond. There were no guards at the gate, and no one stopped me as I ran up to the gleaming, ebony-stone palace on the hill. I'd always found the lack of soldiers unnerving. A subtle implication of power. The message was: come in if you like, there's nothing we need to be afraid of.

Afraid to draw too much attention to myself, I hugged the edge of the property and ran across the grass, staying close to the shadow of the high wall that separated the palace from the Waywoods and blocked the city from view.

No one stopped me. No one was there.

The silence and emptiness raised the hair on the back of my neck. It was hardly ever this empty, and it appeared the quiet was an omen—of what, I wasn't sure.

The sprawling lawn was bare, but for the path that led up the hill to the palace. The castle itself was lit up, every window bright with gleaming firelight, a beacon against the purplish sky. The servants' entrance was around the back of the castle, beyond the enormous gardens.

Pink blossoms fluttered to the ground around a grove of sweetly fragrant pear trees, the flowers twirling down like elegant confetti. Rainbow blooms dotted row after row of hedges, and roses the size of my head hid the homes of cranky Underfae as prickly as the thorns they lived on.

"Lonnie!"

I jumped at the sound of my name echoing off the palace walls and faltered, coming to a skittering halt in the middle of the path, dust and pebbles kicking up around my feet. Spinning, I was met with my sister hurrying toward me.

The moment I saw her, guilt settled in my stomach. I'd completely forgotten to go back to the apothecary. Not that she'd asked, but that was just it; Rosey never asked for help, but she desperately deserved it.

"There you are." Rosey darted toward me, her eyes cast down, her arms wrapped around her body as if to warm herself despite the high temperature of the day. "I've been looking for you everywhere."

Rosey came to a halt in front of me. The sleeves of her corn-flower-blue dress were frayed on the ends, but aside from that, you would never know she'd had the same dress repaired four times—and it hadn't been new when she bought it.

I sighed, trying to school my face into something calm. "Here I am. Is someone looking for me?"

"Yes." She gave a halfhearted smile that pulled at the skin around her mouth. "Me."

I rolled my eyes. "You know what I mean."

Though we were twins, I'd never managed the same refined elegance my sister seemed to exude without effort. Rosey's auburn curls were pinned neatly back from her face, and the expression behind her large brown eyes was calmer than I could ever hope to be. She even had fewer freckles than me, from less time in the sun.

She was a born lady's maid—used to serving wine and standing for long hours in uncomfortable silk gowns. I was better suited to work below floors, as I'd never been able to control my face in the court's presence.

"Where were you?" She asked, then went on before I could reply. "Never mind, do not tell me. I may prefer not to know."

She reached into the pocket of her linen apron and pulled out a scone wrapped in a napkin. "I brought you this. It's rosemary and coriander."

The half-crumbled scone that still smelled better than anything I'd eaten in living memory. My guilt tripled. "Where did you get that?"

"Stole it off one of the trays Beira made for the feast this evening. Princess Raewyn wanted a thousand tarts made in the shape of beating hearts."

I looked down at it. It looked nothing like a heart. "I don't understand?"

"This was what they threw out when the new order came in. They're all going in the garbage. Even so, we weren't supposed to touch them."

I reached out and took the scone, and picked off a piece with two fingers, popping it into my mouth. It melted on my tongue, and my stomach lurched with anxiety. "Alright, now I know you want something."

She laughed. "Fine. Come on, I'll tell you inside. It's cold, don't you think?"

I cast her a sideways glance as we walked toward the door to the kitchens. "No."

She shrugged, "Well—"

She broke off as we hurried past one of the High Fae walking in the opposite direction toward the woods. In unison, we ducked our heads, staring at the ground. "My lord," we murmured, in the same flat, unassuming tone.

Don't walk too fast. Don't look too scared. I reminded myself.

The lord paid us half a glance, and my heart leapt into my throat for a moment. He hovered briefly, like he planned to stop, and his gaze fixed on me. Rosey stiffened at my side, used to it. It was always like this.

Please, please go away. Not today.

Finally, he turned away without comment, and I breathed again.

The Fae was only one of the lesser lords visiting for the hunting day celebration. Possibly from the province of Inbetwixt, I guessed, based on his heavily embroidered clothing. They weren't one of the most dangerous provinces. Still, we'd stayed alive and unscathed this long by assuming all Fae were an equal threat.

Rule number three: never let the Fae notice you.

"Don't give them any reason to look twice at you," Mother would say. "Keep your head down and your mouth shut."

Our mother's three rules had worked perfectly well for Rosey. I had little difficulty with the first two rules, but it was the third that always seemed to cause me trouble.

No matter what I did, the Fae always noticed me. They'd noticed my mother too, and they killed her for it.

5
LONNIE

$\mathcal{B}$y the time Rosey and I made it back to the kitchens, the cook, Beira, was holding court.

Beira was one of the few non-human servants to work below floors. A nymph, she was nearing her 400th birthday but appeared to be in her mid-forties with graying brown hair and light brown eyes. She took on the role of parent to all the children brought to the court and mourned the loss of every one of us when we were inevitably taken from her, by either the royals or the toll of time.

Currently, Beira stood atop an empty crate, brandishing a wooden spoon like a baton. Around her, the kitchen hummed, alive with manic activity.

Four of the kitchen girls stood around the stove, talking animatedly, while on the opposite side of the room, others were still streaming in and out of the doors to the servants' sleeping corridor. The trays of wine and food from the hunts stood abandoned near the stove, and several pots of tomorrow's porridge looked ready to boil over.

The noise dropped when Rosey and I entered. I sighed as all eyes turned to me, gazes judgmental and filled with fear. All except Beira, who turned to the stove to save the porridge.

"Who's that?" the cook yelled.

"It's me," Rosey answered for both of us. "I'm needed down at the clearing, just dropping in."

"Hmmm," Beira murmured, not paying attention. "Be careful tonight."

"I always am," Rosey replied.

"I wasn't talking to you." She turned around and glared at me instead. "Don't hide in the moondust tree at noon, girl."

I stopped in my tracks, about to grab a tart off the nearest tray and hide it in my pocket. I pulled my hand back quickly. "I'm not."

Beira liked her proverbs, and that was one of her favorites when it came to me. It meant not to draw attention to yourself. If only I could.

The maid nearest to me gave me a horrified look and took two steps back as if I were diseased. "Are you coming tonight?"

I scowled at her. "Nice to see you too, Enid."

Enid pushed her mouse-brown hair behind her ears and narrowed her eyes. "I'm serious."

Enid had been at the palace longer than Rosey and me, and was never precisely hostile, though we weren't friends. "I'm not going," I snapped. "But if I was, I would stick to you like sap."

She shrieked as though I'd stabbed her with a fork. "Did you hear her? That's a threat."

Rosey shook her head, exhausted. "Come on. Let's just go."

I closed my eyes against the judgment as I traipsed after my sister. Everyone believed that I carried bad luck with me everywhere I went. That I was dangerous. Cursed.

I was starting to think they were right.

"*I* don't go looking for trouble," I said defensively, before my sister could comment.

I couldn't imagine what she would say if she knew what happened in the woods this morning. It was best not to tell her. She would surely find out eventually, but it didn't have to be now.

"I know," Rosey soothed as she pushed open the door to our tiny room.

The one bright side to being a pariah was we didn't have to share our room with anyone else. The room was small and circular, with a wood fireplace in one corner and two cots pushed next to each other for when the fire had no wood. It rarely did, so we left the beds like that year-round.

There was one small rickety table and a pitcher with a bowl beneath the round window. The only personal items were Rosey's stack of journals—one for every year since she'd been old enough to write—and my latest book. A historical archive snatched from the palace library that spoke of wars, past kings and vengeful gods.

I sank onto the bed, sighing. "Perhaps they would prefer I'd just died in Aftermath," I said acidly, knowing I sounded childish.

"No one is disappointed that you're not dead, Lonnie," Rosey scolded me gently, her smile a little tired. "Surprised, perhaps."

Well, I could hardly blame them for that.

"I don't know why we don't just leave," I said to the ceiling, knowing this was a conversation that was bound to go nowhere.

Sure enough, Rosey let out a sharp breath through her nose. "I don't want to discuss this today."

"But why?" It felt more urgent suddenly. "We have no reason to stay here, and surely, we have other family out there somewhere. Or, at least, there is someplace better than this."

Perhaps it was because of my encounter with the princes, or perhaps it was the misery of staying in a place where I had no purpose beyond feeling fear and inspiring it in others, but my desperation to run was more palpable than ever. Our mother had escaped this castle once, so it was undoubtedly possible.

"Please," Rosey implored. "Can we discuss this again tomorrow? Not right now?"

I sat up on the bed, looking at her. We were the same age, but Rosey was in so many ways my older sister. We didn't know our father, but I imagined she must take after him since our mother had been as impulsive as me.

"What did you want before?" I asked.

The encounter with Enid and Beira had temporarily driven my sister's request and pastry bribery from my mind, but as I watched her, she twisted her fingers in her skirt and shuffled back and forth nervously. Whatever it was, she had certainly not forgotten.

Rosey winced like she didn't want to answer. "I need you to do something for me."

"Anything," I said without thinking, and then wondered if I should have asked what she wanted first. But really, it didn't matter. Rosey so rarely asked for anything.

"I need you to go in my place tonight."

"Go where?" I asked, uncomprehending.

She looked pointedly at me. "To serve the court at the hunts."

I barked a laugh, sure for a moment she was joking. When she didn't smile, my grin slipped. I raised my eyebrows so high I was sure they disappeared into my hairline. "You're not serious."

Her face crumpled. "I wish I wasn't."

"I wish you weren't too, because it will not happen. You know I can't do that."

She reached for my hands. "Please. You did fine swapping with me for that errand for the queen."

I recoiled slightly, feeling guilty for pulling back from her. "This is different, and you know it."

"I know." She sank onto the end of the bed next to me. "But there's something I need to do."

"What?"

She swallowed thickly and tried to stifle a cough. "It's not important."

I laughed. "You're a shit liar, you know."

She glanced to the side, only confirming my opinion that she was lying and doing so badly. "I can't tell you." She looked miserable. "It's better if you don't know. It's just…" She threw her hands up. "You do things all the time and don't tell me."

I shook my head, the shadow of a grin crossing my face. "Yes, but you expect that from me. You're above it."

She gave a hollow laugh that turned into another cough and glanced toward her stack of journals on the little table. I followed her gaze and wondered, not for the first time, what she wrote in there. I'd never looked, but I'd often been tempted.

"Please," she said again. "I won't ask you to do it again."

I frowned, concerned now. "Is this about the moondust trees?"

The trees were named for their large, waxy, white leaves, the size of dinner plates. They only bloomed at night and would shrivel in the morning leaving a fine dust upon the ground. Tea brewed from the leaves was the only thing that helped Rosey's persistent cough, and she had snuck out many nights to pick them.

My sister gave a noncommittal nod, and again, I wished I remembered to go back to the apothecary. I wished that I was not distracted by the princes. Or, that I waited at the apothecary, and didn't go to meet Caliban at all.

I shook my head. "Even if I wanted to, I can't be you. Not so publicly."

Rosey knew how it would go, sending me to serve the High Fae court in her place, and she had not even heard of the incident in the woods. I shuddered at the thought of standing among the same royals from the forest.

Rosey gestured between our faces, identical in nearly every way. Her eyes were wide. Desperate. "You can be me. Avoid speaking. Stand a little straighter."

"It's not that simple. And what of this?" I pulled my hair away from my ear to show her the missing tip.

She winced. "Your hair will cover it."

I stood and began pacing across the tiny room. "Even if there wasn't the obvious danger, I am not meant for this. I cannot control my face around them," I narrowed my eyes, frowning to show her. "I hate them, Rosey."

She sat up straighter. "And you think I don't? I'm asking you to do this once. Just trust me. I won't let them hurt you, I promise."

My chest panged. That was the magic phrase. Trust her. Trust my sister, when there was no one else in the entire world who I could trust. Even though she wouldn't tell me what she was doing. Even though she was openly lying to my face and admitting to it. I did trust her, and this had to be important.

I slumped, defeated. "Turn around."

"Why?"

I didn't own a single dress that looked like anything Rosey would wear, and everyone would surely recognize this dress. She wore it so often and took care of it so well. Rosey's eyes widened, and she smiled slightly, almost like she didn't want to get her hopes up.

I undid her lacings and helped her pull it over her head, leaving only her shift behind. She turned back to face me, wrapping her arms around herself as though to ward off the cold.

I shifted her journal off the bed and then pulled the quilt off to hand to her. "Here."

I took the dress and held it up to myself. "What do you think?" I asked, nervously.

She smiled. "It's an excellent color on you."

I rolled my eyes as I pulled her dress over my head, marveling at how the fabric didn't scratch or chafe my skin. The lace fell delicately across my arms, and the tiny pearl buttons at the sleeves were nicer than anything I owned ten times over.

"Your hair," Rosey tutted.

I peered at my distorted reflection in the windowpane and grimaced. She was right. The dress might fit perfectly, but my hair would give me away. Rosey always wore hers in a smooth bun, while mine was a mess of curls.

"It will take quite a while to fix," I pointed out.

"Come here and hand me a comb."

I sat in front of her as she twisted my long hair into some complex braid I could never have hoped to achieve on my own. It lay flat against my neck and was full on the sides, covering the tips of my ears.

"It's not perfect," she said weakly. "But I would believe it."

"Good." I sighed, dread already pooling in my gut.

"Remember, you must not draw attention to yourself."

I thought back to this morning. To the princes in the woods that Caliban seemingly could not see. Today, of all days, I may be more likely to draw attention.

"I know," I said, slightly frustrated. "Believe me, that's the last thing I ever want."

She didn't comment on that. "Thank you."

"I hope whatever it is, it's worth it."

She reached for my hands, clasping them in hers. I wrinkled my brow as I stared at her. Did she look paler? Thinner? Or was I being paranoid? Was it the light, and the lack of her brightly colored gown?

"It will be," she said earnestly. "I promise."

6
LONNIE

*T*he music of a thousand fiddles wrapped around me like strong, sensual arms. The melody wafted over the breeze, the high notes trailing my skin, and pressing into my pulse points as if fingers wrapped around my throat.

I leaned to one side, then the other. Swaying. Letting the crescendo guide and caress me. Following the urge to dance to the hypnotic beat. The drums pulsed in my center and the darkness of the night called to me: *"Come to us. Come to play!"*

A sharp pain stabbed my ribs, and I sloshed wine down the front of my silk serving gown. I grimaced. Rosey would murder me in my sleep for that.

"Don't dance," Enid hissed in my ear.

I looked up at the brunette maid and coughed as I ran my hand up my throat. There was no hand gripping me. No phantom fingers. Nothing.

Fucking fairy music.

"Sorry," I muttered under my breath, trying and likely failing to appear contrite. "You, er, know I can't stand this sort of thing."

She gave me an odd look. "What is wrong with you this evening?"

I shook my head, uncomfortable. "Sorry."

Even without the strangely mesmerizing music, I would have struggled to contain my disdain. The Fae knew what they were doing, and they loved it. They hoped their music would lure the servants to their beds or off a cliff. Preferably both.

I ground my teeth and tapped the auburn hair curled around my ear to make sure it was still in place. *Absolutely wicked and disgusting, every single one of them.*

Beside me, Enid stared straight ahead, unmoved. She'd noticed nothing earlier when I exited my room in Rosey's dress and met her in the hall. I was used to being mistaken for Rosey, but it was still surreal to walk arm in arm with the same girl who had hissed insults at me an hour prior. I was stuck to her side like sap after all.

We'd walked from the kitchen straight down to a clearing on the edge of the Waywoods where music, drunken laughter and loud raucous voices carried across the grounds.

Now, we stood in the forest clearing surrounded by the rest of the servants who had the good fortune of not yet being called on to serve the court. Before us, the royal court danced, drank, and celebrated the first event of the Wilde Hunts.

Striped silk tents in every color stood out against the darkening sky, lit by a thousand will-o-wisps. Flags flew overhead and flower petals floated in the air like rainbow snow. A band of High Fae musicians played their strange music, while a circle of High Fae twirled by. The silk of the ladies' gowns whipped past in blues and greens, like the colors of Moonglade lake. Their unearthly voices rose above the music, adding to the hypnotic rhythm. Their skin and hair seemed to glitter—either due to some glamour or because of all the wild magic in the air. They chanted a new ballad of King Penvalle and his five triumphs. I snorted a laugh. There were no triumphs. Not yet, anyway. The minstrels had pre-written history.

"Rosey!" Enid hissed, and again I realized I was swaying to the music. "What is wrong with you? You're not yourself today."

I almost laughed. She was correct, I was not myself—or Rosey, at least—and evidently, I was failing at playing my role.

"Sorry," I said, for what felt like the hundredth time.

"Don't apologize. Stop. I do not want to draw any attention, especially today."

I stared into her eyes and nodded mutely. I didn't have to ask what she meant.

Today was the first trial for the new Everlast King, Lord Penvalle. The land of Elsewhere had no hereditary royal family. Instead, one house wore the crown until another house took it from them. Every time the crown changed hands within the ruling house, as it had when Queen Celia had returned to the Source over the winter, the hunting year began. During each of the five hunts of the season, anyone was permitted to challenge the house for the right to rule.

This year, King Penvalle would be the hunted. The hunt would continue all night until either his death, sunrise, or King Penvalle crossed the boundary of the hunting grounds.

When I was a child, Rosey and I used to play a pretend game of the Wilde Hunts. I was always the queen, and she was the hunter. We used the creek in the Waywoods as our boundary. Our hunt would end when I leapt over it, or she "killed" me by tagging me out of the game. Which, of course, she never did, so she never got to play as the queen.

The true hunts were not quite so tame. The boundaries were much further. The obstacles much more treacherous than roots and stones. And killing the King was no game of pretend.

It had been some several hundred years since the last hunts, and for that reason there were many Fae nobles visiting the court, interested in joining the games. Usually, as far as I understood, it was only humans and the occasional lesser fairies who took part. No one expected to kill the King—no one ever beat the Everlasts —but the gold that families won betting on how long their children would last might feed the family for another year.

Worse still, no deaths within the hunts were viewed as murder— only as casualties of the games. Some would wait years to duel out their grudges in the hunts, so that they could not be punished for the crime of killing an enemy or romantic rival.

Others came to watch. As I'd heard this morning, there was little to do for entertainment in the city. Little to break up the monotony of work and starvation and misery that came with being a human in the fairy realm. They came to watch the Fae kill each other and did not care that they were also cheering for their own demise.

Regardless of why anyone was here, the energy of the feast and the way every eye darted toward the royal tents, admiring and terrified at the same time, told me enough. No one thought there was any chance that the Everlasts would not rule for another five-hundred years. Especially the family themselves.

"Rosey!"

I jolted, shocked at the volume of Enid's voice beside me. "What?"

"You're swaying again."

I groaned. "How do you resist it?" I asked under my breath, trying desperately not to listen to the song.

"Count in your head," she said, casting me a suspicious glance. "Or list things."

"Like what?" I replied, trying not to move my mouth when I spoke like she did.

"Anything. Colors. Names of the old gods. The order of the royal succession. If you occupy your mind, they can't get in."

I straightened my back again and tried to concentrate. *Red, blue, purple, brown.* My foot tapped, and I practically growled in frustration.

"Think of something more complex," Enid said, without even knowing what I'd been thinking.

"I'm trying."

"List the order of succession. That should keep you occupied for a while."

I flushed. She wasn't wrong, but her tone was scathing.

The minstrels picked up their pace and my vision swayed. Beads of moisture rolled down my neck. Even under the shade of the forest canopy and the nearly darkened sky, it was unbearably hot. Like the Fae were trying to roast us lesser beings alive. I practically groaned and tried again to focus—the royal order of succession would have to do.

There were nine living members of the house of Everlast. Until the fall of this year, it had been ten.

Queen Celia the Great had ruled the High Fae court of Elsewhere for hundreds of years until this past Samhain when she walked into the Source to rejoin the earth. Celia and her mate had three children.

Her eldest son, Prince Belvedere, was several years deceased. His only son was Prince Scion, who had taken over the role of house assassin upon his father's death.

Queen Celia's only daughter, Princess Raewyn of the Sight, was married to one of the lesser lords of Overcast. Raewyn and Lord Auberon had three children. Prince Gwydion, Prince Bael and Lady Aine, who I had never heard referred to as "Princess."

Queen Celia's youngest son, the new King Penvalle, had many titles. Each were whispered all over Everlast, the way one might speak of a plague:

Penvalle, the Pitiless.

Penvalle, the Powerful.

Penvalle, the Blood King, Lord of the Hunt.

Against my will, my gaze darted to the King's crimson tent in the center of the clearing. I'd known, to an extent, what to expect and still my breath caught, a mixture of interest and revulsion coursing through me.

The tent was decorated like an outdoor bedchamber. Everything from the furniture to the lights to the people were cast in shades of gold and red. Dancing women, twirling silks, bubbles in the air from recently popped fizzing wine.

In the center of the tent, an opulent gold bed was covered in a mass of writhing bodies. It was so dense it was almost impossible to see where one form ended and another began.

In the center of the bed, a handsome dark-haired Fae male wore nothing but an obsidian crown. He watched the surrounding chaos, like a maestro conducting an orchestra.

As I watched, the King's attention was pulled by one of the women in the middle of the bacchanal on the bed. She crawled up to him, a simpering expression on her blood-splattered face. He reached out a hand, and I expected him to pull her onto his lap. Instead, he ran his hand along her jaw, staring intently at her.

So fast, I almost missed it, he twisted his wrist. I gasped, and though I couldn't hear the crack, it was as though I could feel it myself when the woman slumped forward, dead in his lap.

I swallowed thickly, looking away. At least my mind felt clearer as horror rocked me and a cry died in my throat.

I didn't believe in the Wilde Hunts. Didn't support them. Didn't think meaningless death for any reason was justified. However, I might have hoped that someone might kill King Penvalle. I might have. Except that the only one strong enough to beat him was Prince Scion.

And he was worse.

7

LONNIE

"*I*'m going for a walk," I mumbled.

"You can't," Enid snapped. "Have you gone completely mad?"

She looked at me intently, and for a moment I thought she might have figured me out. Might have realized I wasn't Rosey, but if so, she didn't voice it.

"I'm going to offer this around." I raised the pitcher of wine in my arms. "I think I simply didn't eat enough today, and the fumes are getting to me."

Enid sighed in relief, as if that explanation made sense. She waved me away. "Fine. Do that."

I took a step forward, toward the dark edge of the wood, and stopped dead in my tracks as a figure appeared in my path.

"Oh, no," Enid breathed, her attention turning to where I was looking.

I turned and had only a second to look up into the face of the dangerously beautiful prince from the woods before he was suddenly standing too close. "Hello, Slúagh. I knew I would see you again."

My adrenaline spiked, my pulse throbbing as prickles of fear traveled down my spine.

The prince's nostrils flared, and his eyes flashed something dark and predatory. In the space of a blink, he reached for me.

I gasped, shocked, as one hand found the curve of my waist and the other tangled in my hair. Something smashed against the ground, moisture coating my feet, and I swayed as if the jug I'd been holding was smashed over my head instead of the grass below.

He bent and pressed his mouth to mine in a bruising kiss and my breath left me. My stomach dipped as though I were falling, and heat flooded my entire body as an involuntary whimper burst from my lips.

He ran his tongue over the seam of my lips, and I parted them on a moan. The sweet taste of wine filled my mouth, my head spinning as if I'd truly drunk myself to the point of madness.

This *was* madness.

I pushed at his shoulders and dug my nails into his neck, but he held me still, unyielding.

Panic rising, I bit down on the prince's lip hard enough that the metallic taste of blood filled my mouth. He stiffened and dropped his hand from my hair.

I stumbled back, unable to form words. My skin tingled and my lips burned everywhere he'd touched me, and my stomach sloshed in an odd combination of fear and excitement.

Hundreds of eyes turned to look at me. Servants and Fae alike were all craning their necks to see the cause of the commotion, but my attention was fixed solely on Prince Bael.

Prince Bael pressed a hand to his bleeding lip and his fingers came away red. He looked from his hand to me, an expression of delighted incredulity appearing on his stunning face. "You bit me. How positively Fae of you."

I gazed, transfixed, as he ran a thumb over his bleeding lip. He sucked the pad of his finger into his mouth, licking the blood off like honey, then grinned. There was something cruel in the smile. Razor-sharp, that sent shivers down my spine.

He smirked down at me and bent to whisper in my ear. "You just won me a great deal of money, so I'll let your violent urges go unpunished. This time." He reached for my hand and began pulling me toward the glittering tents. "Come."

My pulse was frantic, my adrenaline spiking. I couldn't breathe for fear, the buzzing in my ears drowning out the horrible music that had condemned me.

I choked, swallowing a sob. I'd never see my sister again. Never even learn what she'd needed to do tonight that had been so important that she'd asked me to be here. Numbness settled over my mind like a blanket. I couldn't think of that now, or I would collapse, unable to walk another step.

"Go." Enid's nervous voice came from somewhere behind me. "It will be worse if you don't."

The prince raised an eyebrow as if to say she was correct, and reached for my arm, dragging me behind him across the clearing toward the tent where all the princes sat. It was the largest and most ornate–gold with black and white brocade–and more elaborate than the King's tent of sexual torture.

I shook, all my limbs going numb and cold, and the world felt strangely silent as my feet carried me across the grass without my permission.

Faces blurred around me, and the strange song faded in the background, as though everyone had stopped to watch my funeral march.

I heaved in breath after breath, trying to calm my racing heart. I couldn't decide between the urge to run and the desire to wring the nearest fairy's neck.

As I got closer, I realized the glittering gold on the tents was not gold at all. The walls were ochre silk held up by birch wood posts. Gleaming wisps hovered outside, lighting the tents and giving the impression they were sparkling from within.

The prince gestured widely for me to walk in front of him, as if showing a guest to his home. "I have been proven correct," he announced to the tent at large. "Pay up, you disbelieving bastards."

A few of the noble Fae rose to move toward the prince, but I paid little attention. Instead, my eye caught on a group of writhing dancers in the corner all tied to the ceiling by their arms. Humans, I could tell by the bruising on the vast amounts of visible skin.

Overhead, lanterns hung, bathing everything in a soft pink light, which flickered almost in time to the tinkling music. There was no proper furniture, but piles of blankets and pillows in every color of silk, where the Everlast family and their attendants lounged surrounded by trays upon trays heaped with food and wine.

Miraculously—and to my relief—no one seemed to be dead, or bleeding. Yet.

Still, all the servants were in some state of undress and many were caged or had some sort of collar around their throats. Nearly all were females, though there were several handsome males in the mix. The High Fae cared less about gender or species, and more about physical beauty and magical ability—and this group had beauty in spades.

I looked down at my shaking hands, knuckles white where I knotted them in the fabric of my skirt. The image of a cat batting a mouse between its claws before killing it sprung to mind.

My mother's rules and Rosey's warning not to draw attention to myself rang in my ears and hysterical laughter bubbled in my throat, threatening to choke me. Maybe the other servants were right. I was cursed. Because all those who were noticed by the Everlasts became theirs, and I could never let that happen. *Never.*

8
LONNIE

I closed my eyes and let my face go as blank as
possible, trying to pretend I was Rosey. Rosey, who
never caused problems. Who would never be singled out by the
Fae. Perhaps I could truly play the role of my sister for the rest of
the evening and live to see another sunrise.

"Gwydion!" Prince Bael called, as he looked down at his palm
and seemed to count the coins he'd just acquired. "Pay me, you
fucking cheater."

"I'm a bit busy at the moment," another blonde male called
across the tent.

The other male–Gwydion–could only be Prince Bael's brother.

They looked very similar, except that even sitting it was clear
that Gwydion was two heads taller than any fairy I'd ever seen,
with muscles reminiscent of a troll. The other obvious difference was in their demeanors. Where Bael was slightly
dangerous even to look at, Prince Gwydion was bright and
open. He had copper golden ringlets, wide blue eyes, and a
disposition that had earned him a glowing court reputation. I'd
heard he never yelled and rarely beat servants to the point of

death. In the capital, that was enough to warrant a cult-like devotion.

Reputation aside, Prince Gwydion's claim of being busy was... mostly true. He had two nymphs sitting in his lap, one on each knee, and none of their combined six hands were visible.

"You just made me a good amount of coin, Slúagh," Bael said, turning back to me. "Or you will, when my *cheat brother pays his share.*" He yelled the last bit and several courtiers nearest to us laughed.

I stared resolutely at the ground, having no idea what to say. They'd bet on something—probably something to do with that spontaneous kiss. Whatever it was, I had no desire to know.

"Are you ignoring me now?" the prince asked, still in that same mocking tone. "That's novel. We'll miss so many opportunities. We could take our act on the road."

His personality was...jarring. I forced myself to look up and meet his eyes.

If Prince Bael were human, I would have said he wasn't much older than my twenty years. As it was, it was impossible to say.

He was beautiful like all Fae, but with a darkness that didn't surround most of the High Fae court. It reminded me strongly of the afflicted back in Aftermath. Shadowed. Like no amount of sunlight would ever warm him. If I didn't know better, I would assume he was one of the Unseelie.

"What can I do for you, lord?" The words sounded sarcastic, and I tried to force my voice into a normal, unassuming tone.

He took a step forward. "What's your name?"

I looked from side to side, desperate to find an ally, but no one in the tent was even watching us, let alone stopping whatever they were doing to listen. "Lonnie," I muttered, automatically.

Shit.

Between the music, the wine fumes, and whatever odd thing the Fae did with their eyes, I couldn't concentrate. And that would kill me faster than anything else.

He laughed. "Liar. That can't be your name."

For once I hadn't lied, and it was one of the few moments when I should have. The irony was almost too much to handle. "I don't know what you mean."

He narrowed his eyes, annoyed. "What's your real name, then."

I gnawed on my lip to keep from responding, the compulsion was so strong. "That is my real name. Humans do not have court names."

To the Fae, names were power. Even the prince, no doubt, had some longer official name that he did not give out easily. Our mother had given Rosey and I Fae names that could be easily shortened—one of her only true gifts to us. I tried not to even think my name too often, lest someone have the power to over-hear, but Rosey's—Roisin—popped to the forefront of my brain, unbidden.

The prince mouthed my name, then paused as though tasting it. After a moment, he turned around and raised his arms like a court jester performing for a crowd. "That's horrendous. We'll have to change it."

A shout of agreement went up behind him, mingled with whoops of drunken laughter.

"I would call her a troll," a fairy called. "That seems like a fitting name."

I gritted my teeth. This sort of thing didn't matter. In fact, if I was lucky, they would become so distracted by their childish games they would forget me altogether.

Bael reached for me with one hand and held out his goblet with the other. "I think for now, I will simply call you 'Slúagh.'"

I kept my mouth firmly shut, refusing to give into my impulse to say something back that would lose me a finger. Or worse.

I'd seen other servants have their tongues ripped out to stop them from speaking. I'd seen spells make the victim think they had no lips. It was possible. Maybe someone whispered something on the breeze. Threw some spell or curse in my path.

"Slúagh," wasn't an uncommon insult or even one that bothered me all that much. If he had wanted to really hurt me, I could have listed off ten worse things to call me, starting with *interesting*.

"Slúagh," was simply what the High Fae called those of us who belonged to neither realm entirely. Though I was born here, my mother was not. She was a changeling—a human child taken maliciously in the night and raised to serve the High Fae court.

That made me one of "the Slúagh." The crowd. The servants. The army. There wasn't a perfect translation to the common tongue, but the meaning was clear. We were the faceless, nameless masses, to be used as manual labor and pushed in front of any threat. We were a constant workforce in a culture where work was viewed as necessary but undesirable. We were raised to behave like them, and live alongside them, but were constantly reminded that we could never think like them. We were good enough to labor for them, to fuck them in secret, but we were fundamentally different beings. We'd never be one of them.

The prince looked from me to the wine in his goblet as I poured it stiffly and frowned. "No response? My, usually the ladies fall to their knees before me. Your lack of enthusiasm for even the most basic questions is disappointing."

I clenched my jaw. I hated talking to Fae—especially High Fae. Their tendency to twist words and speak in random, indirect half-truths had infuriated me since I was a child on the cook's leading strings.

This was why I was better suited to jobs out of sight—I couldn't control my face. Couldn't hide my hatred of the Fae, and that got you killed in Elsewhere faster than any hard labor or measly mortal lifespan.

If I could just bore him, maybe he would leave me alone. An outburst would be interesting. Ignoring him was "novel." Servitude was common. "Did you need anything else, my lord?"

His eyes narrowed. "Yes, actually." He lowered his voice to half a whisper, though I was sure all the Fae could still hear quite clearly. "I have a question. How did you see us in the woods today?"

Again, I forced myself to meet his eyes. "I don't know what you mean."

He reached for my chin, holding me tight with two fingers. "I think you do."

"Bael!" a male voice barked from just to my right, "Stop playing games with that one. Go bewitch one of the other servants."

I turned my head, searching for whoever had come to my aid, only to realize he was no savior at all.

Prince Scion sat on the far edge of the tent, slightly removed from everyone else. His huge black bird was perched on the back of his chair like a sentry, and he had a blonde nymph woman in his lap, trailing her fingers over his neck. As I watched, he fisted his hand in her hair and pushed her roughly away, getting to his feet.

All noise stopped, as it had when I'd crossed the clearing, but now it seemed less in my head and more because all those around me were afraid to breathe

"Oh? And why is that?" Bael rounded on his cousin. "Bewitched, beguiled, bedded, beheaded. What's it to you how I prove my point?"

Scion's eyes narrowed on me and there was absolutely no warmth there. If I was afraid before, that terror doubled tenfold as silver eyes met mine.

"You've proven nothing," he said flatly, never taking his gaze off me. "And we don't play with traitors."

"You are taking the fun out of everything, Sci. I would argue we should *always* play with the traitors. Toys get broken."

My eyes widened. I had no idea what they were talking about... but did it matter? They spoke about me like I was something without conscious thought. A slug, or an ant. An item to be passed around in a card game. And, perhaps to them, I was.

The idea made my blood boil as much as it was comforting. If it wasn't about me, only about their entertainment, perhaps I could leave with my life. The sun was nearly set, only the faintest glimmer still visible on the horizon. Once the sun went down, they would begin their hunt. Perhaps then, I could escape.

Bael smiled smugly at his cousin. "How many humans do you know who taste like magic?"

Prince Scion looked down at me with more disdain and hatred than I could remember seeing from one of the Fae. It was all I could do not to return his glare. "What?"

The blonde prince reached down, yanking me to my feet. He shoved me forward and I stumbled, running a couple of steps to keep from falling on my face. "See for yourself."

I tripped over the hem of Rosey's gown, and I felt the fabric rip. I winced. Her lovely dress was covered in mud and wine and soon, no doubt, my blood.

Prince Scion quirked his head to the side, assessing me like an interesting puzzle. I was forced to admit he was handsome—shockingly so—regardless of his murderous intentions.

For a moment, he did nothing. Then, he reached out, bumping his own full wine goblet into my unmoving hand. Crimson liquid sloshed across the grass at his feet. "Clumsy," he said in a tone of mock sorrow. "Do you know how long that takes to ferment? Long enough that you would be halfway to dust before what you spilled could be replaced."

I stared down at the wine, soaking into the earth where only the worms could make use of it, and frustration boiled in my stomach. "But—"

"And look," he continued, playing to the crowd. "You've gotten some on my boots."

He kicked a boot out as if to show me, and the surrounding Fae laughed, the sound deafening.

"Apologize," he said lazily.

Apologize for what?

I warred with myself. This didn't matter. It wasn't so bad. He was determined to make me react, and I was about to burst. I bit my lip, angry tears pricking the backs of my eyes. "I'm sorry."

The words burned my throat, the only time lying had ever made me sick to my stomach.

Prince Bael jerked his hand again and like a puppet on a string, my knees slammed into the ground before I knew what was happening. He bent and whispered so only I could hear. The whisper seemed to wrap around me like he was everywhere at once. "See, Slúagh? That wasn't so difficult. I knew you wanted to fall to your knees before us."

I jerked back, rage and humiliation coursing through me, and stared up at him. My face would surely betray my hatred, but it didn't matter. He was going to kill me, anyway—that much was obvious. Still, I refused to play their cruel, pointless games.

If I was going to die, I would die with dignity.

Scion matched his smile and spoke loudly enough now for the crowd to hear. "Lick it."

I froze, horrified. "W-what?"

He kicked his boot out again and his voice was full of malicious laughter as he moved his foot closer to my face. "You've ruined my boots. The least you can do is clean them. Go on, Slúagh. Lick."

The laughter from the other Fae sounded magnified ten times over. Everyone had to be watching now, which, of course, was the point.

I shook my head. *No. No.* "No."

I'd learned this lesson before. No matter what I did, no matter how I begged or did what they said, the Fae wouldn't stop. They took pleasure in the torment and were only spurred on by fear.

Peels of nervous laughter rang out, mingled with shocked gasps. The prince stared down at me, seeming just as surprised as everyone else. "What did you say?"

My heart pounded, pulsing in my temples and my face burned with rage and humiliation. I closed my eyes, waiting for pain when he would no doubt slam the toe of his boot into my face.

Heat traveled up my spine and down my arms, making my hair stand on end. If it was a reaction he wanted, then he was about to get one. "No. You—"

A ripple of indecision seemed to cross Prince Scion's face, and then he moved so fast I could hardly react. He spun me around, pulling my back against his chest. He too was surprisingly warm. Somehow, I'd expected the Fae to be cold, like marble, but the heat coming from his bare chest beneath that embroidered black jacket was immense. Like standing too close to a fire.

I stared straight ahead, too afraid to move as he reached up, threading long fingers into my hair. His rings caught in the curls, making the bun that Rosey had made come loose and fall around my shoulders. "Do you know why you're here?" he asked, too close to my ear.

I tried to shake my head but couldn't with his hand in my hair. "No."

That wasn't entirely true. I knew that they were all vicious, cruel, irredeemable monsters from the moment they were born, and I was here because they enjoyed suffering. It was no more complex than that.

He bent down, whispering in my ear. "Liar."

I jolted with surprise when his tongue ran up the column of my neck to my ear. Unbidden, heat coiled in my belly, mixing with the terror. Adrenaline flooded me, and I found myself unsure whether I wanted to run or find out what would happen if I stayed.

He pulled my head further to the side and used the other hand to spread his fingers over my hip bone. The scent of smoke and rain overwhelmed me. It drew me in, fighting against every instinct I possessed.

My head was spinning as his mouth reached my ear.

Suddenly he spun me around to face him again. He pushed my hair away from my ear to look. "What is that?" he demanded, his voice slightly rougher, less refined. "Who did this?"

"Don't touch me." I reached up, clapping a hand over it. "It's nothing. Just a scar."

His silver eyes turned dark pewter, and moved from my ear to my face, seemingly looking for something.

Whatever he was hoping to see, I never found out.

9

LONNIE

A shout went up outside and all attention turned to the mouth of the tent. As I wavered between the desire to keep my eyes on my opponent and the powerful urge to look down, something moved in the corner of my eye. A dark object, darting fast past the edge of my peripheral vision.

A stampede of footsteps pounded outside, then more shouts, growing louder and louder in a panicked crescendo. Shadows moved outside the gold brocade tent and the dancers who had stood nearest the door took the opportunity to run, while many servers dropped their trays, wine and fruit scattering on the ground and among the opulent blankets and cushions.

"I fucking knew this would happen," Prince Scion muttered under his breath, speaking to no one in particular. He whirled on me. "Are they here for you, Slúagh? Or are you not important enough for that?"

I stared at him, my mind whirring, as I desperately tried to follow what he thought was happening. "I don't–"

He didn't wait for a reply. Striding away from me toward the mouth of the tent, the crowd shifted to let him pass. His expression was flat, as he knocked servants and courtiers out of his way left and right with a wave of his hand. He took no care to notice if it was a fellow fairy or a human he was bowling over in his effort to leave the tent.

In contrast, Prince Bael seemed bored. Unconcerned, as chaos reigned around us. He glanced at me as he walked backwards following behind his cousin. Bael bent and picked up one of the apples that had rolled across the ground. He glanced back, our gazes locking, as he put the fruit to his mouth. "I hope you don't think we're done here."

I stared, transfixed by his too-sharp teeth piercing the scarlet flesh; by the juice, dripping down his chin. Goosebumps traveled up my arms despite the heat of the evening and I pressed my thighs together, heat coating my skin.

My heart pounded in my ears, matching the beat of the festival drums, and I warred with myself. Loathing and intrigue sitting too close in my mind. Curiosity battling with revulsion.

Then, as if reading my thoughts, the prince pulled the apple away from his lips and grinned. He stepped back, laughing at me as the fruit turned black, rotting in his hand until it was nothing more than dust falling to the earth at his feet.

I squinted into the clearing over the heads of those now mobbing the entrance, desperate to see what was going on. Bodies jostled on all sides, some trying to escape, some trying to see the source of the commotion. Somehow, I fell into both groups, equally curious as I was desperate to leave.

I let the crowd carry me toward the mouth of the tent, and my mouth dropped open in a gasp that was lost in all the noise. In the clearing, it was mayhem.

Someone—or many someones—had stormed through the revel, leaving splintered wood, broken strings, and tiny silver bells littering the ground like the carnage of some great battle. On the hill in the distance, will-o-wisps sped away, illuminating the path as the colorful Fae dancers fled back to the castle, their silk dresses streaming behind them like flags of surrender.

Dozens of cloaked figures rampaged through the clearing, some bearing weapons, others knocking over tents. One ran past me, half a broken fairy flute held aloft like a torch. He turned and looked at me, grinning when we made eye contact. "Ahan!"

I blinked, leaning forward, not sure I'd heard him correctly through the scarf covering the lower part of his face.

I strained my ears. The shouts were not random, they were yelling…something.

"Ahan!" "Ahan!"

Who…?

As I watched, a flash of movement caught in the corner of my eye. One of the black hooded figures darted past them with single-minded focus, moving away from the rest of the rebels. A tendril of auburn hair peeked out from under the hood and my vision grew narrow, my heart leaping into my throat.

I gasped. Even with the scarf halfway covering her face, I recognized the eyes immediately.

They were *my* eyes.

My quiet, mild-mannered sister wove in and out of the other attackers, darting around the fleeing dancers and nobles with cat-like precision. I reached out, thinking she was moving toward me, as if to save me, but she didn't stop.

The scene before me blurred, and time slowed. My reality shattered.

Without knowing what I was doing, I was shoving those around me, forcing them out of my way. I had to get out. *Get to her, now.*

There were too many people between me and the exit, too many bodies. The heat pressed in on me and I opened my mouth to scream, but no sound came out. My elbow collided with something hard, and someone tumbled to the ground, their hands grappling for my arms, my sleeves. Any other time, I would have felt guilty—but not now.

My sister was still moving across the clearing, coming in and out of my line of sight. Every time she ducked behind someone, my panic grew, driving my adrenaline higher, making the heat of my face and arms grow hotter and hotter until I felt like I might catch fire.

Like I could. Like right now, I *would* catch fire.

King Penvalle looked up from the middle of his tent of horrors. He blinked bemusedly at his oncoming attacker, seeming if anything, amused. Rosey's face held the same cool focus it always did as she reached into her cloak and raised a gleaming knife in front of her, as though it were a sword.

I tried again to scream, and my throat was too dry. I choked, coughing, on the burn and tried again. To assassinate the King now wouldn't make my sister the Queen. To assassinate him now was not even possible. This was insane. Reckless, and bound to fail, and from the way the King stared at my sister, he knew that.

Rosey approached the mouth of the King's tent and finally, speech returned, and the word burst from my mouth before I'd stopped to consider the implication. "Rosey!"

She didn't seem to hear me as she approached the King. She must have been saying something to him as they hadn't moved

59

for too many long seconds. Cold goosebumps erupted on my skin, an eerie feeling of finality settling over me.

Rosey threw her head back as if laughing and Penvalle's arrogant, beautiful face transformed into something twisted. Feral.

King Penvalle leapt from the bed and drew a gleaming sword from his belt. I eyed the blade, so clean and fine it was practically a mirror. It didn't look as though Penvalle had ever used it, but when he raised it above his head, I knew he must have used it many times before.

I lunged forward, pushing the last of the crowd out of my way, only to be yanked back.

Arms wrapped around my middle and held me, trapped, against some stranger's chest. The scent of smoke and mulled wine surrounded me, mixing with the pine of the forest.

Fear and rage filled me, stronger than anything I'd felt while the princes tormented me, stronger than in the forest, or when they'd taken my mother away. I kicked out, flailing my arms wildly. "Let me go!"

"Stop," a voice whispered in my ear, seeming to wrap all around me.

I didn't stop. I wouldn't. *Not Rosey. Not my sister.*

I screamed and kicked, but no one paid me any mind, all their attention fixed on the King, and the girl whose hood had fallen back as she stood, facing him, entirely unafraid.

"For Dullahan!" Rosey yelled, loud enough for me to hear over all the madness.

"No!" I screamed, my voice breaking on the word, my throat feeling as though it tore open. "No! Stop!"

"Stop!" Whoever held me echoed me, his voice entirely different from mine.

King Penvalle's eyes were cold and calculated. He raised his arm and moved his sword through the air. It was too fast for human eyes to see. I knew that, and somehow, I saw it.

He sliced once. Twice. Forward and back again. His sword cutting through the air in the swift efficient moments of a trained killer.

For an impossibly long moment, it was as though nothing happened. My sister's body remained there, standing, stock still, as she had been before the sword was drawn. Then, my stomach churned with nausea and heat rose to my skin as gravity took hold.

As if in slow motion, Rosey's body fell first, separating from her head which seemed to hover in midair before it fell. I stared, transfixed, at the face of my sister. At my face. Suspended in time, her expression twisted in pain and rage.

My skin burned white-hot. All consuming. Until I was blind with it.

Someone was screaming. And that someone was me. And I couldn't stop.

I would never stop.

10

LONNIE

*N*o one stopped me as I sprinted toward the tent in a morbid mirror of my twin. Indeed, most of the party had either fled the forest or were hiding in the few tents still standing.

My heart hammered against my ribs, pounding so hard I thought it might burst from my chest. Furious tears stung my eyes and poured down my cheeks. I reached up, angrily brushing them away with the back of my hand. The tears mingled with the sweat from my brow, only making my vision worse as I ran.

Fire licked up the sides of half the silk structures, broken wood and twisted fabric lay across the ground.

In the center of the ruin, one lone fairy stood. He was short, with unusually thin arms and legs and thick, knee-length white hair. His eyes were closed, and he swayed as he played his violin to the emptying clearing. The long resonant notes of the violin sounded more ominous than mesmerizing. Like the low tones of a death march.

That fucking music.

Soon, I would return and throw the musician and his instrument into that fire, but first I had to get to Rosey.

I skidded into the King's crimson tent. It was one of the few structures left standing. One of the few untouched by either the attackers or the surrounding commotion. Indeed, aside from Rosey herself, the other cloaked figures had left the King's tent undisturbed.

I nearly doubled over as I beheld the tableau inside the crimson tent. A strangled sound came from my chest–half sob, half scream. There were too many things to process at once and my eye couldn't focus on a single point as a revolting smell filled my mouth and nose. Pungent and metallic, like rotting flesh and old blood.

The blank-eyed dancers carried on swaying, and the rising mass of naked bodies on the bed had changed rhythm now moving in time to the hypnotic funeral march. I gagged again, nearly vomiting on the floor in front of me as I spotted a disembodied arm and part of what looked like a foot floating freely in the mass of people, as though someone had died, been torn apart, and simply fallen below the wave.

I stared down at my own dead face on the ground, where Rosey's mangled body lay discarded beside the enormous bed where the macabre mix of sex and death carried on as if nothing had changed. For me–for her–everything had changed.

I threw myself on the ground beside her, not caring who or what went on around us.

I couldn't accept this. I couldn't understand it.

We would never leave this place. She would never scold me again, or act as my elder, more responsible twin, or live to see a life better than this one. It made no sense. My sister. My quiet, capable sister did not try to murder the King. She did not run about with rebels—because that was what they had to be. No other group would enter the kingdom, let alone the palace grounds, on a hunting day.

But she had. Why? How? What was so important that it was worth dying for? That it was worth leaving me?

Fingers brushed the back of my arm and I jumped, pulling back abruptly. I craned my neck, hissing as I looked back. "Enid?"

Shock penetrated my haze of misery. It seemed impossible that anything could still be happening around me. That the world had not simply come to an end when mine had, yet the blank, glassy expression in Enid's eyes said otherwise.

My erratic heartbeat sped up, and my panic rose as Enid reached for me again, her nails scratching down my arm. I leaned out of the way and whimpered. A bolt of terror coursed through me. She didn't recognize me.

My fear and rage warred with my sense of self-preservation. Bewitched, Enid was not in control of herself, but I was still loath to hurt her.

She grabbed roughly for my hair and pulled me a few feet toward the bed with shocking strength. I kicked out, flailing, and caught her in the side of the face with an elbow. She shrieked and dropped me, only for another girl to reach for me again.

One of the men rose from the bed, extricating himself from between two partners. I recognized him as one of the guards who had worked with Caliban. One of the Windom brothers. More brawn than brains. And now, he was heading toward me with blank eyes and arms outstretched. Dread filled me.

I'd assumed it was only the Fae I had to worry about. The King, pulling all our puppet strings, and in a way it probably was. But still, I couldn't fight off a dozen attackers on my own, human or Fae.

Ezra Windom reached for me, and I darted backwards out of the way, only for another set of powerful arms to wrap around me from behind. Something hard slammed into the side of my head with a crack and pain shot through me, stars bursting behind my eyes. I felt the warm trickle of blood slide down my cheek from my temple and I stifled a cry.

Then, someone was lifting me and tossing me on the bed. I did cry out then, half in terror and half with disgust at the macabre juxtaposition of sex and death. A hand cupped my face, and I clenched my jaw, trying desperately not to cry.

The King leaned forward from where he sat in the center of the madness. His eyes met mine, and it was as though he were trying to place me. And, perhaps, he was. If not for me personally, then for Rosey—his attempted murderer. A look of horror crossed his face, settling over his glassy eyes and he laughed high and manic. "But I just killed you."

Pain shot through my center. Pain and revulsion and rage. I shook with it. Rage for my sister. For my mother. For all the other dead in this tent—and for how many others? How many times had he done this?

As he had with the girl not an hour before, the king reached out and ran a hand over my face. Terror gripped me, but more than that, I was angry. The rage sent heat up my spine. The back of my neck. My arms and face. It traveled across my body like wildfire, consuming everything in its wake, until I was certain I would burst into flame. Burn the tent to the ground and take him with me.

The King pulled his hand back, suddenly, staring at me and then down at his fingers. I took advantage of his confusion, reaching for his too-handsome face. Heat sparked between us. Like wildfire. Like rogue lightening. Like the molten heat that had destroyed the city of Nightshade twenty years ago.

I looked around, desperately searching for a weapon, and my eye caught on the pointed obsidian crown. Reaching forward, I yanked the crown from his head.

It was smooth to the touch. Sharp and vicious on the edges, with glassy sides so black I could see my own warped reflection looking back at me. See my eyes, wide and horrified.

Swinging my arm back, I smashed the crown into the side of the King's head.

The King screamed like a wild animal, reaching blindly for me, trying to wrench the crown from my hands. His hands closed around my wrists, but he dropped them immediately, as if touching a hot stove.

I pulled my arm back again, and moved without thought, slamming and stabbing blindly again and again and again. Blood poured over my hands and down the front of my dress, and still, I didn't stop.

Finally, with a squelch, the pointed tip of the crown embedded into the King's eye socket, and he teetered forward. Looming. Falling. Until he slumped forward on top of me, crushing me beneath the wave of bodies.

11

LONNIE

*T*he King's sweaty body crushed me into the mattress, his chest pressed to mine in a mockery of an embrace. I recoiled at the hot, sticky moisture pressed between us, coating my hands and my belly. After this, a quick death was all I could hope for.

After this, I felt dead anyway.

"Oh, for the love of the Source. Move!" someone hissed close to my ear. "Move him off her. She can't breathe."

I turned my head almost brushed noses with Enid. Her expression was clear and focused as she reached over my head, and shoved the king's limp body, showing no regard for his royal corpse.

Her efforts to move the body awoke something in me. I quaked in belated terror, the back of my skull rattling against the headboard. The blood was everywhere. Everywhere. It soaked every part of me, my hands, my dress, and it just kept coming.

The tent was full, yet all I could hear was my own labored breath. The pounding of my own heartbeat mocked me.

"Leave her, Enid," another woman's voice rang out, echoing around the tent. "When the princes find out—"

"It's after sundown, you festering wound," Enid snapped, cutting her off. "The princes are the least of our concerns."

My eyes darted past King Penvalle's bare, gleaming shoulder. At least twelve other girls gathered around the king's opulent gold bed, and they were all staring at me. I tried not to focus on those who hadn't stood up. On the smell of death still filling the tent. On the blood coating every surface.

The maids closest to me turned away, fear and anger streaking their faces. My vision blurred, panicked tears pricking at the backs of my eyes. I'd never learned these girls' names in all the years we worked together, too angry about what people said about me. About my mother. That felt foolish now. How many potential allies stood before me? The Fae were our only real enemies, not each other.

Enid swore under her breath as she gave King Penvalle's torso a tremendous shove. She turned back to the other servants. "Help or leave, you cunts!"

I jerked, surprised at the volume of her voice. Whatever spell they'd been under, it had ended when the King died. That, more than anything, made his death real.

My hands came to life, like statues springing from stone prisons. I stretched my fingers, prying them from the crown still embedded in the king's head. I stole a quick glance at the wound. It looked more like a bludgeoning than a burn. *Small mercies.*

There was a beat as the other servants shuffled, some turning away, others moving to help. Enid and the others rolled the king off me, letting him flop on his side in the gilded bed. I gasped, coughing as air filled my lungs.

"Lonnie?" Enid leaned over me. "Are you alright?"

My chest heaved, the combination of anxiety and exertion stealing my breath. I blinked up at her, my mouth opening and closing without sound. Was I alright?

I focused on her dull brown hair pulled back into a tight bun. Her wide brown eyes. Fae didn't have brown eyes. It was a human color. Brown eyes could tell lies, and I always found that comforting.

I held up my bloodied hands to Enid. The syrupy red soaked my skin like corrosive acid, eating away at everything that was good about me before this moment. Even if he was a murderer himself. Even if I'd wanted him dead. I'd never killed anyone. "What do I do?"

"It's after sundown," she whispered.

I furrowed my brow. "So?"

A distant voice rattled through me. "What the fuck is going on in here?"

I didn't recognize the voice, but I distantly felt like I should. The servants toward the back of the tent shifted, the crowd of women pushed in tighter around us, blocking the view of the entrance. They surely weren't protecting me, but trying to suspend the minutes before their own punishment. I'd condemned them too, by association, and there was nothing I could say to take it back.

Enid leaned over the bed and wrenched the obsidian crown out of the king's eye with as little reverence as I'd shown when I beat him with it. She spun and shoved the crown into my shaking hands. "Run."

I required no further encouragement. As if waking from my stupor, I scrambled away from King Penvalle's body, the blood squelching on the mattress as I leapt to my feet. I winced when my boots slide against the ground, and I slipped on the puddle dripping from one corner of the silk sheet.

I took one more look at Rosey, and the crushing pain of it threatened to send me to the ground. *I will find out why.* I promised her silently. *Whoever sent you here, I will find them, and they will get worse than the blood king.*

And with that, I tucked the blood-stained crown under my arm, ducked under the backside of the tent, and ran for the woods.

12

LONNIE

$\mathcal{E}$very tree seemed to watch me as I pushed further into the darkness of the forest. Every rustling leaf was a prince behind me, about to stab me in the back. Leaves and twigs crunched underfoot, every single one threatening to pitch me forward and halt my progress, potentially leaving me vulnerable to attack.

I glanced over my shoulder and darkness stared back at me, endless and empty. Unbidden, fear rose in my stomach, and I pictured some faceless creature crawling out of that shadowed darkness.

Branches whipped at my face and hands, but I didn't care, pushing them roughly aside as sobs wracked my body. I needed to run. Run far away. Be anywhere but here. Be anyone but me.

During daylight hours, the Waywoods were so dense they were nearly impossible to navigate. I'd only ever dared to hover on the outskirts by the wall and even then, only with Caliban. It was dangerous. Sexy. And now seemed abominably stupid.

The vast expanse of the woods stretched on and on in front of me. I looked right then, left, then right again. There was nowhere for me to go. Nowhere the Everlasts wouldn't find me.

Humans did not survive the woods on hunting day.

I couldn't help but remember all my mother's rules. Like lying, never going into the Waywoods after dark was one of the blanket edicts. Something so ingrained it barely needed to be said.

Or, it shouldn't have.

I'd heard ever since coming to live in the capital that the woods were filled with all manner of beasts, Underfae, and Unseelie. The darkest part of the woods housed creatures that mortal eyes hadn't seen in hundreds of years. Some called them gods— brothers and sisters to those living in the mountains at the Source and in the ocean at the undertow. Some said they were long dead or had never been there at all.

I'd heard countless stories of humans pulled off the path by the wisps, led astray by the Underfae, and tricked into bogs or off cliffs. But for me, I'd only ever feared the High Fae. The Underfae were always there. Always watching. They'd never abandoned me.

"Help me," I muttered into the darkness, scanning the tree line for tiny eyes peeking between the leaves.

A pair of gleaming yellow eyes appeared between two trees up ahead, and without thinking, I sprinted toward them, darting between the roots and brambles.

Sharp pain rocked my body. My breath left me in a gasp, and stars burst behind my eyes as I ran straight into a hard object. I bounced back, and the sensation of falling turned my stomach.

I braced to hit the ground but gasped as an arm caught me around the waist. My heart stuttered, shocked by both the pain and the sudden reversal of my fall. I twisted to see my captor, already having a good idea who stood before me.

"A word of advice, Slúagh," the familiar voice sent more tingles up my spine, his hot breath against my ear. "Never cry out for help in the dark. It makes you sound like prey, and you never know who might be listening."

13
LONNIE

"Get the fuck away from me," I growled.

I shoved at the arm trapping me, and was surprised by the boldness in my voice. Still, I could not bring myself to regret the words.

"Why?" Prince Bael whispered in my ear. "I bet you look even prettier on your back."

Another bolt of anger shot through me at that. I'd just watched my sister's murder, there was still blood on my hands, and this fucking fairy was going to try to flirt with me?

I took a large step back, bent, and reached behind me, grappling along the ground for a rock or a stick, *anything*. He might be here to kill me at last, but I would not lie here and let him do it.

His eyes darted to my hands, narrowing, as my fingers closed around a rock. His mocking smile slipped. "Put that down. You're more likely to injure yourself than me."

Something like defiance rocked through me, mixing with my adrenaline. My entire body woke up, humming to life. I only grasped the rock tighter. Without thinking, I hurled it at him.

Bael's yellow gaze went wide. Not in fear, clearly, but more in shock. Amusement, perhaps. He raised a hand, and the rock disintegrated in midair, centimeters before it would have hit his unnervingly perfect face.

"What violent tendencies you have." He cocked his head at me, the corner of his mouth tipping up. "You're a little monster."

There was that look again. The most terrifying one in the world. *Interest.*

"Why bother?" I asked, even as my simmering rage bubbled higher, and my temperature seemed to rise.

Prince Bael's eyes flashed–with something dark and frightening. "What are you going on about now?"

I drew myself up to my full height, but it made little difference. He was so much taller than I was, I barely reached the middle of his chest even with my heavy-heeled boots. "Why bother announcing your presence? You could have just killed me."

Bael laughed, and I hated how the sound seemed to wrap around me like a tendril of warm, teasing smoke. "But where's the fun in that?"

"You think murder is fun?" I shot back.

He looked down his nose at me and the amusement didn't shift from his face. "*You* clearly do. But no, I think it will be fun to watch you run and try to escape me, only to be caught in the end."

A shiver traveled up my spine. I couldn't help but think of his various taunts at the feast. His rotting apple. "B*ewitched, beguiled, bedded, beheaded.*"

I hated him. Them. All of them.

The absurdity of the moment hit me. I was arguing semantics when I should have been running for my life. Normally I would never look this prince in the eye, let alone speak to him thus. Perhaps he was doing…something. Casting a glamour or a spell, making it hard to think clearly.

Or perhaps it was simply that I had very little to lose.

I dug the toe of my boot into the dusty gravel of the ground and darted to the right, kicking up an enormous cloud of pebbles and debris in the prince's face, and turned on my heel to run.

I had not made it two steps before a new hand clasped around my arm, hauling me back.

Long fingers dug into my skin, hard enough to bruise. Prince Scion stared intently down at me, like no one else was present. His silver eyes seemed to take over, owning my attention, beckoning to me. "While I admire the effort, you are outnumbered."

I blinked, and the spell broke.

Instead, my gaze darted to a third figure, blonde, emerging out of the darkness. My stomach sank.

All three of the Everlast princes now stood before me, their fierce otherworldly gazes fixed intently on me. For one who'd wished nothing more than to go unnoticed, this was hell. If I had not known for certain I was awake, I would have believed it to be part of some horrific nightmare.

"What do you want?" I asked, my voice shaking slightly as I glanced between them.

It did not escape my notice that I was not dead, and nobody had made any serious move to drag me back to the castle. I'd yet to be forced to my knees or manhandled. *Much.*

"Relax, little monster," Bael said. "We just want to talk."

I swallowed a laugh. Talk? No. Not possible. And yet, it had to be...because he couldn't be lying. "About what?"

"The question you should be asking, Sl–" Prince Scion broke off, clearly stopping short of calling me a Slúagh for some reason. "—isn't what *we* want. You should think about what you want."

I imagined myself performing some wondrous feat of strength and beheading the princes, as their uncle had Rosey. It would be bloody and glorious...and impossible.

In reality, I would be lucky to walk out of these trees with my life. Even luckier if I left of my own free will with all my limbs and not wearing a chain as some exotic pet.

"Excuse me?" I asked, as I tried to banish the fantasy.

"What do you want?" Scion said again, harsher.

My fear gave way to confusion. Then, Gwydion stepped forward, extending a hand to me as if to shake mine. "Sorry about them, no manners, I know."

I stared at his fingers like they were live snakes and recoiled. Prince Gwydion was the least familiar to me, if only because he had not been interested in my torment. Perhaps he was not as in sync as the other two—two halves of the same cruel coin. Still, I was not likely to accept his hand any time soon. "Don't touch me."

He pulled his hand back. "Ah. I see the distaste for etiquette is catching."

My head spun. Whatever was happening, it was worlds apart from the scene back in the clearing. And why? Shouldn't they hate me more now?

Scion's eyes left my face, momentarily darting to the side. I followed his gaze, and my heart skipped a beat.

The blood-stained, obsidian crown lay abandoned in a pile of leaves a few paces to the right. I must have dropped it when I ran into Prince Bael. I hadn't even noticed.

My eyes darted back to Prince Scion. Was that it? He wanted his fucking jewelry? I bent and picked it up and all three princes stiffened.

It almost looked...mean. Certainly, it was sharp. Each of the six gleaming black edges shimmered and caught the light from the moon, like the teeth of some hideous beast. Indeed, if they were teeth, the monster who wielded them would be able to swallow me in one bite.

Unlike the diadems of the Everlast clan—Princess Raewyn, Lady Aine, and some of their higher-ranked noble court ladies—there were no jewels set into its face. That should have made it less grand, but it had the opposite effect. Almost as if jewels would have paled in comparison, so they could not stand beside it.

I peered at my reflection in the glassy, black-mirrored face. It seemed that the darkness went on forever, while I was caught inside it, rather than sitting outside looking in. I shivered, disconcerted.

Prince Scion took a step toward me, crafting his face into a sensual smile "This doesn't have to be painful for you," he said. "Give me the crown. Whatever Dullahan promised you, we can do better. Do you want gold? Or freedom? We could send you anywhere."

I tried to control my uneven breath. Even in my present condition, I would have had to be dead not to react to his attention. His wickedly handsome face. His perfect smile. Still, his words rang discordant in the back of my mind. Like seeing through an illusion.

I furrowed my brow. My heart pounded faster, threatening to bruise my ribs. A bargain. That's what this was. My mother's rules rang as clearly in my mind as if she were standing beside me. As always, I'd failed not to be noticed, but this also sounded like a brush with her first rule: Never bargain with a fairy.

My head spun. The night just kept getting worse and wilder. Like a bad dream that would not end.

Moreover, there was that name again. Dullahan. I'd never heard it before tonight. Now, I was sure I would never forget it. Was Dullahan who sent Rosey to her death? Were they a friend or an enemy?

"I want nothing," I told the prince. "Nothing except to know why my sister had to die tonight."

I didn't even want their miserable crown, but if it was so important to them, then I was damn well going to hold on to it until they pried it out of my cold, dead hand. Which, I supposed, would be in about five minutes when they got tired of negotiating.

The prince's eyes narrowed, and he set his jaw, anger twisting his too-handsome face. Anger at me for not reacting to his fairy games, or simply because he'd never heard the word "no" before. "You must know that answer already, rebel. Your cause is pointless in the end."

I barred my teeth at him. "I want my sister back. Can you do that?"

Prince Scion paused, seeming to consider it for a moment and I hated myself for the way my heart leapt.

Could he do that? I'd never heard of raising the dead, but then, I had no idea of the lengths the High Fae's magic stretched. If anyone could, perhaps—

The prince stared at me, an unreadable expression on his face. "No."

My chest caved in on itself, pain tearing through me. I closed my eyes and immediately I saw it again. The King, raising his sword and cutting her down right in front of the crowd, the blood. So much blood.

My hands shook, and tears sprang to my eyes again. I wiped them away roughly with the back of my hand.

Any momentary adrenaline I'd felt from the chase, from his silver eyes staring at me had left as quickly as it had come, leaving me emptier than before. I wanted to scream at him. *What! What are you staring at? Am I amusing to you?* But I couldn't find the energy. I wanted to sink to the ground. Sink into the ground and never rise again.

"Ask for something else," Bael said shortly.

If I didn't know better, I would think he was uncomfortable. I stared past him, unseeing. "No. All this over a stupid crown? What can you possibly–"

And it clicked.

I'd killed the King after sundown on hunting day. I'd killed him, and taken his crown, and now the Everlasts wanted to *talk*. They wanted to know what I *wanted*.

A laugh bubbled in my throat. I snorted, and all three princes stared at me.

Were they princes anymore?

I took a step to the right toward the crown, and they all tensed at once. Somehow, that was funnier, and I nearly choked as my hysteria rose.

"Maybe Penvalle did make her go mad," Gwydion said under his breath. "Is that better or worse?"

"Better," Bael said promptly. "I like them crazy."

"Shut the fuck up," Scion barked at them.

I held out the crown to them, holding the infernal thing gingerly as if it would bite me. "Can you not just take it?"

They couldn't. I felt sure they couldn't, or they would have done it already. Still, I wanted to be sure.

No one moved.

"Give it to me," Scion said carefully, his voice persuading. *Hypnotic.*

Illusion! My brain screamed at me. *Lies.*

I took a step back. "No."

Prince Bael moved in front of his cousin. "Sci, wait, what if she's—"

"Bael, move," Scion snapped, seeming finished with his attempt at negotiation. His voice took-on that harsh, demanding tone I'd heard him use earlier in the woods.

Prince Scion opened his arms as though to welcome me in for a hug. The air between his arms seeming to shift and swirl before my eyes. Dark shadows danced between his fingers, and he stepped forward, reaching for my throat.

The ground shook underfoot and the telltale crackle of magic sizzled against my skin, and then his hand closed around my arm, and everything fell to darkness.

14

LONNIE

*N*ausea gripped me for the split second we spun through the dark, and then my feet were slamming into solid ground again.

The scent of death and decay filled my nose and I choked, retching as I fell back against a hard, wet, floor. My head pounded, and I fought to open my eyes, disorientation and dizziness threatening to overwhelm me.

The sound of metal on metal forced me to open my eyes, and my heart stuttered to a halt, my stomach sinking. I was surrounded by near total darkness, the only light visible from a hallway some six feet in front of me. Boots stood, unmoving, by my head.

I looked up the length of the boots, finding Prince Scion staring down at me on the floor. "It's definitely not all magic you're resisting. Only some," he said, thoughtfully. "I suppose I'll have time to consider how that works."

"What?"

He stepped back and I blinked, taking greater stock of the room. My blood ran cold. Within seconds I leapt to my feet, fighting the dizziness and nausea that threatened to send me back to the ground. Fighting the pounding in my skull.

Scion was faster than me, and he moved into the hall too fast for me to follow. He closed the door to the tiny prison cell with an echoing clang.

Rushing to the bars, I wrapped my fingers around the heavy iron, shaking for all I was worth. "You can't do this!" I screamed after the prince. "You can't leave me here."

He couldn't do this. They could not do this to me.

"But I can, rebel. I can't force you to cooperate, but I can stop you from running back to Dullahan with that crown."

"I don't know what you're talking about!" I yelled after him as he walked away, disappearing down the dark corridor.

Prince Scion turned back to me. The prince's silver eyes met mine again, and there was such seductive brutality there it was overwhelming. But something about receiving his undivided attention was overwhelming. He looked at me with so much intensity—sex and violence and disdain—like I was nothing to him, but he still wanted to see how much it would take to break me.

His hypnotic voice echoed off the wall, making threats sound like poetry. "Scream all you want, rebel. No one can hear you." He gestured to the other prisoners as if to say *"Look at them. No one cares when they scream."*

The other prisoners stared at me, their haunting eyes empty and mad, blinking wickedly out of the darkness. Their wails of pain and anger echoed even now as the guards stood leering down at me, locking me in this tiny hole beneath the castle.

My stomach bottomed out, and I thought I would be sick after all.

"It was after sundown," I tried, forcing strength into my voice. "I have your crown. That makes me the queen."

"Yes, it does." He turned and disappeared into the darkness of the corridor. "And let's see how well the crown serves you with no allies."

The prince was right. No one cared when I screamed after him, and no one cared when I screamed many days after.

When the screaming exhausted me, I sunk onto the filthy floor, staring around at my cell. It was tiny, dark, and smelled of things better left unsaid. The hay in the corner crawled with mites and a rodent scurried by my foot. I recoiled.

Down the hall, the other prisoners kept up their screaming, either with madness or hunger, I wasn't sure which. My mind spun, my own misery mocking me. There was no justice in Everlast. No fair treatment for humans.

Wrapping my arms around my body, I pressed my face to my knees.

There had been few moments in my life when I'd known with profound clarity that nothing would ever be the same as it had been before. The day my mother was seized by the Queen's guards. The day I'd gotten the scar on my ear. The day we fled for the capital and today, when I lost the last member of my family and was finally entirely alone.

The incessant buzzing that had started back in the clearing refused to leave my skull, as if it were drowning out anything that was not pain and rage and misery. It was the fucking Fae who did this to Rosey. Who did this to me.

Perhaps I should have accepted the bargain offered to me. Perhaps I should have simply left. Perhaps…

Perhaps it would not have mattered.

Everyone knew the laws of Elsewhere. I was the queen, yet here I sat. It was the greatest lie of all—that the Everlasts would ever truly allow anyone to challenge them.

So, for days, I screamed and cried for my sister.

I cried for my mother, who I'd never been able to mourn, for the injustice of everything, and for myself.

I knew the law, and Prince Scion had no authority to do this to me. But authority did not equal power, and no matter what happened to me. No matter what happened to my family. I could never—*never*—reveal my power.

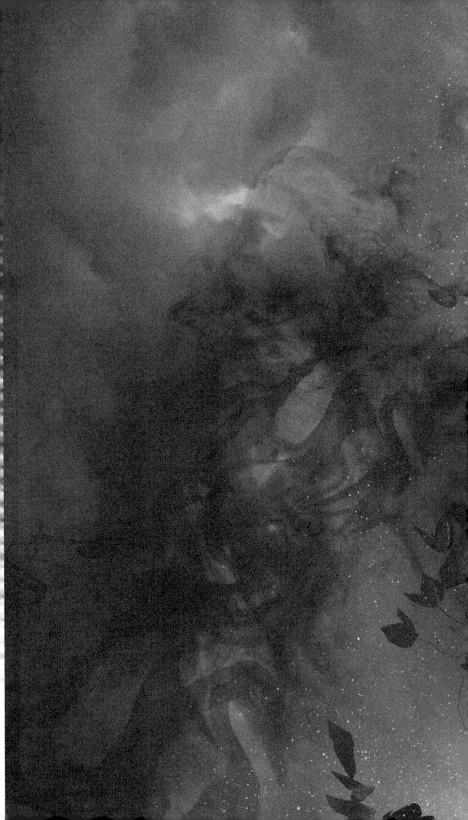

PART II

♛

IT WAS NOT THE THORN BENDING TO THE HONEYSUCKLES, BUT
THE HONEYSUCKLES EMBRACING THE THORN.

— EMILY BRONTË, "WUTHERING HEIGHTS"

15

SCION

MABON (SEPTEMBER) - SEVEN YEARS AGO

*T*he human woman's knee connected with the side of the guard's face, and he grunted as he threw her over his shoulder. He swore loudly, but she barely seemed to notice.

"Shut the fuck up," I told her. *Please.*

The woman stared at me with defiant eyes and screamed louder. Shouting words and curses in a language I didn't speak and had no desire to learn.

Her meaning was clear enough from her expression and the way she tried to fight us off. She thought we—or, rather, me—was evil incarnate. She wasn't far off.

I set my jaw, head beginning to pound. Didn't she understand? If anyone came out to help her, it wouldn't change her fate. It would only mean I'd have to kill more innocent people, and that made my stomach turn.

I raised a hand and pressed it to the woman's bare forearm. She screamed again—even louder. This time, not from anger but from pain. I pulled my hand away. "Be quiet!"

She looked up at me, panting, sweat beading on her brow. She recognized me now, I was sure of it. And I'd just confirmed all her fears.

"Good," my uncle said beside me. "I was about to kill her myself."

Uncle Penvalle was only slightly taller than me now—and likely would not be within the year. He was the crown prince and wore a silver circlet around his forehead to show it. Though he was not my father, even I had to admit I resembled him more than I'd ever resembled my own father.

"What should we do with her, my lord?" the guard asked me, sounding more than a little relieved now that she'd temporarily stopped screaming.

I looked up at my uncle standing beside me, but he said nothing. Waiting expectantly for my reply. My headache worsened.

This, I knew, was the point. The lesson. House Everlast showed no mercy. We felt no guilt or shame over the orders we followed. Grandmother Celia's prophecies were always correct, and we always worked for the betterment of the house. Always toward the end of our curse.

I stared at him, somewhat at a loss—not least because I wasn't used to the honorific. "Have her ride with you, I suppose."

"Yes, lord."

My gaze darted all around the filthy city street. Faces were now poking out of doorways and appearing at windows as the other residents of Cheapside started coming out to see what all the commotion was. Many retreated as soon as they saw me. I was not yet as feared as my father, but the Everlast crest made an impression, regardless.

I couldn't fathom why anyone would have run from the palace to live here of all places. I looked at the screaming redhead, curiously, wondering what made her leave. She probably would have gotten away with it. We didn't have time to go searching for every runaway changeling servant in the city.

It was Rhiannon Skyeborne's misfortune that my grandmother had seen her in a dream and demanded I find her. It was worse luck still that she was born on the day that Nightshade fell.

The guard threw Rhiannon over his horse, and I took a step toward my own.

"No! Mother!"

A scream echoed down the street, reverberating off the houses and lingering in the air. I looked up, more surprised than anything, and froze.

Two identical twin girls ran down the hill toward us, from the direction of the Waywoods.

"No!" The woman yelled back, in the common tongue. "Go back!"

I looked from the girls to the woman, the pieces clicking together in my mind. They were only a few years younger than me, I thought. Perhaps fourteen or fifteen, though I struggled to determine human ages. They had their mother's hair, but not her blue eyes.

At their mother's command, one of the girls stopped moving, stumbling a few steps back as if to run. Smart. That was the normal reaction when humans encountered the Fae. The other looked from the guards to her mother to me and back again. She bared her teeth at me like a wild animal before charging forward with no care for her own safety. Completely unafraid. The hair stood up on the back of my neck, and my vision narrowed to a point. I took an involuntary step forward....

"Let her go," the girl demanded.

"Lonnie, go," the mother cried. She wasn't screaming now, but the shadows I'd cast on her still lingered behind her eyes.

The daughter didn't listen, instead lunging toward me as if somehow, she was going to go through me to save her mother.

I cringed back. If she touched me, it would be agony for her.

Before I could react—even think—Uncle Penvalle plucked the girl out of the air as if she weighed nothing. "Well," he said jovially, "Perhaps you are not ready to do these errands on your own if you can be set upon by a human child."

"I'm fine," I hissed, trying not to react as the girl kicked and screamed in my uncle's hold, just as her mother had done.

I had no idea why I cared, or why her screams were less annoying and more rage inducing.

My uncle raised his eyebrows, but I had no excuse. I simply hadn't felt like killing the girl. Unlike Penvalle, my magic was only good for pain and death. There was very little I could do with it otherwise.

Penvalle looked down his nose from the still struggling woman on the back of the guard's horse, to the daughter he held several feet off the ground. The corner of his lip turned up in a mean smile.

He raised his right hand to cast an enchantment, and my blood boiled. My pulse pounded too loud in my ears, and I stepped forward to rip his hand away from her—

Without warning, the girl went flying backwards against the wall of the house. An ear-curdling scream pierced the air.

Penvalle stared down at his hand, but my focus had shifted entirely to the girl.

Blood poured from her temple, down the side of her head, drenching her hair and the neck of her dress. I blanched.

She smelled like magic.

16

SCION

A fist larger than my head slammed into the side of my skull and I reeled back, pain shooting through me, and gritted my teeth with the effort of holding back my magic.

The crowd screamed their approval, thrilled to see one of the High Fae knocked down at last. I wondered what they would say if they knew it was one of the royals getting thrown around a back alley, or that I could end it any time I wanted. The pain was the only half-interesting thing about this.

I circled the ring of screaming spectators in the filthy back alley of the capital. Most were human, though I'd spotted some Fae among the group. If anyone recognized me—which I doubted out of context, they hadn't said anything.

I wiped blood out of my eyes and danced to the side, already feeling the telltale tingle as the cut closed back up on my face.

The troll lumbered forward. I snapped out a hand, returning the blow. My knuckles cracked against its jaw. It barely flinched, its eyebrow twitching as if it were mildly irritated. Like a fly had flown too close.

"End it!" Someone screamed from out of my eyeline—likely not speaking to me.

These fights only ended when someone stopped breathing, and the troll had been undefeated for several nights. I'd hoped to find an actual challenge. Something distracting, but I should have known better.

The troll charged toward me again, spit and phlegm flying from its mouth, its tiny eyes fixed solely on me. It raised an enormous hand, and this time when it reached for me, I made no effort to hold in my magic.

The troll screamed. A surprisingly high-pitched sound for one so large, like the shriek of a wounded fox on a hunt. Oddly appropriate for the season, and wholly unwelcome when I was doing my best not to think of such things.

It teetered on its back legs, its eyes rolling, foam forming at its lips. I stared, unmoved.

I turned my back, bored, when the troll teetered and crashed to the ground. The crowd behind me had fallen silent. Some stared with open-mouthed horror. Some were already slinking back into the spaces between the filthy houses behind them, sprinting down the street hoping to avoid me.

Only Bael seemed unconcerned, as he leaned against a wall at the edge of the alley waiting for me. He too was being given a wide berth by the crowd, but that was likely more due to his obvious intoxication and lack of a shirt than anything else.

"Good showing," he called as I approached, raising a hand to clap me on the back and missing spectacularly. "But did you have to kill him?"

"Yes," I said flatly.

There had been a time when this turned my stomach. When I'd dreaded using my powers on anyone. When death made me as ill as those I killed. Now, it barely phased me.

"Right then. Well, good job. Very…" he paused, seeming to search for the word. "Dead. Death."

I struggled not to roll my eyes. "Right."

Eyes followed us as we strode back in the direction of the palace. The spectators might not have known who I was before, but they certainly did now. I could hear them whispering as I left.

Prince of Nightmares.

God of Pain.

Scion, The False King, Betrayer of the Hunt.

BAEL

IMBOLC (FEBRUARY) - NINE MONTHS SINCE THE DEATH OF KING PENVALLE

F or an immortal, Samhain was the best day to die.

My skin crawled with discomfort, like the feeling of thousands of eyes on my back. In truth, there were many eyes following my family as we rode the long path from the palace down to Moonglade lake. They watched me, more so than the others, but I'd expected that.

The forest was filled with the imprints of lost souls, shadows of dead things between worlds, and whispers of passionate emotions stuck in the bark of the trees. Every oak and pine we passed had something absorbed in one of its rings, some ripple or disease or knot in its trunk caused by thousands of years of trauma.

Samhain may have been the best day for Grandmother Celia to return to the Source, but it was the worst day for me to travel.

The shadows always watched me; always whispered. Mostly, I tuned them out, but when they were this close to the surface their voices were deafening.

Still, I wasn't worried. I didn't fear the dead.

It was the living that scared me.

I woke up with a start, blinking as the dream fell away like droplets of rainwater. Or, more accurately, like dissipating smoke.

Peering up at rough wooden beams on the ceiling, I frowned. It took no time at all—fractions of a second—to realize where I was. There were five inns in the capital city that bore my last name, and I was familiar with the ceilings of all of them.

I sat up and glanced over at the empty space beside me. *Thank fuck.*

I hated waking to find that my bedmates had taken the liberty of staying the night. Partially because I rarely liked to see partners more than once, but not least because of the dreams.

Leaning over to the leather bag I kept with me for mornings I did not wake in my own bed, I pulled out a quill and notebook. That particular dream was likely not a prophecy, and certainly not projection. Merely a memory. Still, one could never be too sure. I'd learned that from Grandmother Celia herself, who wrote down everything in little journals, every single day of her life.

I sucked on the end of the quill, while trying to remember the exact nature of the dream. Picking it apart from my memory. I remembered the procession, my entire family riding to Moonglade lake where we would travel by water to the Source. The Source was the only way to kill an immortal—either by walking into it directly, or by using a blade forged in its fires. Most would not have chosen to walk into the Source, but after spending thousands of years cursed, I could understand the decision.

My dream was already disappearing, blending with my true memory, and funneling back into the recesses of my brain.

I groaned, giving up, and tossing the notebook to the side of the room.

My prophetic talent was weak at best. Hardly even worth mentioning as compared to my other abilities. Still, I'd never been so motivated to hone it as I had been this past year.

Wherever Scion had hidden the girl, it was out of my reach. But I would do it, eventually. If she was still alive, I had to find her.

Our lives depended on it.

18

LONNIE

IN THE DARK

*W*hen I was a child, my mother told me about the day Rosey and I were born.

"The sky turned black," she'd said. "Plumes of smoke, ash, and magic exploded out of the earth, raining fire down on the city of Nightshade."

A province away, my mother watched the smoke eclipse the sun. She said it was as if my newborn cries echoed that of the Nightdwellers as their city walls fell around them. My mother's screams mingled with the dying Fae, being eaten alive by the Wilde magic spewing from the center of the earth.

My mother was born in the human realms, where there was no magic and a volcano didn't reach the true center of the earth. She spoke of the human realms in the same hushed tones that people spoke of Nightshade in the aftermath of the eruption. That was all anyone called Nightshade anymore: Aftermath.

In the wee hours of the morning, when I lay awake in bed, I used to wonder if I was living in a constant state of *after*. That was how it felt when my mother died. There was a time when I'd had a complete family, and the aftermath.

Now, as I lay day after day in the dark, I wondered if this was the aftermath, or the eruption.

19

LONNIE

IN THE DARK

*I*n the dark, my rage was my only companion.

Food came rarely and with no pattern I could discern. I tried to keep track of the days by the shifting of the guards, but they seemed to change their rotation intentionally to confuse us.

The guards were neither cruel nor kind. Most often they ignored me, occasionally they threw lewd comments at me while they passed out food or stuck their hands through the bars as though I were some unfortunate animal on display.

The worst was the guard who had locked me in, who took every opportunity to knock me into a wall or throw an elbow into the side of my face.

It was impossible to know exactly how long I'd been here, since time lost all meaning and so little light filtered in through the door at the end of the hall, but my bleeding came and went six times before it stopped.

For months the cell beside mine went unfilled. Until, one day, they brought in a new prisoner.

I barely raised my head as he came in, uninterested in anything except food or water. He didn't wail or kick like the others, instead walking tall and proud to his cell, his head held high under the hood that blocked his face from view. I sat up, intrigued.

"How does it feel to know you'll die down here?" the guard sneered as he slammed the door on the prisoner.

"I could ask you the same."

My heart sped up. His voice was smooth and refined. Fae. They had a fairy down here.

"What's that 'posed to mean?" the guard spit.

The fairy didn't answer, but a tingle crawled up my spine. An odd awareness, I couldn't explain. If I'd had anything to bet aside from the disgusting clothes on my back, I would guess the guard would meet his end in this corridor.

I moved to the other side of my cell. I had no need for friends in the dark.

I lay on my back counting the cracks in the ceiling. There were thousands of them, but I played a game with myself, trying to see how high I could count before I lost track. Before the screaming in the halls drove me so far out of my mind that I couldn't count anymore.

It felt like months before I spoke to another person again.

I curled into myself in the corner of my cell when the guards came by with the food, simply hoping they wouldn't notice me.

Heavy boots stomped down the corridor, stopping briefly at each door to hand out bread and water. They came closer and closer, finally stopping in front of mine. "Lon!"

I didn't move my head to look up. Sometimes the walls spoke to me.

"Lonnie. Are you in there?"

I rolled over on the filthy stone floor, my head pounding from dehydration. All my muscles ached from lack of use, and my stomach sent shooting pains of hunger into the back of my spine with every movement.

If it was the Fae guard, he would have to come in here to get me himself. I wasn't going to help with my own torture.

My voice was ragged with lack of use. "Leave me alone."

"Fuck, I thought you were dead."

I cracked an eye open. I looked up. I knew that voice. I blinked against the semi-darkness, unsure if I was seeing clearly.

Caliban.

I coughed, my voice hoarse and dry with disuse. "Not dead."

Not yet.

He pressed his face in between the bars. "What are you doing here?"

What did he think I was doing here? Hadn't everyone seen? Wasn't it obvious? "I—"

A voice came from the cell next to mine. "Shut your mouth,"

I went still. My neighbor hardly ever spoke to me or anyone else, but I was constantly aware of his presence there. It was another game I played with myself. Trying to guess what side of the cell the Fae was on. Wondering what he looked like. Wondering why he was down here, with all the dying, mad humans.

"Why?" I asked finally and was pleased to hear a note of defiance in my voice. I'd thought I'd lost the ability to care about anything. To defy anyone. But apparently not.

"Because they're all listening to you. All the time. They have ears everywhere and believe me they're looking for you."

I frowned, shaking my pounding head, trying to clear it. When was the last time I drank anything?

The Everlast family had no need to listen in. No need to look for me. They were the ones holding me here. "You're wrong," I said to the wall. "They don't give a fuck what I do. They hold all the power."

The fairy chuckled darkly, and his voice seemed to reverberate off the walls wrapping around me. Hypnotic, in a familiar way that made my skin crawl.

I laughed back. Or, I thought I did. I didn't recognize the sound anymore.

20

SCION

"*I* thought I would find you brooding. I see I was wrong."

Bael's voice echoed all around my bedchamber, magnified tenfold. I scowled at the empty air by the door and waited for my cousin to appear. He didn't.

"This is not brooding." His voice continued. "Raging? How unusual."

"Where are you?" I said into thin air, unable to make my tone anything other than aggressive. "Show yourself."

If Bael meant to announce his presence, the pageantry was unnecessary. I'd known he was in my tower the moment he crossed the threshold and had merely been waiting for the dramatic fucker to appear.

I'd more or less been waiting for him to appear all day. Not because I wanted company, but because he simply always did.

Bael laughed, materializing in a shimmer of dislodged air beside my fireplace. He shook the shadows off his red-blonde curls like droplets of water. "I have to say, I'm hurt."

I went back to staring pointedly at the ceiling, refusing to reply.

"Why, might you ask?" he continued without prompting. "I thought you would call for me long before now. I've just been alone. By myself. Without companionship. Waiting for an invitation."

"You can come without being summoned," I snapped. "There *is* a fucking door."

"Yes, but your foul bird is angry with me, and blocking the entrance."

Good.

"It did occur to me to bring a peace offering," his grin widened, as though he were sharing in his own private joke. "For you, not for the bird, obviously, but I waited so long I used her myself and I'm afraid she's currently unable to walk."

I set my jaw. *Fucking idiot.* Soon, there would be no female—or male, for that matter—left in the capital that he hadn't fucked at least once. He'd have to go on tour. At least then I might be left alone.

"Is that what you've been doing all day?" I sat up abruptly, glaring at him. "Yet another innocent village was just burnt to the ground on the border of Aftermath, and you're fucking servants and...what? Wandering around invisible, waiting for me to call for you?"

"Among other things," Bael said lightly, kicking one foot over the other and leaning back against the wall. "I was also recovering from a rather nasty headache. Fawns make absurdly strong wine."

"Don't you have something better to do with your infinite time?"

"Better than drinking and fucking the servants? No, not really. I suppose I could try murdering trolls, but you seem to have the lock on that."

I scowled. "You know I've been informed that I'm to stay within the castle walls until further notice. Do you see how infuriating that is?"

"Sure." He let my mis-directed anger slide off his back. "But don't take it out on me. I'm on your side."

He shouldn't be. I ground my teeth. I hated this castle and everything in it. "This is not one of your jokes."

Bael crossed the room to my bookshelf. "I assure you, it isn't."

The same images kept flashing through my mind. The plumes of black smoke filling the air, choking me. The flames scorching the earth, and crawling up what was left of the crumbling buildings. The distant screams of the fleeing villagers, Fae and human alike —and that was merely the beginning.

I reminded myself of that, reveled in the memories, whenever a shred of guilt crept in. Nightmares didn't deserve my mercy.

"I don't see you volunteering to go in my place," I said acidly, already knowing it was an unfair attack.

"Next time, I will," he muttered, as he scanned over the books. "We'll see how the family takes that. Why don't I suggest bringing Aine as well? We'll make a holiday of it. Or, perhaps Elfwyn would enjoy a run at the battlefield."

My frown deepened. Elfwyn probably would enjoy the battle-field. My younger sister was starting to become a bit too comfortable with violence for a child of nine years–and I would know.

Otherwise, his point was valid, and that made it all the more infuriating. Either one of us could end this chaos in a matter of days. Together, I knew we could find and destroy Dullahan within hours. Instead, we were bound to obey the rambling whims of a madwoman.

The rebel forces from the north had increased in both numbers and ferocity ever since the death of my uncle. My fault, I knew, though I'd managed to keep that fact to myself. Well, between myself and Bael, who would have found out even if I hadn't told him. He had an odd way of always knowing everything.

Well, not everything.

The questions swept the country: where was the human girl who had killed the High Fae King? Why wasn't she on the throne? Why had no one seen her? The answer made me ill some days and filled me with righteous indignation on others. *There was no other choice, but I didn't have to like it.*

"Not to play Unseelie advocate…"

"Fuck off. You would be contrary just to spite me."

He grinned. "True. But really, I can see why Mordant is suggesting you stay in the castle while things are so unstable."

I despised my grandmother's former advisor but saw no legitimate reason to get rid of him. "Mordant is a sniveling sycophant about to learn the limits of his immortality."

I was consistently torn by the dueling feelings of rage that I was not king outright. That our grandmother had picked Penvalle in the first place when he was so evidently unworthy, and that decision had led to this disaster. And, on the other hand, the knowledge that while I knew ruling was my responsibility, I was not particularly suited to it.

Ten years on the fields in Aftermath had taken whatever I was before and left nothing but the Queen's assassin behind.

"It will only get worse, you know," I said to the ceiling, already knowing I was wasting my breath on a well-worn topic. "I don't understand how she didn't see it coming."

Bael was well aware *who* I spoke of. We always spoke of Grandmother Celia thus. *She would have known. She should be here. She fucked us over and left us all to die.*

"I'm not sure what to say, Sci," Bael said. "To be frank, I was starting to wonder if she was losing it a bit at the end there."

I narrowed my eyes at my cousin. He shrugged unapologetically, turning a page of a heavy leather-bound book I was sure he'd read before. "What does that mean?"

"She mentioned something to me I always found odd. It's not anything you need to worry about."

Reading between the lines, that likely meant it was something I *did* need to worry about. Still, I didn't press.

We fell into silence as Bael flipped through the book and I stared at the ceiling. Bael had been trained from birth to keep his emotions in check—the family had guessed, correctly, that without such training he would go mad long before reaching maturity. Now, I only saw the briefest hints of that madness in moments when his mask slipped.

No one had thought to impart the same training on me, and sometimes I questioned if I was half-mad as a result. I'd seen what that could look like, courtesy of my uncle, who shared enough of my physical appearance to give me an eerie glimpse into my own future. I reminded myself of that whenever I felt guilty over the last year—this was all part of the grand design.

I'd thought of little else but the red-haired human girl over the last year. Perhaps longer, if I was being honest. Perhaps that was part of the reason...I shook my head violently.

I'd been watching the new queen for months. More closely than I'd watched the other rebel prisoners, but to no avail.

She'd made no effort to contact anyone from the rebel forces. I decided maybe she was too weak, so I tracked down that fucking idiot guard and assigned him to her cell. But even with more food, she barely moved. We put a known enemy of the crown in the cell next to her, and she wouldn't speak to him.

All I'd learned about Lonnie Skyborne in eleven months was she hated the Fae and talked in her sleep. She hated me specifically, which I found oddly fascinating.

If she had any magic, from Dullahan or otherwise, she wasn't using it to escape. In fact, the only notable thing about her was that she hadn't died. The dungeon usually killed humans within weeks, or at least drove them insane. If that girl was insane, we all were.

The sound of paper swished as Bael turned a page. I shook my head to clear it, and blinked, looking at him more closely. He was already dressed for the festival, and it was a chore not to roll my eyes. He wore a crimson, leather-trimmed jacket open over his bare chest. Something stolen from Gwydion, I assumed.

Of all my cousins, Bael was by far my closest confident, followed perhaps by Aine–though distantly. We'd been raised together. Trained together. Been practically forced into friendship as well as house loyalty. Maybe…maybe I could…should…tell him.

"Do you remember…"

Bael looked up and let his eyes roll back into his head, and held up a hand to stop me. "Aine will be along in a minute," he said. "She's rounding the corner by the fifth-floor library now."

I looked back to him, safe in my conviction that his eyes would have returned to their correct position. I didn't think I would ever get used to that, no matter how many centuries passed or how often he did it. Not only was it alarming to watch, but it was also proof that we didn't really know the extent of what Bael's powers could do. Or how wildly different they were from the rest of the family.

"What were you saying?" he asked.

I shook my head, glancing at the door. Bael was one thing, but Aine… "Later."

It was less than a minute before the door banged open and I choked, my eyes widening in mingled shock and amusement. "What the fuck are you wearing?"

Aine's pink silk gown was transparent enough that whomever she'd worn it for was clearly supposed to take note of the outline of her nipples through the fabric. In one hand she held a bottle of wine, and in the other two goblets.

She sighed dramatically and tossed her curly mane of hair over one shoulder. "I would go so far as to say I'm wearing nothing. Obviously."

I would not go quite that far, but it was a close thing.

She picked up her skirt—what little there was of it—and walked across the room with an exaggerated swing to her hips. "I have been bidden to ask if you would like some company in this time of need."

Bael burst out laughing as I coughed, surprised.

"What time of need?" I asked, horrified enough to forget my dark mood for a moment.

"I don't know." She waved a hand. "Grandmother's slumber. The rebels. The hunt. An unsatisfactory breakfast. It does not matter, choose one."

That settled it. Underneath must be empty, because all the Unseelie were here in this castle fucking with me.

I rarely struggled for words but this shit was beyond me. "Ann..."

"Don't bother trying to think up a compliment." She put up a hand. "My ego can't take it. Rest assured, I am equally repulsed by this situation as you are, I'm sure."

I struggled with whether to laugh or groan and wound-up coughing.

Reaching blindly behind me, I grabbed the nearest blanket and tossed it to Aine. She wrapped it around herself and tucked in the ends, and I moved over to make room for her on the bed.

She sat down with all the dignity of a queen and cast her brother a reproachful glare. "Stop laughing, Baelfry."

I reached for the wine, waving a hand to dissolve the cork into thin air. I poured Aine a glass, filling my own nearly to the brim. "Who sent you?"

I already knew the answer before Aine opened her mouth. She wrinkled her nose and dropped all pretense, becoming almost a different person as she shifted her posture. Her shoulders rolled back, and her eyes narrowed, taking on a hawk-like quality. "Mother will never give rest until one of her children is on the throne, no matter what it costs us."

"Is the cost so much greater than what she's doing to poor Gwydion?" Bael asked, trying desperately to look serious.

I shot him a reproachful look. "Are you finished?"

"No." He cackled. "Can I officiate the cursed wedding?"

That set him off again. I glowered, taking a large gulp of my own wine.

It wasn't all that unusual for cousins to marry, especially within the nobility—or so Aunt Raewyn insisted almost every year or so when this madness was brought up again. I remained unconvinced.

"Well, it will never be me, on the throne," Aine said flatly, and took a sip of her wine.

I looked at her sideways. "No?"

She frowned over the rim of her glass. "No. You're very pretty Sci, but I would sooner fuck a scorpion moth."

I let out a genuine laugh. "I will find one for you just to see if you still mean it."

She raised an unconcerned brow. "Fine. Do it."

We both looked over to Bael, and he stared at us, eyes widening. "What?"

"So, if Aine doesn't want the throne, are you Raewyn's only hope to be queen mother?" I asked.

Bael waved his hand in the air, brushing off the comment. "Are you omitting Gwydion so easily?"

"Where is Gwydion?" I asked, as a second thought.

"No idea," Bael said. "There are places I can't see, you know."

I forgot my reply as a strange look crossed his face. Like he'd only just remembered he had to be somewhere. I narrowed my eyes, an uneasy feeling coming over me.

"Well." Bael stepped away from the bookcase and clapped his hands together. "Shall we go down then? Or, are you two supposed to be late?"

I waved a hand, and a book flew off the shelf and hit him in the back of the head. He didn't even flinch, but it was the thought that counted. "I won't be attending. You two can do whatever you like." I turned away, dismissing them.

They didn't speak for a full thirty seconds, and I imagined that they were looking at each other, sharing in one of their silent conversations.

"Sci, if it's bad now, imagine how much worse it will be if you don't go–"

I cut him off. "I know."

"Then why?"

I leaned over and pulled open the drawer to my nightstand, extracting a familiar piece of worn parchment.

The letter had haunted me. Dictated my every decision from the moment that my Grandmother Celia had left it for me right before she walked into the Source.

Holding it out to Aine, I made eye contact with Bael over her shoulder. "Go on," I told my cousins. "Read it."

As they read, my mind wandered back to the Slúagh girl imprisoned beneath the castle. Enough had seen what she'd done that even without her presence she'd become a constant thorn in my side. She was a symbol, both for the rebellion and for all those who hated us without wanting to go to war over it.

In the last year, Dullahan's forces had tripled, mostly due to support for the human queen. She's become a myth overnight, her actual story seeming to blend with that of her sister to make a better folk legend for the bards.

"Well," Bael said after a minute. "I do love a deathbed confession."

Aine dropped the letter, and I watched it flutter to the bed, like a falling leaf. She turned to her brother. "I suppose you have a plan then?"

Any other year, she would have asked me, but not now. If I'd been angry before, the last year had been unbearable. I couldn't blame her for the shift.

Bael looked over her head at me. I gave him the barest nod of approval before he answered.

Bael clapped a hand on my shoulder. "Of course, I do."

That seemed to satisfy Aine, but it only worried me. Perhaps letting Bael loose was worse than just handling it myself...there were so many ways this could go wrong.

Bael tapped his long fingers along the hilt of the knife in his belt. "What was that girl's name? High Queen Slúagh, the little monster of Elsewhere...The Mortal Queen." Bael's lip curled, as he spoke, and the name seemed to resonate through the room. "You have to admit, that one has a certain poetry to it."

My chest clenched, my blood running cold. "No." I barked, and my cousins jumped, surprised at my reaction. "Don't give her any kind of name. No matter what happens, *that* vicious thing will never be one of us."

21

LONNIE

IN THE DARK

"*H*ey! Girl! Get up."

I tried to speak, but it came out as a garbled moan. "Mmmh."

"Did you hear me?" The voice at the door asked. "I said get up."

My lips felt like fire, cracking as I spoke. "Can't."

"The prince wants to see you."

If I could have laughed, I would have. The prince wanted to see me? That had never worked out well for me in the past. Why should that change now?

Over the last eleven months, I'd had many hours to consider what I'd say to the prince if I ever saw his mocking silver eyes again, but I'd never thought it would actually happen.

Eleven months. That was how long it had been, according to Caliban. He brought in extra bread and water, when possible, even occasionally some meat. Without him, I knew I would have died months ago. Or at least gone mad from not knowing the

117

time. Even so, I could not last here forever. I was dying, albeit slower.

My reasoning for killing King Penvalle had not mattered.

The fact that I'd been set up had not mattered.

The setting sun and the rules of the hunts had not mattered.

Nothing had mattered. Not to Prince Scion, or his guards when they tossed me beneath his castle to rot. And now, it was those horrible silver eyes that haunted all my nightmares as I lay, day after day, dying in the Everlast's dungeon.

"Slúagh!"

"I heard you!" I barked back, using too much of my strength to raise my voice above a moan. I coughed, my chest seizing with the effort of speech. "I'm not seeing anyone."

The guard at the door chuckled as he stomped away. "Fine. I'll tell him the queen has given an order; I look forward to watching him burn you alive."

My stomach curdled, but I said nothing. Quick footsteps followed the guard, and another figure—a smaller one—moved quickly past my cell. I squinted into the dim light around their silhouette trying to get a better idea of who stood there. The woman had blue skin and hair like snakes tied up in an off-white linen kerchief. She held a flickering candle near her face that gave her an eerie appearance, like she was underwater in low sunlight.

"Whether you get up or not, he will come," the woman said, as she distributed moldy bread to the surrounding cells. The prisoners screamed, going wild over every tiny rind. "If I were you, I'd want to look more presentable, but suit yourself."

I did laugh this time, though it hurt. Being attractive to the Fae was the last thing I wanted, especially to the royalty. My entire life had been plagued by being noticed, and as I'd always known it would, it had killed me in the end. I wasn't dead yet, but it had still killed me—merely slowly.

The blue-skinned woman threw a piece of bread at me, and I pounced on it, no better than my screaming neighbors. "Hey!" I called after her. "How long has it been now?"

"Be more specific, girl."

Caliban's last visit felt like months ago, though it could only have been a few days. This place drove you mad with the not knowing. The lack of sunlight and the monotony.

"I have a name," I said, acidly.

"We all have names," she replied. "No one cares to know yours, and you should not offer it."

"Fine. How long have I been down here?"

She looked around at the tiny, dank cell with a grimace. "It could be a month or a year and either way it would feel far longer to you. That is the magic of the castle keep. It twists time and drives you mad."

I gaped at the woman, feeling both vindicated and as though I might cry. Maybe I was mad because my brain was not working correctly.

Perhaps it really had only been days since Caliban's last visit. That would make it nearly a year since I'd killed King Penvalle. Maybe that was why the prince was finally visiting? Maybe I was to be dragged before the court to answer for my crimes.

I pushed myself up on shaking arms and crawled across the floor to the pile of hay in the corner to wait. If I was going to die, I might as well look my murderer in the eye.

"What did you do," a soft musical voice rang through the wall to my right.

I looked over to the wall that now separated me from the Fae and scowled, saying nothing. There was no reason to converse with a fairy, especially not a criminal.

"I take it you're human," he continued. "And being visited by an Everlast. That's interesting. What would warrant that?"

"Nothing I'm proud of," I snapped, and instantly regretted it.

The Fae laughed. He had been here for at least a few months, yet he sounded unbothered by the whole thing. Infuriating.

"Do you know what they're saying out there," he asked. "Everyone is talking about the Slúagh girl who killed the mad king. I wouldn't have the honor of speaking with the missing queen, would I."

I scoffed. "I am not the queen. They made sure of that."

Again, he laughed, and the sound sent shivers up my spine. "No, you're not. Not yet, anyway."

Minutes or hours passed before footsteps pounded down the corridor. That must have been the magic of the cell, tricking me. Making shadows feel like years and voices sound like the whispers of long-dead friends.

I tried to count how long it took for the footsteps to sound in the corridor. If the woman was correct, and time stretched longer here, how long before the prince came? Days? I tried to stay awake and wait, but somehow sleep must've taken me again.

"Slúagh!"

I jolted. The bars of my cell rattled, and I cracked an eye open. Every muscle in my body tensed. That door only opened rarely, and never for any good reason.

The figure looming in the door was no prince, but the same guard as before. He towered over me where I lay on the ground, his bulk made even more extreme by the armor stamped with the Everlast crest that covered his torso. In the darkness I couldn't tell if he was human or Fae, but it hardly mattered. This weak, one of the Underfae flower sprites could have knocked me over with a dandelion.

He stepped inside and reached down as if to grab me. I shrank back against the wall, hating how pathetic I must look, yet too defeated to do anything about it.

The guard grinned. "I'm looking forward to this."

His hand clamped around my arm, and he yanked me forward with enough force that I cried out—a pathetic whimpering sound I barely recognized. As if I weighed nothing more than a rag doll, he shook me letting my head knock against the stone wall behind me with a sickening crack that I could both hear and feel.

Stars burst behind my eyes and pain shot down my spine, numbness settling in my toes.

The stars winked out one by one, a shadow falling over my vision as black seeped in.

"What the fuck are you doing?" A man's angry shout echoed off the stones of the corridor. "Why is she like this?"

I felt myself falling as the guard released my arm, but the impact of the floor was nothing compared to the screaming pain in my skull.

"Err," one of the guards said proudly. "Just following orders, my lord. We weren't soft on her, just like you wanted."

"What did you do to her?" The voice was low and cold.

The guard laughed. "Just roughed her up a bit. No food. We could be more—"

He broke off and the following silence was deafening. Curiosity made me crack one trembling eyelid open, peering into the darkness beyond.

The air seemed to shift in the cell, becoming thicker. Charged.

A sharp crack sounded, startling me to attention, and the distinctive thump of a body hitting the stone heralded the footsteps approaching my door.

I trembled, lying on my side, as soft footsteps crossed the tiny space toward me. I felt the air shift, felt the heat of him as he bent down beside me and held my breath.

"Hello, little monster. I've been hunting for you.

22

LONNIE

*M*y skin hummed, and I didn't have to look to know yellow eyes watched me. The pain in my pounding head warred with the part of me that knew I was now in even greater danger. There was a predator standing beside me, and I could not let myself simply fall into unconsciousness.

I squinted from my visitor to the dead guard on the ground. A puddle of blood, growing larger by the second, seeped onto the floor around the smashed remains of what once had been a leering face. My gaze darted to the wall between my cell and that of the Fae prisoner. I could not help but notice that the guard had indeed died down here, just as my neighbor had predicted.

I turned back to the prince and coughed. My dry throat screamed with the effort of speech. "Why did you do that?"

Prince Bael cocked his head to the side and smiled. He was exactly the same as I remembered him—the constantly grinning bully from the festivals. Red-blonde curls fell into his cat-like eyes, and blood from the guard splattered his chin and high cheekbones. "Because, you need to know I'll kill anyone who hurts you, little monster."

If I could have laughed, I would have. "You'll have to start with your own family then."

"Fine. Anyone who hurts you, except us. You're ours to torture. No one else's."

He gave me a wicked smile and raised his own wrist to his mouth. Keeping his eyes locked on mine, he sunk his razor-sharp teeth into the skin. I gasped, shocked, at the violence of it, yet I couldn't look away as blood dripped down his chin.

Bael took advantage of my open mouth to press his bleeding wrist to my lips. He grimaced, seeming none too happy with the situation. "Drink that."

I came to life, waking from my shock. Choking and spluttering, I tried to push him away, as confused as I was revolted. I tried to pull away, but dizziness threatened to overwhelm me. The prince grabbed the back of my head and held it in place, keeping his wrist in my mouth.

"Don't be so fucking stubborn," he said more sharply than I would have expected. "I did not spend a year trying to find you to watch you die now."

Tell that to your cousin. My head swam, and it was impossible to fight it as metallic blood poured over my tongue. Almost immediately, the pain in my head ebbed away and the dizziness lessened.

Bael dropped me and pulled his wrist back. I scowled at him and spat the last of the blood onto the floor at his feet taking great satisfaction when it splattered the filthy ground.

He looked down at the blood, a bland expression on his face. "I don't think you realize how valuable that is."

I got tentatively to my feet, hating myself for marveling at how the worst of my pain was gone. I was still weak. Still hungry as sin. But my head no longer pounded. My muscles only ached half as badly as they had in months.

Prince Bael kicked the skeleton of a rat with the toe of his fine leather boot, and it spun across the floor toward me. I stared at the boot and scowled darkly, wondering if he would request that I lick up the drops of blood I'd spit out. Then wondering, with a sinking feeling, if I would do it. If it cured pain? Probably.

"Fascinating magic in this place, wouldn't you say?" he said conversationally. "It's modeled after Fort Warfare Prison, which, of course, is built for immortals. Humans don't last longer than a few days before they go mad and waste away, trapped in their own nightmares. Interesting, isn't it, that you lasted the whole year when most humans wouldn't last a week?"

His nonchalance about my death and torture was enough to tip me over the edge into madness already. I set my jaw, resisting the urge to rush him and scratch any part of bare skin I could reach with my filthy jagged nails, regardless of what little good it would do me.

"Yes, fascinating." I sneered. "Is there a point to this, or did you simply come to taunt me with details of the torture the humans in your castle are subjected to?"

In a way, I didn't fear him as much as I once had. I was dying anyway. Death would be a mercy compared with this hell.

"I've come to offer an end to your sentence." He grinned. "Think of it as a royal pardon."

My heart fluttered. Hope, small and fleeting, suddenly awoke in my chest. An end to my sentence. Was he saying I could leave...*no. Never trust the Fae.*

I clenched my teeth. "I would guess I am safer here than with you."

It was a lie, and one I nearly choked on. I didn't care how dangerous he was. I barely cared who he was, and for that, the guilt might eat me alive. Still, I couldn't stay here. Not if there was a possibility of seeing the sun again. Eating proper food again. Feeling the air and walking more than a single step in the dark.

"Normally, I would agree. With me is the most dangerous place to be." His grin widened, and it reminded me somehow of a wolf. "But it would go against my best interest to hurt you, and I am selfish above all else."

My heartbeat sped up. What did that mean? Selfish how?

My brain was too slow since not having conversations with anyone for so long. Speaking to no one but the spiders and rats and the ghost of my sister. It was the madness of this place that was killing me. Before, the court had felt like a prison, but that was nothing. Nothing compared with the dungeon. I would gladly spend every day with the Everlasts if I was allowed to see the sky.

My eyes narrowed. "Should I thank you for not wanting to murder me? Forgive me for not falling at the feet of the man who got my sister killed and locked me in a dungeon."

He stared at me, and I suddenly wondered how old he was. He could be twenty or two hundred and there was no way to know. From his expression–somehow tired and exasperated at once–I got the feeling he was far older than me.

"Death is a risk of the hunts. And of living," he said. Not an answer, just a statement—but one that showed the difference between humans and the Fae as well as anything could. "My uncle killed your sister, and you killed him. I would consider that even, wouldn't you?"

I reeled back, as though I'd been punched in the gut. Something about the casual, dismissive acknowledgement of Rosey's death was worse than a denial.

"Then what is my compensation for a year in purgatory, according to you?" I hissed. "What would make that even?"

His boyish smile returned tenfold. "Ah, you've brought us back to why I'm here. Do you know what day it is?" He didn't wait for an answer. "Tomorrow is the festival of Beltane, which means that tomorrow the hunting season begins."

My eyes widened. "You can't be serious."

"Oh, but I am, little monster. You see, without a queen to hunt, the whole thing has turned quite..." He sucked on his teeth and frowned. "...rebellious."

My head spun and my mouth fell open and no sound came out. No one survived the hunts. I might get to leave the dungeon, but I was dead anyway. I would die before I took two steps into the woods. "I can't...I won't."

"You will, if you want to leave this place. You can walk out of here with me and join the hunts, or you can stay here and, as you put it, rot. Barring any serious injury, that blood should last you about a week, but then you'll go right back to where you were before."

He took a step closer, and I could feel his breath on my face. "No one knows you're here. No one, but me, and my cousin. It took me all year to discover where Scion hid you, and I know him better than anyone else alive. You can hope someone else figures it out, but I wouldn't bet on it."

"And what do you want from me?" I asked, as icy dread settled in my stomach. "No humans survive the hunts. I'll die anyway."

The corner of his mouth tipped up. "But that's just it, little monster. I want to help you win."

23

LONNIE

I barely had time to appreciate the sky outside the windows or the flickering lights of the castle as I chased Prince Bael down a long hall I had never seen in all my years working at the palace. My chest heaved, the combination of panic and exertion stealing my breath.

Without the prince's healing blood, I would have collapsed from exhaustion. Even so, my legs shook, unused to running after all these months. I didn't dare ask him to slow down. Wherever we were going, I was in no hurry to arrive.

We dashed past door after door, upstairs and down again, almost like he was trying to confuse me on purpose.

"Did you see that?" I craned my neck behind me, looking back down the long twisting corridor. I could swear a shadow moved against the wall, like long arms stretching out to grab me. Maybe I really had gone mad.

Prince Bael ignored me, as he had with every other one of my questions since we'd left the dungeons. I hadn't expected anything else, but the last several months had loosened my tongue as well as my self-preservation. If seeing my sister die had made me brave, then the dungeons had numbed me. It didn't matter. I could say whatever I liked to the prince. Ask anything. If he changed his mind and decided to kill me, my insubordination was unlikely to quicken or slow that process.

We came to a sudden halt in the middle of a dimly lit corridor across from an arched doorway set deep into the stone. I could not say with any certainty that I'd seen every part of the palace. That would be impossible, however I had seen the guest chambers, and this was not one of them. "Where are we?"

"A bedchamber that doesn't get enough use," he said. "So now it will be yours. Temporarily."

I furrowed my brow. *What?* "Why not yours?"

His lip curled. "Would you prefer mine?"

"No," I said too fast, "It's just…"

"No one goes in my room." He nodded for me to enter ahead of him. "Ever."

I hesitated on the threshold, struggling to reconcile his breaking me out of the dungeon and insistence on helping, with my hatred of not only the Fae but him in particular. "What will you do to me if I go in?"

He sighed, the corners of his full mouth pulling up as if he were fighting a smile. "Have we not been over this? I do not want to hurt you. Currently, all I want is for you to take a bath. What is so terrifying about a bath?"

I huffed, setting my jaw in defiance. "It's less the bath and more who is offering it. I've never known any fairy to do something for unselfish reasons. I don't know why you would be the first."

"This is entirely selfish, I promise. Does that make you feel better?"

I pursed my lips. Oddly, it did. "How so? What are you getting from this?"

He pushed the door open. "Are you always this difficult?"

"Only when I know I am likely to be murdered, my lord."

He lost his battle with the smile and laughed. "This is becoming quite tedious, little monster, I hope you know that."

"Good. Am I boring you? Let me go then."

"I don't know how to convince you I am not trying to kill you; you seem oddly unwilling to believe the word of *a fairy*," he put emphasis on the word as if it was distasteful. "You must know I cannot lie. Do you see the lack of logic there?"

I crossed my arms. "No. I don't. I can lie and am far more honest than you, I'm sure of it."

He pinched the skin between his eyes. "I am beginning to regret every decision that led me to this moment. Your stubbornness could make an immortal wish for death."

I felt the smallest degree of smugness at that, and that alone shocked me. It had been weeks since I'd felt anything but numb rage.

Guilt flooded me. There was no reason to be conversing with any of the Fae, least of all one of the Everlasts. "Swear that you will not harm me," I directed.

He raised an eyebrow. "Be more specific.

I frowned. "There, I knew—"

"As you wish." He made a mock bow. "I swear on all that I am, as long as I draw breath, I will never harm you while you stand within this room." He pointed, indicating the room in question.

It was not lost on me that the prince had not sworn to not harm me in the oncoming hunts—assuming we got that far—but my mind could only process so much.

"And what about anyone who might be waiting in the room?"

Bael rolled his eyes. "By Aisling, I would like to get out of the hallway while you're still alive."

"Because you're going to kill me?"

He made an exasperated sound, somewhere between a growl and a scoff. "No, you infuriating ingrate, because you are mortal and are in fact aging, and at this rate you will be dust on my shoes before your foul stench stops besmirching my nose."

He looked up at the ceiling and I wondered if I had, in fact, made him pray for death.

My heart pounded, my breath coming too fast. I tipped my face up, refusing to look away first, despite my every instinct telling me to back down. "I know better than to trust a fairy."

After what you did to me.

He moved too fast, stepping closer to me and forcing me to stagger backwards until I nearly hit the wall. "The irony in that statement is delicious."

I sighed. This could go on forever. And honestly, I was hungry, and the bath sounded halfway decent.

Relenting, I glanced around for anything that would give me some semblance of security, no matter how small, and landed on the dagger sticking out of his belt. "That. I want it."

He grinned and handed it to me. "Fuck, is that all?"

I drew myself up as proudly as possible. "Yes. That's all."

"Thank the Source."

He stepped out of the way so that I could walk in front of him. I stiffened as I entered, half-certain that someone was going to jump out and attack me. No one did.

We must have been in one of the towers, I realized.

The room was perfectly round with ceilings so high, twelve men could have stood on each other's shoulders and not reached the top. A towering marble fireplace stood directly across from the door, and a bed took up most of the far wall.

There was a round silver braided rug in the center and dark linens on the silver four poster bed. A black spindly wardrobe was half-open showing rows of men's jackets in every color of the rainbow, and some colors I had no names for.

I had assumed the room would be empty and was not sure if I was relieved or disappointed to discover I was correct. I did not want to see anyone, least of all any other members of the house of Everlast. But, on the other hand, now I was well and truly alone with the prince.

I raised an eyebrow. "Whose room is this?"

"Never you mind. They're not here."

I didn't like the sound of that. "Mmmm."

"The bathing room is through there," Bael said as he closed the door with an ominous crack.

I turned back to look at him. He pointed again to another door set into the stone of the right-hand wall beside the wardrobe.

"Excuse me?" I said, shaking my head to clear it.

"The bathing room," he repeated, slower, over enunciating each word. "Unless you require assistance." He crossed the room and sat on the opulent silk bed and began unlacing his boots. "I'll admit I've never spent much time with humans, but I thought you were capable of washing yourselves." He looked me up and down slowly. "I suppose I'm not opposed to helping, though."

A flush rose across my body, heating my skin. "It's not that, it's...I might be starving and tired, but I'm not as stupid as you seem to believe."

He glanced at me, lip curling up in a genuine smile. "And how stupid is that?"

"You promised me you wouldn't harm me in this room. Not that one."

"And I also said I didn't want to kill you. You might not be stupid by nature, but your fear of me is making you so. Get a handle on it, my family will exploit that weakness."

"It could also be that I haven't eaten in a year," I snapped.

"Don't use hyperbole, you sound absurd." His lip curled again and this time there was absolutely no humor in his smile. "Let me explain something to you," he drawled. "To an extent it is easier for me to tolerate your eccentricities, but you are quickly approaching the line where I will find it not worth my time."

A chill traveled down my spine, and I clutched the handle of my borrowed dagger as adrenaline coursed through me and my pulse pounded in my throat in some mixture of terror and anticipation.

He took a step closer and grasped my chin with two long fingers. "You can do your best to trap me into whatever oath you like, but you will never win. Whether I swear not to harm you in this room or that one does not matter, because you will have forgotten some detail."

As with the other times I'd been in close quarters with this prince, I couldn't help but notice there was something wilder about him than the others. Something bewitching, that made it difficult to think clearly. As though my mind was working twice as hard as normal to form the same thoughts. Like walking through wet sand.

My gaze darted between his wild eyes and vicious teeth, far too close to my throat. When the servants found my body, I could practically hear what they would say. *"Did you hear about Lonnie Skyeborne? Finally got what was coming to her. Had her throat ripped out by a fairy."*

I narrowed my eyes. "What do you—"

"As long as I draw breath, I will never harm you while you stand in this room," he mimicked his own words, giving me a mocking smile. "So, one might ask themselves, what would happen if I were to knock you to your knees and hold my breath?"

My own breath caught. There was nothing in Elsewhere that made my blood boil like a fairy oath, except perhaps the Fae themselves. I despised them and their twisted words, and I hated the royals most of all.

2 4

LONNIE

*T*he bathing chamber was nearly twelve times the size of the bedroom that Rosey and I shared for all the years we'd lived in the palace.

Everything from the floor, to the walls, to the enormous bathtub was carved from gleaming white stone. The bath itself was so large it could have easily fit six people, with room to spare. A wall of shelves held colorful glass bottles and piles of towels, and beside that, a spotted silver mirror took up nearly an entire wall.

The mirror was gold around the edges and nearly twice my height. It was so large and imposing, it was impossible not to see my own reflection as I padded across the white stone floor to the bath. I choked on a sob, shocked at the reality of my appearance.

I'd hardly believed the fairy woman when she told me how long I'd sat in that cell, but now it was impossible not to. My hair— usually a reddish auburn, was caked with so much grime it had turned a color I could not classify. My skin too, had taken on a gaunt appearance, purplish in places, merely filthy in others. Scratches covered my arms and hands I did not recall getting. I wondered vaguely if I'd given them to myself, tearing at my own skin in the night, either from cold, discomfort, or madness.

If this was how I appeared now, I did not want to consider how bad it had been when the prince found me. Somehow, the lingering aches in my bones doubled upon seeing the sources of the pain. The scratches stung, when I saw the dirt stuck in them. My hunger nearly crippled me, when I realized why my face felt thinner, my wrists brittle and easily broken.

I'd never considered myself a vain person, but now I was forced to confront that I'd taken my appearance for granted. I hated myself for hastening to the side of the bath and turning on the water.

I pulled off the remnants of what had once been one of my sister's lovely dresses, and tossed it to the floor, before sitting naked on the bottom of the porcelain tub and waiting for the water to fill around me.

Within seconds, the water pooled black around my legs, and I had to fill and drain it several times before the water would remain clear. I expected the water to run cold after the second time, but it never did, proving to me that the servants' showers were left cold on purpose.

I'd tried not to think of my sister or our mother or much of anything while in the dungeons. I thought only of food and time and the next day's survival. Of what I would say to the prince should I see him again, and my growing hatred for the Fae. Now, I recalled with sharp clarity that when I lived in the palace, I always awoke before the sun on bathing day. While the water never ran out, the heat and the soap did. Being the first to reach the soap was one of my few pleasures in life—a victory I would strive for each week.

I pictured myself swinging my legs over the side of my bed, looking at my sister in the semi-darkness.

"Better hurry," I would say.

"Quiet," she would mumble, blinking sleep out of her eyes. "I'm sleeping."

Perfect, I would think. Less competition.

Within minutes, I would stand under the lukewarm spray of the shower as the water pelted the chapped skin of my hands. I'd squeeze my eyes shut and imagine the dank showers were a luxury bath house with all the soap I could ever want.

Here, in this luxury bathtub, I sank under the water and wished I could think of nothing.

25

LONNIE

I was pulled from the water, sometime later, by the sound of voices. No, *a* voice.

"Are you finished? I'm growing concerned you're attempting to drown yourself and I will have to perform some sort of daring rescue."

I jumped, splashing water over the sides of the bath. "What the—"

My entire body flushed hot, embarrassment washing over me.

"I should warn you," the prince said lazily, from where he sat on the marble floor with his back against the mirror. "I am not the rescuing type. More of the drowning type, honestly."

"What the fuck are you doing in here?" I folded in on myself, doing my best to cover my most important bits, only to realize that the enormous mirror and the fact that he'd been in here for who knew how long made the whole exercise mostly pointless. "Get out."

"You get out." He grinned, all his teeth flashing. "I said to bathe, not to marinate."

"I am!"

I was indignant. Furious even, and evidently it did not matter. The injustice of the whole thing sent fire licking up my spine, and the urge to break something was nearly unbearable.

"If you will not leave the bath, I am forced to speak with you here." His gaze moved leisurely over my body, lingering long enough that I burned even hotter. "Rest assured, you have nothing there that I haven't seen presented more successfully countless times before."

I sank lower under the clear water until only my eyes were above the surface, as though that would help. After a tense moment, I popped back up again, drawing a large breath. Of all the injustices, this had to be one of the worst. "I feel no need to discuss my imminent death. As you've already said, I have no choice."

I had meant it to sound angry, but it came out defeated. They defeated me before we even began.

Bael held out a hand and plucked a full wine glass out of the air. He smiled at me as he took a sip. "You're exaggerating again, which is essentially a lie. You are not dying. I told you I would help."

I scowled. "Help me by giving me a towel."

"No. I quite like you like this." He reached for his wine glass again, and as I watched a bottle and a second glass appeared beside him. "Wine?"

I shook my head, no. The glass disappeared. "Why would you want to help me? I don't understand why you would want to give your throne to a human servant."

"And there you go again." He stood and began pacing back and forth as though we were having an intellectual discussion over supper. "You know what I dislike about humans? You lie, constantly, without even realizing it. It's absurd. You will say the most outlandish things so casually as though they are fact, and not even blink an eye."

"I love that about humans. Fae have no imagination."

He ran a hand through his curls and sighed. "Imagine then, for a moment, that perhaps you have not thought about this as thoroughly as I have. That you do not know everything and do not need to. I don't want you to be the queen. I am simply offering to help you win the hunts. By winning, you get to live. That seems to be a good outcome for you, is it not?"

"And once I win, then what?"

"Then, you say 'thank you very much for saving my life.'" His lip curled. "We can discuss all the ways you'll thank me later."

I clenched my fists. "You accuse me of lying, yet you are the one who will not say what you truly mean. Infuriating, mother fucking–"

He laughed. "Is that how they talk in the kitchens?"

I glared. "Say what you want, and for the love of Aisling give me a towel."

"Fine."

He seemed put out, but reached backwards and grabbed one of the large, fluffy towels off a rack and passed it to me. I reached over awkwardly, trying to cover my breasts with one arm and take it with the other.

"When you win," he said, in a tone that would have been more appropriate for discussing the weather. "You will abdicate and give the crown to me."

I looked over my shoulder as I rose from the bath and wrapped myself in the towel. "Wouldn't it be easier to simply kill me?"

"Do you want that?" He seemed genuinely curious.

"No! It's just…why go through the effort?"

"If you are trying to avoid getting killed, you're going about it the wrong way."

"That doesn't answer my question…lord." I tacked on the end with as much venom as possible.

"Perhaps I want the crown, but I don't want to be king. If I killed you, I would have to be king, as unfortunately I am in most ways as bound to the rules of the hunts as you are."

"In most ways?"

"Only that I know the rules better than you." He took a sip of his wine and leaned back against the mirror. His brow furrowed. "Knowledge is power, but it is also a curse. But then, power is a curse unto itself. Do you think perhaps they are the same thing?"

I tried to untwist that statement and failed. "I am growing tired of pointing out when you do not answer my questions."

He grinned. "Look out the window."

He pointed, and I craned my neck to see what he was looking at. When it proved impossible, I crossed the room to stand beside him, taking care not to let our arms touch.

I pressed my nose to the glass, and gasped, staring out over the sea of Fae. Hundreds if not thousands, all clamoring to get inside.

Their movements seemed to be as one, like a writhing, angry sea in a storm. Their shouts were audible even from here, the general mood of the mob a violent tempest.

I jumped, my heart stopping for a beat as a pixie zoomed past my window without warning. He trailed a string of decorative flags behind him like a banner, making sweeping motions in the air. I had a feeling if I stood below, I'd be able to read whatever rude messages he and his brethren were spelling out in the sky.

The contrast between this and last years' was stark. I tore my eyes away from the window. "What are they doing?"

"They want to see you," he said acidly. "This entire thing has emboldened the rebel attacks. Think what you want about me, but I don't enjoy when entire villages get slaughtered."

I narrowed my eyes. I refused to be endeared to the bare minimum of decency. I looked out the window again at the screaming mob. "What do they want?"

"Different things. Some are here because they hate you. Some because they hate us. That mob will want a part of you, many literally."

"That's barbaric," I said, glancing down at the mob. "I don't want to be anything."

"But you already are," he said bitterly. "You will be the savior to some and the pariah to others. They'll fear you, and lust after you, and some might even love you, right before they try to kill you."

"Is that what they do to you?" I blurted out.

He paused, so long I thought he wouldn't answer. "No," Bael said finally, and again his voice lacked that humor I'd come to associate with him. "They can't love us."

I watched him for a second. Something about that seemed genuine to me in a way I couldn't describe. It wasn't the exact answer to my question but didn't feel like a trick or a diversion as nearly every other statement so far had. It reminded me of something my mother said: The most honest people were liars.

And somehow, I found common ground in that.

"Fine," I said. "But swear that I will never be put back in the dungeon. And…" I cast around for what else to ask for.

I had no family left. No real friends. Nothing to use against me. All I wanted was to leave and be free of this cursed castle and these Fae. To go somewhere where I wouldn't be stared at or followed or spark the interest of a fairy ever again.

"I want to go to Aftermath."

He gave me a strange look. "Why?"

It was a fair question. The province of Aftermath was a desolate wasteland since the destruction of the city of Nightshade twenty-two years ago. It had once been a city to rival Everlast, but now it was known for little more than ruins and its proximity to the Source. Still, I'd never known it any other way.

"That's where I was born," I said vaguely. "If I win and give you the crown, I want to go back."

He shook his head, clearing his skeptical expression. "Done. The fifth hunt is held in Aftermath as it is."

I nodded, and a finality washed over me, like a blanket of ice. "Alright then. I agree."

"Good," He smiled, like he'd already won the hunts. "Now, tell me little monster…what's your real name?"

"Lonnie," I answered automatically.

"Liar. That cannot be your name, and without sealing the bargain, it doesn't mean anything."

I bit my lip. He was right, but I'd only ever given one person my real name, and they'd betrayed me. I shook my head. "Seal it another way."

"What would you suggest?" he asked, a mischievous glint in his eye.

"I don't know, I am not the purveyor of oaths."

My heart beat against my ribs as I waited. I hoped, desperately, that he would give up.

"I could always kiss you again."

I looked at him sideways. "Does that work?"

He laughed. "No, but I am still offering. I am very curious to know if you always bite, or if that was a spontaneous decision."

I narrowed my eyes. "Try it, and I'll do more than bite."

He raised an eyebrow and smirked. "Really? Like what?"

I closed my eyes, wishing for all the world I could go back ten seconds and say anything else. I'd meant that to be a threat, but it sounded more like a promise. "Isn't there any other way to seal a bargain?"

"Fine, don't take my offer. I'm very curious to hear your real name."

"It's not that exciting," I grumbled.

"Then it shouldn't matter to tell me."

I sighed. I couldn't see a way around this. I leaned forward to whisper the name, the lingering paranoia of never saying it aloud getting the best of me.

In a movement so fast I barely had time to breathe, the prince closed the space between us. He reached for the back of my head, tightening a fist in my still-damp hair, and crushed his lips to mine.

I should have stepped back immediately. Should have thrashed and kicked and bit, but it had been so long since anyone had touched me at all, and I hadn't realized until this moment how much that had been part of my torment these last months. As much as the starvation and the cold and the filth and stench, it was the loneliness—the lack of connection that had tortured me.

So, for one shameful second, I sank into that kiss, and bathed in that inhuman warmth, before I reminded myself who I was and why I was here. And how much I hated these Fae royals who had taken that connection from me in the first place.

I smacked the arm that had snaked around my waist, and he dropped me immediately.

"What was that?" I spluttered, brushing my hand across my mouth. I knew my face must be flaming red.

"That, my little monster, was exactly what you asked for." He smiled and turned on his heel to leave the room. "And an opportunity to satisfy my own curiosity."

I stared after him, wondering if he was bluffing. If he could really seal a bargain with a kiss or if there was some trick in his statement. "But, does that really work?"

"It doesn't matter," he said, and I could hear the smile still in his voice. "Keep your name. I don't need it to control you."

A lead weight dropped into my stomach, and a chill fell over me. Before I could react, however, my eye caught on movement by the door. Every muscle in my body tensed.

Like a scene out of my nightmares, my dark shadow had caught up with me at last.

LONNIE

*P*rince Scion stood framed in the doorway, unbridled rage written all across his face. He carried that enormous raven on his shoulder and wore his usual black on black clothing. I gaped at him, too stunned to do little more than stare.

Scion stared back, his gaze flicking between me and his cousin. In the bath, the water started to churn, slopping against the sides like a turbulent ocean.

"Oh, you're back." Bael seemed completely at ease. "You will be interested to know she still tastes like magic. I would say that means you still owe me gold."

"Bael!" Scion screamed, his voice echoing off the marble, and reverberating all around me. "What—"

In the space of a blink, Prince Bael disappeared, and reappeared again behind his cousin. He yanked him back, slamming the door with so much force that the mirror on the wall rattled, and several bottles toppled off the edge of the tub, slamming to the ground.

I trembled, my heart beating too fast. I stared at the closed door as my brain caught up with the situation, perhaps it was all his cousin's cryptic warnings, or obvious exhibitions of strength, but I now realized my fantasy of stabbing Prince Scion was just that —a fantasy.

My revenge would have to be more subtle.

Padding over to the door, I pressed my ear to the wood.

"Give the queen a moment to collect herself." Bael's voice echoed from the other side as clearly as if he stood in front of me.

"Fuck off," Scion replied, and heavy footsteps followed his statement. "This is my room. What are you doing?"

A fresh wave of shock and horror flowed through me. Surely, I must have misheard. Misunderstood. *Something.*

"Well, I wasn't going to put her in my room. Obviously," Bael retorted, as though that were entirely reasonable.

"And one of the thousand guest rooms wouldn't suffice?"

"Like I know where the guest wing is." Bael's voice was quieter, as though he were walking away. "I didn't think you would mind, you're hardly ever here...well, you weren't. I suppose lately you've been, but—"

"Bael!" Scion interrupted, and his voice was so loud I swore the mirror cracked. "You're going too far. Surely you can't be this bored."

"I am, in fact, but that's not what this is about. You know, you could have told me you put her in the dungeon. I'd been wondering what you did with her. This is so much worse than I imagined, and frankly I'm proud."

There was a jarring thump, like someone dropped something heavy, or punched a wall. Bael laughed.

I pressed my ear harder into the door, waiting with bated breath for Scion's reply. Footsteps sounded, and I held my breath. I imagined them walking away, to allow for a more private conversation.

The doorknob turned, and my heart leapt into my throat. I jumped back, stifling a scream. Bael looked at me, amusement and disappointment combined on his face.

"Another word of advice," he said. "We can hear you. And smell you. There's very little you're going to be able to do to hide from us. You should remember that in the hunts."

I stared up at him and nodded mutely.

His eyes darted over me, assessing, starting at the top of my head and combing all the way down my body. I grew warm under his scrutiny and braced for an insult. None came.

"Food and clothes," he said flatly. "Now. You have two hours, and if you're naked and unfed when I get back then that's how you'll enter those woods.

I jutted my lip out, defiant. "Perhaps I'd prefer that. Why bother pretending this is anything other than torture by dressing it up in silk and a crown."

Bael's lip curled, and his gaze traveled up and down my body. Though now I wore a towel, somehow the look made me feel more naked than I had in the bath.

"Stop talking little monster," he drawled. "Before I decide I like that idea too much and call your bluff."

27
BAEL

"*A*re you fucking insane?" Scion asked for what had to be the sixth time.

As I'd not answered him, he seemed to take that as license to keep asking. He certainly took it as license to chase me around the castle. At this rate, I would be insane by the end of the night.

I simply grinned as my cousin practically chased me down the long hall to my bedchamber. Scion's voice echoed off the stones, reverberating back to me and rattling my teeth.

"Where are you expecting me to sleep?" He demanded.

I shrugged. "Why don't you find one of the thousand guest rooms you are suddenly so fond of? Or go visit that nymph that keeps hanging around your neck like a rather large noose."

He spluttered. "I'm not—"

"Or stay in your own room. Perhaps you can convince the Slúagh queen to be more accommodating. I don't care what you do with her as long as she's alive tomorrow."

As I spoke, a shred of doubt crept in. I wouldn't be able to make that proclamation a second time. Not without looking wildly suspect.

I had half a mind to turn around myself, but I kept trying to remember that the...craving...had nothing to do with the girl personally and everything to with the blood I'd fed her earlier. As long as I ignored it, the effect would wear off in a few days. *Hopefully.*

She was too interesting before the blood... The unwelcome thought rose to the forefront of my mind. *Instinct or coincidence?*

I shook my head. This was a dangerous line of thinking. I looked back to my cousin. If Scion noticed anything odd, he said nothing.

I turned and opened the door to my bedchamber for Scion's benefit. It was absurdly rude to travel through the shadows into someone else's private chamber. Of course, I did it to him all the time, but Scion was better behaved than me.

Scion did not follow me inside, instead choosing to hover at the door and wait for an invitation. I didn't like anyone in my space. Even him, though I likely would have allowed it if pressed.

"You should have told me," Scion said bitterly.

I rolled my eyes without looking at my cousin. Scion was always angry. I'd always thought our grandmother had given him the wrong name. He should have been the Prince of Wrath. Perhaps the Ruler of Resentment. The Sullen Sovereign.

I leaned back against the wall beside my bed and crossed my arms. "You could have just as easily told me," I pointed out. "You're the one who hid a human in the dungeon for a year. I'm shocked she lived."

Anger churned in my chest at that. If it were anyone else, I wouldn't be standing here discussing it so calmly. Anyone else, and I would have thrown curses first and asked for explanations later. Not only had putting the little monster in the dungeon possibly destroyed everything, she'd been nearly dead when I found her. I shuddered at the thought. Things like that did not usually bother me, yet the monster in the back of my head battled for dominance, growling to make its displeasure known.

Scion had the audacity to scoff. *Fuck it.*

"Oi!" Scion yelled, as I launched myself forward and shoved him backwards into the wall.

His surprise allowed his magic to leak out, as I'd known it would, and agony shot up my arm as my fist connected with his face. I stumbled back, shivering, as pain lanced my entire body. If I were human, perhaps even a lesser Fae, that likely would have killed me. *Worth it.*

"Are you fucking insane," Scion spit blood into his hand and braced himself against the doorframe.

"If you're going to keep asking that without getting an answer, I'm going to think it's you who's insane."

He shook his head. "What was that for?"

"You nearly ruined everything."

He gave me a stony look. "Now we know there's something off about her."

"And you think that's what?"

I assumed he planned to tell me—why else chase me all around the castle?

"I've seen her before," he admitted.

That had me raising my eyebrows—or at least trying. The pain was still making my muscles spasm slightly. "In the woods, when—"

"No." He cut me off aggressively, as if he didn't want to discuss it. I almost laughed, but swallowed it. I didn't want to discuss that either. Not that I had any right to comment—I'd fucked more people than that girl had hairs on her head, but still. The idea of that guard continuing to draw breath after touching her...irked me.

"Years ago," he said darkly. "Grandmother was interested in that family long before any of this started, and that girl smelled of magic even back then."

I stared at my cousin, shock coursing through me, as a new possibility occurred to me. A new—horrible—possibility. "When was this? *Exactly.*"

His eyes shuttered. "It doesn't matter. In a few hours it will be over, regardless."

My mouth became a thin line. Over, because he intended to kill the human and once again ruin everything. "I wish you would look past the end of your nose for once."

"What the fuck is that supposed to mean?"

"Only that you were never good at prophecy."

He scoffed. "I don't have to be. Enough were made about me to more than make up for it."

I rolled my eyes. *If that wasn't the most arrogant thing I'd ever heard...*

I glanced over at the stack of prophetic journals on my shelf and sighed. They'd grown considerably in the last year, since I'd been making more of an effort, but I had yet to see anything to contradict Grandmother Celia's demands. *Unfortunately.*

Scion turned to leave, and I closed my eyes, pinching the bridge of my nose. "I wouldn't hunt if I were you."

He glanced over his shoulder and the suspicion in his gaze told me he knew me too well. "Why? What did you do?"

28

LONNIE

*D*espite my threat, I did not actually want to run naked through the woods and was grateful when I found a stack of clothing on the bed. They were all gowns in colors and fabrics I had never seen outside of the palace and had certainly never worn. Far from practical, but better than a towel.

Beside the clothing was a tray of food. Fruits and cheese and meats, again, all richer than anything I'd been allowed to taste before.

My eyes itched, burning with exhaustion, and my stomach growled in protest. It was as if the understanding of time passing woke my body, making everything come alive, humming with discomfort.

I scowled. Had someone delivered these while he'd kept me cornered in the bath? Had he waved a hand and made them appear? Both seemed equally likely, and both annoyed me in ways that were hard to put into words.

A memory sparked unbidden to the forefront of my mind. The discarded scones that Rosey had stolen from the cook because they would be thrown away otherwise. The Everlasts threw away food while their people starved. Did they even consider that? Likely not.

I hated myself for reaching for a scone. A better person would have refused the food in protest. Said something to him about it. Given it away...something. Rosey probably would have done that. But I'd eaten nothing but moldy bread and water for months, and my every protest died.

Half a scone in my mouth, I crossed the room to the door—just to check. I already knew what I was likely to find, but still, I gave the knob a few useless tugs. It did not budge.

Perhaps I should simply have been relieved that Prince Bael did not insist on sleeping in the room with me. I feared he may want to make sure I didn't try to escape overnight.

As it was, I was far too exhausted to attempt it even if I didn't fear a return to the dungeon. Too weak from the months underground. And perhaps he saw that, for he did little more than lock me in the tower room before leaving for the evening. Tomorrow, I told myself, putting a hand to my mouth. Tomorrow, after I'd had one proper night's sleep and eaten more of the too-rich food I would consider ways to test the efficiency of that bargain.

Turning back to the bed, my gaze caught on a box I had not noticed before set on the spindly bedside table. I was certain it had not been there before.

It was wooden. Simple, with a golden clasp and runes laid into the sides. My stomach fluttered with anxiety as I reached for the box, glancing back at the door once before opening it as if someone would burst in and stop me from handling the item.

My breath caught. The gleaming obsidian crown sat nestled on a velvet pillow.

Even if the crown had not caused me so much pain already, its sharp edges and dark bottomless depths would have seemed like a bad omen to me. For the crown of the High Fae court, it certainly had a malevolent look to it.

A knock sounded at my door and I looked up, the scone falling from my mouth. "Who's there?"

No one replied.

Maybe they didn't hear me? No doubt an assassin here to end my misery.

"Who's there?" I asked again, a bit louder.

"Your Majesty?" A female voice asked, tentatively.

I coughed, spluttering in indignation. I threw my blankets off and jumped to my feet and was halfway across the floor before I remembered to check for murderous fairies. "Are you alone?"

"Yes!" the voice was out of breath, like the owner had run here.

I tried to yank the door open, only to wrench my arm almost out of the socket. "It's locked!"

"Oh, I know," came the reply from the other side. "I simply didn't want to bother you."

I ground my teeth as I massaged my arm. "Well come in if you can I suppose…whoever you are."

The door opened and despite opening it herself, the woman—I didn't recognize her—jumped back as if *I'd* startled *her*. I blinked at her in confusion.

She had a heart-shaped face and large honey-brown eyes. Her hair was the color of unsweetened tea tied back in a tight bun that my sister would have envied. She carried a huge armful of gowns in every color imaginable. The pile was so high she had to lean awkwardly to the side to see around it. I gaped at her as she elbowed her way inside the room.

"Don't call me that," I said too loudly. "No, 'Your Majesty.' No 'My Lady.' Nothing like that."

"Sorry!" She bobbed a quick curtsy, seeming mortified, and I felt slightly bad for being rude. "What would you prefer?"

I crossed back over to the tray of food. I was more hungry than truly angry…well, at least not angry with this woman. "Lonnie is fine, but nothing would be better."

"Sorry," she said again. "I didn't know. I'm Iola. I'm really Lady Thalia's maid. I've heard all about you."

She said everything very fast and with an authority, as if it explained her presence. I had no idea who Lady Thalia was. Moreover, if this Iola was one of the maids, I should at least recognize her. There were certainly enough servants in the castle that it was difficult to know everyone, but one did at least recognize every face. I was quite certain I'd never seen this woman in my life.

I was starting to think I really had gone mad this year. "What are you doing here?"

"I'm here to bring you these and help you dress before the hunts." She looked at the pile of clothes the prince had left for me on the bed the night before and snorted a laugh. I was inclined to agree with that reaction.

I'd examined the clothes, only to decide that they were at once too revealing and too complex to wear to any event, and certainly not to bed. I'd chosen the least offensive of the under-garments and only now realized I was wildly underdressed to be speaking to anyone, particularly a stranger. Not, I supposed, that it mattered much. I'd spent a year without bathing and relieving myself with only iron bars for privacy. Modesty be damned.

"You've missed the feast I'm afraid," Iola said sadly.

"The feast?"

"Yes." She nodded knowingly. "Before the hunt. It really should be today of course, but what with…" she glanced at me. "Recent developments, they've decided to hold the feasts the day before now. So it was yesterday, you know, so there were no, er, interruptions."

It was my turn to snort a laugh, and then an ill feeling washed over me immediately after. I shouldn't laugh. Not at the memory of the event that had ended my sister's life. But really, "interruptions" was such a terribly Fae way to talk about a rebel attack and the mad king beheading the servants and then being beaten to death with his own crown. *Quite inconvenient. Most disagreeable.*

"What do you think of this?" Iola held up a blue silk gown to my chest. "It's a wonderful color for you."

"No!" I said too harshly. "Not blue."

She jumped back, seeming startled. "Alright. Plum then?" She grabbed another dress.

I thought of running through the Waywoods. Was I intended to do that in a dress? "Are there no trousers?"

She bit her lip. "Sorry, no. I can go look for some?" She glanced at the window, as if assessing the time. "I don't know where to find any, perhaps I could borrow–"

I sighed, shaking my head. "It likely won't matter." I heaved a laugh that felt more like a sob. "If they don't kill me, they will torment me regardless of what I wear."

She pursed her lips, not bothering to ask what "they" I meant.

"Well, I like this gown," Iola mused, holding a purple gown up to me as though checking if it matched my skin tone. "You may as well be a lovely corpse."

I'd never had anyone aside from Rosey and my mother touch my hair, and certainly not in a long while. It had been months since anyone had touched me at all, save for the beatings from the guards, and the shocking kiss from the prince last night.

It did not take much begging from Iola before I sat in a chair before the small vanity and let her comb out my tangled curls.

I wondered briefly why Prince Scion had a vanity table in his room, but then noticed it was a different color than the rest of the furniture–white, rather than all the austere black. The lengths that Prince Bael had stretched to–as far as I could tell–simply annoy his cousin for no reason other than his own enjoyment were almost impressive.

I bit my lip as she combed, gazing at myself in the enormous mirror on the bathing room wall. I looked barely better than the night before. Pale, and haunted, tormented by lack of sleep, lack of food, and my own grief and bitterness.

"Why don't I know you?" I asked. "I worked here for years."

I said it slightly guiltily, wondering if I should perhaps not be allowing a fellow servant to wait on me—even if it was only temporarily.

"Oh, I know," she laughed. "Everyone talks about you."

I scowled. "I'm sure they do."

She began twisting my hair into some sort of complex knot and I nearly moaned as tingles traveled over my spine. "What does that mean?"

"No one likes me much."

"They do now," she grinned. "Or, most of them, anyway."

I blinked, surprised. That was similar to what Prince Bael said would happen, but I difficulty believing it could be true. I was the cursed one. The one the Fae preyed on. Surely, this would only prove that correct.

"But to answer your question, I arrived a month after you..." she trailed off and I knew what she meant. She did not need to finish.

I supposed many things had changed in the castle while I'd been underneath it. With any luck, I would live to learn what those things were.

29

LONNIE

*I*ola reluctantly locked me in my room—or rather, Prince Scion's room—when she left, apologizing for having to do so. I waved her off. I'd expected it.

I wondered vaguely if the prince would ask for his room back at any point. I hoped at the very least this was inconveniencing him. I pictured him sleeping on the floor in the corridor and almost smiled. It was unlikely, but a nice idea all the same.

The closer it grew to nightfall, however, my anxiety rose. It churned, turning my stomach and sending my breakfast back up again. I'd just been sick for the second time when Prince Bael arrived to collect me.

"You look…" the prince stared me up and down twice over as he stood in the doorway to the tower room. "Surprisingly bewitching. Well done, little monster."

A lovely corpse—that was what Iola had said, and I couldn't get the visual out of my mind. I scowled at the prince.

He'd also dressed up—as much as I'd ever seen him do. As he had last year, Prince Bael wore a red jacket with no shirt underneath.

Unlike Prince Scion, who seemed to wear as much silver as he could fit on his person at one time, Prince Bael wore no jewelry. This time, up close and in better lighting, I noticed the edge of what looked like a pale tattoo—or perhaps a scar—on the right side of his chest.

He gripped my arm, pulling me out into the hall. Then, as if remembering something, he stopped short. "Where's your crown?"

I snorted a laugh. "You cannot be serious."

He didn't bother responding to that, instead marching back into the room and returning holding the obsidian crown. He held it gingerly, like he was afraid it might bite him.

"Do you often dress up your pigs before you slaughter them?" I asked, as Prince Bael placed the crown on my head. It was somehow even heavier than I expected, and my neck immediately began to ache with the weight.

He stepped back, no longer smiling as he stared at me. "No, but I always sharpen my sword before a battle."

I took deep breaths of fresh air through my nose as I stepped out onto the front steps of the castle. The scent of grass. Of night and of oncoming rain. It was the best scent in the world after months and months underground. If I'd had the chance, I would have laid down on the earth and cried for the joy of simply seeing the sky again.

The grounds were quiet as we made our way down the front steps of the castle and into the night, but soon enough, the sound of music and high-pitched laughter reached me. The colorful tents and tinkling music brought back foul memories of this time last year, and I nearly retched. I would have if there was anything left in my stomach to expel.

I hadn't realized it was nearly night once more, and the setting sun disoriented me for a moment. Another day, gone, on top of the many lost to the dungeon beneath the castle. The time felt both endless and instant, melding together until I could not even fathom how much I'd truly lost.

I racked my brains, trying to remember what I knew about the other hunts beyond this one. What locations, and what obstacles were to be expected. "What is the boundary?"

"There is a stream that runs through the middle of the Waywoods. If you cross it, the game ends for the evening."

"How far into the woods is it?"

He shrugged. "I never checked. It's only because of you that I'm forced to walk at all."

Right. They preferred to travel in and out of the shadows, disappearing and reappearing at will. Yet another way I was at a disadvantage. "What's stopping the entire hunting party from simply disappearing at the starting line, and reappearing at the end to wait for me?"

"Not all of them can. Most wouldn't be able to travel that distance without knowing where they were going, and many are not here for you. They will be here to battle each other unbothered, so you may only need to worry about those with both the power and the desire to wait you out at the finish."

In short, the most powerful Fae of the bunch. *Perfect.*

As we walked, the shouts of the mob I'd witnessed outside the window carried to me on the breeze, sending shivers up my spine. What would they do if they saw us? I glanced up at Prince Bael. How odd, to be glad I wasn't alone, and stranger still to be grateful for the fairy prince as my companion. Cruel? Yes. My enemy? Of course. But against a mob of High Fae, I would gladly take any of the Everlasts as my guard.

Prince Bael looked sideways at me, as if reading my thoughts. "A word of advice,"

I went stiff at that. Not that I was unaware that Bael was danger- ous. Abhorrent even, but he was not my most hated of the Ever- lasts. Still, his advice was beginning to sound like threats.

"Do not show your weakness on your face," Bael said. "If there is one thing my family does well, it is exploit a weakness."

I looked up as he said that and caught his smile. "And are you counting yourself among that group?"

"Oh, absolutely. I simply got to you first."

I was not ashamed of my fear, it would be stupid not to admit it. Strength was one thing, but bravado quite another. I felt neither brave nor anything close to it at the moment, and there was no point pretending otherwise. "Why should I be afraid?" My tone dripped with sarcasm. "There are only hundreds of Fae planning to kill me."

"You are certainly not making this pleasant, you know," he sounded disappointed, as though it were my fault that I was wildly outmatched in a game designed to destroy me. "And here I thought you would want to live."

"I want to leave," I snapped.

He whirled to me, stopping in the middle of the path. "Don't even think about it." His eyes were dark, more gold than yellow and I couldn't tell if it was the lighting or something else.

For the first time in a long while heat licked up my skin, the faintest glimmer of excitement at the thought of a battle urging me to open my mouth and fight back. "Do you have the authority to forbid me? I thought we were here because I now outrank you."

He growled low in his throat, and I took an involuntary step back. "I'm going to choose to ignore that. Consider it your coronation gift."

I furrowed my brow at him, momentarily distracted. "My what?"

"Your coronation—assuming you get a proper one. I would not put it past my mother to attempt to circumvent the issue."

I fell silent. Somehow the word "circumvent" sounded an awful lot like "murder."

"That crown on your head is more than a piece of jewelry, little monster. It's as good as a chain around your neck. If you try to run, I'm happy to throw you back in the dungeon in between hunts."

I tipped my chin up, fixing him with a fierce gaze. "I understand. I can still want to leave, can't I?"

He scowled. "I will never become used to the way you humans speak. Say what you mean."

I pressed my lips shut. It seemed pointless to argue with him, although from my perspective, I'd said exactly what I meant.

*A*s we moved toward the lights of the silk tents, set up along the sides of the forest, the familiar tinkling notes of a flute sounded, and I stopped dead in my tracks. "No," I said. "I cannot."

"You can't, what?"

"The music, I—"

Bael smiled, and it looked slightly mean. like he knew exactly what I was about to say and enjoyed it. "It doesn't affect everyone, you know. Some humans have it worse than others. Perhaps you are just weak-willed.

I shook my head. He couldn't phase me. That, I knew, was not the problem. If anything, it was that I was easily distracted. Or, I had been. Perhaps now that I had little else in my head but survival and anger, it would not be as much of a problem.

"That's odd, though," Bael said thoughtfully as he practically marched me through the gap in the tents and into the clearing. The lights of the will-o-wisps hung low over the party and seemed to twinkle brighter as we approached.

"What is?"

Bael kept his head high as we walked into the middle of the celebration, groups of dancers parting to let him pass. I walked directly behind him, dodging servants and Fae alike. Many watched me, some with interest, and some with derision. I cast my eyes down, not wanting to make enemies of anyone. "I thought you might be immune to magic in some way. You could see through our glamor. Scion doesn't seem to affect you, and I'd warrant a guess that my uncle didn't either."

"I'm not," I said shortly. "Immune to magic, that is. I don't know what's wrong with your family, but I have had fairy magic used on me before, so it certainly has nothing to do with me."

He looked sideways at me. "Pity. That would have made this far easier."

For once, we agreed.

30
LONNIE

*R*ather than entering the circle of tents, Bael led me around the edge toward the darkness of the woods.

I squinted, and a line of shadowy figures standing backlit against the setting sun came into view. As we approached, they fell silent and turned to face us. A wall of overwhelming power and beauty all in one place. All fixated on me.

Their expressions ranged from anger to hatred to curiosity, to clear confusion as they assessed me, like they were sizing up an opponent. Which, I supposed, they were. If I lived a thousand years, I never would have anticipated having even one of the Everlast family know my name, let alone the entire house. If I'd known, I would have begged, borrowed, and stolen anything to avoid this inevitable nightmare.

Only Prince Scion, standing slightly off to the side from the rest, seemed neither interested nor surprised. Then, he'd known both that I was alive and what Bael intended to do. The others were likely as shocked by this whole turn of events as I had been.

Beside me, Prince Bael shifted slightly, and I would have given nearly anything to know what he was thinking. Was it strange, to be standing opposite the proverbial line from the rest of his family? And why would he want to?

The divide lasted mere seconds.

Two of the shadowy figures extricated themselves from the group and walked purposefully across the grass. One, I recognized immediately as Prince Gwydion. Even in the semi-darkness, his smile was blinding. As if he'd been waiting for us all night.

The second figure, I knew by sight, though I'd never had the misfortune to speak with her. Lady Aine was tan, with perfect angular bone structure and cupid's bow lips. Her curly, honey colored hair was piled on top of her head and decorated with a wild rose crown that matched her pale pink silk hunting jacket and trousers.

Unlike Gwydion, she walked across the grass with all the enthusiasm of one heading to the gallows. She sighed heavily as she reached us and glared daggers at her brother before moving to stand next to him. The tension was evident to anyone who had ever had an argument with one's sibling and still had to support them. An odd sense of envy hit me. I would never have that again.

Prince Gwydion looked at me again, smiling in what seemed to be a genuine way. "Hello."

Lady Aine let out a huff through her nose that told me in no uncertain terms that she did not agree with this stunt and would kill me herself if given the chance. At least she had the decency to be obvious about it.

Ignoring Aine, I blinked at Gwydion. I was unsure if I should answer. My fear of the Fae and suspicion of their intentions warred with the part of me that was conditioned to react to "hello" with a greeting of my own.

"You'll have to forgive the little monster, brother," Bael said under his breath. "Her highness is both suspicious by nature and a bit rude. You may or may not get used to it."

"Sounds like Scion," Gwydion said jovially. "I think we'll manage."

At the sound of his name, I looked over at the Prince of Ravens. Or was it 'King,' now? What did they call him all year while he'd been hiding me beneath his castle?

Whatever he was called, his mere presence was enough to stir rage in my gut.

Scion watched me as intently as I watched him. He took in every inch of me, but not as if he was interested. More as if I were food. I shivered to my very core, and his eyes flashed—like he was hoping for my reaction.

"Darling," A high female voice echoed across the grass like musical laughter. "We were beginning to think you had decided not to attend."

Prince Bael stiffened beside me. "Show no fear, little monster," he said so low that only I could hear.

"Good evening, Mother," Bael said, the note of delighted glee I'd previously associated with him now back in his voice. "I heard."

Princess Raewyn wore a long, blue gown, completely inappropriate for the hunts, and walked as though carried on an unseen wind. She was flanked by a gaggle of a dozen or more handmaids and a tan, dark-haired male I recognized as her husband, Auberon.

Lord Auberon seemed about as willing to support whatever his wife was doing, as Aine was willing to support her brother. At the very least, the father and daughter shared the same expression of exasperated wariness.

"Is it evening?" Raewyn asked as she approached. "I couldn't say." Her tone was light, playful, but something about it sent shivers up my spine. "I haven't ascribed to the sun cycle in some hundred years, you know that. Schedule is unconducive to prophecy, and I don't like to be disturbed when the moon is high."

Prince Bael cleared his throat loudly. "Good of you to make this exception then."

Gwydion seemed to try to subtly elbow his brother, but he was so large it came off more as a shove. Bael didn't move an inch, but the action still did not go unnoticed.

Lady Raewyn's brow crinkled in the tiniest line—the only outward evidence that she was either confused, or concerned. She looked up at her son, raising one brow. "Beloved," she said, her smile indulgent. "I am eagerly anticipating the culmination of this latest stunt."

Bael made a sweeping bow, clearly putting on quite a show compared to five minutes before. He reached down and grabbed my arm, yanking me forward. "Not a stunt, a scandal. One might even say a secession.

She threw her head back laughing, and it echoed around the grounds setting my teeth on edge. Her maids joined in, but everyone else in the vicinity stiffened. "No," she said, her laughter stopping as abruptly as it started. "I wouldn't think so."

Bael turned to me. "You should understand, Lonnie, that my mother is more dangerous than she appears, but far more harmless than she believes, and your own perception of her power has a large impact on your likelihood of survival."

"You flatter me, darling," Raewyn said with a brittle smile that could have cleared a room. "You are still not my favorite, but you are the best."

Something dark flashed behind Bael's eyes and I wondered if I'd just witnessed an actual insult hit its mark.

"Mother, might I introduce—"

"—the murderer!" a harsh voice yelled.

I jumped at the sound. As, I was surprised to note, did Lady Raewyn. Before anyone could say anything, she hurried away, her gaggle of maids fussing as they followed her.

Prince Bael muttered something under his breath and reached for my elbow, grasping it hard with two fingers as if to hold me back. The move was wholly unnecessary, though the feel of his disconcertingly warm skin on mine sent tingles up my arm. I wrenched my arm from his grasp and stumbled back with the force of it when he made no effort to hold me there. Embarrassment washed over me.

"Murderer!" the same male voice said again. "What the fuck is this little kingslayer doing here? What game is this now, Bael?"

My eyes darted back and forth, searching for the source of the voice in the gathering crowd. Without my realizing it, those who had been dancing and drinking by the tents, or gathering outside the castle had started to make their way over to us, evidently realizing the real show was happening elsewhere. The crowd was growing larger by the second. The feeling of being trapped set in, and my heart pounded against my ribs.

"Lysander," Bael said calmly. "You're punching above your weight, cousin."

A dark-haired teenager stepped forward, his face contorted in rage. I saw it then—his resemblance to both King Penvalle and Prince Scion—and anger licked up my spine.

"This is neither the time nor the place," Aine snapped. "Don't get yourself killed before you even learn what your magic is."

The kid wasn't listening. He turned to me, a vicious sneer on his face and a spike of fear shot through me. That was the look of someone who wanted me dead. I'd learned long ago not to underestimate the Fae based on age. The fairy who'd first tormented me and given me my scars had been only a child by their standards, and Prince Lysander was far older than that. If he wanted me dead, there was little I could do to stop him.

He sneered, his ire moving from me to his cousin. "We should have known you would pull something like this, poison tongue bastard."

Bael raised a hand as if to strike the smaller prince, but Gwydion held him back.

"Leave it." Gwydion said under his breath, even as Mairead shooed her son away in the background. "You can't fight Lysander, Bael, he's barely more than a child."

Bael gave his brother a contemptuous glance. "I can. I shouldn't."

"Fine. The point stands."

Bael shook Gwydion off. "I won't, but only because I look forward to killing him in a few years when it's a fair fight."

Gwydion rolled his eyes. "We don't fight amongst ourselves."

"We fucking should, if you ask me. Prune the dead branches to save the tree."

As if remembering I was there, they both fell silent at once, watching me.

At any other time in my life, I would have moved mountains for such unfettered access to a conversation between the Fae. If I wasn't mistaken, I'd just learned several things about them in quick succession. They practiced using hyperbole—it must have been difficult, or at the very least, a skill gained with age. Lysander had no powers, but he would in a few years.

And most importantly, the Everlasts did not all get along.

For some reason, that idea made me glance back over to where Prince Scion had been, but the space where he stood was now empty.

Though it was growing dark when we walked from the palace, it seemed to take years for the sun to actually set.

The gathering crowd kept growing larger and larger, moving and writhing like a living thing. Their anxiety mirrored my own. The longer we stood here, the worse it got. The stares. The whispers following me…

Dark clouds crossed what was left of the light, and the scent in the air warned of oncoming rain. In the distance, thunder rumbled, and I turned toward the sound. I frowned. Now, I would be wet as well as dead. Perfect.

"That's lucky," Bael said in my ear.

"What is." It came out more statement than question. I couldn't see any way in which the rain was lucky.

"The rain will drive some of the beasts off the paths," he said. "It will also raise the water level in at the river, so I would get there as fast as you can."

"Why do you keep saying 'you' as if you won't be with me?"

He gave me a look that was almost pitying and gestured toward the crowd of hundreds of hunters. "Do you think I might be a bit busy? Do you believe you can walk in a straight line unassisted?

Or, would you prefer I walk alongside you, and not remove those attempting to murder you?"

"Why can't you do both?"

Before he could answer, Bael's attention was pulled as a High Fae on horseback cantered into the center of the field. He wore a black cloak and a mask of a stag's head covering his entire face. I tilted my head up, waiting for him to speak.

A hush fell over the crowd, punctuated only by ripples of nervous anticipation. In the distance, an ominous drum began to pound, signaling the impending start of the hunt. My heart matched its rhythm, and sweat broke out on the back of my neck.

The fairy in the stag mask pulled a large hunting horn from his belt. He was silhouetted against the stormy sky, monstrous and otherworldly, as he raised the instrument to his mouth.

And for once, I didn't stop to ask questions or consider if I was playing the game correctly. I didn't ask if I could be prepared better, or if I had permission. Because the Fae didn't think like that, and I had to stop thinking like that.

The horn hadn't even finished its note and I was already running for the trees.

3 1
LONNIE

I drowned out the noise of the screaming crowd behind me. I couldn't recall there being a crowd like this at last year's hunts, and a part of me knew why that was: *They were here for me.*

Here to see the human queen pulled limb from limb by the Everlasts. Or perhaps because they hated the royals as much as I did and wanted to see the one small moment of rebellion before it was snatched away again. Either way, I knew it would end the same. Prince Bael could try his best to promise my safety, but he was only one fairy. One prince against a whole horde of hunters out for my blood. Soon enough they would reach me.

Still, I'd never run so fast in my life. My heart pounded against my chest, my breath coming too quick. I couldn't think. Couldn't breathe through the fear and adrenaline. My mother's warnings pounded in the back of my mind. *Never go into the Waywoods alone. Never at night. Those humans who enter the hunts never come out alive.* Her voice mingled with Prince Scion's threats, the taunts of the guards in the dungeons.

I gasped. Rain poured over my head and panic gripped me. I shook with worry and cold.

My breath heaved, but I ignored it, pushing further into the darkness near the edge of the forest. The trees loomed like boney fingers reaching out for me. Every inhale was ragged, painful in my chest, and a lump formed in the back of my throat. More from anger at the situation than anything.

Prince Bael had pulled me from my cell to die in a different, more traumatic way and nothing could change that now.

I pressed my hands to my chest. *I had to calm down.*

If I couldn't breathe, couldn't calm my racing thoughts I would never survive this.

I squinted through the rain and darkness. The path ahead split, one side going up toward some rocky overpass, the other down into a mossy slippery mudslide of unknown darkness. Neither seemed a good prospect. But as the shouts and jeers of the hunters behind me echoed in my ears like fearsome phantoms chasing me, I had no time to pause and think.

I stumbled slightly on the hem of my gown, and I looked down, wishing I had worn something else. Something warmer and less constricting.

I paused, reaching down, and wasted precious seconds tearing savagely at the gauzy skirt of the fine gown until it lay in tatters around my knees. I looked down, saddened at the loss of warmth, no matter how small. Still, better to be cold than to trip and break my neck.

I chose the right fork, jogging up the rocky hill, searching for higher ground. The rain blurred my vision, making it nearly impossible to see, but still I soldiered on, forcing my arms and legs to pump faster despite the screaming of my muscles. The pounding in my ears.

I only had to get to the river. I didn't have to fight, only escape. Perhaps I could hide long enough, stay out of sight long enough that they wouldn't catch up, or would run past me, get lost in the rain themselves. It was possible. Except, if I couldn't see, there was no chance of finding the way on my own.

The last time I'd run through the Waywoods had been a clear night, illuminated by stars and a full moon. Tonight, the rain posed as much of a threat as the hunters.

Ahead, a cluster of wet, bedraggled bushes, thick with greenery, sprung up beside the path. An idea springing to mind, I sprinted toward them. Wisps often hid among leaves, creating their own tiny natural lanterns.

Skittering to a halt, I sank to my knees beside the bush. Pounding footsteps behind me made me fall flat to the ground, pressing my belly to the dirt and putting my hands over my head. *By Aisling.*

"This way," someone shouted, pronouncing their Ws with a V sound, reminiscent of the accent common in the mountains of Nevermore.

Their companion replied in a language I didn't understand, but the tone was clear. Excited. Full of adrenaline.

Humans probably. Maybe lesser noble Fae, but not ones concerned with me.

I lay on the ground until my panting subsided, my panic falling into nothing but numbness. I let my heartbeat fall back to normal. While I waited for the sounds of the distant hunters to quiet, I needed a plan better than just laying here. And yet I was frozen.

As I lay there, waiting for my pulse to slow, something touched the side of my face. I jolted, alarmed, and clapped my hand to my cheek.

Then, something long and rough slithered toward my neck. Panic rose in my chest, and I tried to jump to my feet, only for another and another of the slithering creeping tendrils to reach for me. The plants—if they were plants at all—were *alive*.

I rolled to my side, screaming now. "Let me go," I demanded, for all the good it would do.

I reached for the knife in my belt, trying vainly to pull it free as twisted vines wrapped around my arms and squeezed my chest. This was how people died in the Waywoods—not by the hands of other travelers, but by monsters and poisonous plants and broken limbs. If I was going to die, I would prefer it be by the hand of an Everlast than by my own damn ignorance,

I pitched myself forward, bending at the waist, and pulling the plant with me. Its roots creaked and I used the momentum of my body to reach for the knife again. My fingers brushed it and I gripped the hilt with two fingers, fumbling to pull it free. My heart soared with excitement, but I was not free yet.

I grappled for a better grasp on the knife as the vines rose together, lifting me clean off my feet. In the distance, a sound roared like thunder combined with the screams of the hunters. They were close, and in a way, I almost hoped they found me; perhaps they would free me and I could run from them rather than being suffocated to death by a plant.

A flash of lightning tore through the sky with a tremendous crack. The plant quivered, and water poured down over me in torrents like nothing I'd ever seen. Almost otherworldly in origin.

The plant shivered, as though it were cold, and quaked under my weight. I laughed, my knife shifting in my hand as I brought the blade down on the nearest vine.

It shrunk back from my touch. And shifted, as the water continued to pitch down, almost painful against my skin. The plant loosened slightly, letting me drop a foot or so back to the ground. I gained enough slack to raise my arm and try to hack at the vines. It pulled back and I imagined it hissing, like a cat, with its tail stepped on.

"Let me go," I demanded again, though I knew it was pointless to speak to a plant, but it seemed better than nothing.

Thunder sounded again and lightning followed immediately, the storm right above us. The plant trembled, pulling back from me almost entirely. I wrenched myself out of its grip.

"You don't like that?" I demanded. "Well, I don't like being grabbed."

With the last of my strength, I stabbed my blade into the center of the largest vine. "Ha!"

The sky opened further, droplets of water pelting down over my head. The downpour drenched my face and I quickly wiped it away.

Struggling to see, I stared into the bushes as I tried to catch my breath. A spark of movement made me focus, and blink against the unrelenting rain.

A tiny figure peeked out from behind the murderous bush. I frowned.

I wasn't sure I wanted anything to do with a guardian of that horrid thing. I was almost angry with my little friends. "Where have you been?"

For years they'd stayed with me. Always. Never abandoning me; but when I'd needed them, they were inconsistent at best.

The little creature widened its eyes at me and made a buzzing sound as if trying to reply. It was a fiddlehead sprite, I thought.

Not a—carnivorous plant sprite. Not one of the fearsome beasts, anyway, but certainly one of the stranger-looking ones with its furry green ears and its curly fingertips.

"Well, help me now," I said, no idea if it could understand. "Where's the boundary?"

The creature hopped up and down, excited, or perhaps agitated —it was hard to say which. Either way, I was simply pleased not to be alone.

The sprite unearthed a tiny lantern from its tree, and I half ran, half jogged back down the path chasing the spec of light. As we went, I pulled in deep breaths, pressing my hands to my face.

I had survived the plant. Killed the high king of Elsewhere, survived the dungeon and I'd made it out of the woods once before on hunting day. My mother was wrong. Humans did survive the hunts, because I had. *I would not die here.*

3 2
LONNIE

I chased the fiddlehead sprite back in the direction opposite from the one I'd been walking. I could have kicked myself but vowed to kick Prince Bael instead for not giving me better directions. If he wanted to help during the next hunt, he should actually help.

We walked for a quarter of an hour seeing no one. The wind howled loud enough that it drowned out any sounds around me. Leaves kicked up, swirling like pinwheels near my feet and brushing by branches and grass against my face. It picked at the ends of my hair spinning.

The knife at my belt, taken earlier from Prince Bael, felt impossibly small compared to the swords that the others were no doubt carrying. My anxiety over both the emptiness of the forest and what would happen when inevitably we met another hunter warred in my mind, driving me near enough to madness.

The obsidian crown dug into my scalp and finally I gave up, using a strip of gauzy material from my ruined dress to tie it around my waist. I was less likely to drop it that way, anyway.

A tree branch cracked behind me and I whipped my head back. My heart beat against my chest, threatening to escape. There was nothing there. At least I thought there was nothing. I stared hard at the space between two trees, squinting, unsure if there was movement, maybe a bird, maybe one of the hunters.

This was it. This was how I died.

I stared at the ground, waiting for either the hunter to grab me or the plant to come alive and eat me again.

Except—the group of humans darted past my hiding place, but they were not pursuing me. A man sprinted between the trees ahead of them, one man versus five or six hunters. I grimaced, turning away, trying to tune out the sounds of carnage that no doubt would follow.

Not everyone entered the hunts for the crown. Many did so for their own grudges. My stomach churned. What would happen if I tried to intervene? Nothing. I'd only die faster, surely. That man was already dead and there was nothing I could do.

I stared back at the ground again, this time saying a silent prayer to Aisling for the souls of that man and the others who would inevitably die here tonight. Possibly my own prayer would apply to me soon enough.

The sprite tittered, pointing excitedly as we approached the base of a wide hill. My heart leapt. "The boundary?" I asked.

It squeaked. They didn't really speak, but that was as close to an affirmative as I felt I was going to get. I grinned and started up the hill.

Water—a combination of rain and sweat—poured down my face as I climbed. My fingers scrambled for purchase whenever my feet slipped and my chest was nearly ready to burst, but if I could just get across the water I could collapse then. Just a bit further.

I crested the top of the hill and nearly sobbed in relief when I spotted the boundary down at the base of the other side. The hill was flat on top, with no trees to mar my view of the landscape. A tiny plateau in the middle of the wood.

I sprinted across, pumping my arms, and panting. Putting on a burst of speed, excitement filled me. As I reached the other side, I skated to a stop, horror coating my skin. Icy dread washed over me.

It was too easy. Too quiet. Even with Prince Bael removing hunters, my curse of misfortune was bound to catch me eventually.

33

LONNIE

*I*t was less a hill, and more a cliff.

I teetered on the edge, peering down over the side. The side I had climbed wasn't very steep, but the opposite edge was rocky, with sharp boulders dotting the bottom.

That wasn't why I stopped.

Bodies. Dozens of them lay broken and twisted on the rocks, some of their necks at odd angles as if they'd run straight off the cliff in the dark and plunged to their deaths. I looked over at the sprite and its lantern, and gave it a relieved nod of thanks.

Winged insects hovered lazily over the bodies, some landing on their exposed skin, others drifting in the air above them. I squinted, unsure what I was looking at. Flies didn't float like that, and it was too soon for flies to set in anyway. Not when presumably these hunters had just died.

The wisp buzzed around my head, humming in agitation, and I looked up at it again as its light illuminated more of the rain-soaked hillside.

Before I could investigate further, a shout sounded behind me. Footsteps pounded across the flat ground of the hill, too fast to be a human, and I lost my breath as someone slammed into me. Pain shot through my back as I hit the ground, landing hard on the sharp points of the crown I'd tied to my waist. I whimpered as a heavy weight landed on top of me and dizziness washed over me.

The leering face of a Fae I did not recognize looked down at me. "Where is it?" He said roughly.

I gasped, unable to speak as he pressed down on my windpipe.

He pulled a knife and held it to my throat and my heart pounded wildly. "Give it to me, Slúagh bitch."

I struggled to focus, my eyes darting back and forth in panic, even as the pain in my back threatened to make me pass out. He was looking for the crown. The crown currently stabbing me in the back—literally.

Well, in that case, he'd kill me anyway as soon as he held the crown in hand. He didn't even really need to hold the thing— only to kill me, but maybe he didn't realize that. He didn't seem too bright.

The fairy spoke again, yelling something in my face I couldn't process. Blackness seeped in around the edges of my vision.

Then, an odd buzzing filled my brain. I was losing too much blood. *Hallucinating.*

Or, I blinked confused, as the buzzing grew louder. *Perhaps not.*

White, winged insects were suddenly everywhere. Swarming the man on top of me, diving at him, attacking his face and arms.

"Ah!" He waved his arms wildly. "Get off!"

He leapt off me and tried to bat the things away. I lay there, unable to move for the pain in my back as the bugs overtook him. I blinked, trying to clear my vision. Moths, I thought. Moths with…

"Ow! Ah!" The man screamed, dancing back and forth as the moths attacked every part of him, stinging him over and over with scorpion-like tails. He backed away from their cloud. My eyes grew wide, and my stomach roiled.

He backed up, further and further until he reached the edge of the cliff. It was dark, and the stingers just kept coming for him. I winced and closed my eyes as understanding dawned. Those people at the bottom hadn't run off of the cliff for no reason.

But then, why had the moths ignored me?

Raindrops pounded on my face, refusing to let me pass out. I took a deep breath and pain rocked me. I needed to roll over. Needed to move. I was so close to the boundary, if only I could make my way there.

I rolled over and let out a shriek of pain as the crown dislodged itself from my skin. *Shallow,* I told myself. *It's shallow.*

But now, I had other problems, because the buzzing was growing louder again.

And this time, I was the only one on the hill.

Where the hell was Prince Bael? If this was his definition of protection, he needed to reevaluate his grasp of the common tongue.

If I had to choose death by a thousand moth stings or death from falling over the edge of a cliff, I wasn't sure which was worse. At the moment, however, I couldn't have gotten up to run if I tried.

I closed my eyes and bit my tongue, holding in a whimper as I curled onto the ground with my hands over my head.

No pain came.

I looked up, and yelped. The moths fluttered in a cloud some two feet away. My fingers grappled in the dirt as I tried to roll away.

The cloud morphed, growing larger as they swarmed. A scream tore from my throat and burning pain lanced my body as the first sting hit my arm. Then another and another, each one seeming to magnify the pain tenfold.

Wings fluttered everywhere, batting against my face and arms, and I sobbed; the pain was too great to form coherent thoughts. I blinked in and out of consciousness.

Something touched my face, and I opened my eyes a sliver. White specks. Like ash, or snow, rained down over my head, only for the rain to wash it away a moment later. If I could have laughed, I would have. I was hallucinating, clearly.

Something too hot touched my skin and then I was floating.

"You are far too breakable, little monster."

34
BAEL

J raised a hand and the scorpion moths disintegrated into dust all around the girl. I sucked in a deep breath, more annoyed than I should be. This was something I had not foreseen.

Any fairy child would have known that scorpion moths were only dangerous if one was foolish enough to make noise in their presence. They were blind and had no sense of smell. No sense of direction or ability to reason. They lurked in the dark, catching travelers unaware. All one had to do to avoid them was stand still.

The girl's skin was covered in angry red welts, and blood soaked her dress. I could already see this as being a large flaw in my developing strategy for the coming year. This...Lonnie—that could not be her real name—was going to get herself killed with no help from me or any of my family.

I reached down and lifted her into my arms. She barely reacted. "You are far too breakable, little monster."

I looked out over the edge of the hill and swore. The boundary was in sight, but I couldn't carry her across it—could I?

The rules of the hunts were not specific about such things, but the uproar would no doubt make such a spectacle not worth it, anyway.

I wrinkled my nose, and the cut on my lip pulled, stinging. That cut was proof enough I'd already pissed off the family enough today.

Earlier, when the horn sounded, I'd watched her sprint into the forest. At least she hadn't waited for permission. I had been certain I would have to tell her she was allowed to move.

Aine looked sideways at me, crossing her arms over her chest as we waited for the second horn to allow the hunters to give chase. Even out of the corner of my eye, I could see that my sister was smiling. "Well," she said, sidling closer so only I could hear. "That was quite a display."

I didn't make a habit of battling females, but for Aine I'd make an exception. "Stop," I bit out, staring straight ahead. "I'm not in the mood."

"When you said you had a plan, I will admit I didn't picture this."

I shot her a mutinous look. "You did not have to involve yourself."

"I know and I still may not."

"Fair."

I hadn't pictured this either. I'd assumed when I went to find the girl she would be in better condition. For the love of the Source, I couldn't imagine what Scion had been thinking.

I opened my mouth, intending to say I was going to murder our cousin, and the words got stuck in my throat. I coughed, pain tearing at my tongue. *Fuck.* "I'm going to find Scion's foul bird and bake it into a pie for yuletide."

There. I'd yet to catch the pestiferous pigeon, and it wasn't for lack of trying, but if I could find the thing I wholly intended to follow through on that threat.

Aine raised an eyebrow. "I look forward to seeing you try."

In unison, we both looked around. Neither Scion nor his damned bird were anywhere to be found. I narrowed my eyes.

I scanned the crowd waiting to run into the forest. The first hunt was my least favorite. It was odd, as I'd never actually attended any of them, but I'd spent enough time conversing with the dead to feel as if I had been there.

I was probably too glib in saying that Lonnie should be able to run straight to the river. The Waywoods posed an unfortunate hunting ground—both due to the difficulty of navigating between the trees and because of all the miserable things lurking in there. Now though, I was almost glad the season always began in the woods. There were hundreds of Fae waiting to chase after the little monster. I supposed the best that could be said was the Unseelie hadn't shown up as well.

"I knew there would be many, but this is extreme," I hissed.

Aine followed my line of sight. "Why involve yourself at all?"

"I like chaos."

That was true, but not the reason and her expression told me she knew that. "You also have no great affection for that girl, I can tell, so what's the point?" Her eyes widened. "Is this to do with Sci's letter?"

"It's not."

It wasn't. *Not entirely.*

"You know Grandmother Celia was vague at best."

"I know."

I knew that better than anyone. I knew, and hoped that she'd been too vague with all her predictions for me.

The second horn sounded, and the crowd surged around us, darting toward the trees. I let them run for a minute. It wouldn't be hard to catch up. Glancing sideways at Aine, I frowned. "You don't think Sci is so self-loathing he'll do something reckless...do you?

"Like what?"

"Like try to kill my queen despite knowing what will happen if he does?"

She laughed. "So, she's your queen now?"

I waved a hand. "In a metaphorical sense. Like chess."

She thought about it, swinging her arms at her sides as though she were out for an afternoon stroll. "Not tonight..." She didn't sound sure. "But in a day or so? Yes, that's exactly what I think Scion will do."

I sighed and ran a hand through my hair. "Yes. That's what I think too."

I couldn't blame him exactly. If I'd been left that letter, I would likely do the same.

Fuck, I was also following the directions of a dead woman. It just seemed that for the first time in our immortal lives, my cousin and I had been given opposite directives.

I looked down at the human again, yanking my thoughts back to the present. It had taken me too long to get here. Looking down at the half-dead woman in my arms, I grimaced. All my carefully laid plans were going to come crashing down because this damn human couldn't stay alive on her own.

I crossed the hillside, back toward the edge furthest away from the cliff, and lay her down on a flat stone. To my surprise, a tiny sprite danced after me, lighting the way and reflecting off the rain.

I had no problem seeing in the dark, but it wasn't entirely unwelcome. Still, how novel. The Underfae were usually terrified of us and would clear the area for miles whenever one of the High Fae was around. I looked down at the human and furrowed my brow. Strange.

She let out a moan of pain and I flinched. I wished, not for the first time, that I could heal by normal means. She would need Gwydion for that–though, I wasn't entirely sure he'd be able to heal her. A moot point, I supposed.

Giving the human more of my blood now was not only foolish, it was borderline insane. Still, I couldn't think of any other way to help her. Grimacing, I raised my own hand to my mouth and bit down hard on my palm, the metallic taste of my own blood filled my mouth.

"Here," I pressed my hand to her mouth. "Come on, drink that."

She didn't move and I froze, dread washing over me. *Fuck.*

Her heart was still beating, I could hear it, but for how long? What would happen if I couldn't make her drink?

I glanced around, as if an idea would appear out of the trees, and a terrible thought struck me. An idea that I had no business considering. I shook my head. No. No, that was asking too much of me.

Feeding the human my blood had been wicked enough, particularly as she clearly had no understanding of the implication or potential aftereffects of that act.

I glanced back at the girl and the obsidian crown glinted where it was tied around her waist. Blood dripped down its points. My stomach lurched. She should really be dead already. Like she should have died in that cell, and surely countless other times if she was always as rude as she'd been to me. Most Fae would have ripped out her tongue. I found it oddly fascinating.

I rubbed my hand over the back of my neck and looked over my shoulder again. *Why?*

I looked down at my hands, then to her, unsure how to do this even if I wanted to.

I'd obviously never attempted it–none of us had. If she really was human, only human, with no magic, it would kill her. Though, if she was human she was dying anyway, and I was sure there was something there.

Then I reached for her hand. Her skin was hot, despite the rain and the cold evening. I'd certainly touched enough humans to know that was abnormal. Too hot. Like the Fae. Like she was burning from within. Perhaps that was a good sign that I wasn't wasting my time with this.

I closed my eyes, already regretting this, and bit down on her hand as well. Her blood flooded my mouth for a moment, and I struggled to stay in control of myself. The animal in the back of my mind roared and I shook with the effort of maintaining a hold on the monster.

My whole life, I'd been well aware of my dark nature. Of the fact that my siblings weren't my full siblings. That my father was not my father.

It had been abundantly clear to the entire family as soon as my magic developed that it was not a power found within house Everlast. I was sure I would have been exiled, if not for my mother pleading with her mother, insisting I could be trained. Controlled.

So, my grandmother had me trained to control my emotions. I was taken out of the line of succession, before they even knew what my magic would turn out to be. I was taught not to indulge in my baser instincts or allow my father's nature to come out. Even so, I was sure Celia would have removed me eventually, if not for the fact that I was stronger than all of them. Except perhaps Scion—we made a conscious effort to never test it.

And we'd never come as close to breaking that pact as we had tonight.

I pulled the girl's hand from my mouth, licking her blood from my lips. She tasted like magic and honey. I would never get that taste out of my mouth again, and that wasn't even the best reason for not indulging in what I was about to do.

I pressed her bleeding palm to mine, our blood mixing, and watched with bated breath. This wasn't enough blood or enough contact. Not really, but unless I stripped her down right here, this was going to have to work. Anyway, with so little blood it would wear off in a matter of days. A few weeks at most—at least I hoped so.

An achingly long moment later, the human went as still as a statue.

Her chest rose off the rock, her back arching, and she slammed back down. Then, her huge brown eyes opened wide, taking up even more of her face than they already did. She'd stopped breathing, I could hear it.

I waited a long moment, then another to see if she would breathe again. Frustration pricked at my skin. Humans were so easily rattled, keeping them alive was practically impossible. She gasped finally, as though remembering to breathe, and it was all I could do not to offer her congratulations for not dropping dead.

"What...what's going on?" She asked, looking around. Then, as if realizing where she was, she yanked her hand back. "Don't touch me."

I almost laughed. Now, I couldn't even if I wanted to. "Believe me, I won't"

35
LONNIE

I pulled back from the prince, confused and disoriented. Though, I noticed with mingled relief and suspicion, I was no longer in pain.

"What did you do?"

"Saved your life," he said curtly. "You could thank me. Or not, it makes no difference to me, really."

I sat up a little straighter. I was not foolish enough to thank a fairy. They would take that as acceptance of a favor and demand repayment. "I would not have needed saving if you had fulfilled your oath to help me in the first place, so no, I don't think I owe you any thanks."

He laughed humorlessly and I was surprised to see that for once he wasn't grinning. "My apologies," he made a mock bow. "I erroneously thought that by removing anyone who wished to kill you from your path you would be able to walk in the woods unimpeded. I should have realized that you would find a way to die that a child could avoid."

I spluttered, sitting up, and my head spun. Something was...off. I felt both dizzy and filled with energy at the same time. "What is wrong with me?"

"Nothing that won't wear off."

"But—"

"The boundary is just on the other side of the hill," he cut me off and I blinked at him as he seemed to blur around the edges. "Do try not to die between here and there, I'm not sure I can stomach it."

"Wait—"

But the air shifted, and he was gone.

J dragged myself down the hill and nearly collapsed a dozen times before making it to the boundary.

My throat burned and my breath heaved, my chest ready to bust, as a bone-chilling cold seeped into my skin, everywhere the gauzy gown still clung to me. Tears poured down my cheeks, more out of exhaustion than pain. Though the pain would come, I knew, as soon as the adrenaline ebbed from my body. It was not something I looked forward to.

A crowd of Fae watched on the opposite side of the boundary and I could not even find the energy to scowl at them. They stood beneath tents like those in the clearing at the feast last year, trying to stay out of the rain. Some held wine goblets, while others simply jeered as I staggered through a break in the stone and collapsed on the hard, muddy ground in a sweaty, bloody, heap, not caring who watched. There was every chance this would be my ultimate resting place.

"Does she have it?" someone yelled.

"Where's the crown?"

I imagined myself lifting the cursed thing over my head in victory. Screaming my win for all to hear. I imagined it and did not move. I couldn't move. I might never again.

The voices melded together, some angry, others curious. I couldn't focus on any one voice. Not, I reasoned, that I would have recognized anyone in the crowd, anyway. Anyone who cared about me was either dead or didn't know I was here, and anyone I had the misfortune of meeting in the last several hours had hopefully drowned in the river or was in the belly of some infernal stinging moth behind me.

Heavy footfalls sounded near my head, and I cracked one eye open. I couldn't move my head to look at whomever it was, nor did I wish to.

"Well. I can't say I'm glad you made it, but I can say I'm surprised."

I groaned into the ground. I did know that voice. "If you're going to kill me, do it now. If not, leave me alone."

Prince Scion laughed. "Your insistence on bringing up your own murder is only going to give others ideas."

"You don't need any encouragement, I'm sure you'll get there on your own."

He didn't reply. I took that to mean I was correct.

I waited for the retreating footsteps, instead I felt him shift beside me, bending to pick up the crown I'd dropped some-where to my right. I supposed I should have cared, but I couldn't bring myself to move. I didn't want it anyway—maybe he would leave me alone if all he wanted was the damn crown.

"Shall I congratulate you on your win?" It sounded like he'd walked around to my left side. "Or would that be inappropriate given the circumstances?"

I sat up enough to look at him. He leaned against the nearest tree, spinning the obsidian crown between his long fingers. He hadn't taken any of his absurd silver rings off, even to hunt. One would think they would get in the way of wielding a sword. But then, he probably didn't use a weapon. Didn't people say that this prince leveled villages with just a wave of his hand?

"What circumstances?" I muttered, the metallic taste of blood still strong in my mouth.

He smirked. "There is no chance you managed this if it had been a true competition."

What an insufferable prick. "What does that mean?"

"Only that any real competitor was threatened not to take part. That will not happen again."

I furrowed my brow, confused. I hadn't realized.

"Also," he continued. "That even with that advantage, there is no chance you managed this on your own."

Scion's eyes darted to the side, as though whoever helped me might appear out of thin air behind me. It wasn't as absurd a notion as I would have thought before today. Still, it was all I could do not to roll my eyes.

"Is it not true that your house usually hunts as a group?" I asked, trying to ignore the pounding in my head.

He stared at me, pausing the spinning of the crown. "Your point?"

"One could say that you cannot manage the game on your own...my lord."

His casual smile slipped, turning into a sneer. "We shall see about that next month." He tossed the crown back at me hard enough that the air left my lungs as I caught it against my chest. "Enjoy your win. It will be your last."

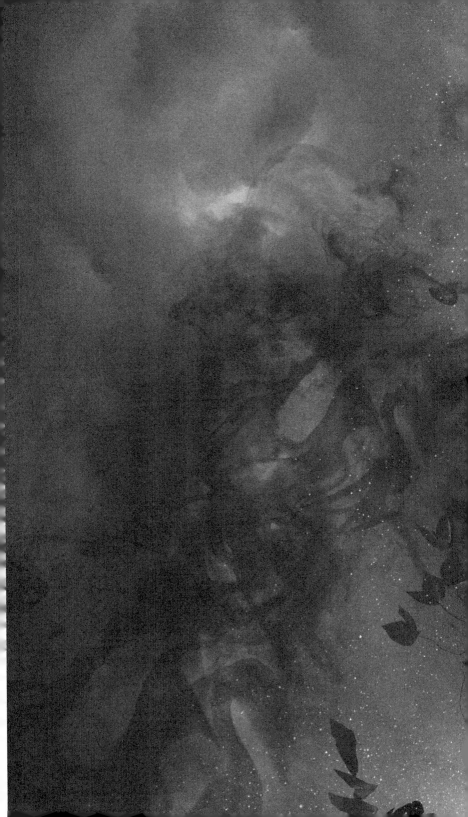

PART III

THOSE WHO DREAM BY DAY ARE COGNIZANT OF MANY THINGS
WHICH ESCAPE THOSE WHO DREAM ONLY BY NIGHT

— EDGAR ALLAN POE, "ELEONORA."

36

LONNIE

*T*he sharp bark of the tree pricked painfully at my back, but I didn't care. It didn't matter. Nothing mattered. Nothing but the hands gliding over my hips, and the lips pressing soft kisses on the curve of my neck.

Long fingers ran up my thighs, pushing my skirt up around my waist, and heat pooled in my core. Warmth coated my skin and I moaned as smoke wrapped around me. Whispering, caressing every part of my body.

"I…" I heard my own voice, breathy and too far away. I bent my head to the side, no idea what I was asking for, but I needed something. Now. "I want—"

A darkly hypnotic laugh wrapped all around me. "Ask nicely."

I looked up at Prince Bael's disarming yellow-gold eyes and whimpered. "Please."

His grin was feral. "Good girl."

He grasped my hips, pressing me down exactly where he wanted me, and that heat overtook me. I wriggled impossibly closer, wanting to soak up every drop of him.

He ran his mouth over my neck and my back arched. I gasped, my pulse beating a violent tattoo where his teeth grazed. Just barely nipping. Just enough to sting.

"I'm going to devour you, little monster. You taste like magic."

A knock sounded at my door and I sat up violently in bed, disoriented. My heart thrummed too fast. I pressed a hand to my forehead and it came back wet from the sweat coating my brow. Mother of all that is…

A knock at my door and realized it was likely the second knock of the morning.

There was no smoke. No Prince Bael. My skin still tingled… and…shit. My entire body ached, both from the hunts and for…I squeezed my thighs together, horrified.

The knock sounded again and I looked toward the door, panicked. It was too much to hope that I could simply sleep. Or rather, wallow in my current shame uninterrupted. Surely, this was my first assassination attempt. Perhaps a mercy after such a dream.

"Who's there?" I asked tentatively through the door. No one replied. Maybe they didn't hear me. "Who's there?" I said again a bit louder.

"Your Majesty?" A female voice asked, tentatively.

"Iola we've discussed this!"

The knock came again, louder this time, accompanied by a garble of uncomfortable greetings. "Your maj…Lonnie—Er, miss, Eil…Well…"

I blinked the sleep from my eyes, turning to look at the sun coming in through the tower window. "I'm coming!"

Though I'd only met the girl once, I was quite sure it was the slightly erratic maid outside my door. She seemed the only one who would be so painfully unable to settle on a way to say good morning.

I threw my covers off and swung my legs over the side of the bed. Giving myself a firm shake, I tried and failed to ignore my racing pulse. The mind plays tricks. I was grateful to be out of the dungeon and that was all. It meant nothing.

Though, I thought, as I went to let Iola inside, this particular trick had reminded me of something that until today I'd been too tired and distracted to think about in depth: How could one taste of magic?

*I*ola was a whirl of excitement when I finally let her inside my—or rather, Prince Scion's—tower room.

I was locked in anyway—clearly, the Everlasts did not want me wandering the palace overnight—but I'd closed the deadbolt, feeling like perhaps I needed the extra level of security. Mostly on the off chance the prince decided he wanted his room back overnight and came to take it back. Not that the deadbolt was likely to keep him out, but I might have some warning.

"You did well!" Iola cried. "I knew you would, but I was worried, but not exactly, but I was. You know that feeling?"

"Mmmm," I mumbled

"Not a morning person?" Iola asked brightly.

"Not a life person at the moment," I replied darkly.

"Right," she said, grimacing animatedly at the bruising still evident on my legs. "Sorry about that."

I stared at her. I'd never met anyone quite so excited or so loud this early in the morning. With a pang, I was reminded oddly of my sister. Who had never been precisely loud, but always happier than me. Always more the optimist. Iola was different, but I could find Rosey in the strangest places.

She stared at me expectantly and I thought I must have missed a question. "Sorry?"

"What would you like to wear today?"

I picked at the edge of my nightgown. "This?" I smiled. "And you don't need to dress me, I can do it on my own."

She tsked. "I was told to help. We could find you an official maid I suppose, but that might be worse since you worked with them."

I nodded. That would be exponentially worse. I already felt horrible enough, sleeping in the lovely tower room Prince Bael had brought me to that first night. It made my skin crawl. As if I'd sold my soul already to the Fae for a few creature comforts, and nothing I said to myself banished that feeling.

With that in mind, my preference was certainly no maid. Well, except perhaps when it came to my hair. If she was offering, I was more than happy to let Iola brush my hair. I'd do hers in return, if she liked.

"In any case," she said, crossing to the wardrobe and throwing it open. "You cannot wear that. Not down to breakfast."

"I am not going to breakfast."

She gave me an odd look. "How else do you intend to eat?"

"I could go to the kitchen. Beira would feed me." She waved that off as if it were ridiculous and I scowled. "What is wrong with that?"

She wrung her hands. "It just doesn't seem right, and I don't think I'm allowed to let you wander around alone."

I frowned. Well, that answered one of my questions I supposed. I might not be locked in the dungeon, but my leash was still quite short. "It doesn't seem right to me to eat alongside Fae who want to kill me."

She fell silent, seeming to struggle to find an argument for that. "Alright. I'll tell Lady Thalia."

"Who is Lady Thalia?" I asked, more fiercely than I really intended. But really, I hadn't gotten a sufficient answer yesterday and I expected one now.

Iola raised her eyebrows at me. "She's betrothed to Lord Gwydion. I thought you met her last night."

"Oh," I said. Well, that wasn't very interesting. "Why does Gwydion's mate care what I do?"

She glanced to the side, uncomfortable. "Ask her yourself. At breakfast."

I scowled, but no matter how much I needled, Iola refused to continue discussing her true mistresses' secrets.

"No."

She sighed. "Fine. But at least get dressed."

I glanced at the enormous bathing chamber. Perhaps I could swallow my pride in favor of another bath.

*A*n hour later, I'd been bathed, combed, and primped to Iola's liking. She laced me into a pink silk gown I considered far too nice for breakfast, but she found "delightful," and finally she wore me down. In truth, the promise of food after a year without much at all was still a fierce motivator.

As we walked down the long hall to the dining room, shouts of laughter in the corridor up ahead made me go stiff, freezing where I stood. Two nobles walked in the opposite direction, their long gowns trailing on the floor behind them. They spoke in high, carrying voices despite having their heads bent together as though to whisper.

"No wonder they're worried, can you imagine?" one said.

"No!" her friend replied. "I could never...but I would watch I suppose. Maybe."

I started to bend my head as Iola did, staring at the floor as they passed, as I'd been trained to do since childhood. Just a servant, on my way to do my chores...

We came to an awkward impasse as they walked by, leveling with me. They glanced at each other, then at me, taking in every inch of me, their expressions were matching masks of distaste. Hatred. And that old look I knew too well—interest.

A prickle of old fear crept up my spine and my ear seemed to burn. What did they want? Why were they staring at me?

Then, without warning, they bowed their heads in a quick curtsy.

"My lady," they muttered mutinously, before hurrying away.

I stood there for a full minute, gaping after them, the shock washing over me.

"Are you alright?" Iola asked, seeming bemused.

"Er...yes. Sorry."

She shrugged. "No need."

Iola split off from me and disappeared down to the kitchens as I crossed the entrance hall and headed toward the dining room. I'd never been inside, apart from occasionally being asked to sweep or tidy up after a meal, and my heart pounded against my chest as I approached the door.

I did not notice the footsteps behind me until a hand touched my shoulder. I whirled, coming face to face with a pair of yellow eyes.

I jumped back, my entire body quivering as my dream came back to me in full force. My lips parted, and heat washed over me. I swallowed, my throat suddenly dry.

37

LONNIE

*B*ael cocked his head at me and I wanted to die. "You're quiet this morning."

I couldn't breathe for humiliation. "Hello."

"I've been waiting for you."

I walked pointedly toward the dining room, my cheeks hot. "Why?"

"How are you feeling today?" He looked at me with expectation, as if he were worried I might turn blue or grow an extra eye in the middle of my forehead.

I bit my lip. "Er…"

Now that I thought about it, I felt…too good. I hadn't thought to check for scrapes or bruising this morning, but I certainly didn't feel like I had any. My muscles didn't ache like they should, either from my year underground or the exertion of last night. I wasn't even as hungry as I felt I should have been.

I narrowed my eyes. "Fine. Why?"

"Merely curious."

"Right."

Bael fell into step beside me. "Where are you going?"

I scowled at him. I hoped he didn't think we now had to spend time together. Didn't he have other things to do? I jerked my head toward the dining room doors behind me. "Was I not summoned?"

He wrinkled his nose as if eating with the rest of the court was beneath him. "We don't eat there."

I swallowed my opinion of his elitist tone. "We, as in…"

As usual, he took no care to elaborate, simply seizing my elbow and guiding me down the hall to our left. "As I was saying." He spoke with the same annoying, grandiose nature he often used, as though everything was a joke. "I was waiting for you. I wanted to tell you I've decided you will begin training."

"For?"

"Not dying."

"Isn't that what you promised to do for me?"

He nodded sagely. "Yes, but unless you want me with you every moment of every day. By your side. Breathing your air. Sleeping in your bed—which I'm not entirely opposed to, I might add—you need to become less useless than you are now."

He said all of that in one breath and I goggled at him, unsure if it was an invitation to his bed or an insult. Either was unwelcome, but lessons in how to kill him? That would be alright. "So, fighting lessons?" I clarified.

"Correct. The second hunt will be here before you know it."

"When is it? *Exactly*."

He ran a hand through his hair and his smile turned wicked. "You say that as if you don't trust me. It's two weeks from yesterday, so you have thirteen days to become less breakable than you are now."

I frowned. That sounded next to impossible. "Fine. But let us begin tomorrow."

I wasn't sure I could stand to be in his presence for much longer. Not without constantly blushing.

We came to a sudden halt in front of a set of ornate obsidian doors I'd never seen before. I stared up at them, towering over me like the face of jagged cliffs. "What is this?"

Bael didn't look at me, his tone flat, posture unconcerned. "The other dining room."

I raised an eyebrow at the too-ornate doors. As though hearing my unspoken question, Bael glanced back at me, the doors still half-closed, blocking my view of the room beyond. "You've never been invited."

"Invited?" My voice sounded far away to my own ears—the very definition of shock and awe. Shock at my recent acquaintance with a dagger, awe from this entire interaction.

"There are countless rooms in the palace that appear only when invited."

He left his statement hanging—the implication that I needed to be here now lost on neither of us.

"Then who cleans it?" I blurted out, feeling like I needed to fill the silence. "If no humans are let inside?"

Bael furrowed his brow. "I didn't say no humans were let inside. I said you weren't."

The prince turned his back, pushed the doors the rest of the way open, and stepped forward, expecting me to follow. I followed him, trying not to feel like an obedient hound trotting after its master.

I gasped, unable to hold in my reaction. The room glittered—or more accurately, glowed. As if built to reflect the Fae themselves, everything was bathed in a dark, luminescent light. It took me a moment to realize that it was also an illusion, though likely not due to magic this time.

The entire room—floor, walls, ceiling, even the long dining tables were built from gleaming obsidian. Like the doors, every-thing had been carved with intricate angles and shapes, like a million jewels when it was just one continuous surface.

I froze, as I took in the entire house of Everlast sitting around the long, shining table, halfway through a breakfast of decadent fruit, bread, and what looked like some sort of roast bird. I wasn't sure what I had expected, but it certainly wasn't that. Unlike last night, they had not all turned to look at me. Instead, they seemed to be ignoring me intentionally. Eating as if nothing were amiss.

Bael reached for me, seeming about to ask another question, but was interrupted as a Fae male came rushing toward us with quick efficiency.

He wore an anxious expression and waved to prince Bael with one boney hand in an erratic way that appeared half greeting, half urgent insistence that he move faster. In response, Bael stopped walking entirely.

"Good morning, Mordant," Bael said cheerfully, as the male reached us. "You seem..." he trailed off, before finishing with: "The same as always."

My eyes widened at the name. I'd heard Rosey, and even my mother on occasion mention Mordant of Nevermore, the advisor to Queen Celia. He was tall and statuesque with pale skin and narrow lips. His long, white hair was tied back in a knot on the top of his head that gave his already angular face an even harsher appearance.

"My lord," the male said in a slightly fussy tone, glaring daggers at Bael.

I wondered if this Mordant didn't like Prince Bael personally—which I empathized with—or if he was annoyed at his lateness. Or perhaps that he had to speak in deference to a prince who was no longer a prince and clearly hundreds of years this male's junior. Any of those reasons would be enough to cause Mordant's frustration, in my opinion. I smiled up at him, offering a silent look of camaraderie. Even if he was High Fae, he was also a servant.

"I see you've brought the Slúagh. That's…It's only, we haven't set enough places at the table."

My smile evaporated. This was what I got for having the smallest bit of empathy. "I do not want to be here, anyway," I told Bael. "I can just go."

"Don't concern yourself with Mordant, little monster," Prince Bael said, rather loudly. "I certainly never have. I have considered killing him on many occasions but then I remember that his entire existence surrounds serving the whims of my mother, and that is the cruelest punishment I could ever think of for anyone."

Across the room, Lady Raewyn laughed, and threw an indulgent look at her younger son.

Mordant, to his credit, did not react. "Lord," he said flatly. "I will…see what we can do about locating another place setting."

If I had not known exactly how many plates there were below floors, the whole thing would not have seemed so absurd. I tore my eyes away from the old advisor's surly face and looked back at the Everlasts...and the room as a whole.

About ten servants stood against the wall, their eyes cast down at the floor, trays of more food and jugs of wine clutched in their hands. I recognized all of them and knew at least half by name. None had been particularly kind to me in the past, but I still couldn't stomach eating with the Fae while they stood by and watched.

"Never mind," I said under my breath, taking a step back. "I would rather starve."

38

LONNIE

"We can arrange that," Bael said cheerfully. "But I would take no pleasure in it, and it certainly wouldn't make any of our lives easier."

"Why would you think I care what pleases you?"

He frowned. "Most do."

"Give them my portion." I pointed at the servants, and from the way they shifted slightly I was quite sure they could hear me. "I'm sure they haven't eaten today, and they've been awake far longer than I have."

A mocking laugh rang across the room, and I whirled knowing I would come face to face with Prince Scion. I glared. *What? What's funny?*

Scion sat at the head of the table, watching me over the rim of his water glass. His expression said all too clearly that he thought I *should* starve.

Beside me, Bael sighed in exasperation. "I am not made for this, I hope you know."

"Made for what?"

He didn't answer. When I looked up, he wasn't looking at me. Instead, he stared across the room at Scion, as if talking to him. I supposed they could likely hear each other just fine, but still...odd.

Bael blinked and looked back down to me. "Eat, and then you can give whatever you want to the servants. I don't fucking care if they eat or not, so they may as well feast."

I narrowed my eyes. That wasn't a kind statement. Far from it, but it was indifference in my favor and I would take it. "Fine."

On one end of the table, Scion sat at the head. There was an empty chair to his right that Bael immediately filled, and on his left was a brunette woman I recognized as Scion's mother, Mairead.

The Lady Mairead was a mystery to me. She had been mated to Prince Scion's father, Prince Belvedere, until he died some twenty years ago. She later remarried to Belvedere's brother, Penvalle, and had two more children: Lysander, the angry teenager from the hunt, and Elfwyn, who was barely ten years old.

No longer a queen, Mairead still dressed and held herself like one. She bore little resemblance to her eldest son in looks, but she was a match in the haughty way he looked down on everyone around him. Judging them without having to say a word.

On the other side of the table, Princess Raewyn sat next to her husband, Lord Auberon. Lady Aine sat to Auberon's left, the seat beside her empty. Of that trio, the only one eating was Lady Aine. Her parents were holding a whispered conversation, their attention entirely on each other as though no one else was in the room.

The other head of the table, Prince Gwydion turned around in his chair and smiled at me. He also had a vacant seat next to him, across from a blonde girl I had not immediately noticed. She was lovely, in a way that was so undeniable even a blind man would have known from the reactions of those around him. Her expression, however, was sullen.

Gwydion nudged the blonde and she looked up, beckoning to me. I hesitated only a moment before walking over to join her. Anything was better than standing alone in the center of the room.

"Good morning." The blonde gestured to the open seat across from her, beside Lady Aine. "Sit?"

I assessed Aine warily. As if feeling my gaze, Aine tilted her head very slightly in my direction. "I will not poison you, if that's what you're thinking."

"No," I said flatly. "I was thinking you might stab me with your butter knife."

She laughed lightly. "No. If I were to kill you, it would certainly be poison. I simply meant I would not do so today."

A sweet smile appeared on her face, a bit like Lady Raewyn, and a shiver traveled up my spine. I vowed to keep a better eye on Lady Aine from now on. While Raewyn gave off the impression of false innocence, I somehow doubted Aine was innocent at all. Merely unsure if or how she wanted to involve herself in the present situation.

"My name is Thalia," the lovely blonde said, pulling me from my musing. She nodded to me as I sat down.

"Oh." I opened my mouth in surprise. "Thank you."

She looked surprised now. "For what?"

"You sent Iola."

She gave me a flat expression that I took to mean she did not want to discuss it and we fell silent, my discomfort building. I wished I could ask her what Iola had meant earlier, but I did not dare bring it up. Not now. Not in front of the obviously listening royals.

"Lonnie!" Princess Raewyn called down the table, turning to face me with a vicious smile on her lovely face. "That's what they call you right? Or shall I call you 'Your Majesty'?"

Whatever hunger I had, left me, and I wished I could follow.

"Will you not answer?" Raewyn asked, when I said nothing. "I was simply going to inquire where you have left your stolen crown."

I looked up at that. "Stolen?"

"But of course," she trilled. "Try not to lose it darling. It's thousands of years old, you know."

I scowled. Stolen. I bit my tongue, resisting the urge to point out I had just as much right to the crown as she did. More, if I understood the rules correctly. I didn't want it but still, she had no right to speak to me as if I'd stolen anything from her.

Cutlery clattered against the fine golden plates and Prince Lysander leaned forward, putting his elbows on the table. "Queen of the Slúagh," he scoffed. "I'm not sure I can stomach eating with this filth."

I scowled. Raewyn was one thing, but this boy—this child— reminded me of another. Arrogant and cruel. I had no patience for that. Anger warmed my skin, and I met Prince Lysander's gaze.

He faltered, then laughed. As if trying to mimic Scion, but not quite managing to do so.

"Leave it, Sander," Lord Auberon said. "The Slúagh isn't worth your time. Someone will end her soon enough. If she happens to have an unfortunate accident before the next hunt, the crown will return to us."

My eyes met Prince Scion's across the room. If I died between hunts, the crown would go to him. So why was I still sitting here?

"Actually," Mordant said stiffly, taking a small step forward. We all turned to look at him. "That is not entirely true."

"What are you talking about, Mordant?" Raewyn said airily, barely sparing him half a glance.

Mordant had everyone's full attention. His back was perfectly straight, his expression haughty and dignified as he addressed the royal family. And me, I supposed.

To my surprise, he didn't answer Raewyn directly. Perhaps because she'd turned her back on him and was busy feeding a slice of fruit to her husband with almost unnecessary gusto.

"Do you have any family? Parents? Siblings?" He looked down his nose at me. "Children?"

My heart panged. I'd already had to bring this up once to Prince Bael, and it was no less painful now. "No. My family is dead."

"That's as I suspected." Mordant said with absolutely no sympathy. "So, if this…" he struggled for words. "*Interloper* dies."

I rolled my eyes at that.

"Then you will not become King, Sci," Aine finished for him. "No one will."

"Someone will," Scion snapped. He glared at me as if I'd done this on purpose. "You must have a living relative somewhere."

I shook my head. "Not that I know of."

"She's lying, obviously." Raewyn trilled in the same tone she used to say everything. "We will end up with a worse humiliation than the current one. Could you imagine? Next it'll be..." She cast around for what could be worse than me.

"An Unseelie," her husband chimed in.

To my surprise, Raewyn did not immediately agree with him. "No, Darling, I still think that might be better."

Bael cleared his throat. "Can we move along?"

Mordant drew himself up, clearly annoyed at having been interrupted. "Quite right," he said, a fussy tone to his already nasal voice. "Unless a next of kin can be found, a death outside the hunts would plunge the country into chaos."

"We're already in fucking chaos," Scion growled.

His only contributions to this conversation were evidently to complain rather bluntly. I glanced up at him, scowling, and my breath caught. He was already watching me.

His piercing silver eyes seemed to see through me, to the very core of my being. As if he were looking for the answers to all his unspoken questions.

"If I cannot kill you now, then I will simply have to end you during the next hunt," Scion hissed. "Don't worry, rebel, I can be patient."

39

LONNIE

$\mathcal{T}$he door to the banquet hall slammed behind me with an ominous, echoing, thump and I stared around, dubiously.

I stood alone in the hallway, staring up at the empty, stone stairs to the second floor without really seeing them. No footsteps from beyond the closed door sounded—no one chased after me, or had asked where I intended to go when I rose from the breakfast table. I supposed they didn't care? Or more likely, had forgotten to notice.

Still, Bael had said I could give the servants whatever food I liked. Which, I supposed, meant a trip to the kitchens.

The castle of House Everlast was as lovely as it was treacherous. Everywhere you looked, their symbol—a black crown surrounded by a wreath of ivy—jumped out at you. Tapestries and paintings hung on every free surface, and the eyes of the occupants seemed to follow me. Woven green and gold carpets covered the floors of the corridors, adding warmth and matching the emerald and sapphire stained glass of the high, arched windows.

I reached the top of the main staircase and paused, turning slowly in a half-circle. The palace was silent—almost suspiciously so. I'd half-expected to find guards stationed outside the door, either keeping me safe or confined, but not a single maid or guard crossed my path as I made my way down the winding corridors.

"Where are you going?" I whirled as the quiet of the hallway was broken by a snide question.

Thalia stood in the center of the hallway, staring at me as though she had been there for quite some time. I blanched. "The kitchens."

The statuesque blonde strode toward me, her long crimson gown swishing around her legs with every step. "Do not tell me you are trying to go back to work. That is so painfully depressing I cannot stomach it."

"What if I were?" I retorted, setting my jaw.

I wasn't going to the kitchens—far too many eyes would recognize me and see me leave if I went through that door, but that was the first thing that came to mind.

Thalia laughed. "As I said, do not tell me."

I barked a laugh in return. I did not understand this woman, nor did I care to, but she seemed less dreadful than the other High Fae. "Was there something you wanted?"

She looked down her nose at me. "No. I am on my way to the north tower, if you must know; you are simply in my path."

I was tempted to ask what the north tower was, but it barely mattered. Instead, I took a step back. "Well, I'll just go then."

"Wait," she called. "I'll walk with you."

I deflated. "Why?"

"Do you often ask so many questions?"

"Yes," I said honestly.

Thalia snorted an entirely unladylike laugh and put her hand to her mouth. "Well," she said flatly. "That will get you killed one day, I hope you know."

"I know."

She stared at me for a moment too long, then sighed and began walking again. "I don't have anything better to do than walk to the kitchens with a servant I suppose. There, do you feel better?"

I waited for half a second before following her. Thalia was probably just as bad as the rest of them, but I had the oddest feeling that maybe she didn't want to be here any more than I did. And that was interesting.

"You're not from here?" I asked her as we descended the stone steps to the second floor and turned into another long hallway.

"Why do you say that?"

I stiffened, wondering if she was angry, but she didn't seem to be. "Er, your clothing." I gestured her voluminous, crimson gown. "And your accent."

Elsewhere was made up of five lesser provinces, as well as the capital city. The bustling merchant city of Inbetwixt, the quiet marshlands of Overcast, the winter island of Nevermore, the dry deserts and mountains in the province of Underneath, and the toxic ruins of Nightshade, now known as Aftermath. Only the capital of Everlast had the kind of springtime climate where flowers grew year-round and the trees of the Waywoods could thrive. That, in addition to the ruling house, was the reason for its name. Nothing died in the capital. At least, not until recently.

"My uncle is Lord Auberon," she said. "I'm from Overcast."

"Oh," I answered. "So you're their cousin?"

She didn't ask what "they" I meant.

"In some sense," she waved a hand in the air as though warding off flies. "My mother is also Queen Celia's second cousin, or something to that effect. But I was actually sent as a bride for Prince Scion."

She said this nonchalantly, as if it were nothing of note. I gaped at her, unsure which strange thing needed to be addressed first. "But you're cousins," I said again.

"We are all related. There aren't that many Fae with strong magic left," she explained, somewhat defensively. "At least, not in this part of the country. It was decided years ago that I would be the next queen consort, regardless of who actually wears the crown…but circumstances change."

I blinked a few times, having no idea what to say. "Why?"

She snorted what sounded like a genuine laugh. "Our magic is quite compatible. Not that it matters."

I chewed on that for a few minutes as we walked. "What is your magical affinity then?"

She looked sideways at me. "What are you asking? What is mine? Or what is Prince Scions?"

"Both."

"In simple terms, we're illusionists. Most of the Everlasts wield some type of illusion. Scion has an affinity for causing pain."

"Ah." I had very little to say to that deeply unsettling revelation. "And you cause pain as well?"

"Not quite." She didn't seem to want to elaborate.

I rushed to change the subject. "And what of Lord Gwydion? You're betrothed now, correct?"

Her face turned sullen again, and for the life of me I couldn't understand why. "As I said," she muttered. "Things change."

Thalia deposited me in front of the kitchens, and I was struck with an overwhelming sense of homesickness. It was strange, as I'd hated nearly every moment of my time here. Now, in comparison to my current circumstances, it seemed wonderful.

The delicious smell of roasting meat and something I hoped was stew wafted out into the corridor and my stomach growled, despite having just eaten. I nearly moaned, my mouth watering. I pushed open the door to the kitchen and was met with the same flurry of activity I'd been used to for years. I almost sighed in relief at the familiarity.

All eyes turned to me as the door swung shut behind me.

I supposed I should have expected silence. I was used to people fearing me. Hating me. Thinking my tendency to attract Fae attention would somehow rub off on them. What I was not used to was people falling to their knees and bowing to me.

Like the Fae women upstairs, the servants immediately responded to my presence, though perhaps with a bit more gusto. Some bowed their heads, some dropped to the floor, some seemed actually pleased to see me—a novel experience.

Perhaps I had missed some of the reactions to my existence due to being cloistered by the Everlast family. Was that intentional— the isolation? Why?

The only faces who had not changed at all were Beira, busily stirring something on the stove, and Enid, who watched me warily from the back of the room. I smiled at her, and she gave a quick nod of acknowledgment in return.

"Don't bow," she said loud enough for them all to hear. "For the love of Aisling, it's Lonnie in a gown. And not even a nice one."

I opened my mouth to tell her she was nothing special either, and instead found a lump forming in my throat. I hadn't cried in a year. Not since I gave up crying in the dark of the dungeon, but there on the floor of the kitchen I sobbed.

*B*eira made tea and was happy to get started on food for the servants, only after I assured her that Prince Bael had said I could feed them all however I liked. Once I'd calmed down and was feeling calmer than I had in a year, I put my teacup down on the worktable and got to my feet. "I want to go look in my old room."

"You don't have to ask our permission." Enid said from where she was hovering by the fire.

"Oh. Er, I know."

I took a few steps in the direction of the hall, but she called after me. "There's nothing in there though."

My stomach sank. I'd known this was a possibility. It had been a year of course, but still. My lungs felt like a weight rested upon them. "What happened to everything?"

She narrowed her eyes somewhat defensively. "Your clothes went to other girls."

I nodded. Fair enough. That was a common practice when some-one...well, died. It happened often enough that no one got too close around here if they could help it.

She looked awkwardly to the side. "I don't think you under-stand how it was."

I shook my head. "Are you alright?"

Her eyes widened. "What do you mean?"

I gestured vaguely. "You were there. You know, when..."

She barked a harsh laugh and her eyes shuttered. "Oh. I don't remember anything."

She started walking in the direction of my room and I kept pace with her, caught somewhere between desperately wanting infor-mation and not wanting to upset her. She'd helped me once, sort of, but we weren't friends. Certainly not in a way where we would confide our feelings in one another.

"I remember Rosey—well you, I suppose—being taken by Prince Bael," she shuddered. "That was awful. It makes more sense now since it was you, you know? But that sort of thing never happened to Rosey."

In a morbid way I almost wanted to laugh. Enid hadn't changed much at all, and again, I found that oddly soothing. "I know. Rosey didn't, er," a lump formed in my throat. "Make waves."

"Exactly!" She said fiercely, as she stopped in front of the door that had been my bedroom. "I mean, you were always getting singled out, but not her. So, when the attack happened we thought it was you."

I nodded. "I know."

"The rebels didn't go after servants so most of us were fine. Shaken, you know? But alive. So, we were all trying to get back to the castle and then the hunts started...I think. I heard the horn. And then I don't remember much after that."

I raised my eyebrows. I supposed that made sense, but it was also strange. "Where were you?"

She leaned against the closed door and looked up, as if trying to remember. "The path out of the woods I think. I don't know. I remember coming to, like waking up from a dream, and I was back in the tent and you were there. I thought I was dreaming."

"How did you know it was me and not Rosey?"

She reached up and tapped her own ear. "That. And I just couldn't imagine that I would be anywhere like that tent with Rosey, even in a dream. If I was going to get pulled into shit like that, it was going to be your fault."

I choked. "I don't know what to say to that. Thank you, I suppose, for helping me."

She waved her hand. "Don't. I took all your clothes and the blankets off your bed and I'm not giving them back."

Fair enough.

I nudged her slightly out of the way so I could open the door and peer inside. She hadn't been lying, there was almost nothing left in the room. Enid looked vaguely smug about that.

My eyes darted to the windowsill where Rosey used to keep her journals and my heart throbbed painfully. "Enid," I asked. "What about Rosey's journals?"

She furrowed her brow. "What journals?"

I spun to face her, excitement coursing through me. "You know, she wrote all the time? She had all those journals, they were lined up over there." I pointed to where they used to be.

I couldn't believe I hadn't thought of this before. Rosey wrote down everything. Everything.

The mystery of why she'd done what she'd done had plagued me. Why had she been with the rebel group in the first place? Who was Dullahan and how did she know them?

Enid shook her head. "There wasn't anything there. When I came through here, there were clothes, blankets and a couple of novels, but no journals. I gave the novels to one of the new girls if you want to check."

I groaned in frustration. The journals had definitely been here the afternoon I went down to serve the court in Rosey's place. Did she move them, knowing what she was about to do and that she may not survive? Or were they moved afterwards?

Wondering any of this about my sister was so unusual. She hadn't been a rule breaker. As far as I knew, she didn't have anything interesting to write in a journal in the first place.

The only unusual thing I could recall in the months leading up to Rosey's death and my imprisonment was that she was ill. She'd gone out several nights to collect leaves from the moondust tree in the palace garden to make tea. A few times, I'd gone with her. I supposed she could have been meeting with someone then, but I hadn't seen anyone.

"Are you absolutely certain?" I asked Enid. "They weren't given away? Or...I don't know, sold?"

Not that I could think of a reason to buy them, but who knew?

She scowled. "Hey, I would tell you if there were. I don't give a fuck about what your sister was whining about when she was twelve. If you don't believe that, believe I care about not dying. I don't want to bow to you, but I understand that you have power now."

I scoffed. "By the Source! I wouldn't hurt you, Enid. I couldn't even if I wanted to."

She rolled her eyes, but said only, "And I wouldn't lie. They weren't there."

I nodded. "Alright."

Then I would have to assume that Rosey did something with them before she died...but what?

40

LONNIE

*J*walked back to my room alone. Or rather, to Prince Scion's room, as I had nowhere else to go.

After thirty minutes and several trips up the same staircase, however, I was forced to conclude—

"Lost?"

I whirled around. Prince Gwydion leaned on the banister of the same staircase I could swear had just been on the opposite end of the corridor. Behind him, the window outside showed the night sky. The one to its left displayed a bright orange sunrise. "Yes, I suppose so." I threw up my arms, frustrated. "But I have no idea how. I lived here for years."

He looked at me with a thoughtful expression. "True…but there are a lot of enchantments on the castle meant simply to ward off enemies and intruders. That's likely your problem."

"I'm not an intruder," I said hotly. "I'm a prisoner."

He waved a hand airily. "An enemy, then. Someone will simply have to walk with you at all times." He held out his arm. "Come on, I'll take you back to your room."

I gave Gwydion a suspicious look, torn between a desire to avoid him and anyone who shared his ancestry, and the fact that I had no idea where I was.

"Why bother?" I asked.

"You'll need to be more specific."

I supposed he'd sent Thalia too, now I thought about it. Or she'd sent him. One or the other. Like his brother, Gwydion was also nearly always smiling, though his expression seemed more genuine and less sinister.

"Why bother helping me?"

"Curiosity?" He said it like he was uncertain.

"You'll need to be more specific."

He laughed in an almost friendly way. "I'm a healer. I saw all the blood on your clothes last night, and I assumed you were also weak after the dungeon."

I thought about his words for a full minute before I replied. "You saw me bleeding and what…"

"And knew you should need a healer."

Hmmm. I contemplated that as we walked. He seemed like the most pleasant of the Everlast princes, and perhaps he was, but he was still a good side-stepper of questions.

"And do you intend to actually heal me, Prince Gwydion," I asked as we climbed the huge white marble stairs to the second floor. "Or do you mean to harm me?"

"To be frank, I am not all that concerned for your health. I am, however, curious why you should be dead but you look to be in fine health. Why is that?"

I shrugged. I wasn't sure I was supposed to mention what Bael had done to help me—not for his sake, but for my own. "You didn't answer my question."

"Ah. Don't worry, I heard Mordant. I don't think the country would be better off in the hands of some distant human cousin, or the rebel forces."

"So, it's better with me?" *Not that I was doing much of anything.*

"No, it's better with us. You are an inconvenient figurehead."

Ah. Fairy honesty. It was unpleasant in so many ways, and yet, usually correct. I wondered if there was anything I could actually do for whatever short time I had this shred of power. The idea seemed preposterous, but maybe...maybe there was something.

"Isn't healing me a bit pointless if you're going to murder me, anyway?" I asked, not really caring about the answer.

He laughed again. "I didn't say I was going to murder you."

I stared at him. His demeanor was a bit disconcerting. I'd never seen a happy noble. Well, except for Prince Bael, and I was fairly certain he was not so much "happy" as enjoyed showing off his teeth.

I crossed my arms. "You're not?"

"I haven't decided yet. The things that Bael wants to cultivate but Scion despises are usually either powerfully dangerous or very entertaining."

I shook my head. "I don't think so. Powerful is not a word I would use to describe myself."

He shrugged. "Maybe not. You smell different though."

I stopped walking abruptly. "Like what?" I said too quickly. "Is that why fairies are always so interested in me?"

He raised an eyebrow. "Fairies are what?"

I stepped back, wishing I hadn't spoken. "Never mind."

Gwydion gave me a mildly curious look, but to his credit he didn't press me on it. In fact, I realized as we passed door after door of guest rooms on our way back to my tower, he only seemed to be barely paying attention to what I was saying. That wasn't unusual for humans, but it was wildly out of character for the Fae. My entire adolescence and adult life, fairies had been fixated on me. Maybe because he had a mate?

"Your mate is Lady Thalia, correct?"

He paused. "Who told you that?"

I was taken aback. "Her maid has been helping me."

He laughed again. "Oh. I wondered if somehow she managed to give you that impression."

"She seems displeased?" I hedged, sure I was overstepping.

"She is. She will not get to have a mating ceremony at all until next year at the earliest."

"Why?"

"Because my entire family cares for her, though she refuses to see that."

I said nothing. I wasn't sure if that had anything to do with me or not—perhaps next year was arbitrary. Had nothing to do with the waves I had made in their coronation plans. Or perhaps it had everything to do with it.

As we approached the entrance to my tower, an enormous crash sounded from the floor below; Gwydion rolled his eyes. I looked over at him, alarmed.

He waved a hand as if to say it was nothing and reached for the handle to my door. "The library is one floor below here. Ignore that, it's Bael and Scion."

My eyebrows raised so high I was sure they disappeared into my hair. "A bit of light reading, I suppose?"

He laughed. "Those two are best friends and mortal enemies at the same time." He stepped aside so I could enter my room. Another crash echoed below and I shivered. Gwydion merely grinned. "I wouldn't worry. They've never had a reason to actually hurt each other. I can't think what would be that important."

*L*ater that evening, my curiosity got the better of me.

I'd been in the library before, of course, but my orientation within the castle since moving to the upper floors was all turned around. Intentionally so, I supposed. Trying to confuse me. If Gwydion had not mentioned their enchantments I would think I was losing my mind. Yet more proof of what I already knew—that Bael's theory of my magical immunity was false.

After dark, I tiptoed down the hall and the quiet of the castle rose around me, seeming to breathe like a living pulsing heart. Alive with deadly magic.

After what could have been minutes or hours, I found myself standing in front of a tall, curved wooden door. It reminded me of the dining room I never wanted to see again.

I pushed it open, hinges creaking with disuse. I was greeted by nothing except dust and darkness. Squinting into the black, a feeling of foreboding settled in my stomach. I hovered at the darkened mouth of the room, hesitant. Maybe I should turn back now.

The library was a vast cavern of books that stretched further than seemed truly possible in this part of the castle if you looked up at the tower from the outside. The walls should have ended, yet they simply didn't. Dusty tomes and scrolls in every color, some ancient and some new, covered mismatched shelves of wood and marble that ran from floor to ceiling in a labyrinth that probably shifted when it rained and every other Friday.

I took a deep breath, the scent of paper and, oddly, sulfur filling my nose as I took a few steps inside.

Without warning, a light within flared. I shielded my eyes, surprised by the sudden brightness.

Prince Scion sat in a chair by the window, a book in his lap and a candle on the table beside him. His eyes were narrowed at me, evidently angry at being disturbed. "You," he hissed.

I jumped, my heart leaping into my throat. "Sorry."

The noise had stopped hours ago and I'd assumed Bael and Scion had taken their squabble elsewhere. Not only that, but I hadn't pictured this male reading, but in practice it seemed quite natural.

He looked down his nose at me. "If you've come looking for secrets to send back to your traitorous kin, there's nothing here.

I already regretted apologizing for simply existing, and I set my jaw. "Once again, Prince Scion, you are more wrong than you could possibly imagine."

I wished I were working with the rebels. I wished I knew who the fuck to contact, especially since it was clearly going to get me killed anyway—really this was getting tedious.

"Of course," he said snidely. "And I suppose that's why you've demanded to go to Aftermath where the rebellion has the strongest foothold?"

My heart pounded against my chest "No, I—"

I broke off, giving him a flat stare. A spark of annoyance lit inside me that Prince Bael would reveal the details of our deal, but I supposed he had no reason not to. Anyway, I didn't owe Scion an explanation, nor was it smart to give him one. I shouldn't say anything about my family, and telling him I was born in Aftermath would likely only fan the flames.

I turned to leave. "I was only looking for something to read, but I can see this is more trouble than it's worth. Goodnight."

"Wait."

I stopped, my heart pounding. I heard the chair creak against the floor as he stood and his footsteps clacked toward. His arm brushed against mine as he passed me, and I couldn't breathe.

"You stay," he said darkly. "You are in far more dire need of reading material than I. Perhaps begin with the children's scrolls, Elfwyn outgrew her tutor years ago but I'm sure they left something around here somewhere."

I flushed. "I may not be as well read or well educated as you, but at least I use my words effectively."

He turned on his heel in the doorway, smirking at me. "Really? How so?"

"Go fuck yourself."

His expression turned sour. "Enjoy your temporary safety now, rebel. Your fate has already been foretold, and by the end of this year I will destroy you."

LONNIE

*T*he darkness seemed to press in around me. The space between trees shrinking, as the sounds of the hunters grew louder in the distance.

I glanced behind me, suddenly sure I could feel eyes on my back. Darkness stared back at me, endless but seemingly empty. Unbidden, fear tinged with the tiniest hint of excitement rose in my stomach.

They were coming.

Heat traveled over my skin, sparking with static energy.

I looked back again, a prickling awareness traveling up my spine. Peering into the darkness between the trees, My stomach leapt as hungry, jewel-bright eyes peeked out of the darkness. They were here. Hunting for me.

I waved in and out of consciousness, aware and yet, not, that I was dreaming.

I could never outrun them, but here...here they chased me. Louder and louder. Closer and closer.

Need pulsed in my core, and a tingle of excitement traveled down my spine.

They were right behind me, until finally arms wrapped around my waist, forcing me to the ground.

I screamed, as a heavy weight landed on top of me. The scent of smoke and mulled wine invaded my senses. My face pushed into the dirt and my breath left me in a woosh and my heartbeat was deafening, as the pain only added to my excitement.

My captor flipped me onto my back, keeping one hand tight around my throat. I stared up at his wild eyes and my knees fell open of their own accord. I moaned in pleasure as he pressed his hard cock into me.

"A word of advice." Teeth grazed the skin of my throat. "Never run from monsters. It only entices us to chase you."

" $\mathcal{T}$ he first thing you need to know, if you want any chance of winning the hunts, is you will never defeat my family."

"Mmm," I hummed, noncommittally.

It was unseasonably warm for mid-spring, and the sun beat down on the top of my head, forming beads of sweat in my hairline. I sat on a boulder beside the lake, leaning back on my hands as Prince Bael paced back and forth, spinning a dagger between his long fingers. Behind him, the reeds waved in the breeze, and a group of gray-blue water sprites chattered loudly in what could only be a family squabble. I glanced over at them. What I wouldn't give to join that conversation instead.

Bael crossed in front of me again. "Never," he repeated, sounding far too-gleeful about that fact. "So, we'll need to go about this differently."

I let my head fall into my hands. Immediately, the heavy obsidian crown tumbled into my palms. I sprang back up, shocked and a little sheepish. I'd forgotten about the thing, which seemed ludicrous, but the moment my brow was free of it I felt relief. It had to weigh as much as a sack of flour, yet without realizing it I'd attributed the pounding headache forming in my temples to stress and lack of restful sleep.

I'd tossed and turned all night, haunted by yet another mortifying dream. Clearly, my subconscious was trying to tell me something. Perhaps that getting in bed with the enemy was only going to fuck me over in the end.

I placed the crown awkwardly on the grass beside me, ignoring its presence. "I thought you couldn't lie?"

Bael stopped pacing and spun to face me fully, cocking his head to the side. "I can't."

I scowled and hopped to my feet, putting my hands on my hips. "How can you say that then? I will never defeat your family. That seems extreme."

He grinned and took a step toward me. The afternoon sun glinted off his golden hair in an angelic way that was both distracting and a bit ironic considering what I'd learned of his personality during our brief acquaintance. "Ah, but I wholeheartedly believe that, little monster. Thus, it's not a lie."

"If I have no chance then what's the point of training me?" I asked mulishly.

He gave me a look like I was missing something very obvious. "Must I explain all my ideas to you?"

"Yes," I snapped. "If you expect me to trust you."

"I don't," he said simply. "I would be shocked if you did."

I frowned. That was…disheartening.

The prince was not as sullen or as mysterious as the rest of his family, but he seemed unashamed of his aptitude for violence and trickery. I couldn't decide which I found more worrisome.

"So," I prompted, as he started pacing again. "Why will I never win? I've dealt with Fae before." I lifted my hair away from my ear to show the evidence of my first run-in with a fairy long ago. "And you should not forget, I did kill the king."

Bael's yellow gaze zeroed in on my ear, and he bared his teeth. "What is that?"

I dropped my hair again to cover it. "Nothing," I said, as nonchalantly as possible. "Merely the first time I ran afoul of a fairy."

"Yes, well," he mumbled. I nearly laughed. I'd rarely seen a fairy uncomfortable. "You seem woefully undereducated, little monster," he said conversationally, still not letting me up. "Let me offer you some advice. No one believes you killed my uncle due to anything other than blind luck, and that will not happen twice."

Without warning, he spun on his heel and hurled the dagger at my head. I gasped, my breath dying in my throat as the blade spun toward me. My heart missed a beat, and I barely registered what was happening before the blade disappeared in a puff of smoke. Like a candle flickering out.

My entire body went stiff, the adrenaline and shock coursing through me, as my heart stuttered to life again.

But Bael wasn't done.

Suddenly, he was directly in front of me and his hand wrapped around my throat. He started to fade around the edges and panic shot through me. We were traveling somewhere. My heart stopped. "No." I breathed. "No. You can't!"

He stopped moving. "What exactly is it you think I'm going to do?"

I hadn't realized until this moment how much I feared returning to that dungeon. Never seeing the sky again. How grateful I was to Bael for taking me out of there in the first place.

I didn't fear death. Not exactly. But I did fear helplessness. I feared being put back in the darkness to rot. My lip trembled. "You can't lock me up again. You said you wouldn't."

"For the love of the fucking Source," Bael's yellow eyes flashed with clear anger. "Believe me, little monster, if I desired to hold you captive, I would not need iron."

"But—"

He moved his hand from my throat to my chin, almost gentle in the way he held my face between his long fingers. "I actually like you." He bent lower so his face was mere inches from mine.

"You can't, you hardly know me."

"But you can dislike someone immediately? Is that how it works?"

I set my jaw. He didn't let me go.

The grin slipped from his face and he stared down at me with a warning in his yellow eyes. "I am merely trying to point out, imagine what I could do to you if I wanted to hurt you.

I stared stonily back. "Don't you?"

He reached down and held out a hand to help me up. He laughed without a hint of humor. "No, but I can't say the same for the rest of my family. They didn't participate in the first hunt only out of self-preservation. They're unlikely to fall for the same trick twice."

I narrowed my eyes. "What trick? You mean whatever you threatened them with?"

The corner of his lip turned up. "'Threat' is an ugly word. I would say it was...creative advice."

I stifled a laugh, then froze as he pushed my hair away from my ear, inspecting it, A shiver slid down my spine as he ran the tip of his finger over my ear, then traced the surrounding air, as though drawing where the tip had been. He raised one eyebrow, then blinked, focusing back on me. He said nothing, but it was as if he realized the scar proved his point.

I reached up to push my hair back into place and our hands brushed by mistake. A jolt of electricity shot through my arm. Our gazes connected for half a second, before I jerked back, surprised.

I nodded, dazed. "Right. And what did you tell them?"

I'd assumed it was another bargain, or perhaps even a duel, but a trick made both more and less sense. What would cause the entire house of Everlast to avoid killing me for reasons of self-preservation?

"Never you mind," Bael said, shoving his own hand in his pocket. "They will likely all join the second hunt, and whatever you've seen from them will be child's play compared to if they are actually trying to kill you."

My blood ran cold.

I'd always understood that the Fae were dangerous. I'd always known that the Everlast family was powerful, even by Fae standards. But I'd never considered the horrifying possibility that all the atrocities I'd seen committed against humans my entire life had been the Fae's idea of jokes.

And they weren't joking anymore.

42
LONNIE

A ray of moonlight streaked across the base of my bed, illuminating the obsidian tower room and casting long shadows on the circular walls. I lay flat on my back, sinking into the cloud-soft mattress

Teeth scraped my skin. Tendrils of smoke wrapped around me and electricity sparked at my skin, sending tingles of pleasure all over my body. Brutal. Feral.

Awareness pricked at my skin. A far away sound pulling at the recesses of my consciousness.

Bael reached for my chin, pulling my face back to his, and licked up the side of my neck. I moaned, writhing against him, chasing the friction I desperately craved.

"Turn over, little monster," he demanded against my skin.

I did, pressing my ass into the hard length of him, letting him pin me into the mattress.

He laughed in my ear, and I moaned as his fingers teased my nipples. "Good girl."

An intake of breath made me turn my head toward the door. I smiled. "What are you doing here?"

Prince Scion pushed off the wall and prowled toward me, his expression hungry. "This is my room. Why shouldn't I be here?"

"Because you despise me."

He said nothing, only moved closer. For a moment, I thought he was going to reach out and grab me, but instead he reached for the drawer of his bedside table. Opening it, he pulled something out, and shoved it in the lapel of his jacket.

The prince turned back to me and raised an eyebrow. "I take it you've been sleeping well?"

I blinked, confused. Bael was gone, and I wasn't sure when it had happened, or when I had gotten back under my covers.

I pulled the blankets up to my chin and glared at him, my heart pounding out of control. "Get out. Or, if you want this room back, find me another, it makes no difference to me."

His lip curled. "Would you prefer to return to your cell, then?"

"No," I said too fast as fear flooded my stomach.

He would do it. I knew he would. Would Bael come find me a second time, or let Scion lock me away and just heal me between hunts. Wouldn't that be easier for them both?

He leaned over and ran one finger up the side of my face. I gasped, as tiny sparks of pain followed the path he traced. "No, rebel. I like knowing where I can find you."

hen I awoke the next morning, the drawer was still open.

43

LONNIE

*T*hat day, I couldn't look myself in the eye, let alone Prince Bael.

I was nearly certain that Prince Scion had been in my room, and while I didn't think he was a mind reader, perhaps I had spoken in my sleep or something equally mortifying. My embarrassment outweighed my indignation at the breach of privacy, and therefore I decided to avoid the entire court.

For the last few nights, no one had locked my door, either due to negligence or because they assumed I would not risk leaving. So, I didn't wait for Iola to arrive and dressed myself, before creeping out into the hall before most of the castle was awake. Today was the day to see how far my leash would stretch.

I let my mind wander as I walked down the long hall, as that seemed to be the key to not getting lost. I appraised all the glittering golden paintings and jeweled sconces along the walls, as I moved in the direction of what I hoped was the front door. Such absurd opulence for no reason in this rarely seen corridor, when the village was starving.

The city of Everlast had two distinct social classes. There were the free humans–those who were not part of any Fae court, or bound to another magical order—and the High Fae not of noble birth. The humans lived on the far edge of the city and the surrounding villages, while the Fae lived in the center taking up most of the resources. Non-nobles had no strong magic, if they possessed any at all, but they were still dangerous. Still far stronger and faster than humans, and still immortal.

The Everlasts only seemed to care about the Fae in their city, but no one bothered with the thousands of humans. Any one of these absurd trinkets would feed an entire family for life.

Setting my jaw, I spun back around and returned to the tower to find a bag.

The air was crisp, far cooler than yesterday, and the breeze nipped at my skin as I burst into the crowded village square. It was as if no time had passed over the year, and I fought the bile that rose in my throat.

Paper pinwheels and flowers decorated every merchant's stall, while colorful banners–dirty with age, but still festive, were strung between the nearby houses. I scowled at the ground as I wended my way between the booths, searching for something to stand on.

Spotting a crumbling stone wall in front of someone's overgrown garden, I dragged my sack of stolen art and housewares another twenty yards and climbed up on the most sturdy looking rock.

"Hey!" I screamed at the top of my voice. "Hey! Listen!"

No one turned to look.

To my left, someone snorted a condescending laugh. I looked down, and spotted an old merchant peering up at me with hawk-like eyes from underneath the red, dirt-crusted, awning of his booth. He had blue-green skin, and long scraggly hair, and wore a dusty black jacket embroidered with a tree on the sleeve. He caught me looking and his expression went from amused to flat in a flash.

"What?" I snapped.

"You'll never catch anyone's attention like that," he said gruffly. "Scream yourself hoarse and you'll see."

I grumbled in frustration. "Then what am I supposed to do?"

He shrugged. "Nothing? No one has time to listen to preachers. Go home."

I reached down and hauled my heavy sack up onto the wall beside me, then dug inside it, unearthing a golden candlestick. "Does anyone have time for gifts?"

The merchant's eyes widened. "Put that away. Are you daft? You'll get robbed."

I shoved the candlestick at him. "Good! Take it."

The merchant gaped at me, but didn't protest as he took the candlestick. I wouldn't have either. Free was free, and we both knew how much that gold was worth.

The merchant now watched me with a peculiar expression. Wariness. Nervous respect. "There's many that would kill you for that, you know."

I laughed harshly. "They can get in line."

He shook his head and he reminded me a bit of Beira when one of us did something that disappointed her. "Go door to door, then. Or take that to the nearest tavern and ask the mistress how to reach families. For the love of the Source, don't just go screaming for anyone to hear."

I'd never been to any taverns, even before this year. "Any suggestions?"

He pointed through the crowd to a plume of smoke just visible over the tops of the thatched roofs and crumbling chimneys "Try over there. More locals than not at that place."

I nodded. "Thanks."

I hopped down from the wall and took a step in the direction of the tavern.

"Wait!" The merchant called me back.

I turned around. "Yeah?"

He held something out to me. I glanced over what he was selling for the first time, marveling over the hilts of all the weapons. Swords, some as tall as me, daggers in iron and bronze and obsidian, and battle axes that looked like they could cut a man's head off in one stroke.

The merchant pushed a dagger into my hand. It was similar to the one that I'd taken from Prince Bael on my first night out of the dungeon, but black instead of silver. Black, like the obsidian palace. Like the obsidian crown.

"For the candlestick," he said. "That's Source-forged."

I raised my eyebrows and let out a small laugh. Source-forged weapons were worth their weight in gold. Literally. "Did you want a larger candlestick, then?"

He shook his head. "No, I'll be selling it anyway. I find, that if I want to speak with friends, I can only reach them in the dark."

44

LONNIE

I puzzled over the old merchant's odd words as I stepped inside the tavern.

It was dark, and smelled of firewood and tobacco. A long bar took up most of the room, with mismatched chairs—mostly empty—covering the remainder of the floorspace. In the back corner, a dodgy-looking staircase led to what I assumed were rooms for rent.

As it was barely mid-day, the place was far from full, yet still, the woman behind the bar seemed harried as she rushed back and forth pouring drinks for the dozen or so patrons.

"Excuse me," I said quietly, approaching the red-faced woman. "Could you–"

"Huh?" She yelled, glancing at me as she poured a tankard of ale and practically threw it at one of the men sitting in a rowdy group to my right. I wrinkled my nose. To be that loud this early was almost impressive.

"Excuse me," I started again.

"Speak up, girl, I can't hear ye."

"I'm looking for someone who could–" I said at twice the volume.

She laughed, and her sharp eyes darted over me in a quick assessment. "You and everyone else in here."

What?

She turned away and started pouring another drink. Irritation pricked at my skin and I leaned forward, rapping my knuckles on the bar. "Excuse me. Can you—"

She turned back around and gave me a withering look. "I don't answer questions for the palace," she snapped. "If they're looking for someone, tell them they can find them on their own or not at all. Now order something or get out."

I stepped back surprised. "I'm not from…I mean, I don't…"

She raised her eyebrows at me, looking me up and down again. "I've seen you before. Girls like you never come around here unless they're from over there," she gestured vaguely toward the door, and I assumed she meant to the west. Toward the palace. "What are you, one of the royal whores?"

I thought of the dancers in cages, the barely dressed women on the tables of fruit, and the woman on Prince Scion's lap in the Waywoods. Bitter anger pooled hot in my stomach and I shook my head. "No, I'm…" I sighed. "Never mind."

I dropped my sack of treasures at my feet and pulled out a stool. The bartender raised her eyebrows at me expectantly, the demand obvious in her expression.

I pointed to the drink she was pouring without caring what it was. "I'll have one of those."

She nodded sharply and pulled out a second glass, slamming it down in front of me.

Who would have thought it would be so difficult to give away gold? Soon, I would start walking around handing it out like oranges at Yule.

I bent my head, nervously fixing the hair covering my ear as I glanced surreptitiously down the bar. The woman poured my drink and shoved it toward me. Catching the glass before it landed in my lap, I took an experimental sniff. When it didn't smell too offensive I sipped cautiously, just to be polite. "Thanks."

Clearly, this woman wasn't interested in helping me, and I doubted that would change if she knew who I was. It would probably be worse.

I looked around, wondering if I should find another bar, or perhaps go door to door as the merchant had suggested. Most of the patrons of this tavern were the sorts of people I wouldn't care to meet on a dark road at night, rough and alarming as any Fae. I saw more rounded ears than not, but the occasional Fae stood out among the crowd, their ethereal beauty noticeable even in this dull lighting.

Sighing, I was about to give up, when I thought back over what the woman had said. My stomach lurched, anxious and excited at once. "Hey!" I yelled.

The barmaid whirled back to me, obviously angry now. "What?"

I reached down to my sack of treasures and closed my fingers around the first item I could reach. Pulling out a silver-backed mirror, I shoved it at her. "Can I please just talk to you?"

The woman looked from me to the mirror and back, her expression wary. "Not from the palace? Sure." She shook her head. "I'm not getting mixed up in that. Get out."

My frustration rose. I understood her position. The palace and the Fae were dangerous enough that even taking gold was a risk. Still, I needed her to listen to me. I pulled out a picture frame from my sack and slammed it on the bar. "You said you'd seen me here before. When?"

I'd never been to this tavern in my life, but that didn't mean the woman was lying.

The woman blinked in awe at the jewel-encrusted picture frame. Her brow furrowed, and I could see her resolve wavering as she craned her neck, trying to see over the bar to my sack. "How much you got down there?"

"Enough." I smiled. "And I'm trying to give it away. So, if you can tell me when you last saw me and who I was with…I think we can help each other."

I knew someone was watching me as I left the inn forty minutes later.

The barmaid had seen Rosey twice–maybe three times–last year. Always at night. Always speaking with the same group of travelers. I wanted to stay longer, perhaps wait until evening, and see if the same travelers turned up, but the prickle of eyes on the back of my neck was overwhelming.

I thanked the woman and headed for the back door of the inn. Yanking it open, I stepped out into the dismal little alleyway behind the building. It was now mid afternoon, and the sun had fallen behind the buildings, casting long shadows on the cobblestones and chilling the air slightly.

Instead of heading down the main road back to the palace, I hurried around the back of the building. I wasn't sure if I was imagining the footsteps pounding around the corner behind me, or if I was really hearing them, but I behaved as if they were real.

The tavern had a small set of stables around the back that more often than not went unused. Fae horses did not like humans. They were larger and more temperamental than the horses in the human realm, or so I understood. Many journeys were delayed or even ended prematurely because Fae horses simply would not carry human riders, deeming them unworthy. Therefore, it was uncommon to see the stables filled in the capital city, where most of the population was human or some lesser Fae hybrid.

I pushed the stable door open and was hit with the scent of hay and manure. The long, empty room was dark, the only light from the low flicker of a wisp lantern along the wall. Anxiety bubbled in my stomach and I paused. Anyone could be hiding here, crouching in one of the stalls or lurking in the shadows. Outside, however, a worse danger waited for me. Better an unknown demon than the one I knew would slit my throat without a second thought.

I took a few quick steps forward, ducking into the nearest empty stall and bending low to wait. The knife in my belt felt heavy against my thigh and I inched my fingers toward the hilt, ready to pull it out if the door opened.

Seconds ticked by and nothing happened. There was no sound but for my own ragged breathing. The distant music and muffled voices from inside the tavern. As the minutes crept on, I heard the back door open and close, the music growing louder whenever it did. A woman laughed, and something smashed against the ground, like broken glass. Just the normal sounds of a busy evening on the outskirts of the city. My breath calmed, and my heartbeat returned to normal.

Finally, I straightened up, startling slightly at my own shadow cast on the wall behind me. You're being stupid Lon.

I was foolish enough to be afraid of my own shadow, perhaps, but not so foolish as to walk back out of the stables the same way I'd come in.

Instead, I moved deeper into the darkness of the building until I reached the back door and unlatched it. The rusted hinges screeched, and the heavy wooden door scraped against the stone floor and I winced, my heart landing in my throat.

I stepped back out into the night, my heart leaping in victory when no one waited for me beyond the door. A smug smile curved my lips as I turned on my heel and took off, running as fast as I could around the edge of the stables back toward the road, my chest swelling with triumph.

A noise behind me made me pause and turn my head back.

I screamed as something hit me in the side of the head so hard, I went rocketing to the ground.

"I am not sure if I am pleased or disappointed to have been proven right about you, rebel," Prince Scion said harshly as he loomed over me.

An odd sense of relief washed over me, and I hated myself for it. It made sense, I supposed. Prince Scion could not kill me today. Still, embarrassment flooded me adding to my hatred. Each time I met this family, they had landed me on the ground within seconds. Just once, I would like to see them fall to their knees.

"How?" I snapped. "What are you accusing me of now?"

"You are meeting with Nightmares and trying to contact Dulla-han. I don't give a fuck what Bael promised you, I–"

"You know who Dullahan is?" I sat up and leaned forward, cutting him off. "Tell me."

He seemed taken aback by that. "I'm not going to play into whatever lies you're spinning now."

"No," I said, sounding far too eager. "I truly don't know."

His forehead wrinkled in one of the most human expressions I'd ever seen him make. Like perhaps he truly doubted himself. Without another word, he disappeared, leaving me staring at empty air once again.

BAEL

"**F**uck me," Lonnie swore loudly. "Mother of all that is cursed and—don't laugh at me!"

The rest of what she said was lost in my laughter. She stared up at me from the ground, rage written all over her face. She was not good at sparring. Horrible actually, and for all the time we'd spent practicing over the last week I was certain she was only getting worse.

I should have stopped trying to teach her. I should have realized that it didn't matter anyway, as she'd rightly pointed out during our very first session. But I wouldn't, because it was the most interesting thing I'd done in years.

"Try not to turn your back foot out so much," I suggested, as I reached out a hand to help her up.

She scowled at me, honey-brown eyes turning a shade darker. "I wasn't."

She was. She was such a liar. I loved it.

"Forget the blade," I told her. "Enough for today."

It was enough for the century, really. She would never improve. I would have to think of something else.

She sighed in relief and went to retrieve her bag from the edge of the lake. I looked pointedly away, resisting the urge to watch her.

It was almost painfully difficult.

She was looking healthier by the day—more like last year when she'd sparked my interest. I'd been with hundreds of human women, but none who I remembered for days on end. None who talked back to me, or demanded pointless bargains of me. The way her mind worked was hysterical and fascinating. All consuming.

I took a step toward her, then stopped, realizing what I was doing. My eyes darted toward the trees, and I closed them, trying to banish thoughts of the dreams that kept plaguing me.

I could not have this girl. Not now—not ever—but especially not now, while my blood was in her veins. That would spell disaster for my entire family.

Lonnie stood up, and turned back to me. She jumped at seeing me closer, and I scrambled for something to say. "Do you know how to kill the High Fae, little monster?"

"Are you going to tell me? That seems foolish."

"I am in no danger, I assure you." Curiosity sparked in her eyes and a thrill shot through me.

I was under no delusion that she didn't still hate me—hate all the Fae—but I was quite sure that over the last week something had shifted.

I kept having to remind myself that it wasn't an entirely natural shift, and worse, she had absolutely no idea why it was happening.

Soon, it wouldn't matter, I reminded myself firmly. I'd barely given her any of my blood. Certainly not enough to bind her to me. If I'd wanted to do that—which I couldn't, ever—it would have been far more complex.

"Well?" she prompted, pushing her hair behind her ears.

My eye caught on the scar on her right ear and something flared in my chest. What happened there? Who did that? More importantly, why did I care?

I shook my head, realizing I'd lost the train of my sentence. Fuck. Humans did that, but never the Fae.

"There are two ways." I forced myself to focus. "With the fire from the Source—either directly, or with a blade forged there."

She nodded. "I knew that."

I narrowed my eyes then, wondering what she'd used to kill Uncle Penvalle. I opened my mouth to ask, but she interrupted.

"What else?"

"Or." I grinned. "You can pull us apart so completely that it would be impossible to heal. The Fae are immortal, and can heal from most any wound. We don't get sick and we do not age, but we are not invincible."

"Ah. So magic."

"Essentially."

An errant thought tugged at the back of my brain. Maybe that was how she killed Penvalle. She smelled too suspiciously of magic for it to be nothing. Scion was out of his mind lately, but he was right about that. She tasted of it. There was something... not right.

"So, if I have no chance of fighting your family, then what am I supposed to do?"

"I'm not sure you're ready to hear my strategy."

She looked contemplative, and I was tempted to run a thumb across her forehead and wipe away the line marring her bow. It didn't matter, really. She wouldn't have to fight anyone. I'd do that.

Surely she wouldn't like that answer though.

She set her jaw. "Oh? Pray tell, when would you like to bestow that wisdom upon my poor, lowly, human ears?"

I laughed. "Good! Now again, with more sincerity."

She scowled at me, her brow furrowing even more deeply. I wanted to laugh. Her face was flushed from our sparring, her breath still too short, but still she managed to look irritated with me. I'd never met anyone who lied so often, and yet was so painfully easy to read.

Every single truth was evident on my little monster's face. Every emotion. And I wanted to catalogue each one of them.

"I suppose I could always burst into one of your revels. Is that not how it's done now?"

Darkness shuttered her eyes, and I knew she was likely thinking of her sister. I probably should have said something about that, but instead, I was too focused on the idea of her coming to one of the revels.

"You are not attending."

She looked up at me, surprised. "Pardon?"

My hand formed a fist at my side. "The next revel. You are not to attend."

She scoffed. "You say that like it's a punishment. I have no desire to attend any of your abhorrent fairy feasts."

"Good."

She cast me a sideways glance "But why?"

I set my jaw. Fuck. She wanted more. More explanation, which I couldn't give her without tipping my hand. "It's dangerous," I said flatly. "You cannot go."

I realized later I should have told her she had to go, if I wanted the opposite effect.

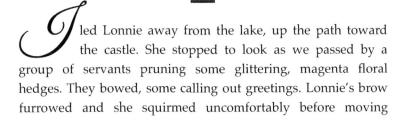

led Lonnie away from the lake, up the path toward the castle. She stopped to look as we passed by a group of servants pruning some glittering, magenta floral hedges. They bowed, some calling out greetings. Lonnie's brow furrowed and she squirmed uncomfortably before moving along.

I watched her with interest. "Do you want to go back?"

"No." She sounded horrified. "I just don't want them to speak to me like that."

"Like what?"

She narrowed her gaze at me. "Like they talk to you. I can't imagine anything worse."

I was simultaneously relieved and disappointed that the blood seemed to be wearing off. Though, I supposed, if it was wearing off for her...then, why not for me?

LONNIE

My breath heaved and my heart pounded against my chest as I ran. The wind of the valley whipped in my ears, and the ever-present fog that swept down from the Source hovered low over the moss-covered rocks that lined the path. I held my crown of dandelions and yarrow out in front of me, with reverence equivalent to the obsidian crown, as if I were the true Fae Queen, about to win the Wilde Hunts.

The leaves rustled all around me, tiny eyes peeking out left and right, between the trees. Watching. Judging. Cheering me on.

I didn't stop to greet any of my friends as I ran. I hoped The Underfae would forgive my rudeness. I couldn't stop now. I was winning.

There was no better thing in the world than winning. Better than Yuletide. Better than falling in love. At least, I assumed so. I had never had the opportunity to compare.

Far in the distance, I could barely see my destination. The edge of the clear brook that ran through the northern tip of the forest, trickling down from the mountains of Aftermath. Just a bit further, and I'd be able to cross it. Just a bit further, and I'd win the game.

"Lonnie!" Rosey screamed behind me, her voice full of untamed laughter. "Wait, I—"

The rest of her shout was lost to the pounding of my heart in my ears. The rush of victory hit me as the stream came into clear focus at last. I stretched my arms out to either side, sprinting toward it, and made a tremendous jump. My skirts fluttered around my knees and I tumbled in a heap, hitting the muddy ground on the other side of the water.

"Yes!" I shouted my victory, clutching the flower crown tight in my fist.

I panted, throwing myself to the ground. Safe at last.

Lying flat on my back, I stared up at the sky as I raised the crown straight up in the air in triumph, before letting it fall uselessly back down onto my face. The dandelions tickled my nose, the tiny yellow petals lodging themselves in my mouth and making me splutter.

My sister shrieked as she crossed the creek, undoubtedly trying to tiptoe across the rocks. I sat up and shook my head. "You have to jump or you'll get wet."

"I'm trying!"

She never tried to jump and that was why she always lost this game. One of the reasons, anyway.

Rosey finally hopped across the last of the rocks and walked over to me. "I'm tired."

I nudged her, playfully. "You're tired of losing."

She laughed. "Yes, that too. I want to be Queen Celia next time."

Queen Celia Everlast was the Fae queen of Elsewhere. Everyone knew the story of how her magic was so strong, no one even challenged her when it was her turn to defend her crown in the Wilde Hunts. She simply walked through each arena with her head high, while violence *reigned all around her, and crossed the finish line without sustaining a single scratch.*

"You can't be the queen until you catch me," I told Rosey. "That's how the hunting game works."

Rosey laughed. "Well, you're growing far too smug for my taste, winning every time."

I shrugged, sticking my tongue out at her. "You choose the next game, then."

"I'd rather go home and read. I'm almost finished with my novel and it's getting dark, anyway."

I wrinkled my nose, even as I nodded in reluctant agreement. I'd already finished all the books we owned ten times over. Mother insisted it was my own fault for rushing through everything. Never satisfied, she called me. Impatient. Hungry.

I was in a foul mood when I arrived for training, a cloud of grief hanging over my head.

Bael looked up at me through his blonde bangs, and his eyes narrowed. "What's happened?"

"Nothing," I said sharply.

I didn't know why he would care, and I didn't know how to explain at any rate.

It was two days since Prince Scion had found me at the tavern, and to my shock it seemed he hadn't told anyone about the incident. I hadn't dared to go back yet, despite the useful information the barmaid had shared.

Perhaps it was my preoccupation with the tavern that had sent my dreams in a new direction. For nearly a week I'd been plagued with dreams of nothing but this prince, supplemented only occasionally, and even more shamefully, by his cousin.

Now, my reprieve came at the cost of another sort of torment, and I wished desperately to return to the phantom arms of the Fae.

"*H*ow do you think we won for the last seven thousand years?" Bael asked me as we walked back to the castle after the shortest and worst training session to date.

I stared straight ahead, considering this as we reached the top of the slight hill and passed through the elaborate gardens back toward the castle. Several more servants gawked at us, bowing and curtsying as we passed. I couldn't blame them. We had to make quite the pair: The black sheep prince and the human servant queen, strolling in the garden like we were friends instead of trying to murder each other as nature intended.

"You have the strongest magic," I guessed as we ascended the steps to the front doors.

Bael tipped his head toward me, conceding the point. "Yes, although that wasn't what I was going to say."

"Well magic isn't going to help me next month, not unless you're a miracle worker."

He grimaced, and took a long moment to answer, chewing on his words. I watched him carefully. Whenever Fae took too long to answer a question, I assumed they wanted to lie, and were thinking up some rotten half-truth.

"Magic isn't everything," he said finally.

Not an answer to the question.

"My family has a longstanding tradition of rejecting our true mates in favor of a marriage to someone with more complementary magic, so our children will have stronger powers."

I raised my eyebrows. That was similar to what Thalia had said, although, she hadn't gone so far as to reveal they rejected their true mates. What happened to the mates? I twirled the hair by my ear uncomfortably. "That's…"

"Unconventional?"

And disturbing. "I was going to say 'that's an excellent deflection from my question.'"

His eyes widened slightly. "I will admit I—" he stopped speaking abruptly, and I blinked, hanging on his words.

"Don't stop on my account."

I looked up at the distant sound of a familiar, amused voice, and was slightly surprised to realize we'd reached the front doors of the castle. Two guards held the enormous double doors wide. Within, the shadow of a figure stretched across the impressive marble floor, heralding their arrival.

It felt absurd to be entering through the front doors, rather than by the servants' entrance. Would things ever stop feeling that way? Did I want them to? What would it mean for me if I got used to this lifestyle?

"Aine," Bael greeted his sister, just before she came into view for me.

How much better was their eyesight than mine that he could see her all the way inside and down the hall? Or, perhaps, he just knew her voice.

"As I said," Lady Aine drawled, as she drew nearer. "Don't stop talking on my account," she waved a hand for him to continue. "Please carry on your conversation, I can wait."

Bael narrowed his eyes at her. "Not a chance. What do you want?"

She pouted, and in that moment I saw her resemblance to Lady Raewyn.

Seemingly overnight, I'd become fascinated with the resemblance between—or lack thereof—the house of Everlast. Aine looked like her father, Lord Auberon, but one would never know she was related to Bael, let alone his sister.

She turned, fixing large midnight eyes on me and smiled. "Good morning."

I blinked, surprised. "Er, good morning."

She passed by my discomfort without comment. "I was coming to find you," she told Bael. "I wouldn't have expected to find you here…in present company. You'll start rumors."

He stepped around her and walked purposefully inside, forcing her to follow. "How?"

I waited for half a second before hurrying after them.

Aine looked sideways at me. "It's simply an interesting choice. Though, given that you've fucked nearly the entire staff and two-thirds of our guests, this shouldn't shock me as much as it does."

I choked. They ignored me.

"Thank you for your input," Bael said dryly.

"Of course," Aine smiled, "I was coming to find you to inform you of a recent development past the southern border, which you would already know if you'd been paying any kind of attention."

Bael stopped in his tracks and looked at her, as though noticing her for the first time. "Shit."

"Precisely."

Bael glanced at me, then toward one of the long hallways leading off from the entrance hall. "I need to attend to something. You'll have to amuse yourself for the rest of the day."

Before I could say anything, he was gone, running down the hall faster than I could have thought possible. Ten times as fast as I could have done anything.

I actually like you. Imagine what I could do if I wanted to hurt you. I shivered. What, indeed.

"Do you know what his magic is?" Aine asked lightly.

"Excuse me?" I looked over at her, surprised to find she was still there watching me.

She stared back at me expectantly, seeming unwilling to repeat her question. I scanned over the details of her face. Where her mother was ethereal and airy, Aine was sharp and intense. She wore a high-necked gold and blue jacket with pointed shoulders, and tight trousers tucked into leather boots. Her curly hair was loose, and she had several silver jeweled necklaces hanging one on top of the other down to her navel.

"No," I said finally. "Aside from the…" I waved my hand in the air. "Disintegration, you mean?"

As if that wasn't enough.

She laughed. "So, no then. You don't. I thought not."

My lips became a flat line. Not that I had any ground to stand on when it came to secrets. Still, the curiosity was apt to eat me alive. "Are you going to tell me, then?"

She strode away, calling over her shoulder. "Have a nice afternoon, Your Majesty."

47
SCION

*R*age churned in my gut, dark shadows clouding the edges of my vision and practically blocking out anything that Mordant was saying. I stared, mutinously straight ahead, trying and failing, to find meaning in the words slipping in and out of my brain, like water through my fingers.

I couldn't believe that I'd fallen for it, even for a fucking second. All humans were liars, and that girl was no exception. She was possibly the worst of them all.

Most of my family—plus Mordant—sat around the round war council table, speaking with the same attitude as if at a late breakfast.

"If we could just discuss—" Mordant was saying.

"No," I snapped. "We're not all present."

There were eight seats around the table, but only five were occupied.

Aunt Raewyn and Uncle Auberon sat to my left, as usual not paying the slightest bit of attention to anything that was going on around them. Auberon whispered something in my aunt's ear and she laughed, turning her back fully on us.

Beside them, Gwydion made eye contact with me across the table, looking absolutely appalled. I shrugged. His parents might have been useless at best, but at least he had them.

I supposed that wasn't entirely fair.

I glanced at her where my mother sat directly across from me. She was still alive, she just wasn't...herself.

In the hour we'd been sitting here, she'd done nothing but stare straight ahead. Said nothing, but "Good Day." Part of me had wondered if Penvalle had done something to her, but when he died and she didn't return to normal I'd had to put that theory to rest. There had been a time when I could recall my mother being a vocal member of the family, but that was before my father was killed. Since then, she'd said little, and rarely used her magic.

It was enough to drive anyone to the point of violence.

The chairs on either side of Mother were vacant. It was odd seeing so many seats open. Once, Grandmother Celia had been in charge of these meetings. My father sat to her right, with Uncle Penvalle on the other side.

Currently, Aine's chair was empty. Though, I hadn't expected her to show up. Bael however...I slammed my hand on the table. "Where the fuck is Bael?"

Only Mordant jumped, everyone else turned, slightly bemused.

Gwydion gave me a sideways look. "Occupied?"

"Unacceptable," I growled.

"Lord," Mordant said tentatively.

I looked up at the weedy little male. "What?"

"If we are unable to continue without Lord Bael then—"

My family made no move to stop me as I stood from the table and marched out of the room.

I walked through the shadows by a large vase, reappearing three floors below. We all had the ability to disappear and reappear at will, but it was far easier under the cover of darkness. Doing it in the daytime was exhausting, and only allowed for extremely short-term travel—even for me.

I needed to find Bael if we were going to accomplish anything.

The northern rebels had attacked the southern border of the capital, and we had no idea how they did it...officially.

I was becoming more and more certain they had help inside the castle.

Figuring out how the rebels communicated had been an obsession of my grandmother's, and now of mine.

The obvious answer would be magic, but most of the rebel forces were human. Until recently, I'd thought it was impossible for humans to possess magic. Until recently, I'd thought a lot of things were impossible.

I walked in the direction of the front hall, only half-aware of the shadows trailing in my wake. Several guards dove out of the way as I passed, and I made no effort to call them back. For the best, really.

The air shimmered in the hall ahead and my shoulders tensed. "Nice of you to finally make an appearance."

"I didn't realize I was needed," Bael said casually, striding forward.

"What the fuck were you doing?" I asked, momentarily distracted by the sweat coating his forehead. It was difficult to exhaust one of us to the point of actual physical exertion.

He rolled his eyes. "I never thought I would meet someone worse at swordplay than Lysander, but I have been proven wrong."

Irritation prickled at the back of my neck and I closed my eyes, pulling deep breaths through my nose. For perhaps the thousandth time, I wondered why no one had thought it worth putting both of us through some sort of emotional training.

"You need to stay away from her," I snapped.

He cocked his head to the side. "What is it this time? The scent, or the prophecy?"

I set my jaw. Either of those should have been more than enough, but no. "No, it's that the rebellion is gaining strength behind the idea of a human queen, which you would know if you were at the meetings."

I started walking again and he fell into step beside me. We both knew where we were going now—it didn't need to be said.

"Why is that a bad thing?" Bael said thoughtfully. "I would have thought you would prefer to—"

"Stop." I cut him off as we passed a group of noble women from Nevermore walking in the opposite direction. They smiled, bowing slightly as they passed. I frowned, glancing after them. How much had they heard?

"We shouldn't discuss this here," I stopped walking, and rounded on my cousin. "Or ever."

"Fine," he said, unconcerned. "You were the one who wanted me to make a plan though. Perhaps I'm simply executing it."

"Stay away from her." I demanded.

"Is that an order or a suggestion?"

He didn't seem the least bit concerned and that only drove my rage to new heights. "Do you realize your pet was wandering around the city yesterday looking for contacts in the rebellion?"

He raised an eyebrow at me. "No, I know she was stealing our dinnerware and giving it to merchants and innkeepers. A bit of a misguided attempt at philanthropy, but well intentioned I'm sure."

"I highly doubt that's all it was." I scowled. "I don't know why you're so obsessed with protecting this…woman, Bael."

I'd intended to say "Slúagh" and changed my mind at the last moment. I did not care to analyze why.

"I'm not obsessed with protecting her. I'm not even interested in it," Bael said with no room for misinterpretation. "I'm protecting myself. You might try it sometime."

I furrowed my brow. "Well, do it from afar, then, because if she's passing information to Dullahan we won't know with you hovering over her all the time."

"Fine, I will have to make myself scarce this week anyway."

I winced. I'd forgotten, and now I felt like an ass. "Right. Sorry. I wasn't thinking."

"Clearly." He faded slightly around the edges, about to disappear into nothingness. "You know, you might consider, Sci, that it's you who has the obsession."

48

LONNIE

I blinked, and a week passed.

Prince Bael's immediate attention to my training had given me the false impression that he would be working with me daily up until the hunt, but apparently I'd been wrong. Either that, or he'd had a sudden change of heart and neglected to mention it. Whatever the reason, I went from seeing the yellow-eyed prince daily, to barely seeing him at all–either in person, or in my dreams.

It was not only him. All Everlasts seemed to be avoiding me.

No more spontaneous visits in the corridors or invitations to their odd dining room. No more appearances in alleys, or the library, or the shadows of my room. It was like I'd woken up in my teenage body, and all the servants and townsfolk were terrified that associating with me would bring the wrath of the Fae down on their heads.

It should have thrilled me—no fairies to torment me on a daily basis, no princes tossing cryptic threats or confusing flirtation in my direction—in reality, it became a bit dull, and for the most part, I spent my days alone.

While Prince Scion had not seemed to tell anyone about seeing me in the village, guards did appear on the castle steps and by the gates for the first time ever. I had no way to return to the tavern, and no clues as to where Rosey had hidden her journals. Therefore, my investigation into my sister's involvement with the rebel forces stalled.

As the days edged closer to the second hunt with little change in the weather, and no mention of where they would be held, my primary feeling became boredom. That seemed preposterous, after years of fear and work and exhaustion, but without those things, without anyone to talk to...without my sister or even Bael, I was lonely.

I took to visiting the library more often than not. I had no friends, no family, so the words of others became a comfort.

With only days to go until the next hunt, I sat at a rickety table in the back of the cavernous room. For once, the sun crept in through one of the dusty windows to shine a beam across the floor, and the scent of sulfur wasn't as heavy as usual. My eyes strained to read the tiny writing of the scroll spread over the table in front of me.

The men reached out to the gods, but due to their own negligence, their gods would not come. Then, on the day of bargaining, when the people feared they would be pulled beneath the surface of the waves, three new gods arrived on a river of fire.

I'd often wondered if the Fae could lie in writing, or if the magic that bound them to honesty extended to ink and paper as well as conversation. I wondered about that again now, as I squinted at the cramped, looping handwriting of the manuscript.

Those most loyal bowed at the feet of the new gods and pledged their souls to their service. Thus, the fire overtook the water, and the demons were banished to the kingdom below.

On a river of fire? Was that an allegory? Was allegory technically a lie? I groaned softly. All of these old texts were the same. None of them made the least bit of sense, and most referenced at least half the High Fae court as gods.

"History is written by the victors," I murmured.

Turning back to my scroll, I moved my candle closer and searched for the spot I'd left off.

"You again."

I jumped, whirling toward the sound of the voice and coming face to face with Prince Scion. His lip curled. The absurdly large raven on his shoulder opened its beak and squawked, mirroring his expression. He looked at it, seeming surprised, but made no comment.

I opened my mouth and closed it again, unsure what to say. The prince stood four paces in front of me, one hand atop the books I'd already gone through.

Today he was wearing a black and gold brocade jacket which complimented his hair but clashed horribly with his silver eyes. I swallowed hard, noticing that he had a sword in his belt. Why, I had no idea. He never usually carried a weapon. He didn't need one.

"You," I replied, with not nearly so much menace. "I was here already, you cannot accuse me of interrupting."

The floor creaked as he moved toward me. "I am surprised to see you again."

"Why?"

"Don't you have other things to keep you occupied?"

I cocked my head to the side, trying to decide what he meant. Other things like what? "I am equally surprised to see you here. You do not seem the type to read."

There was a pause, and I wondered for a moment if he was going to lash out at me, but he snorted what might have been a laugh. "Finally, truth from the queen of lies. So, you are capable, then."

"I haven't lied to you," I said. "Much."

He did laugh at that, and I was taken aback by the carefree nature of it. It seemed so oddly out of place for someone so filled with rage. "Two truths today. I will have to start keeping track."

My gaze followed Scion as he walked down one of the dusty aisles, and I shuddered. A heaviness seemed to fall over the room, like a constant feeling of eyes on my back.

There it was—a healthy reminder of why loneliness was preferable to spending time with the Fae.

There was a reason that everyone feared the Everlast princes. Alone, they were fearsome enough, but together they were the vengeful gods my scrolls warned about.

"I don't want to go."

My breath fogged the glass of the window as I spoke, and I raised a hand to clear it before peering outside again. Below, a crowd of fairies trailed up the front walk of the palace, their glittering gowns and lovely silk jackets obvious even from here.

In the reflection of the glass, Iola dropped the already gleaming shoe she was polishing and whirled to face me. She looked scandalized. "But you have to."

I turned around, and stared at the shoe, where it had landed sideways on my bed, to avoid meeting her eyes. "I'm not sure I have to do anything. Except take part in these cursed hunts, apparently. And even that, I'm starting to doubt."

It was early evening, and Iola had given me barely any notice before she came whirling into my room announcing that I had to dress for dinner with, "Only a few guests."

From the parade now making their way into the castle, it was clearly more than a few. My anxiety grew with each group that arrived. More and more Fae, here only for the reason of murdering me. And some dancing, I supposed.

Iola coughed, taking a moment to answer. "But if you don't go, they'll all talk about it."

I gave her a flat look and put a hand on my hip. "As opposed to every other day when no one discusses me at all."

She blanched. "But I already made you a dress."

I winced. That was hardly fair. I didn't want to take advantage of her work, but I really didn't want to go. "Did it take you long?"

She looked sideways. "Er, not long. Only for most of the last two weeks."

I groaned and rubbed the back of my neck, uncomfortable. "Iola, I–"

"You'll see. Your dress will be perfect and it will help."

I closed my eyes, resigning myself to my fate, and gestured wordlessly for her to carry on.

The only tiny silver lining I could see was that perhaps this dinner–or ball, as it seemed to be–was the event that Prince Bael mentioned. The one he did not want me to attend.

In that case, I could see at least one reason I might enjoy myself this evening.

49
LONNIE

*W*hile I thought the idea that any dress would change how I was viewed by the high court was delusional, I had to admit that Iola had outdone herself.

Layers of violet and silk, cascaded to the floor in a skirt that seemed to change color as I walked, shifting like the evening sky. The sleeves were sheer, gathered at the wrist, and exposed my shoulders. It was the bodice, however, that I was truly excited by. It was form fitting, molded to my body, and the color of obsidian and fairy iron. It appeared that I was wearing an armored breast-plate over my gown—one that had been so artfully crafted and molded to my body it might have been a second skin.

Unable to find a polite way to avoid the whole event, I sat in front of the mirror and allowed Iola to arrange my hair. For once, she left my curls. It seemed more appropriate somehow after seeing the gown. Wilder. She agreed on tiny braids on the sides "To hold the crown," she said, while letting the rest fall down my back.

It was the crown that worried me. I avoided wearing it—even looking at it. It sat in the wooden box beside my bed, and I did my best to pretend it did not exist. Still, I could see the reasoning behind wearing it. I would likely be the only human at the feast —who was not serving, that was. Without the crown, I ran an enormous risk of being singled out for torment.

Before I could voice that thought, my attention was pulled by a clattering on the windowsill. Iola and I looked up.

An enormous blue-black raven landed on the sill, just barely fitting inside. It squawked and fluttered its feathers, watching me with dark, intelligent eyes. I gestured toward it meaningfully.

Iola covered her mouth as she let out a hacking cough.

I waited for her to stop coughing. "Are you alright?"

"Yes. Sorry. Isn't that Prince Scion's bird?"

"Maybe. Are there not many ravens?"

She gave me an odd look. "No, not of that size." She crossed the room, clearing her throat, and tried to shoo the bird away with both arms. "Get out!"

The bird watched Iola suspiciously and tried to nip at her fingers when she got too close. I threw him a look. *Harmless but erratic*, I tried to say with my eyes. The bird stared back at me, and I could swear it understood.

"Leave it," I told Iola. "It's just a bird. It probably lives here."

"Isn't he the Prince of Ravens? Does he need the bird?"

I crossed my arms, feeling entirely defensive for no reason I could explain. "I have no idea what Prince Scion needs, beyond a swift kick in the ass and some etiquette lessons."

The raven squawked and it sounded eerily like a laugh.

"Yes, but—"

I beckoned her back over. "That title doesn't mean anything, it's only a stupid nickname."

She looked at the bird again, her face a mask of confusion. "Strange."

"You know, if that cough persists, you should go pick leaves from the moondust tree and make tea," I told her.

She furrowed her brow. "Really?"

"My sister used to do it and said it helped her."

A knock sounded at the door and I glanced over, surprised. The only one who ever came to my room was Iola, and few people, if anyone, knew I'd moved to this guest chamber.

I rose, intending to move toward the door, and flinched as the enormous raven leapt off the window, swooped across the room, and landed on my shoulder, its razor-sharp talons digging into my skin. "Ouch." I looked helplessly from the bird to the door and back. "Who's there?"

A chuckle sounded outside. "You could open the door and find out."

Gwydion.

I glanced back at Iola, then again at the bird. It looked at me expectantly, as if waiting for me to continue walking.

"What am I supposed to do?"

Iola shrugged. "Take it with you?"

I furrowed my brow. That would be...a statement. A statement saying what, I had no idea, but a statement none-the-less. "I thought you were concerned about the Fae talking about me?"

Iola grinned, her eyes dancing with mischief. "Was it not you who said they are all talking, regardless?"

*P*rince Gwydion looked even more handsome than usual standing alone in the hallway. He wore a midnight-blue jacket, more formal than anything I'd seen him wear before. His unruly blond hair was combed, and for once, he had no sword in his belt.

He looked down at me and blinked twice, seeming slightly taken aback. "You look lovely."

"What are you doing here?"

He refocused his gaze on my face. "I assumed you would have no escort."

I frowned. "Why?"

"Because Bael isn't coming tonight." He glanced at the bird on my shoulder. "Although, perhaps I wasn't the only one to have that thought?"

I blanched. "No. It's only the bird."

For some reason his eyebrows rose at that. "Really?

"Yes…why?"

He shook his head, bemused. "It's only that no one likes that bird except Scion. It's positively vicious."

I frowned. It was annoying, certainly, but did not seem vicious. "I think he'll be fine. Do you know his name?"

Gwydion shuddered dramatically. "I dare not speak it, it might anger the beast."

I rolled my eyes. "You're not serious."

He wrinkled his nose, as if trying to decide if he was, in fact, serious. "Quill, like–"

"Like a feather quill?" I interrupted, before looking up at the bird. "If you are angry, I can see why. That's like naming a bull 'Leather.'"

Gwydion chuckled. "I suppose it is."

"Where is Bael, then?"

Gwydion looked sideways at me. "Do you care?"

I wrinkled my nose. "Define 'care.'"

He crossed his arms over his chest, his face giving away nothing. "He's not coming. That's all I'm allowed to share."

I pursed my lips. How odd.

I offered for Iola to walk with us, but she insisted that she had to return to the kitchens to get orders from Beira and would likely be back upstairs later. Gwydion smiled and offered me his arm as we walked down the hall, but I declined, deciding to simply walk beside him. The raven took up quite a bit of space, anyway.

"Didn't you have to escort Lady Thalia?" I asked as we moved down the winding halls toward the main stairs.

Gwydion looked sideways at me. "No. Why?"

I furrowed my brow. "Oh. I thought...aren't you betrothed to be married?"

"Yes."

He looked oddly displeased about it and I felt like I was missing something. "Then, why–"

"I don't want to waste time discussing Thalia. I have something I wanted to discuss with *you*."

I narrowed my eyes. After over a week of silence from the Everlast family, a discussion, and with Gwydion no less, was concerning. He was perfectly pleasant, but didn't seem precisely in charge. I would have said that was Scion. Perhaps Bael, though in a different sort of way.

I turned and pretended to adjust Quill on my shoulder to buy myself a moment to think. "Prince Gwydion…"

"Gwydion is fine, unless you'd like to be called 'Queen.'"

"Er, no, please don't."

"Is it because 'Queen Lonnie' sounds awful? Because I think we would all be sympathetic to you not wanting to hear that very often."

"No," I said acidly, shooting him a murderous glance. "But thank you for pointing that out, as if I'm not aware. I doubt my mother was planning for this possibility."

When he grinned he looked alarmingly like Bael. "I'm sure your full name would sound better, if you'd care to share."

"I believe I would care to walk alone."

"No, wait." He swallowed a laugh. "I have a proposition for you."

"What?" I said mulishly.

"I'm not sure you yet realize the position you're in, or how valuable an alliance with you is." His eyes widened. "Let me assure you…we do."

I stopped walking and narrowed my eyes at him. "What does that mean?"

"It means that the hunts are a game and for centuries our house played as one team, until *you* forced us to play against each other. It means that you're letting my brother win by allowing him to lead you around like a prize pony…but you don't have to do that."

My cheeks heated. "I haven't seen any of you in days, I don't know how you can accuse me of letting anyone do anything."

He raised his eyebrows. "My mistake. Are you *not* relying on Bael to keep Scion from killing you? Have you *not* traded a cell for a tower and one jailer for another?"

I crossed my arms. "What else am I supposed to do?"

"Bael likes to think he's the only one who could beat Scion, but that's never been tested. You have options...and most of those options wouldn't keep you quite so *caged*."

"What if I have no desire to play your games?" I demanded.

Gwydion sighed, and there was no malice or condescension in his voice when he replied. "You don't get it. You're not one of the players. You're part of the game."

50

LONNIE

hank the Source, the bird seemed to know the way down to the ballroom, because Gwydion left me to walk the rest of the way alone.

At the end of the hall, A huge, sweeping marble staircase descended to a wide gleaming great hall. The room was as large as a throne room–or what I imagined a throne room to be. Despite my precarious position, I'd yet to actually enter any throne rooms.

It had high, vaulted ceilings, with stained glass windows and flickering candles lighting an obsidian dance floor. Green and black tapestries emblazoned with the crest of the Everlasts hung from every possible wall and rafter. I raised an eyebrow. It was as if they'd never lost their crown.

In the center of the room, dozens of Fae stood in neat rows facing the arched double doors. The faint buzz of noise—mostly from the human servants, rustling and muttering, emanated from the mostly silent crowd.

I raised my eyes, casting them around at the hundreds of faces cast toward the floor. While they were not looking up at me directly, their expressions were still evident. Their rigid posture telling. All I wanted was to find a smile in the crowd, just one, but all that looked back at me was anger. Confusion. Contempt.

The wickedly beautiful faces of the nobles, so different and yet all so alike in their ethereal perfection, were twisted into judgment. I could practically see the plans forming behind their eyes. Who would be the first into the quarry at the next hunts? Or, would they try to end it sooner, and put Prince Scion on the throne in my place?

I had to admit, even I could see their point. This whole spectacle was absurd at best, and more akin to a mockery of their entire institution. Their highest law was magic, and I had none.

If I were a druid or a witch—a human who had learned some magical arts from the Fae, enough to perform the duties of a court advisor, they still would not have been happy but perhaps not as insulted. As it was, the foundation of their world was crumbling. If a mere human could kill their king and take their throne, then what next?

As I stood there, staring down at them, whispers carried through the crowd. First quiet, then louder, and louder until it was a sea of hissing voices. Finally, I realized the direction of their comments.

The bird on my shoulder flapped its enormous wings, but did not make an effort to move or leave my side.

Someone cleared their throat to my left and I jumped. I turned to face a tiny, wide eyed Underfae in a golden tailcoat. "Name?" He said in a high, reedy voice.

"Er, no thank you."

He looked at me oddly. I assumed everyone else had been announced already. Some sort of processional of wealth and power that I had no business taking any part in.

I shook my head more firmly and began a slightly teetering descent down the stairs.

I tried to force my face into a calm, collected expression. As if I belonged. As if I understood the rules of the game.

$\mathcal{A}$side from the servants, I'd been right to guess I would be the only human here. The glittering gowns and jewels of the Fae nobility almost paled in comparison to their ethereal beauty.

I wandered around the outskirts of the party, doing my best to blend in and failing spectacularly.

Every person I passed gawked at me. I should have known better. I was still noticed. Still stared at. Still seen, no matter what I did. Now, the Fae simply had a better reason for their interest.

I found myself by a table of refreshments and pressed my back to the wall, hoping to blend in with the gleaming obsidian architecture.

As I stood, doing my best impression of an ornamental statue, I sighed in relief as I spotted a familiar face among the crowd. I raised my hand, waving urgently. "You made it back up here quickly."

Iola darted over, nearly out of breath as she weaved in and out of the nobles. She had a large pitcher of wine in hand, that reminded me with a jolt of the type my sister would often carry at parties.

She pushed a few stray strands of hair out of her face as she came to stand beside me. "Yes. Beira had nothing for me to do, and Thalia was already dressed, so—" she gestured around, as if to say *"here I am."*

I frowned. "Is there much for you to do?"

"No. Thankfully, unless you would like wine?"

I shook my head. "No. Fairy wine makes my head spin."

She laughed, and it turned into a cough. "Agreed."

"How is that cough?"

"Miserable. I'm going to try that tea you recommended. Or honestly, I may just chew on a damn leaf and see what happens." She grinned, but it looked a bit strained.

"You should go to bed."

"I can't. Let me pour you some wine, though, even if you don't want it. I am not sure if I am allowed to be standing here talking to you."

I scowled as she reached for a cup. "Who is going to scold you? Certainly not me, and I doubt Thalia would care."

Before Iola could answer, two fairy nobles approached behind her and she stepped dutifully to the side. I nearly called her back, but her clear discomfort discouraged me from the idea.

Instead, I stared flatly at them, unsure for a moment if they were actually making a beeline for me, or simply eyeing the food.

Their clothing indicated they were with the group from Inbetwixt. Though I'd never visited, I'd met some servants from there during other official visits. Their clothes were all less decorative than the Everlast nobles, but more colorful. The woman wore a cobalt gown with a wide magenta sash. The man clashed spectacularly with his companion in a bright leaf-green jacket.

"Your...majesty," the woman greeted me with a saccharine smile that couldn't be anything other than sarcastic. "We were so hoping to meet you."

"Why is that, Melina?" Aine appeared out of nowhere and put her hand on my shoulder.

I nearly flinched at her touch, but if it was a choice between these two and her, I supposed I would prefer Aine. How odd. Until recently I would have said I would prefer a bog troll to an Everlast.

The woman fixed Aine with a hateful look. "Good Evening, *Princess* Aine." Her tone dripped with syrupy disdain. "It's been far too long."

"Has it? I hadn't noticed."

"I only wanted to meet the new queen, before the next hunt. It's a shame she won't get an opportunity to see the city in Inbetwixt."

My ears pricked up. It was the first I'd heard of anything to do with the city, let alone specific plans for the next hunt. "Why would—"

She cut me off. "I heard that you don't hunt alone. Is that true?"

"I don't hunt at all," I said without inflection. "I am the hunted. Surely you know that."

"Yes," the woman drew herself up. It was so easy to offend fairies, and insulting their intelligence, particularly in public, was the fastest way to do it. "Where is your brother anyway, Princess Aine? Or is it a bad night for him?"

Aine took a small step forward that I still perceived as a threat. "It will be a bad night for you if you do not leave, Melina. You are likely to die soon anyway if you intend to hunt, I suggest you enjoy your final days."

The couple walked away in a huff and Aine turned to me. "What did you do to draw their attention?"

"Nothing. I was just standing here."

"Hmmm."

"Why?" I looked over her shoulder. "Who was that?"

"Melina. She's one of the daughters of the Lord of Inbetwixt. I don't know the male, likely just her escort for the evening."

"You don't like her." It wasn't a question.

"No. And she doesn't like us."

I took "us" to mean "the family" and didn't ask for clarification. "Did you do something to her?"

"Not specifically. It's not me she hates, anyway, it's Bael. That's likely her issue with you. Everyone saw you at the first hunt."

"Where is Bael?" I asked, glancing around.

Perhaps she would have more of an answer for me than Gwydion. I hadn't seen him at all in days, but it seemed as though he should be here tonight.

"I can't be expected to know where everyone is at every moment," Aine said vaguely.

I narrowed my eyes at her. That sounded like a deflection to me. I wondered what Melina had meant by "bad night," though I got the feeling I wasn't going to get any more information about it. I changed tactics. "I've never heard anyone call you 'Princess' before."

I expected her to deflect that as well, but she didn't. To my shock, she laughed. "Oh, *that*. I am, I simply dislike my title. It's a bit...obvious."

I pursed my lips. "Can I ask you something?"

She frowned. "If it's my title, then no. Otherwise, you can. I may not answer."

I looked around at the fairies. "Is this party not a bit..." Dull was the word I wanted to use, but that didn't seem quite right.

"Dead?" she supplied.

"I suppose."

There was no music. No dancing. No...general debauchery. The only fairy events I'd encountered were the complete opposite of this. The back of my neck heated at the memory of my last High Fae encounter. I supposed this was better than that. At least here, I could think straight.

"That is hardly an interesting question."

"I am never looking to be interesting."

She smiled. "Really? Why?"

"Don't change the subject, I honestly want to know what's wrong with this party."

She waved a hand as if to say it were nothing. "It hasn't truly begun yet. You could change that if you wished. Are you a good dancer?"

I blanched. "What? No."

"Pity. This will be terribly unpleasant for you, then."

My heart beat against my ribs, my anxiety rising. "What are you talking about?"

She shook her head. "No, you got your question. Now it's my turn. How did you convince Sci to give you the bird?"

I shook my head, distracted, still thinking about the ominous dancing. "I didn't. He just..." I waved my hand in the air. "Appeared. I don't know."

"Really?" Aine scowled at the raven. "That's unusual. I'm convinced it's part wyvern, you know. Either that, or Sci did something truly hellish to it to make it that size, and it never recovered."

I blinked at her, and reached up almost unconsciously to pet the raven, who was eying Aine like he planned to bite her. I was tempted to let him. "I like him. The bird, I mean. Not your cousin."

She raised an eyebrow at me. "Do you? That would make you one of exactly two who do. How interesting."

I frowned. There was that word again. Interesting. My eternal curse.

"Your brother said more or less the same thing."

"Bael? Yes, he hates the flying rat-beast more than I do."

"No, Gwydion."

Her eyes widened even further. "By Aisling, not another one."

Before I could ask what she meant by that, a ripple of commotion traveled through the crowd. Whispers and movement, as everyone seemed to turn to look at something behind me. Their chins tilted up, looking at whoever was now standing at the top of the stairs.

I turned as well, moving with the group. My breath caught.

Prince Scion had arrived. He stood at the top of the otherwise deserted staircase looking out over the crowd of High Fae with an expression of arrogant boredom. He looked more regal than I could ever hope to be, even wearing the obsidian crown, and the crowd reacted to it. A hush fell over them as they seemed to wait for his next move whether it be to descend the stairs to smite them down like ants under his shoe.

For perhaps the first time ever, he was not accompanied by his bird. As if to make up for it, he wore a jacket with black feathers on the shoulders, almost giving the impression that he would take flight himself.

His gaze traveled over the crowd, and I saw the exact moment he spotted me. Shock flashed across his face, and his eyes darkened. He dragged his gaze up my entire body and it was as though I could feel his fingers tracing my skin. From my hips, up the curve of my waist, along the swells of my breasts and over my exposed shoulders. My lips parted, remembering the heat of his tongue traveling over the curve of my neck as he watched me.

And then, his gaze moved to the crown on my head. His eyes narrowed, and my blood ran cold.

51

LONNIE

I stepped out the double doors off the ballroom and onto a large stone balcony, desperately in need of some fresh air. After that too-intimate display, I almost wished I'd taken that glass of wine from Iola after all.

Prince Scion's raven hopped off my shoulder and landed on the stone railing, looking up at me with its beady, knowing eyes.

"What?" I said to it. "I don't need your judgement."

Quill made a tittering sound, I could swear was a chuckle.

I stared down at the palace grounds, watching the illuminated bushes where the will-o-wisps hovered between the leaves. From here, I could see the intricate design of the maze of hedges in the garden, and the moondust tree at the center, currently in bloom. With a jolt, the tree reminded me of Rosey, sneaking out to make tea for her cough.

"There you are. I thought you'd managed to escape."

I stiffened as Aine's voice rang out behind me. I turned to face her as she walked out of the ballroom. "I tried. There are guards at the door."

"Yes. Well...don't worry about that."

Aine was followed closely by Gwydion, who smiled at me over the top of his sister's head and Thalia, who was too beautiful to be seen by mere mortals in her blood-red gown, despite her sullen expression. Behind them, to my surprise, was Mordant, who seemed the odd one out of the group.

"I'm quite worried about that, actually," I said, my tone as sullen as Thalia's expression. "If I could leave, believe me, I would."

"Well, if you open the dancing for us I don't see why you couldn't," Aine said with an almost too-friendly look.

I narrowed my eyes at her, suspicious. "What does that mean?"

Mordant sighed and looked me up and down. His assessment was just as careful as Prince Scion's, but the feeling was entirely different. I felt more like a rather ugly painting being judged by a disappointed instructor. He wrinkled his nose. "The musicians will not start until the highest ranked member of court has allowed them to, and Aisling help us all, that is you."

"Oh." I waved my hand. "Well, they can start. Please, carry on."

Gwydion snorted a laugh and even Thalia cracked something resembling a smile. Mordant, however, seemed incensed.

"No, you undeserving simpleton. You must dance."

"Mordant," Scion's voice sounded from the back of the group. "I would be careful when throwing insults around that could better apply to yourself."

I glanced up, shocked that the prince would defend me, and our gazes locked. He looked me over again.

Aine clapped her hands together. "Sci, your timing is impeccable."

The prince stiffened. "Why?"

She smiled, I felt as if the stones of the balcony were falling out from under me.

*T*he musicians seemed more than a little relieved as Prince Scion and I made our way out onto the center of the glittering dance floor. The court crowded in around us, and nervous excitement traveled through the crowd.

"Stop shaking," Scion said out of the corner of his mouth.

His posture, his expression, and everything in his overall demeanor said all too clearly that he did not want to be standing anywhere near me. I scowled. Of the two of us, I had far more of a reason to dislike him. His hatred of me seemed far more trivial.

I shot a nervous glance at the musicians as they lifted their instruments, poised as if about to play. "The music…"

"Is just music." He rolled his eyes. "It's a ball, not a revel."

Scion let go of my hand and turned to face me, his silver eyes widening as if he expected something. "Well?"

"Well, what?" I hissed, unmoving.

He set his jaw. "You don't know how to dance, do you?"

"When would I ever have learned to dance? While I worked in your kitchen? Or perhaps while you kept me chained in your dungeon for a year?"

Several ladies gasped, but Scion ignored them. "I don't know what you had time for," he snapped. "You seemed to find time to plan rebellions and fuck my guards—neither particularly well, I might add."

I choked, on what could have been a laugh or a groan of frustration. Maybe both. "Are those things equal crimes in your mind?

Or have you simply been looking for an opportunity to bring it up?"

He took a tiny step closer, looming over me. "The real crime is how you've yet to be punished."

I furrowed my eyebrows. "For what?"

I wasn't entirely sure what we were arguing over, but it didn't seem to be about dancing. Someone in the room—Gwydion, I thought—coughed, and I became painfully aware that we had an audience. An audience of High Fae, who could no doubt hear every word we were saying.

I shook myself. "Well, as everyone knows I don't know how to dance I'm sure it won't matter if I don't do it well."

Scion blinked and seemed to remember where he was. "Right. Fine. You're supposed to curtsy."

I stiffened. If I could help it, I wasn't going to bow to Prince Scion ever again in any capacity. "No."

He rolled his eyes. "Once again, you fail to surprise me."

He clasped my fingers in his, directing me to place my other hand on his shoulder. Long fingers curved around my waist, coming to rest on the small of my back. I shivered, painful aware of everywhere we touched. He was so much taller than me, I was forced to tilt my head back to avoid bumping my nose against his chest or impaling his chin with one of the points of my crown. *Something to keep in mind if he continued to insult me.*

The music started—not a fast song, thank the Source—and immediately I realized that there was more to the footwork than simply swaying on the spot. Scion looked down at me, and I could almost see the insult forming on his lips.

"Why defend me if you're just going to insult me yourself?"

His brow furrowed. "What?"

"Back there, to Mordant. You defended me."

He opened his mouth, and closed it again. Like perhaps he hadn't realized he'd done it. "That's different."

"How?"

He sighed dramatically, and as if I weighed nothing, moved his hands to my waist, lifted me a few inches off the ground as if I were floating. "Stop moving your feet."

I noted the change of subject—a clumsy misdirection compared to his usual verbal traps—but was too distracted to pursue it. "You'll drop me."

He laughed. "I swear, I won't."

I was surprised that his laugh sounded genuine instead of darkly condescending. I was loath to admit it was a lovely sound.

I relaxed, letting Prince Scion carry me as we spun in circles around the ballroom. My lilac gown fanned out behind me, catching the light of every flickering candle, and the music of the fairy band was mesmerizing, perhaps hypnotic after all, but for once it did not bother me

"Why do you hate me?" I asked.

He raised a dark eyebrow. "I have many reasons to hate you."

"Fine. But which one is it specifically?"

He adjusted his grip on my waist. "Why?"

"Because I would understand if you were angry about your uncle, but you clearly aren't." I glanced at his silver eyes for any hint of reaction, but he only nodded for me to continue. "I would understand if you wanted your crown back, but then why let

Bael convince you not to play in the first hunt, or even pretend you need to follow the rules. You could have killed me at any point since last year and declared yourself king and no one would have questioned it."

He laughed softly, and this time the sound seemed to travel through me, wrapping all the way around me, like the notes of the fairy flutes. "I see Bael didn't bother to tell you how he convinced the family not to participate in the first hunt. Let me assure you, rebel, we had little choice."

"How, then?" I asked sharply.

"No," he drawled. "I look forward to the fallout when you finally work that out on your own. As for why I didn't simply kill you over the last year? I didn't have to. Don't make the mistake of thinking I was being kind by leaving you alive, you were more useful to me as you were. This situation–" he darted his eyes back and forth, as if to indicate the entire room. "is not something I anticipated."

I bit my lip, unease washing over me. So many new questions. So little time with his undivided attention. "But why do you hate me?"

"Could it not be because of your rebel affiliation?" he said darkly. "Do you realize that I've spent years watching entire cities fall to ash because Ambrose fucking Dullahan thinks he could rule better than us, yet doesn't have the balls to come challenge us? Instead, he taunts us and murders innocents, all while spewing lies about a better world."

I blinked, shocked at the wealth of information in that diatribe. "You hate Dullahan because he murders innocent people...like your uncle did, you mean? Does he also perhaps toss servants in dungeons?"

The prince sneered. "You say that as if you were innocent, rebel."

I sucked in a breath, trying to calm my frustration. His logic was impossibly flawed. "So that's the only reason why you hate me? Because you think I'm part of the rebellion? An assumption you seem to have made long before I ever went near your uncle."

He paused, as if trying to find the right words. My temper flamed as I remembered back to my first interactions with the prince. Not only Scion, but Bael, and to a lesser extent, Gwydion.

I wished I'd paid better attention to what they were saying that day. I wished I'd known how much it would matter. I remembered seeing Scion and Bael in the woods when Caliban could not. I remembered Scion's strange reaction to me, and them leaving...being grateful to be alive. And later, at the feast before the hunts, them targeting me before my sister ever showed herself to be a rebel.

My heartbeat sped up. Was there more to that than I realized? I'd often been targeted by Fae, picked out of crowds, but was that why? Or was it something else?

My feet touched the ground again and I sucked in a breath, realizing the music had stopped. Prince Scion let go of me and my skin burned through the fabric of my dress everywhere he had touched me. As if my body was tattooed with his mere presence.

"No," Prince Scion said, pulling my attention back to him. "I don't hate you."

My heart pounded too fast. His silver gaze bore into me, and I got that all-consuming notion that he could see through me. Read my every thought and feeling and desire and would crush them all into powder beneath his boots. "Then, why?"

"But it doesn't matter." His voice was so quiet only I could hear. "Because I'm going to kill you, anyway."

And then, in one graceful movement, he bent his head and knelt at my feet.

52

LONNIE

*B*ehind Prince Scion, three-hundred fairies followed his lead, kneeling on the floor of the ballroom. In the space of a breath, I was the only one left standing. "What is happening?" I hissed.

The prince kept kneeling, but I could see the top of his head literally shaking with indignation. After a too-long moment, he looked up to meet my gaze. The top of his head reached my hip bone, but somehow that look made me feel like the one at a disadvantage. "You have to tell us to rise."

I blinked in utter surprise. "And if I don't?"

His lip curled and I flinched as a sudden spark of pain licked at my toes, as if I were standing on hot coals. "Then you can be sure that our collective displeasure will be felt eventually."

I looked down at the prince and set my jaw. The image of hundreds of Fae fusing to the ground, like a little army of kneeling statues, crossed my mind. Moss and vines growing over Scion's sleek dark hair, and his sneering contemptuous expression warping into a stone mask over time.

By Aisling, that was a dark thought…but an exhilarating one all the same.

I stood, unmoving, as heat tingled in my fingers and up my arms. Scion's silver gaze sharpened, and his nostril's flared.

Holding my gaze, he lowered his voice to barely more than a whisper. "Do you know what they're all thinking…my queen?"

He said "my queen" with the same venom as "you cunt."

I shook my head. "I expect you will tell me."

"They're wondering when I'll kill you. Not if, but when."

I snorted a laugh. Well, of course they were wondering that. It was hardly a threat, just a statement of the obvious.

If any other person in Elsewhere had won the crown, their family would be the royal house. The Everlasts would have been demoted back to nobles and standing in the hall with everyone else, but with me…well no one expected me to last an hour, let alone make it through the first hunt. They were all waiting for Prince Scion to slit my throat right here and now and declare himself the King of Elsewhere.

"And?" I whispered back. "Have you bet on yourself? Is that what you wanted to tell me? Not to lose you money?"

It was his turn to laugh. "Hardly. I don't have to gamble. I already know."

I looked up sharply. That was…an oddly direct statement, but he couldn't be lying. "You don't know that," I hedged. "You can't. You can want it. Plan it, but you can't *know*."

"Can't I? I keep telling you, rebel. Your fate is already sealed. I'm going to ruin you. All that remains to be seen is how much destruction you cause before I do."

My mouth became a thin line. I glanced out over the crowd of High Fae, clearly getting restless now as I argued over my death with their beloved prince. The same prince who'd locked me in a dungeon. The same prince who'd wanted me to lick his fucking boots.

I lifted the hem of my skirt slightly to reveal my slipper. He glanced down, seeming unsure what I was doing.

My heart pounded in my ears—even *I* was unsure what I was doing. "Lick it."

He raised his eyebrows, eyes dancing with amusement. "Excuse me?"

"You heard me. Lick."

"You're going to have to be more specific, rebel, or this will turn into a very different kind of party."

I gasped and his gaze danced with what seemed to be genuine mirth. He thought he'd beaten me and now I would give up and Gods, I wanted to win, just once. "Lick my cunt, then. Show me how you pay fealty to your queen."

His eyes flashed with raw hunger and a thrill shot through me. My entire body practically ached with the anticipation as need pulsed in my core.

As though reading my mind, Scion rose slowly, reaching for me. My lips parted on a gasp.

The moment shattered.

Behind us, a terrible sound tore through the room. Like the moan of a dying animal. I stiffened, turning on the spot, as all the hairs on my arms stood on end.

The lone figure of a woman lay on the tile floor in a crumpled heap, next to a puddle of vomit and...I gagged at the amount of blood. Her mouse-brown hair was lank and plastered to her face, which held a sickly sheen of sweat.

She lolled her head back and looked up at me, and I recognized her instantly. "Iola!

53
LONNIE

*P*rince Scion melted into the crowd, leaving me standing alone, but I barely noticed as I rushed to Iola's side and bent down, my gown pooling around my feet. Dread lodged itself in my gut and churned, doubling over on itself. Like poison, sitting in my stomach.

Iola lay writhing on the ground. My hands shook as I reached for her, and I swallowed several times, willing myself not to vomit— both from the smell and my own panic.

I turned back toward the crowd of Fae, only to find that most had turned their backs. Of course. Who amongst them would care for the death of a servant?

"Do something!" I demanded.

No one turned around. Beside me, Iola convulsed. Her eyes were wide open and bloodshot, tongue lolling out at an odd angle.

This could not happen again. I could not watch another person die while the Fae stood by ideally unbothered. I wouldn't.

My skin seemed to heat again, anger licking up my spine. My fingers tingled, as if with lack of movement, and all my muscles trembled.

"Someone do something!" I was shouting now, my voice echoing all around the ballroom.

My eyes caught on a blood-red gown, and Thalia pushing through the crowd, dragging Gwydion behind her to reach me. Relief flooded me. Gwydion was a healer.

Thalia looked expectantly at the prince, even as I shuffled out of the way to make room for him. Gwydion didn't move.

I gaped. "Heal her." My voice was incredulous.

"What's wrong with her?" he asked, far too slowly.

"I don't know." My frustration was rising, reaching a boiling point. I looked to Lady Thalia for help, but she too was staring at Gwydion with mingled disgust and confusion.

"That's my servant," Thalia said loftily. "If someone has poisoned her, I would take that very personally."

If she was poisoned or simply ill soon wouldn't matter because they would have allowed Iola to die while they stood there discussing the details of the situation. "I order you to help her." I told Gwydion, with as much authority as I could muster.

He raised an eyebrow. It wasn't an unkind expression, exactly. More...a curious one. "With what authority?"

"With...this?" I pointed at the absurd crown.

"That does little when you have no power behind it. No...alliances."

I closed my eyes, understanding now what he was getting at.

The offer was clear. He would not keep me in a dungeon or a tower because he did not care enough to bother. He would only help me exactly and as much as I helped him.

There was no loyalty from Gwydion. Only strategy.

"You are despicable," I hissed. "Perhaps worse than any of the others."

"Do you think so?" Gwydion said, sounding genuinely curious. "I don't see it that way. I simply don't like to lose. Now, let's get on with it. I'd say your friend has less than a minute before her heart stops for good."

I gritted my teeth. I was angry at myself for believing that Prince Gwydion was nicer or different from the rest of his family simply because he wasn't as overt in his scheming.

Still, he was right. I had no choice. No time.

I leaned in and whispered my real name, and the finality of it settled over me like the lid of a coffin.

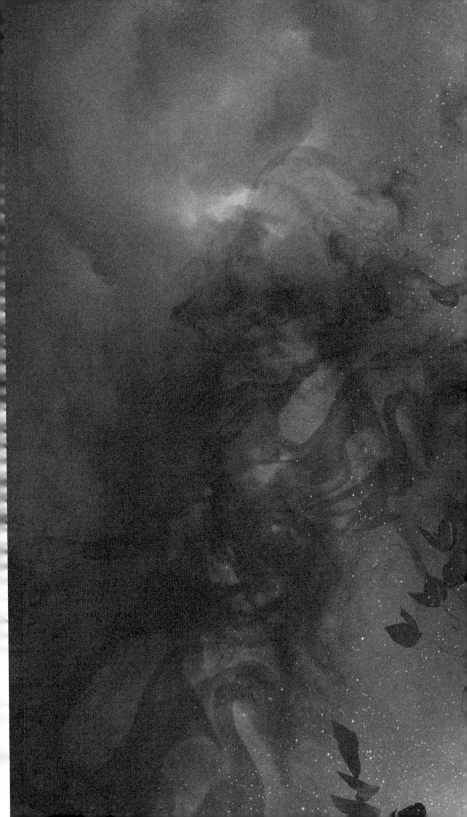

PART IV

♛

THE ONLY WAY TO GET RID OF A TEMPTATION IS TO YIELD TO IT

— OSCAR WILDE, "THE PICTURE OF DORIAN GRAY"

54
LONNIE

*W*hen I was a servant, I used to long for bathing day. Later, in the dungeon, I nearly forgot what clean water felt like. Now, in Prince Scion's fussy, beautifully furnished tower, I had a complicated relationship with the bathtub.

On the one hand, the bathing room had become my favorite. I spent lavish hours soaking in the lovely clawfoot tub with all the sweet-smelling perfumes. Afterward, I sat in a clean towel and Iola would brush my hair. It was bliss, and surely what I would miss most when this inevitably came to an end.

On the other hand, I was constantly reminded that while I sat in this luxury, others starved. They were cold. Dying. And there was nothing I could do about it.

It was the same with the castle.

On occasion, the beauty of it was overwhelming. The food, the warmth and the luxury threatened to make me forget my hatred. But then, I would see the Everlast crest, and be transported back to the dungeon. To my sister's death. To Penvalle's vile tent. To the day my mother was taken.

I was grateful for my lapse in judgement during my dance with Prince Scion, and that it had gone no further. It was a reminder of how easily I could be drawn in.

And why I could never allow myself to forget.

Today, I was painfully aware of the shame of enjoying my bath while Iola was not here to chat with me, or argue when I offered to brush her hair for once.

"Lonnie?"

My heart leapt and I sloshed water over the side of the tub as I sat up too fast, screaming at the top of my voice. "I'm coming, Iola!"

I pulled open the door and reeled back. "Where's Iola? Is she alright?"

"Good morning," Enid said, almost cheerfully as she elbowed past me and into the room. "Iola is still recovering. She won't be back to work for another several days at least."

I let out a breath of relief. "Oh good. She's alright though?"

"Yes. Thanks to you."

I raised my eyebrows, shocked, and waited for the other shoe to drop. It didn't. For the first time ever, Enid looked at me with something other than contempt in her gaze. Not quite affection. Not even respect, but perhaps the hint of something more fleeting. I had no name for it.

"Did Beira make you come?" I asked, uncomfortable.

"No, I volunteered." She scowled, as if she regretted it. "Do you want someone else? I won't bow if that's what you're expecting."

I smiled. That sounded about right. "No, I'm glad to have you stay."

She seemed suspicious about that. "It was poison, in case you were wondering."

"Oh. Yes. I assumed."

Gwydion had been able to heal Iola in seconds. Without feeding her any blood, I noticed. The real question in my mind was who attacked her? And more importantly, why?

I could have kicked myself for not paying better attention. If I hadn't been distracted—foolishly so—I might have seen the whole thing happen. In fact, if the whole room had not been kneeling, facing me, it might have been far more difficult to get away with such an attack.

"There's no gossip in the kitchen, is there?" I asked.

Enid looked up from where she was running a hand over the edge of the wardrobe, as if assessing the authenticity of the gold trim. "Like what?"

"Like, who might have poisoned Iola."

"Nothing specific. A lot of people think it was you."

I sighed, running a hand over my face. "Perfect."

I would just have to add this to my ever-growing list of questions. Hopefully, if I answered one, some of the others would start to fall into place.

"Listen, Enid," I asked, changing the subject. "Iola was never able to get me any trousers. Do you think we could find something for me to wear other than this?

Enid eyed the skirt of my gauzy gown and wrinkled her nose. "Most definitely."

I marched down the front steps of the castle, my head held high. The morning air was quiet, the fog hanging undisturbed over the grass, and the sun hadn't quite gotten hot enough to decide whether it would be a pleasant day.

I nodded to the guards and they stared stonily back at me. My stomach clenched. If they stopped me I wasn't sure what I would say. I didn't know either of them. Certainly, they had no loyalty to me, and likely they had been told I wasn't to leave the palace.

They didn't stop me, however. They didn't say anything.

I walked with purpose toward the gates, hoping that no one would stop me if I looked like I knew where I was going.

Iola's treatment at the ball had lit a new fire within me. Not only her poisoning, but the indifference of the Fae following the incident, filled me with an indescribable rage. Not that it should have surprised me, and in many ways, it didn't, but it did encourage me to try harder to find my sister's journals.

I strode down the road toward the city, heading for the tavern I'd visited over a week ago. There was no one around. No noise emanating over the water of the nearby lake except the occasional cricket or call of a mourning dove.

Perhaps, if I could wait at the tavern until nightfall I–

"Oi!" A voice shouted far too close to my ear. "Look what I've got."

I gasped, my breath catching as powerful arms circled my waist and lifted me off my feet.

I kicked out, alarmed. I struggled against the arms wrapped around my middle, holding my feet above the ground. "Get off me."

My captor laughed. "Listen to her giving orders like she thinks she's really the Queen."

He dropped me in a heap at his feet. I tried to stand, but was met with the point of a knife at my back. My stomach sank. *Why. Why hadn't I brought that dagger the merchant gave me?*

A group of Fae, two males and a female, stood in front of me, grinning at their friend as he taunted me. I blinked at them through my daze.

It was difficult to tell, as all Fae had that otherworldly beauty, but I guessed this group was not nobility. High Fae, certainly, but their clothing was closer to what I'd seen in the village than up at the palace.

I swallowed the bile in my throat. I had no idea if that was better or worse for me. It could mean they had less magic. It could also mean they were more adept fighters. There was no way to tell, and frankly it didn't matter. The weakest Fae could kill the strongest human with no effort, every time.

"What are you doing out of your palace all alone, Slúagh?" the one who grabbed me jeered.

I pressed my lips together, refusing to answer. He had bright red hair, several shades lighter than mine, and was holding a weapon as large as my entire forearm.

"Can't you talk," one of the others said, prodding at me with his iron-toed boot. "Or did they cut your tongue out already?"

The female bent down and picked at my hair. "Pretty for a human, don't you think?"

"I don't know," the one who'd grabbed me answered. "All humans smell disgusting, I can't get past that."

I recoiled from her hand. "Get away from me," I repeated with more venom.

I backed away toward the lake. Maybe I could jump into it and they wouldn't follow, but then I might have to contend with whatever called the water home. That might be far worse.

They laughed, their voices mixing together into a mocking cacophony.

"Here's what I want to know," the one with the red hair said. "This little thing killed an Everlast? I don't believe it. All humans lie."

"Then what happened?" One of the others asked.

"I think we should make her tell us," the redhead said, his smile turning nefarious.

I reached down slowly, feeling on the ground for a rock. A sense of familiarity stole over me, and I remembered Prince Bael telling me I was more likely to hurt myself than him. He was surely right about that. There was little I could do if someone didn't come along to help.

Unless…perhaps there was something I could do?

The redhead crouched down and looked me in the eye. His were green, like grass—or noxious fumes. "Can you be honest, human, or is that impossible for your kind?"

"You're insane," I spit with more confidence than I felt.

So quick I couldn't *even* brace for it, the fairy reeled back and slapped me across the mouth. I grunted, and a noise escaped my mouth I didn't know I was capable of making.

His friends laughed. High, cruel sounds.

"Let's try again," he said calmly. "How could a useless little thing like you manage to kill a king?"

"Fuck you," I muttered. "You might kill me, but it won't matter. No one cares about you any more than they care about me."

The fairy pulled his arm back and his knuckles collided with my cheekbone.

I heard the bone crack before I felt it, and I was falling to the side, blood spraying as pain exploded across my face. My vision swam, and tears filled my eyes.

I couldn't breathe. I couldn't see. The pain was everywhere.

The female pulled her foot back, swinging it toward my stomach as I curled into myself like a beetle on the ground. She kicked me again and again and I prayed to pass out, knowing that at any moment the one with the weapon could end me.

If there was ever a time for one of the strange occurrences that had terrified the village it would be now. One of those odd surges of power that seemed to attract the Fae and had made my mother so paranoid that she taught us to lie, always, no matter the consequences.

I willed my fingers to warm. Willed that surge of anger to travel up my spine and make my skin too hot to touch. Prayed for that strange pounding behind my eyes to start up again.

But nothing happened.

Another blow to my abdomen made me cry out, pleas falling from my lips, and still nothing happened.

Darkness closed around my eyes, and a tiny spark of defiance flickered at the back of my mind. Prince Scion had been wrong. He didn't kill me after all.

SCION

*M*y eyes had started to glaze over, darkness seeping around the edges despite the blistering sun beating down overhead. I blinked, the water of the lake coming back into focus, undisturbed as though no time had passed. And, in the grand scheme of things, what were a few minutes, really?

Steel clashed somewhere behind me, but I made no effort to stand or turn to watch. Instead, leaning back on my elbows in the grass, I picked up a stone from the shore beside me and held it in front of my face to inspect. It was warm in my palm— purple and pale gold with flecks of quartz. For the hell of it, I swapped the gold with silver, warping the shape into more of a disk before raising my arm and throwing it as hard as I could into the center of the still water.

For a moment, my own breath caught in my lungs as I hoped nothing would happen.

Then, an arm, dripping and glittering, clothed in white samite, rose from the center of the lake to catch the stone disk before sinking beneath the surface again. I set my jaw. *Hello again.*

"Sci, get off your lazy ass," Gwydion called to me from across the lawn.

I tipped my head back to look at him. I could barely see him upside down, but shadows flashed past my eyeline, and steel clanged alarmingly close to my head.

"No," I drawled. "I don't think I will, thanks."

"Your sword is painfully neglected."

"And that won't change by using it today," I pointed out. "It will still be neglected tomorrow and every day after that."

Bael cackled a laugh. "Truer words never spoken."

The sounds of swords stopped and footsteps pounded closer until a shadow fell over me. Bael's heavy leather boots rose on either side of my head. "You might as well come practice, he won't stop asking."

I rolled over and sat up to look at my cousin. Bael was flushed from sparring—a difficult feat, but then, they'd been at this for hours. His golden-bronze curls stuck to his forehead. I gave him a flat look. "I don't need to practice."

"Neither do I, but I'm being sociable."

I scowled. He was trying to make me feel guilty, the miserable bastard. Bael had only been back for a day or so, and already I knew he was bored. I had little advice. I hadn't spent so much time in the castle since...never. I'd never been confined to the capital this long.

At least it would soon be coming to an end.

As if reading my mind, Bael voiced exactly what I'd been thinking. "Only two more days until we travel to Inbetwixt. You can pretend to enjoy sparring for that long."

We both turned to Gwy in unison. He wasn't watching us and hadn't been paying attention to our conversation. His sword was back out, and he took long swipes at the air, battling an invisible enemy.

I made a non-committal noise in the back of my throat. The impending trip to Inbetwixt was both a blessing and a curse. It meant I could finally leave this wretched castle, but it also meant the second hunt was upon us, and I dreaded that for reasons I couldn't explain.

I closed my eyes and exhaled a long breath, fighting against the images that fought to flood my subconscious. Lying to myself was pointless as trying to lie aloud.

I was well aware that I'd become…conflicted…as of late. I simply had no logic for it. The rebel was haunting me. Consuming my every waking thought and twisted dream. Every nightmare and fantasy.

What would I have done if the ball had not been interrupted? I already knew the answer. I dreamed about it in such excruciating detail, I could swear it was prophecy.

"What's wrong?" Bael asked.

I cracked an eye open. I tried to say "nothing," and found I couldn't. Instead, I said, "Nothing worth discussing."

He scoffed. "That was a piss-poor deflection. You seem strange lately."

"I could say the same about you."

Bael opened his mouth to reply, but before he could a scream pierced the air. We both stiffened. I turned, looking for the source of the noise, but I knew that Bael had remained completely still. Sure enough, his eyes had rolled back into his head. Searching.

"What is it?" I asked.

He shook his head, not answering as his eyes continued to roll. Gwydion stepped up behind me, equally concerned.

Without warning, the air shifted and Bael disappeared.

"Where the fuck di—"

I didn't finish my sentence. Another yell sounded around the opposite side of the castle and I followed him through the shadows before I had time to think.

I reappeared on the other side of the castle. *It's Bael I'm concerned about. That's logical.*

Without warning, Quill swooped down from above, landing hard on my shoulder. I winced at his talons digging into my flesh and scowled.

There was nothing special about Quill aside from his size, which was my doing, but he was a useful pet. Partly because most believed him to have more power than he did, and I had yet to correct that assumption. His presence was more menacing than his actual abilities.

"Did you find Bael?" I asked the bird, as I strode in the direction of the lake. I glanced around the empty forest. There was no one there. No one to hear me. "What about the girl?"

Quill squawked, alarmed, and I stared at him nonplussed. I should have enchanted him to speak—this was getting ridiculous.

Up ahead, the surface of the lake shone in the setting sun, and…I paused, intrigued by the noise floating back to me on the wind.

My heart sped up, and I ran toward the commotion, some unfamiliar emotion rising in my chest—an instinct I couldn't contend with.

I turned in a full circle, searching for both my cousin and the source of the screaming. My heart pounded too fast, and an odd cold settled over me, trailing down the back of my neck.

Four strange Fae surrounded a limp body on the ground. The auburn hair spread across the ground was disturbingly familiar. I stopped in my tracks, blood rushing in my ears. Rage narrowed my vision, darkness seeping in on the edges.

Out of the corner of my eye, I saw Bael begin sprinting toward them. *Fuck.*

There was a reason that Bael didn't engage in direct combat— ever. Why our grandmother hadn't wanted him as an assassin, when he was just as competent as me. Why the entire family, even me, made sure he was on a short leash.

I had to reach them first.

My vision blurred, and I threw out an arm. The familiar buzz of magic filled the air, and two of the Fae flew backwards into the depths of the lake. I didn't have to look to know that arms would soon reach out of the depths and pull them below the surface.

The remaining two—a redheaded male, and a female—looked up at me. Their eyes widened.

The woman stumbled and took no more than two steps before she crumpled in a heap, writhing and twitching, a silent scream twisting her face.

The male stared open-mouthed at his companion. Or, what was left of her.

Nothing was happening to her. Not really. But her mind didn't know that.

As far as the bitch knew, her organs were being eaten alive from the inside out. Her skin was peeling away from the bone. Her hair and eyes were burning, and melting, and because she was immortal, she would never die. The pain would never stop.

On the ground, my rebel moaned. Turning my attention away from the last of the attackers, I bent down. Humans were impossibly fragile; it was incredible she was still alive. Unless...it wasn't.

I bent closer, searching for evidence of what I knew was there. She moaned again and I pushed some of the bloody hair back from her face, searching for the scar on her ear.

Her eyelids fluttered and cracked open and she looked up at me with surprising lucidity. "What, did you come to finish the job?" she croaked.

Something seized in my chest, and I opened my mouth to reply.

A familiar presence loomed over me and I looked up. "There you are. Where the fuck did you go?"

I furrowed my brow. What had just happened? One minute, Bael was running toward them, and the next I'd easily overtaken him. Where had he gone?

"Doesn't matter. Move." Bael barked, elbowing me out of the way.

I blinked in surprise, and let him crouch down next to me. Bael didn't usually talk to me like that. He didn't usually talk to anyone like that. My cousin had such a tight leash on his true emotions that his chosen persona had started to become his personality.

Now though, I watched, dumbstruck, as Bael picked up Lonnie, cradling her in his arms, and vanished into thin air.

How had I missed this?

I turned around, searching for the lone remaining male who'd decided to attack an unarmed human. No, attack *the Queen.*

Yes, that was worse. That was a better reason for the rage still coursing through me. More logical.

The male had the good sense to run, but clearly not the power to walk through the shadows in the light of day. I caught up with him easily, appearing in the middle of his path some five miles away from the castle.

He skittered to a halt, his face draining of color. "Lord, I—"

I walked slowly toward him, rage bubbling in my throat. He was dressed in the clothing of the Slúagh of Underneath. *Strange.*

"Who are you?" I asked him, tone deadly calm.

He stared at me, tripping over himself to answer. "Aedric. Son of Corrin. I'm—"

I cut him off with a hand. Peasant names. None that I recognized and none that mattered. That was enough. "And who sent you to hurt m—" I broke off, stumbling over my words slightly, trying to decide what to call her. "—the Queen."

"No one. She's just a fucking Slúagh, we—"

I reached out, grabbing his neck. It would have been easier to kill him with magic but tearing his head off would be more satisfying. *Except.*

I thought back to what I told her. I was going to kill her. That had to be the source of my anger. It was the injustice of it. He was taking my kill. Then there was Bael, who clearly had some sort of attachment to the girl.

I dropped the male, flexing my fingers. He gasped as he hit the ground and starred up at me, wide-eyed.

"You get to live," I said, my voice deadly calm. "Because you're going to tell everyone in all five providences that the Queen is ours. No one touches her. No one hunts her. She's our kill."

LONNIE

*P*rince Bael laid me down in the center of the plush bed in the tower room and bit savagely into his own wrist before pressing it to my mouth. "Drink."

My entire body ached. It ached in places I didn't know it was possible to ache, and spasmed everywhere else. This was worse than after the hunt, and maybe even than after the dungeons, though that was a near thing.

I sucked greedily at the prince's wrist, lapping my tongue against the wound so it wouldn't close. I didn't know where that thought came from but it seemed to be working.

I tried not to think about how objectively revolting this was. How beastly. How oddly intimate. How…Fae.

"What the fuck were you thinking?" Bael growled, sounding oddly like Scion. "You could have been killed."

I shook my head, narrowing my eyes at him and he pulled his wrist back from me sharply so I could answer. A whine I didn't quite recognize sounded in the back of my throat. He raised his eyebrows. Beneath that bemused expression however, I thought his eyes might have been a bit dazed.

I tried to force my voice not to shake. "I could be killed here, as well. Or did you not hear about the poisoning?"

His yellow eyes were wide with some unidentifiable emotion. Not concern exactly. More like anger. *Possession.* "You are too breakable."

"What happened to the Fae who attacked me?"

"Dead." His lip curled, his smile dangerous. "I told you, we'll kill anyone who hurts you."

I noticed that he said "we" now instead of "I," but I wasn't sure he noticed the shift. Regardless, he must have thought the statement to be true.

"Who were they?"

He sat on the bed, looking oddly human for a moment. I wondered if perhaps he was tired. Could the High Fae experience blood loss like humans did? "I don't know. Probably no one important, but we'll try to find out."

I chewed on my lip. It seemed too coincidental that Iola would be poisoned and then I would be attacked with only days left to go until the second hunt. Why not simply wait until the hunt?

"Where have you been?" I asked, leaning back against the pillows.

Bael didn't move. "Oh, many places. Shall I list them? That could take a while. You see, I was born in—"

"Stop it. You know what I meant."

"You need to work on your specificity, little monster."

"Where were you this past week, then?"

He smiled. "Why? Did you miss me?"

"Answer the question."

He stretched his arms out across the bed. "I was unavailable. You will have to be content with not knowing more than that."

"And you're back now? Just days before the hunt?" My anger sparked. "What happened to preparing me? What about helping?"

"I hear you found a new ally in Gwydion."

I barred my teeth. "That is hardly the point. What province will we be traveling to for the second hunt? What is to happen there? How—"

He sat up, looking bemused. "You did miss me."

"Fuck yourself."

He laughed, and all his too-sharp teeth caught the light. "Inbetwixt. It's at the quarry on the far side of the province. It's barely a day's ride from here, so we will not be encroaching on the Lord of Inbetwixt's hospitality overnight."

I remembered the sneering woman from the ball and narrowed my eyes. "Is that really why? Or is it because that court hates your family?"

He shrugged. "Both."

"Aine said it was you specifically they dislike."

"Aine is a bitch." He grinned. "And she's usually correct. Aside from Scion, she's my closest friend."

I frowned. "When will we leave?"

"The morning after next. Now can you be quiet a moment? I have a miserable headache."

He lay flat on his back, eyes closed. He looked almost innocent—that same close to angelic visage I'd thought of when I first met him.

I swallowed, thickly, and tried to calm my racing thoughts. "So, can your entire family heal that way then?"

He opened his eyes and grinned and immediately the angelic persona dropped. That was it, I realized. It was his slightly cat-like eyes and too-sharp teeth that made some primal part of me wake up and know I was in danger. *Bewitching. Beguiling. Bone-chilling.*

"Yes..." He grimaced, giving himself a little shake. "But they wouldn't. And I would appreciate it if you didn't mention to any of them that I've done it for you again."

I hadn't mentioned it in the first place, which must mean he had. "Yes, because I spend so much time gossiping with Aine."

He laughed hollowly. "That wouldn't shock me, actually. But truly, please do not bring it up?"

I sat up a little straighter. A request for a favor from one of the Fae was unusual. Maybe he really was tired.

"Why?" I asked, shrewdly.

If he noticed my tone he said nothing. "For one thing, Scion will become more violent than he already is. Not that I care, but you might when he becomes homicidal."

"Why?"

He squeezed his eyes shut tight. "Are you not willing to let this go?"

He really must have a headache. "No."

He made a noise in the back of his throat—half groan, half growl. "It's not a common practice, and considered taboo except among mates."

My eyebrows hit my hairline. "Oh."

I wasn't sure—and wasn't sure I wanted to know—if he'd meant true mates, or if it was a slip of the tongue.

He was quiet for a second. "Do you know how the hunts started?"

"Do not change the subject. I despise when you all do that."

"This is not changing the subject. Do you know?"

I sighed, then thought about it for a moment. I knew what everyone knew—that the Everlast family had sat on the throne for so long hardly anyone was alive who remembered a time when they hadn't ruled Elsewhere. But honestly, no. Now that I thought about it, I didn't know where the tradition came from. Only that it had been plaguing the country for generations.

I shook my head. "No."

He gave me a feline smile, stretching back out on the bed. He reminded me too much of a house cat in the sun. Or some sort of well-fed beast. "Fine, little monster. I'm going to tell you a story."

LONNIE

"Generations ago, Queen Aisling was the first ruler of Elsewhere."

"And I suppose she was an Everlast?" I said acidly.

"No." He gave me a feline smile. "But I'm glad you asked."

"Aisling was from the northern province of Nightshade. Her magic was strong, due to living near the source of all magic, and therefore she took three mates to help share her power. One from each of the High Fae cities of Overcast, Inbetwixt and Nevermore in order to bind the land together into one kingdom."

"What about Underneath?" I asked.

Bael gave me a sideways glance. "Do you ever allow anyone to speak uninterrupted?"

"No," I retorted. "Not when there are quite so many dramatic pauses."

He laughed. "This was some thousands of years ago. The city of Everlast did not exist yet, and it certainly was not the capital. The province of Underneath extended further than it does now, as far as the border of the Waywoods, and all the Unseelie monsters were allowed to roam free as long as they didn't cross the woods."

"So, Aisling and her mates lived happily in Nightshade for some time, ruling the High Fae with the help of the magic at the Source, until one day the Unseelie King of Underneath crossed the border of the Waywoods. He was angry that Aisling had not offered him a place at her court, so he came and killed her mates and violated her and then took her crown forged in the volcanoes of the Source."

I blanched. "How were four High Fae royals killed by one Unseelie?"

He shrugged. "I don't know how they were defeated. It seems from the rest of the story that the Unseelie King possessed some strong powers of persuasion, perhaps he simply suggested that they surrender."

I shuddered, thinking immediately of King Penvalle and his odd hypnotic hold over the servants in his tent. If it was anything like that…I could believe it.

"But all four weren't killed," Bael said. "Just the mates, and most of their children. Aisling survived, as well as one of her children."

I sat up. "How do you know?"

"Because she's written about in further history. She went straight to the ancient Gods at the Source and asked them to punish the Unseelie King with the same pain he'd inflicted on her. The curse took a tremendous amount of power, and it caused the Source to erupt, turning the sky black."

I swallowed. That was…an odd coincidence. "What did the curse do?"

He spoke with an affect, as if quoting someone else. "As long as the crown is not returned to the worthy wearer, the obsidian kingdom will know everlasting misery. If ever any member of the royal house should experience true happiness, all those with Everlast blood in their veins will die."

I stared at the prince, conflict warring in my mind. That was horrible, and yet. "He deserved it," I said fiercely. "Did it work?"

Bael cocked his head at me. "You think so? Interesting. Would it change your mind to know she was pregnant with his child?"

I opened my mouth to ask how and closed it again. Horror filled me. It was thousands of years ago, and still, I felt for this poor woman. "If her curse worked, would her own child die?"

"When she realized she was pregnant and that the curse would affect her child she went to the gods but they could not change it so she left her older child in Nightshade and took her younger son to the Unseelie King. She demanded that, to save his son's life, he return the crown. Instead, the king took the boy from Aisling and raised him in the obsidian palace."

"And what about her?"

"The Unseelie King kept her too, as a hypnotized slave, until the day she died."

I raised my eyebrows, looking around the tower room. Not every room in the castle was obsidian...but enough. Enough that the persuasive power of the king and his resemblance to King Penvalle was more than coincidence. I shuddered. "I thought you were going to tell me your ancestor was the first child. The one who the king spared. Maybe that your family were the heroes who killed the king."

He laughed, and the sound echoed all around the room, wrapping around me like smoke. "No, little monster. I come from a long line of villains. If there are any heroes in this story, they share no blood with me."

I frowned. Something about those words rattled me and I couldn't place why.

"So, what happened?" I said urgently. This felt important, and I desperately wanted to know how it ended.

"The prince grew to despise his father for keeping his mother a prisoner, but he didn't have the same magic talent and could not free her. When he grew old enough, he lured his father out on a hunting trip and killed him, thinking that would break all his enchantments."

"And did it?"

"They never found out. Aisling died the moment the king died." He grimaced. "Her son, the new king, turned his attention to breaking the curse of the crown. Until it was broken he and his entire family would never find happiness. Eventually he started the hunts, searching for someone worthy of the crown."

My heartbeat sped up. "You're not about to say that's me, are you?"

"I wasn't, no."

I bit my lip. It was a lot to process at once. And, I supposed, some of it could simply be a story. Although… a tiny voice whispered in the back of my mind. The sky turning black when the Source erupted was an odd coincidence. I wondered if Prince Bael knew what day I was born. I doubted it. I doubted he knew exactly how old I was.

"How old are you?" I blurted out.

He gave me an odd look. "Why? You're not wondering if I'm telling you a first hand account of history are you? That would make me one of the oldest beings alive. No one that old is simply walking around, casually chatting with rude human women."

"No." My face heated. "I know that."

The Fae were immortal, but most, like Queen Celia, would choose to return to the Source after some thousand years or so. The only truly invincible beings were the Gods that Aisling had asked for help all those years ago.

"I was twelve during the fall of Nightshade, so by your standards I wouldn't yet be middle-aged. Much better than the rest of my family, they're all growing quite old."

I raised an eyebrow. "That surprises me."

"Why?"

"I don't know." I said honestly. Maybe because all the Fae, even the children, were a bit enigmatic.

"I will be interested to see if your magic keeps you from aging."

My stomach lurched. "I don't necessarily have magic."

He turned his head to look at me. "You do. It's painfully obvious. We all know it, we just don't know what it is."

My heartbeat sped up and fear washed over me. Always lie, I reminded myself. Never let them notice you. "I don't know what you're talking about."

He gave me a look that told me he saw right through me, but didn't comment. Instead, he sat up and got to his feet. He looked me over as though scanning for injuries, and then stepped back, evidently satisfied. "I'll let you keep your lies for now, little monster. All I care about is that you're safe."

LONNIE

I stood on an unfamiliar balcony overlooking the city.

Unnatural heat surrounded me, and I reveled in the warmth as Prince Bael held me tight, my back to his chest. He pressed his lips to my shoulder, then the curve of my neck, speaking low against my skin. His too-sharp teeth grazed the shell of my ear and I shivered.

He pressed his mouth to my ear, speaking so softly I felt the words more than heard them. "Do you want more, little monster?"

His voice lacked some of the refined musicality I was used to, but was just as hypnotic. Honeyed. Like sex and dessert personified.

Prince Scion looked up at me from the floor, his silver eyes owning my attention, beckoning to me.

A whimper escaped my lips and my pulse pounded in my core. Holding my gaze, the prince pushed my knees wide. I moaned as he pressed a stinging kiss to the inside of my thigh.

He laughed softly. "I'm going to destroy you."

I gasped and he bent his head and ran his tongue up my center in long slow licks.

It was too much and I tried to squirm away, but Bael held me still, his fingers traveling over my sides, ghosting my ribs, and finally moving to circle my hard nipples.

I rocked against his hard cock pressing into my ass, as Scion circled my throbbing clit with the tip of his tongue.

"Please," I begged.

Fire licked up my stomach. Scorching me. Consuming me from the inside out.

I stormed through the castle the following morning. I had only one full day left before the second hunt and I refused to waste it. I refused to allow any distractions. I *refused* to dwell on this foolishness.

As I walked, a rustling behind me made me jump a foot in the air, my breath catching in my throat. I spun on the spot, coming face to face with a set of jet-black, inhuman eyes. "Ahh!"

I scrambled away, alarmed, and the gigantic raven screeched in my face, as though affronted, flapping its enormous wings.

This time, it was impossible not to recognize Quill. How often did one come across a raven the size of a small wolf? Its beak alone had to be the size of my hand, and its wings spread out across most of the corridor.

It landed on the floor and cocked its head at me, its eerie, knowing eyes assessing. "What are you doing, you stupid child," it seemed to say. "I have no time for your foolishness."

I agreed.

"Er…" I wasn't sure if talking to a bird was insane or polite. Magical animals were not particularly rare, but this one seemed normal aside from the size. "Hello."

My, how far I'd fallen. Making bargains with Fae, talking to birds. I was halfway to mad and I hadn't even realized it.

I hadn't really expected to see the bird again after the other night, but its presence wasn't entirely unwelcome. That wasn't until it jumped into the air, fluttering for a moment, its wings beating me around the head. I raised my arms to cover my head from the spontaneous attack. "Ow! Stop!"

It screeched again, sharp talons ripping at my hair and clothes, and swooped away down the hall. I stared after it, unsure if I should follow or if that was further proof of my growing insanity.

"Do you want something to eat?" I asked the bird, hoping it could understand me. It seemed to understand the word "eat" at any rate.

The enormous thing leapt into the air and landed on my shoulder. Its talons dug into my skin. I winced slightly as I opened the door.

It was unusually quiet in the kitchen—perhaps more so than I'd ever seen it in all the years I'd lived here. I was grateful for that. Perhaps my bad luck had decided to go easy on me today.

As I stepped inside, I stopped short, my blood running cold. It was no coincidence that it was empty today. I looked from Beira at the stove, to the black-haired girl eating a cookie on a stool by the fire.

Trays upon trays of food covered the kitchen, dried vegetables hung from the ceiling, and there was a pot of broth large enough to boil me cooking on the stove.

Beira turned around, saw me, and shrieked something akin to a hello.

"Hello." I glanced nervously at Princess Elfwyn. "I just wanted...what are you doing?"

Beira swore loudly. "What does it look like I'm doing?" She also glanced over at the little girl by the fire and rolled her eyes.

She muttered something in a language I didn't understand, but had heard her use before. The expression was something to the tune of "When the fucking hills turn inside out." And meant "I'll die before I do this again."

She said it often, and always did the same things again.

I shook my head. "Sorry. I mean, what are you cooking for?" And why are you doing it alone?

Beira stopped stirring and turned around to face me. "Shouldn't you of all people know?"

One would think. "No one has told me anything."

"The second hunt is at the quarry in Inbetwixt," Beira said. "Out on the far side of the province."

"Oh. Right. I knew that. What's the food for?"

"The journey there. You should have all left already and some damn cook at their court should be cooking for the fucking nobles tonight, but *no*. It's all on me, and—" She jerked her head toward Princess Elfwyn. "My kitchen was just cleared out because all the damn help is scared of a child."

I stared at Beira. That raised almost more questions than it answered, and clearly it was a bad time for a visit. "Well, I'll leave you to it."

"Please," the woman said, her hair falling out of its bun.

I took a step back in the direction I'd come, but my eyes caught on the little princess by the fire.

Elfwyn had finished her cookie, and now sunk sharp teeth into a jelly pastry and looked up at me from her seat by the fire. "What are you doing here?" She asked between bites.

I could ask you the same question. "Er," I glanced at Beira. "Just bored."

The princess looked up at me with round, silver eyes. Unblinking. Like a haunted doll. "I'm bored all the time," she confided. "There's no one interesting to play with."

"You have such a large family, I'm sure there's someone."

She rolled her eyes and I took that as the entire answer. "I'm not even allowed to go outside alone."

I grinned in spite of myself. "Me neither."

"Well, of course," Elfwyn said knowledgeably. "Because you are weak and useless and there are rebels in the area. I am more than capable of caring for myself."

I coughed. That was…something from such a young child.

"I'm sure your family just worries about you."

I was not sure of that. The Everlasts did not seem the worrying type, and of all of them, the only one I'd yet to hear utter a single word was Elfwyn's mother. Still, all species cared for their children…right?

"Wait, Elfwyn?" I asked tentatively.

She looked up at me with her wide, pale eyes "What?" Her teeth were red with jelly and it reminded me too much of the blood on her father's face the night I killed him. I shuddered.

"What do you mean rebels are in the area?"

She wrinkled her nose. "Don't you know anything?"

"Obviously not."

She cackled a creepy little laugh that made the hair on the back of my neck stand on end. "True enough. The rebels have come to the capital; they're infiltrating the city. My brother said they're just waiting for us to leave for Inbetwixt. That's why we aren't staying for long."

My heartbeat sped up, and I stared at her. "Are you sure?"

She shrugged and took a tremendous bite of pastry, her next words muffled by the food between her too-sharp teeth. "I said we should have left and let them take you, but no one cares what I think."

I frowned. That sounded about right. "So, they're still here?" I asked. "In the city?"

She nodded. "And it's all your fault. Now I don't even get to go to the second hunt. If not for all the passages out of the castle I would be stuck here day in and day out, and I would waste away."

I raised my eyebrows. "What passages?"

"Everywhere. The halls, the bedrooms, the library. Finding them is half the game of course, but—wait!"

I was already halfway out the door.

59

LONNIE

$\mathcal{T}$he library passage Elfwyn mentioned had taken me most of the afternoon to find.

I ran my hands over every shelf and window ledge in the cavernous room until finally I found one with hinges. It was surprisingly simple. A mechanism, not magic. A foolproof escape plan, just for me.

The door behind the bookshelf had opened onto a spiral staircase which led out to the garden below. At the bottom, the door melted back into the stone, with seemingly no way to open it again from the outside—that would have to be a problem for later when I returned.

Though every fiber of my being longed to go through the passage immediately, I was all too aware that the daylight hours were likely the worst time to do so. Not only because I was likely to be caught by the guards or the princes, but because the woman at the tavern last week had mentioned that Rosey had only ever visited after dark.

I had only one night. One opportunity. And I couldn't waste it.

I lay in bed reading another history book as I waited anxiously for nightfall, Quill the raven perched on the window beside me.

My door flew open without a knock and I jumped, my heartbeat skyrocketing for a moment before I realized it was only Enid.

"Get up!" she yelled, bursting in with a basket nearly too large for her arms to wrap around. "Look what I found."

I jumped off the bed. "Rosey's journals?"

For good measure, I'd mentioned to Enid to continue to look for the books in hiding spots near the kitchens. Perhaps I wouldn't have to risk sneaking out after all.

"No. Sorry." Enid frowned over her basket. To her credit, she did look a bit sorry. "I looked in all the bedrooms, and asked anyone who might have taken them, but I don't know where they are."

I sighed. "It's alright. What did you want to show me?"

"Pants!" She dropped the basket on the bed and pulled out a pair of trousers small enough that they looked like they'd been made for me. "You can stop wearing those ridiculous gowns."

She glanced at my gown with clear envy and I got the feeling she thought it was less ridiculous in general, and more unfair of anyone who had once been a servant to own a dress meant for royalty. I didn't blame her. That *was* ridiculous.

I reached for the gray trousers she held out to me. "That was far faster than I expected. Thank you."

Enid crossed to the window, sparing half a glance for Quill. She was evidently not nearly so alarmed by the bird as Iola had been —then again, Enid cared for very little. "Yes, well, I didn't make them. They came from guards uniforms."

That made me think with a pang of Caliban, who I had not thought of in some time. Not until the other night at the ball when Scion had brought him up. I hoped wherever he was, he was safe.

"Enid," I said slowly, my plan still forming. "I need another favor."

She looked back at me and scowled. "What?"

"Can I swap dresses with you? You can have my gown."

Her eyes widened. "What the hell am I going to do with that?"

"Sell it? I don't know."

She stiffened. "Don't try to be nice."

"I'm not," I said honestly. "You don't have to take my dress if you don't want it, but I really need yours."

A muscle in her cheek twitched and I could tell she was tempted. "Why?"

I hated the irony of my constant refrain, and how unlikely it was to work. "I need something that will help me go unnoticed."

60

LONNIE

$\mathcal{T}$he tavern was loud and alive with activity when I arrived on the doorstep. The air had cooled, night nearly upon us, but the inn was as raucous as noontime at the capital market.

Light poured out onto the road, and music—normal, human music—welcomed in passers by, beckoning in the weary traveler and the local barfly alike.

I kept my hood pulled low over my head, hoping that no one would recognize me as I ducked inside. I could be any other girl. I was any other girl, and the only second glances I received were from men and women several drinks in and searching for a bedmate.

I took stock of them, just to be safe. Two Fae—a male and a female, speaking in low voices by the fire. No concern to me, they were here for each other. A demi-Fae, I guessed, based on his slightly rounded ears, sitting with a group of soldiers.

Taking a seat at the bar, I waved to the same woman I'd given the gold to over a week ago. I noticed with some satisfaction that she seemed less anxious than she had been the last time I was here, and her dress appeared new.

Her eyes widened in recognition as she saw me and she hurried over. "It's you!"

"Shhh," I hissed.

"Sorry, I was just hoping I'd see ye."

My heartbeat sped up. "Are they here tonight?"

She scanned the crowd. "I don't see them, but don't worry. I'll get you a drink, yeah? You can wait."

I smiled, only a bit disappointed. "Thanks."

She placed a glass of something in front of me I'd never seen before and gave me a nod before hurrying away again. I tapped absently on the edge of the glass.

It was strange—my entire life, I'd assumed everyone feared me because of something inherently wrong with me. Like perhaps it was part of whatever odd quality drew in the fae and caused my mother to demand I lie from the time I was a small child.

Now, removed from the stories that had always followed me, everything felt different. Like I'd been cast in a different light.

A man stepped up beside me, his presence casting a shadow over me and blocking out the light from the fire. "Never had Fawn-made ale before?"

I stiffened and looked up. "Of course I have," I lied.

"You know what you're doing then," he said jovially. "Potent stuff, I was just going to warn you to drink it slowly."

I looked up at the man. He was tall and broad, with red hair and a matching beard. He wore a blue traveling cloak over an embroidered tunic, far too intricate to be from here. My heart sped up. A traveler, then, like the barmaid had seen with Rosey.

"Who are you?" I asked, trying not to sound too excited.

"I could ask the same."

"Inbetwixt?" I asked, gesturing to his clothing.

"Not originally," he said pleasantly, but didn't elaborate. "You?"

"Here," I said. "Not originally."

He laughed and sat down beside me without invitation. "Fair enough. What's your name?"

"Rosey," I said without hesitation.

I watched the man's eyes for any spark of...anything, but there was no change. *Shit.*

He smiled at me and it was a bit too nice. "What brings a girl like you here?"

My stomach turned over. I thought I'd done a decent job of hiding my identity this time. I'd piled my hair into a messy twist of curls as I always did before, and Enid's maroon and tan dress looked so close to something I would have worn before this year I was not entirely sure it wasn't pieces of one of my old garments made over to look newer. There was nothing about my clothing that screamed wealth or status.

I put my hands in my lap. "What kind of girl am I?"

"A clean one."

I looked down and could have kicked myself. He had a point. I hadn't thought about how noticeable freshly washed hair and clean fingernails would be, but there was nothing to be done about it now.

"Bathing day," I said vaguely.

He smiled. He didn't believe me and we both knew it, but he let it go. "Of course. You didn't answer my question though."

I had to think for a moment to remember what he'd asked. "I'm looking for someone."

"Who?"

I blinked at him, suspicious. "Why?"

"I know lots of someones. Might know yours."

My heart pounded against my ribs. This felt a little convenient, but then again, if anyone had known Rosey they would certainly recognize me...

"Fine," I said, my excitement making me speak a little too loudly. "You know the name Dullahan?"

His eyes shuttered. My heartbeat sped up. That was definitely a reaction. He knew the name, if not the person.

The red-bearded man pushed to his feet, and took a step back from the bar as if he wanted to get as far away from me as possible. "No, sorry," he frowned. "I don't know that one."

I got to my feet. "Are you certain? It's not a common name."

"Quite certain."

"But–"

"Listen." The man was no longer smiling as he leaned down to speak low so only I could hear. "If I was you, I wouldn't come asking around here again. They're listening. They have ears everywhere."

I wanted to take a step back, as his breath hit my face, his entire body invading my space, but I held my ground.

Usually, when someone said *"They,"* they meant "The Everlasts," and I didn't have to clarify. This time, I wasn't entirely sure what he meant.

My eyes narrowed. "Who's listening?"

"I don't know your man, but if I did, I would tell you to keep your friends close at night. Don't hide in the moondust tree at noon. You know?"

The excitement I'd felt for half a second came crashing down. That wasn't a secret, or any rebel clue. It was a proverb.

"Don't hide in the moondust tree at noon." was a common enough expression. Beira said it sometimes, and my mother had adopted it in the years before she was taken. It meant not to draw attention to yourself, as hiding in a tree that had no leaves during the day would make one quite obvious.

"Sure," I grumbled, turning toward the door. "Thanks."

If only this man knew that his advice was wasted on me.

LONNIE

I barely watched where I was going as I crossed back onto the palace grounds and walked up the long path to the castle. Without any guidance—nothing from Rosey, and no sign of her journals, I was completely lost.

Up ahead, the lights of the palace twinkled in the moonlight. The will-o-wisp circled the east tower, like a halo against the dark sky. I swallowed. It was supposed to be beautiful, but to me it appeared somehow ominous. Another pretty thing designed to entice as much to harm.

I could scream with frustration. It felt as though I was so close. So close to finally discovering real information, and yet I was out of time.

There were so many moments over the last year I wished I could return to and do differently, beginning with when Rosey had asked me to be her at the hunt and I hadn't pressed her on why.

I stopped short in the middle of the path, as an idea struck me. We'd been taught to lie, always, and yet somehow I'd thought so highly of my sister that I assumed Rosey was honest with me.

But clearly, she wasn't.

In the months leading up to Rosey's death, she had a persistent cough and insisted on drinking tea from moondust leaves. Unless she wasn't. Unless it was simply an excuse to go out to the trees at night.

I grinned and my heart sped up, excitement flooding me. Could that be it? Could it be that my sister hid her journals in the tree? Or perhaps that was where the rebels left their messages? On the leaves that would be there overnight and disappear by morning.

My smile widened. This was the answer. I was sure of it. The only question remained, which tree?

*T*here were three moondust trees on the grounds of the castle. One on the furthest edge of the grounds by the lake, one in the center of the gardens in the middle of the labyrinth of hedges, and one in Lady Raewyn's private courtyard.

I felt it unlikely that my sister or anyone else would use the tree in Raewyn's courtyard, however during the months that Rosey was ill she had visited each of the other two trees several times. It was difficult to say which tree would be a more likely hiding spot.

I decided to start with the further tree–the one at the lake. As I moved in that direction, flickering lights danced in the depths of the forest, and distant voices called to each other. I strained my ears. Who would be out here?

My heart pounded faster, slamming against my chest. What if the rebels were staying nearby? Or planning another attack? What if they were coming now? Would they be welcoming or hostile toward me if I encountered their group unawares?

I hadn't planned to meet them as such—not in a large group. What if they stabbed me before ever asking what I was doing there?

Then again, if I turned back now, there would be no point to any of this.

I continued on, marching resolutely toward the sounds down by the lake. As long as I didn't have to venture into the Waywoods —that was where I drew my line. Curiosity—it would kill me one day, and what a wonderful way to go.

Fortunately, the sounds didn't seem to be coming from the woods. The sounds led me further from the palace, in the direction of Moonglade lake. I rarely went this way, if only because I had no reason to. The lake stood independent from most anything else, on the opposite side of the palace from the village. I'd heard servants talk of its magical properties, and there was nothing I wanted less than to get closer to magic.

Finally, the lake came into view up ahead surrounded by swaying cattails and reeds. The moon reflected on the surface, creating a bridge of light across as the name suggested. The enormous moondust tree trailed its waxy, white leaves into the lake by the edge, the only disturbance in the perfectly unmoving surface. Like a bubble in blown glass. For a moment I forgot what I was looking for, captivated by the beauty of the reflection on the water.

Then, a shout of laughter shook me from my reverie. Louder now. Closer.

I turned, searching for the source, and gasped. My eyes grew wide, and I froze gaping at the scene in front of me.

Fairies. Dozens of them filled the meadow beside the lake. Some danced or drank around the fire, but most…I flushed. It was as if I'd walked into one of my dreams.

A roaring bonfire raged in the middle of their circle, illuminating their wickedly beautiful faces—and their perfect, naked bodies.

I felt drunk, like the hypnotic music of fairy fiddles and the scent of Elven wine was wrapping around me, making my heart beat faster. My stomach fluttered with anticipation and need.

My eyes darted from group to group, unable to focus. Moans of pleasure, shrieks of laughter, and animalistic growls echoed around the grounds. Some hundred yards in front of me, two males held a dark-haired woman between them, both pounding into her in a synchronized rhythm. Mere feet from them, a nymph woman devoured another woman's cunt while a man took her from behind.

I was simultaneously shocked and transfixed. They were wild. Untamed and uninhibited. They moved as if dancing with no music, and my body reacted as I watched. My stomach clenched, heat flooding my core, and my nipples growing hard against the tight fabric of my dress.

I shook myself violently, knowing I should leave—and yet curiosity lingered. I darted back, hovering behind the trunk of the very moondust tree that had brought me here to begin with.

My breath coming fast as I tried desperately to collect myself. I should leave. Go look at the other tree, and try this one later. I didn't know what I'd walked in on, but it wasn't for me.

I took a few deep breaths through my nose, and peeked out around the tree once more, making sure no one would see me if I darted back across the grass toward the palace.

My wide eyes grew even larger as I beheld the figures approaching the crowd in the field. My stomach leapt in an odd combination of excitement and jealousy.

Every other thought fled my mind as two familiar silhouettes strode toward the fire and the crowd parted to welcome them.

62

LONNIE

*M*y pulse thrummed low in my belly and tingles traveled over my skin.

The princes were still mostly clothed, though the fairies who walked up to them were not, wrapping their arms and bodies around them like cats in heat.

A low surge of anger rose in me and I sucked in a breath through my nose, gritting my teeth. I had no right to be watching this. No right to have any sort of opinion, negative or otherwise. No right to feel…anything.

Still, I watched, hating myself more and more every second.

A painfully sensual nymph approached Prince Bael and threw her arms around his neck. To my great satisfaction, he shoved her away, disentangling himself immediately and stepping away with a shake of his head.

Scion, who already had two nymphs draped over him like blankets, leaned over and said something to Bael and Bael scowled at him, seeming irritated. Scion threw his head back and laughed.

My eyes widened. I'd never seen him laugh like that before. I wasn't even sure I'd seen him smile in a way that was not cruel or calculated or mocking. He was attractive normally, they all were, but like that...my chest seized.

Tugging the nymph woman closer, he attached his mouth to her neck. My skin grew hot. Not with excitement this time, but with anger I didn't want to acknowledge or examine too closely. Why I cared, I had no idea, but my body knew more than my brain was willing to admit.

Energy crackled, sending static through the ends of my hair and making it stand on end. I gasped, fear mingling with my anger. *Shit.*

As if summoned by the energy surging around me, Bael looked up. Across the field our eyes met and I knew without a shadow of a doubt he saw me. His yellow eyes widened and then narrowed.

An emotional turmoil surged through me. Dread. Embarrassment. Defiance.

Excitement.

I trembled, and our gazes locked.

And then, in the space between breaths, the air shivered in front of me. The darkness shifted, twisting, moving until it reformed. Fingers reached for my throat, becoming more corporal by the second, and I gasped.

Bael pushed me back against the tree, rage in his face, and bared his too-sharp teeth. "What the fuck do you think you're doing? How did you get out here?" he growled, practically vibrating as his eyes blazed with rage.

From far away, I hadn't noticed. But now, I saw that he had some sort of rune designs drawn in white paint on his cheeks and forehead. He wore red trousers—thank the goddess—but no shirt, and for the first time I could see the full extent of the tattoo on the side of his chest.

Or not exactly a tattoo I realized, but a raised scar in the shape of a vine-like pattern that covered half his chest and most of his shoulder.

I struggled against his hold, stammering, my entire body flushing with heat. The bark pressed into my back and my eyes widened, remembering my dream of earlier in the week.

Shock and mortification washed over me, overtaking everything "I'm—I just wanted to…"

What. What could I possibly say?

Was it worse to say that I had been trying to find Dullahan—trying to meet the rebels Prince Scion was always accusing me of working with? Or worse to have Bael think I'd followed him here on purpose to watch their… "party" felt like the wrong word.

Both possibilities were equally horrifying in different ways, and for once, I struggled to think of a lie.

I coughed, choked, and pulled at his hand around my neck. He loosened his fingers slightly but did not step back.

"Why do you care?" I demanded.

Not the worst I could have said, I supposed.

"Because I told you that you were not to attend the revel."

I cast my mind around, unsure what he was referring to. Then, a single conversation from one of our sparring sessions came back to me. I'd assumed he was talking about the ball—evidently not.

"I didn't realize I would be intruding. I simply wanted some fresh air."

"Liar." He grinned, but not as if he was happy. More like a baring of teeth. Vicious and hungry at the same time. "Go back to the castle. You're not safe here."

I glanced over his shoulder at the meadow. Without meaning to, my gaze found Scion among the melee. As always, he sat slightly apart from the others, however he was not alone. My eyes widened and my heart beat a violent rhythm against my chest in time to the drumming, which seemed to grow louder in my ears.

The girl I'd seen with Prince Scion now knelt between his legs. His fingers were tangled in her hair, his silver rings catching the light from the fire, as he guided her head back and forth over his length. Heat washed over my body; I balled my hands into fists at my sides. His face was tilted up, his gaze fixed on me.

Bael was entirely right. It was not safe for me here, but not for the reasons he probably meant.

Bael craned his neck around to see what had caught my attention. He chuckled and looked back at me. "Jealous?" There was an edge to the question I didn't understand. "You shouldn't be."

"No, I'm—" *Horrified. Repulsed. Intrigued. Bewitched.*

Not that I was, I told myself. *I wasn't.*

Bael raised an eyebrow. "Because he wishes he were over here right now."

I looked over again, and sure enough, Scion was still watching us. Our gazes collided and my lips parted as I sucked in a sharp breath. He smirked at me, his silver eyes flashing with dark amusement.

I scoffed. "To kill me, perhaps."

"I doubt it. He may not be able to lie to you, but he can lie to himself." Bael took a step closer. "Now, I'm not going to tell you again. Leave. My patience is growing very thin."

I met his predatory yellow eyes and the same energy as before seemed to crackle through the air, and all the hairs on the back of my neck stood up. My eyes widened. I had no idea how I was doing that, or if it was even me doing it at all.

The prince's nostrils flared. His gaze darted from my eyes down to my mouth, and I felt a magnetic thread of energy pull tight between us.

He reached up, fisting his free hand in his hair. "Fuck. Stop doing that."

I ran my tongue over my teeth. "Stop what?"

"You're making it far too hard to stay away from you, little monster. It's driving me fucking insane."

The fingers around my neck tightened slightly again, digging into the skin. I whimpered, but not with pain. My pulse pounded in my core, sending tremors through my entire body.

His thumb pushed into my throat and stars danced behind my eyes as he crushed his lips to mine.

I gasped, air flooding my lungs as he let go of my neck and reached down to lift my legs, twining them around his waist. I moaned against his mouth and he ran his tongue over my lips, hungry and desperate.

I wrapped my fingers around the back of his neck, wanting to get closer. *Closer.*

This was the same and yet so different from my dream. Better. More tactile and raw.

I bit down on his lip, but instead of pain this time he moaned in pleasure as the faint hint of blood hit my mouth.

He gripped the collar of my borrowed dress and before I could say anything had yanked it down over my breasts, tearing a good few inches along the neck and shoulder seams.

He bent his head and sucked my nipple into his mouth and my moan mingled with my squawk of indignation. "That wasn't mine."

"Good. It's disgusting."

"But–"

He laughed, and held me still, pressing his chest hard into mine until I was pinned against the tree. "You're not in control here, little monster. I am."

He leaned over and resumed his meticulous licking over my nipples, and it was slow, blissful torture that sent shocks of pleasure straight to my core. "I want—"

I ground against him wanting more. More. *More.*

Bael held me with one arm while he twisted the other in my hair. He pulled my head to the side and ran his tongue along my throat from pulse to ear. I whimpered when he reached my scar, wondering if he would stop, but he only pressed a kiss to it, whispering: "Ask nicely."

My stomach dropped and I stared at him, shocked, as I remembered my dream. That was too coincidental. Right?

He chuckled at my expression. Not waiting for me to speak or to recover, he reached between us and under my skirt to cup my core. He ran one delicate finger over me, stroking back and forth too lightly.

I trembled and cried out at the touch, already overly sensitive. Too hot. "More. Please."

"Gladly."

He thrust two fingers inside me, and I bit my tongue to keep from crying out. My back arched and my breathing became uneven as he pressed the heel of his hand hard against my clit.

I whimpered and fisted my hands in Bael's hair, wanting to bring his mouth back to mine, but he buried his face in my neck

Over his shoulder, my gaze caught silver eyes watching me. Scion was no longer smirking. The fairies still danced and fucked, writhing on the ground around him, but Scion stared only at me.

Heat built in my belly, and my thighs trembled as Bael ran a thumb over my throbbing clit. I burned, if possible, even hotter, writhing against Bael's fingers as silver eyes bored into mine.

Bael's teeth grazed my neck just as I shattered around his fingers, light dancing behind my eyes, and I keened, tipping my head further to the side.

I panted, the tremors of my orgasm floating through me, and ran my fingers down his stomach to the waistband of his pants.

He pulled back from me, his eyes flashing hot. He caught my hand, stopping me before I traveled lower. "Careful, little monster. Sex isn't an option."

I hated myself for being disappointed by that, but still I asked. "Why?"

"Because..." he paused, and blinked a few times. And then, just as suddenly as it had started, Bael yanked back. The prince stared at me, his expression close to horror. "Fuck."

Dread washed over me. "What?"

"Go back to your room Lonnie." He said flatly, all the heat falling from his voice. "Now."

My heartbeat thrummed too fast, but now for an entirely different reason. "Why?"

"Playing human for you is difficult enough as it is. Next time I won't bother."

He let me slide back to the ground as he put a hand to his mouth, running one finger over his canine teeth—almost as if checking they were still there. Then, in a blink, he disappeared.

I panted, my head spinning, my breath coming too fast.

I didn't have the nerve to look for Scion, but I knew without a doubt that he was still there. Watching the whole thing.

63

LONNIE

I ran back toward the castle, my heart pounding out of control. The sound of the drums still loud in my ears, and my skin still burning too hot.

Small mercies, my ruined dress was still wearable—for now—though I would have to give Enid several new ones to make up for the obvious damage.

My mind raced, too many thoughts and emotions warring with each other. I sprinted toward the garden where the passage to the library was, only to remember that there was no outside entrance.

I gritted my teeth. "Shit."

I spun in an awkward circle, searching for a solution. No door would be unguarded. No entrance open to me where I wouldn't be seen.

My eye caught on the hedges that I knew hid another tree in the center of their twisting, winding, maze of leaves. I pressed my lips together. There was really no decision to be made.

*T*he maze of hedges might have been more difficult to navigate, if not for the tiny Underfae peeking between the leaves. A thorny rose sprite and a lazily floating wisp were only too happy to lead me to the center, though I took care to watch the path we walked in case they were not so willing to help me walk back out again. That seemed the kind of trick they would play. An annoying, but mostly harmless one.

In what felt like no time at all, I stood beneath the moondust tree, staring up at the gently swaying leaves. The white, effervescent sheen of them reflected the light coming from the palace, making them truly appear as moons. Or, perhaps stars, I supposed, all grouped together as they were.

I circled the base of the tree, running my hand over the bark, searching for any sort of hole or notch in the wood where something might be hidden. My gaze darted over the leaves as I went, searching for writing as I'd spotted on the other tree down by the lake.

I sighed when nothing immediately jumped out at me. It must be only the other one then.

Irritation pricked at my skin. If not for the fairies, I would likely already have my sister's journals in hand. Already know what I was meant to do next. What she'd been trying to do. Who had sent her to attack the king and why?

Just as I was turning to leave, I spotted a spindly, long-legged Underfae lurking in the branches. The guardian of the moondust tree, I supposed.

I nodded to it–best to be polite, since I wanted something. "Do you know, if anything is hidden here?"

The sprite watched me for a long moment, unspeaking, and then disappeared. I sighed. It was unlikely, anyway. Rosey could not see the Underfae. She would not have left anything with them. Unless...

The guardian returned a moment later, blinking back into view with a tiny pop. I pressed my hand to my mouth to hide my shriek of excitement when a pile of books appeared beside it.

Falling to my knees, I reached for them, running my hands over the familiar covers. I looked up at the little sprite, which watched me down its long, insect-like nose. "How?"

The sprite had no answer for me.

Looking down at the books, I squeezed my eyes closed, and prayed that my sister would.

64
LONNIE

*M*y joy came crashing down at the realization I would still have to find a way back into the castle without passing the guards–and now, I was further hindered by a stack of heavy books.

Looking up, I focused on the castle wall above me. Not for the first time, I longed for trousers, as my heavy skirt caught around my ankles. Perhaps my plan had been too foolhardy after all.

There were two enormous walls surrounding the fortress. The outer one, at the edge of the lawn, and the inner that held the courtyard. The library had several large windows overlooking the garden. The sills were wide and easily climbed, and the trees below would lend their height.

Glancing at the journals in my arms, I had to admit that either I was getting inside without them, or not at all. I let out a sigh of frustration.

Taking only the most recent journal and stowing it in the top of my boot—it was a tight fit—I stashed the rest of the books under a large rose bush. At least now, I knew where they were.

*P*ink blossoms fluttered to the ground around the base of the sweetly fragrant pear tree, the flowers twirling like elegant confetti.

I stepped too hard on a small branch and it cracked, sending my stomach lurching. I dropped a few feet before catching myself on a lower bow. Golden pears rained down, bouncing all over the ground and rolling into the bushes on the far side of the garden.

From the ground, the library window had not seemed so far away, especially with the tree perfectly poised to assist me. In practice, I was less coordinated off the ground than a newborn lamb, and I hadn't even reached the window ledge.

I stuck a toe out to test my weight on the next branch before balancing precariously and reaching for the wall. Digging my fingers between the rough stone of the castle wall, I lifted my feet off the branch.

My arms burned, screaming with the effort of holding my own weight, and my feet flailed. The sensation of falling rushed through me. I resisted the urge to scream, instead hauling myself up, up over the edge.

I lay flat on my stomach, panting, the wooden shutter of the window pressing against my right arm, and open air on my other side. Terror gripped me, as I realized I'd have to sit up at least to open the shutter. Thank the Source it was nearly summer, and the glass had been removed.

I jostled the latch and the shutter burst open, depositing me in a heap on the floor of the dark, silent room.

I stumbled back to my room on wobbling legs. I was so distracted, it took me a beat to process that something was wrong. Very wrong.

I crossed the room in a daze, staring around open-mouthed at the scene in front of me. The door was open, hanging off its hinges. Linens, papers and clothing covered the floor. The door to the bathing chamber was thrown wide, and through the opening I saw the glitter of broken glass covering the floor.

My breath caught in my throat. Someone had been here while I was gone. Someone who was clearly searching for something.

I tiptoed toward my bed, nervous tingles traveling up my spine and over my arms. Could they still be here? Were they here for Prince Scion, or for me?

In seconds, I had my answer.

The obsidian dagger I'd all but forgot about lay on the bed. The Source-forged one, that the merchant had given me during my first trip to the village after I'd been let out of the dungeon. Beneath it, a note in unfamiliar handwriting stared up at me— the only carefully placed items in an otherwise chaotic room.

I held my breath as I reached for them, as if either might leap up and bite me. The note shook in my trembling hand, making it nearly impossible to read.

I look forward to meeting my queen under the cover of darkness in Inbetwixt.
Your Friend, Ambrose Dullahan

65

LONNIE

*I*n the wee hours of the morning, I shivered and turned over on a hard cot in the servants quarters. It had been hours, and I hadn't managed to get a wink of sleep.

I hadn't dared to go to anyone for help. Not with an incriminating note in hand. Not while the revel still raged on. Not after Prince Bael's odd reaction to…I blushed at the thought.

I curled into a new position beneath the rough, thin blanket, and listened to the soft breathing of the other girls in the overcrowded dormitory.

While in the dungeon, I'd longed to return to a bed like this. Now, after spending weeks in the tower, the cot seemed like a hard block of ice; the blanket scratchy and nearly useless against the chill of the room.

Perhaps, if I made it through the hunt tomorrow…today, now, I supposed…I could demand better bedding for the servants. Maybe I could leverage my new bargain with Gwydion. It was a possibility.

I rolled over again, this time landing flat on my back. My mind raced. What would have happened if I'd stayed inside tonight? Would I have been there for the attack? Was it an attack at all?

Some part of me—a large part—wondered if I had set things in motion by asking about Dullahan in the tavern. If he'd been tipped off by the red-haired man, and come to meet me. Perhaps searched the room for good measure.

But that didn't account for anything else that had gone wrong this week. Iola's poisoning. My attack on the path. Even if one of those was unrelated, it seemed absurdly foolish to think both were...my gut said all three were connected.

I wished I had someone to talk to. My only confidant had been Rosey, and those days were long gone. There was no one I could share my thoughts with in hopes of coming up with a better answer.

Down the hall, the echoing thump of a door slamming against the wall sounded, and the distant sounds of screaming reached my ears. I tensed, thinking wildly that perhaps whoever had ransacked Prince Scion's room had come to find me here. Maybe they were after me. Maybe it was one of the Everlasts, uncaring about the rules of the hunt, coming to kill me in cold blood.

"Where is she?" a male voice screamed, voice echoing off the stone.

My heart pounded, slamming against my ribs.

"I don't know what you're talking about, lord, I—"

"Where the fuck is she?"

Heavy footsteps approached, and I shook, waiting for the storm I knew was coming. Around me, others were waking up.

"What's going on?" someone asked, and immediately I recognized the voice as Enid.

I groaned internally. Yet another thing to add to her list of grievances with me.

The door to the dormitory slammed open and a tall figure stood framed in the entrance. I hated myself for the thrill that shot through me, going all the way through my body and settling in my core. Partially at the sheer power of the moment, and partially from the memory of mere hours ago.

Bael bared his teeth as his eyes immediately found mine. "What are you doing down here? I told you to go back to your room hours ago."

My brain caught up with my mouth and I glared at him. "Did you see my room?"

He growled. "Yes. I thought you were fucking dead."

I jutted out my lip. "I didn't know you cared."

His eyes narrowed. "That's childish."

It was, and I didn't care.

"I don't understand what you're angry about. You left. Or are you simply angry that your plans for the crown may have been ruined before the season was even truly underway?"

Mingled defiance and embarrassment churned in my center. If he hadn't abandoned me he would know full well where I was, so how was this my fault?

He was in front of me in a second, his hand tangled in my hair yanking my head back to meet his eyes. Around me, gasps sounded from the other servant girls. No one was sleeping now, and thirty girls were witness to my—whatever this was.

"Be glad I left," he growled. "For all our sake."

"I don't understand."

His yellow eyes seemed more animalistic than ever, his entire demeanor different from anything I'd ever seen. "There is quite a bit you don't understand. Or so you say."

My cheeks grew hot. "Well explain it to me then. All of it."

"You don't want that. You are clearly far more comfortable with lies."

I thought of the stack of journals in the garden. The lone journal and rebel note burning a hole under the mattress of my cot at this very moment. I thought of all the lies I'd been conditioned to tell since childhood. And yet, somehow, I managed to sound defiant when I said, "What is that supposed to mean?"

In the shadows of the darkened room, the servants were fleeing. I could see them out of the corner of my eye, darting for the door, as if our argument might light the room ablaze. They weren't entirely wrong.

"I think you understand far more than you are letting on, little monster. I think you're lying, and I think you've been lying so long you've started to believe yourself."

My own anger flared. It was better than fear, I supposed. "You say that, yet you manage to omit all the pertinent information from every conversation."

He stared down at me, his lip curling into a smile. "Fine. You want the truth? I hope you enjoy all that comes with that."

66

LONNIE

*P*rince Bael kept a tight hand on my hair as he half dragged, half marched me back out of the dormitory. My scalp screamed, but I refused to make a single sound, adrenaline fueling my defiance. My skin practically burned with it—and I thought I could feel that familiar crackling heat. Though, if he noticed, he said nothing.

We exited the kitchen in a whirlwind and blew down the corridor. I'd expected to go back upstairs, but instead Bael walked further into the depths of the castle.

"Do you think you're scaring me?" I hissed. "You're not."

He laughed, and there was a hard edge to it. "I know I'm not. You should question why that is."

I had no energy for his word games. "What about the second hunt?" I demanded as we came to a halt in the middle of a deserted hall. "We need to leave for Inbetwixt."

It was a bad day indeed when I was requesting to be sent to a potential fight to my death, rather than wherever the prince was dragging me.

"Oh, you'll get to Inbetwixt, little monster." He leaned to the side and reached for the handle of a door I hadn't noticed until now. Pushing it open, he stepped to the side and gestured for me to go inside. "Don't think I'm abandoning the crown that easily."

I blinked in surprise. "Where are we?"

His smile was all teeth. "My room."

"I thought you said no one was allowed in your room?"

"They're not. You would be the first."

Stepping out from under his arm, I peeked around the door-frame. My eyes widened and mingled shock and confusion coursed through me.

The room was lit only by flickering candles set in brackets along the walls. A large square, iron cage stood in the center of the room with no more than a hand's width between each bar.

What little furniture was inside the room was all outside the cage, except for an enormous bed like the one I had in Scion's room, though it seemed to be chained to the bars.

I looked back at Bael and took a huge step away from him. "So you're not putting me in the dungeon, but I'm going in there?"

He laughed, and my anger ratcheted higher. It was hardly amusing. Sick and twisted fairy games. "It's not for you. I believe I've told you before. If I desired to hold you captive, I would not need iron."

I swallowed. I knew that was true, and I didn't want to examine why. "What is it for?"

The prince prowled toward me, his yellow eyes seeming more animalistic than ever as he backed me into the room. "You're not the only one with violent tendencies, little monster. Don't worry, it's a good night tonight."

I remembered suddenly what the noble woman from Inbetwixt had said to Aine at the ball. How Bael had been mysteriously absent the whole evening, and no one had seemed willing to discuss why.

"Is it a bad night for your brother?"

"I can't be expected to know where everyone is at every moment."

Pieces of a puzzle began to fall together in my mind, a picture forming, and yet it was as if the image were out of focus. Several pieces still missing.

I glanced back at the caged bed. "How can you expect me not to worry about this?"

"The same way I am ignoring all your painfully bad attempts at rebellion. All your lies."

My stomach swooped as he crossed the room in two strides, backing me into the bars. My spine hit the hard metal, and I gasped, reaching back to wrap my fingers around the bars behind me.

His hands found my cheeks, and he kissed me hard, like we were fighting for dominance. I whimpered into his mouth as he parted my lips with his tongue.

I wondered distantly if I should be scared. If I should have been running for my life like all the other servants, and yet I couldn't bring myself to leave.

He'd kissed me under so many other circumstances. When it felt like a trick or a bargain. When it was more to tease me than anything else. Dozens of times in my subconscious, and even frantically, in the meadow only hours ago. And yet, nothing–nothing–could have prepared me for this.

I buried my hands in his hair, tugging him closer, sealing his lips to mine. He ran his hands up my sides and I became needy. Feral. A molten writhing mess in his arms.

My heart pounded wildly in my chest, like it was trying to escape and fuse itself with his.

Bael pulled back and ran his razor-sharp teeth over my bottom lip tugging it into his mouth. He gave me a seductive smile when I opened my eyes to meet his gaze, and then bit down deliberately on my lip.

"Ow!" I pulled away as blood pooled in my mouth. "You bit me."

He licked his lip, and a thrill I couldn't explain shot through me. That should have been disgusting, yet...

His breath was hot on my face. "It's not as though it's the first time."

"Not the first time that...what?" That we'd kissed? That he'd bit me? That I'd ignored all reason and wanted him to fuck me hard and brutal, even knowing he'd likely leave me broken.

"You wanted the truth. To know why I left?" His expression was unreadable, even as his eyes had turned more gold than yellow. "It's simple, little monster. Because I've been feeding you my blood *for weeks*."

He said it as though that were the entire point. The whole answer. Yet still, I didn't fully understand. "I know. You were healing me. Because I was going to die. Right?"

He laughed, but there was no humor in it. More of a shocked incredulity. "I told you, that's not how healing works. When Gwydion uses his magic to heal, like he did with your servant friend, he does not get tired. Have you ever heard of one of the High Fae becoming exhausted from one simple enchantment?"

I bit my lip. No, I hadn't, but I hadn't ever thought about it in those terms. "Simply tell me, then. What is happening?"

But even as he'd been speaking, I wondered if I already knew. Or had suspected and not been willing—or able—to face it.

"I'm not healing you. Not really. You've been feeding on my magic since the day I pulled you out of that dungeon. Sharing power…that's not something to be taken lightly."

My stomach turned over, and I gaped up at him. "Then why do it? I certainly never asked you to."

He shook his head. "Instinct? Or maybe it's you. I don't think you understand what it's like. Whatever that power you have is, it's…"

"I don't have any power," I snapped.

"Don't bother lying. It goes both ways, you know," he licked his lip. "I can taste it."

My thoughts raced, too fast to keep up with. His emotions as well seemed erratic. Tumultuous.

"It doesn't matter, though. Do you understand what would happen if I fucked you the way I want to right now? The way I know you want me to? That's a completed mate bond, which would kill not only you but my entire house."

That rocked me. My head swirled, and I felt as if I might faint. "I don't understand."

"Don't you? I told you the story of Aisling and her curse."

"History," I said too fast.

"My family history."

His eyes grew cold, and he pulled further away from me, even as I shook my head. Struggling to come to terms with all of it. I trembled, and desperately wished for the logic to return to my mind, banishing the need still pounding in my center.

"As long as the crown is not returned to the worthy wearer, the obsidian kingdom will know everlasting misery. If ever any member of the royal house should experience true happiness, all those with Everlast blood in their veins will die." He said it very fast, as if he knew the words so well they meant nothing to him anymore. "We don't form mate-bonds. *Ever.*"

My lungs burned with the effort of breathing. There was too much. Too much to process. I wanted the truth from him, but perhaps he was right. I was more comfortable with the lies. "Then...why?"

"I didn't realize it would affect you like that...at first. And if you'd been only human, it would have been fine."

"I am human," I exclaimed.

That seemed like the only thing to grasp onto the only rational part of this conversation.

"No...you're not. I don't know what you are exactly, but you're not entirely human. Scion and I thought so last year when you could see through our glamour, but I knew for sure when you were attacked by those Fae."

I could swear I wasn't breathing.

He held out an open palm to me, as if trying to take my hand. I looked, nonplussed. Without warning, a dancing blue and white flame appeared in his palm.

I scrambled back, fear flooding me. "What is that?"

"I don't know. I have never been able to make fire, but when you were attacked my own magic failed me. Instead, this was all I could create." He leaned forward, his eyes searching mine. "So, why don't you tell me, *mate*. What are you lying about?"

EPILOGUE

SCION

I strode purposefully down the dimly lit corridor, a slip of well-worn parchment shaking in my fist.

Upstairs, the castle teemed with nervous excitement for the second hunt. Our hunting party would leave for Inbetwixt in less than an hours time, and yet, I suspected that not a single member of my family was prepared to leave.

Of course, I had to include myself in that. Upstairs, it might be chaos, but here, there was only quiet. There was only me, and the lone guard, standing at the end of the hall.

I could have placed more guards here, but I'd always felt that no one in their right-mind would enter the dungeon; and no one in the dungeon was in their right-mind to attempt an escape.

"Lord," the guard greeted me.

I sneered at him. It wasn't that I hated all guards. It was this one specifically. "I need to see the prisoner."

He stepped aside immediately. "They're loud today."

I didn't look back. "They're always loud."

The smell of the dungeon was even worse than I remembered and I cringed, holding my breath as I walked down the long rows of cells. Some ancestor had molded it after Fort Warfare prison, but I shuddered to think how it truly compared.

Coming to a halt in front of the familiar cell, I crossed my arms over my chest. Irritation prickled at the back of my neck as the prisoner looked up at me, smiling serenely.

He nodded his head in something between a greeting and a salute. "It's been awhile."

"Not long enough," I spat.

"You are the one in control of that."

He wasn't wrong. I wished I hadn't had to come. That the compulsion for answers hadn't driven me near to madness.

Ambrose got to his feet, pushing silver hair out of his eyes. When he approached the bars, his walk was too confident. His smile too comfortable.

I wished he was in worse condition.

I hadn't expected him to be—the prison was built for High Fae, not for Everlasts—but I could dream.

"What do you want, Sci?" he asked.

I stiffened at the familiarity of the nickname. "Don't call me that."

"My apologies, King of Ravens." His smile twisted. "Or is it still 'Prince?'"

My jaw tightened, but I refused to rise to his bait.

We were opposites, he and I. His eyes were black, his hair silver, yet I'd always thought it was strange no one had noticed the resemblance—even if he had gone out of his way to change his name. To hide his true identity.

"I need you to do something for me," I said, begrudgingly.

He laughed. "I don't do favors. Especially not for my captors."

I narrowed my eyes. We both knew he was staying here of his own free will. At first, I'd thought it was about *her*, but she'd been free for weeks now and he was still here. *Why?*

I held up the parchment for him to see, and his eyes tracked my movement. "What is that?"

"I think you know."

I'd long suspected that I was not the only member of House Everlast to get a final letter from Grandmother Celia. Bael certainly had—it was the only thing that accounted for his behavior lately. Perhaps Gwydion and Aine, as well. The Source knew who else.

Until this moment, it had been a mere suspicion, but Ambrose's reaction to the letter confirmed my theory. Because, if I had thought to consult the opinion of another oracle—the best oracle since Celia herself—then someone else had as well.

He crossed his arms over his chest, giving me an almost feline smile."I will expect you to let me out, you know."

"I know. I will simply hunt you down again."

While Grandmother Celia had often been vague, she had never been wrong.

Except that I could not see any way her last prediction for me could end in anything but misery—which made no sense if it were accurate.

If she were correct. If I were to be the last Everlast King—if our curse were to end with me—then surely, I could not be miserable.

Ambrose took another step closer and wrapped both hands around the bars of his cell. It was as if he was relaxed. At ease to be speaking face to face after all this time.

I stiffened, yet did not move. I wanted clarity badly enough that I was willing to do almost anything to get it—even this. Even free my brother.

Perhaps he knew that. Perhaps it was his plan all along.

He grinned, flashing too-sharp teeth. "You know, I'm not sure you needed my assistance for this, Sci. There are other ways to be king besides winning the hunts."

I scowled. "Like?"

His eyes darted to the side, and I followed his gaze, toward the cell where I knew *she* lived all last year. My stomach lurched, guilt flooding me.

Ambrose watched me closely, seeming amused by my reaction. "Like," he drew his words out, taking relish in my torment. "You could simply marry a queen."

Continued in book two...
Wilde Fae: Lady of the Nightmares

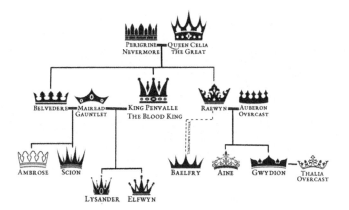

ABOUT THE AUTHOR

USA Today and International bestselling author Kate King loves sassy heroines, crazy magic, and alpha-hole heroes.

An avid reader and writer from a young age, she has been telling stories her whole life. Ever a fan of the dramatic, she lives in an 18th century church with her husband and two cats, and often writes in cemeteries.

ACKNOWLEDGMENTS

This book took more out of me than I had to give it, and so I have to first acknowledge my husband, John, for being extremely patient throughout the process.

A major thank you to my best friend Mallory Hart/Marilyn Marks for being the constant ear to bitch to, and helping me work out some of the finer details of this world.

To my parents for their never-ending support, and especially to my dad, who loves fantasy more than I do.

To Renee, my best cheerleader, Lucy, my OG, Jessa for introducing me to UFs, and Emily for redefining juice.

Thank you my extremely supportive ARC and beta teams, and to my PA, Kayleigh, my editor, Noah, and my ad manager (and friend!!!!), Melissa.

Thank you to my agent Susan, and to Christina over at JAB.

To KD at Storywrappers, Viki at Flowers and Forensics, and Rin for all the lovely art.

Thank you to my therapist.

And thank you to my cat, Jonquil, for very occasionally being quiet.

KATE KING

WICKED GOOD ROMANCE

STALK ME!

Visit my website at www.katekingauthor.com

Follow me on Tiktok and Instagram @katekingauthor

Printed in Great Britain
by Amazon

26404210R00234